EVERYTHING GLITTERED

ALSO BY ROBIN TALLEY

The Love Curse of Melody McIntyre

Music from Another World

Pulp

Our Own Private Universe

As I Descended

What We Left Behind

Lies We Tell Ourselves

EVERYTHING GLITTERED

Robin Talley

LITTLE, BROWN AND COMPANY
New York   Boston

Copyright © 2024 by Robin Talley

Cover art copyright © 2024 by Kamin. Cover design by Gabrielle Chang. Cover copyright © 2024 by Hachette Book Group, Inc. Interior design by Carla Weise.

Little, Brown and Company
Hachette Book Group
1290 Avenue of the Americas, New York, NY 10104
Visit us at LBYR.com

First Edition: September 2024

Little, Brown and Company is a division of Hachette Book Group, Inc. The Little, Brown name and logo are registered trademarks of Hachette Book Group, Inc.

The publisher is not responsible for websites (or their content) that are not owned by the publisher.

Little, Brown and Company books may be purchased in bulk for business, educational, or promotional use. For information, please contact your local bookseller or the Hachette Book Group Special Markets Department at special.markets@hbgusa.com.

Library of Congress Cataloging-in-Publication Data
Names: Talley, Robin, author.
Title: Everything glittered / Robin Talley.
Description: First edition. | New York : Little, Brown and Company, 2024. | Summary: "In Prohibition-era Washington, three best friends investigate their beloved headmistress's murder as dark secrets and new feelings start to arise among them." —Provided by publisher.
Identifiers: LCCN 2023057285 | ISBN 9780316565318 (hardcover) | ISBN 9780316565332 (ebook)
Subjects: CYAC: Mystery and detective stories. | Murder—Fiction. | Boarding schools—Fiction. | Schools—Fiction. | LGBTQ+ people—Fiction. | Washington (D.C.)—History—20th century—Fiction. | LCGFT: Detective and mystery fiction. | Historical fiction. | Novels.
Classification: LCC PZ7.1.T35 Ev 2024 | DDC [Fic]—dc23
LC record available at https://lccn.loc.gov/2023057285

ISBNs: 978-0-316-56531-8 (hardcover), 978-0-316-56533-2 (ebook)

Printed in Indiana, USA

LSC-C

Printing 1, 2024

For Louisa, who is way too young to read this book. (Sorry, honey.)

SOMETHING'S MOVING IN THE DARKNESS.

I pull back the curtain and press my forehead into the windowpane to get a better view, letting the politely strained murmurs and tinkling of punch glasses carry on without me. The party can wait.

The alley below us is only a few feet wide, with the Washington Female Seminary on one side and the Capital Electric Streetcar Repair Facility on the other, and it stretches from a narrow gate on P Street to a dim little courtyard behind the seminary's laundry room and kitchen.

No one ever looks down into this alley. There's never anything to see.

But I was sure I heard something.

Tonight's faculty party is being held in the old library, where the windows are always kept tastefully draped. The real view is to the south, where the wide, smooth balcony hangs over busy P Street, and to the west, where the grandest window of all faces Dupont Circle. During the day, this little alley to the east is used by the maids and footmen and delivery boys to bring things in or out of our seminary, but at night, far from the reach of streetlights, only the occasional scurrying of mice and rats disturbs its darkness.

The shape out there now is too big to be a rat. It's moving in a distinctly human way, too. Pacing in the tight expanse of pavement.

It's difficult to be sure of much more. The shape could be a man, or it could be a woman. It could be more than one figure, moving in tandem. From two stories up, in the dark, it's impossible to tell.

"Gertie?" Milly's voice wavers behind me.

I don't turn yet. I want to make sense of what's happening outside. Why someone would be out there on so cold a night.

Then Milly says, "You've been asked for."

And that gets my attention. Being needed always does.

I let the curtain fall and turn to face her, smiling. The old library's a remnant from when this building was some rich man's mansion, until he died and it became a finishing school for girls whose well-heeled parents want us to have some semblance of an education before we're married. Today this room's used solely for parties and teas, but the dead owner's musty tomes still crowd the remaining bookshelves. Milly's standing beside one of them now, gesturing apologetically with a black-gloved hand toward a cluster of girls on the other side of the room.

Milly's the most fashionable girl at our seminary, with a wardrobe full of dresses custom-made in Paris. Tonight she's chosen a black gown with a gold-and-onyx brooch that I'm sure cost far more than anything I've ever owned. Her thick yellow hair is coiled neatly above her neck—our hair is required to fall past our shoulders when loose, yet stay pinned up above our collars unless we're inside our dormitory rooms—and she's pulled it back on one side with a sparkling comb that shows off the silvery glow of her onyx drop earrings against the ivory of her skin. Her wrists are heavy with a half-dozen bangles that jingle prettily when she moves. But then, Milly does everything prettily.

We've been best friends since we were freshmen, stuffed into our tiny attic room. Our nights back then were spent burrowing into plush blankets to keep out the chill, whispering secrets under the row of miniature winged mermen carved into the hard gray mantel above our little fireplace.

Now, as seniors, we share a room with a broad window overlooking P Street, and tonight we'll make good use of it.

As soon as we can make our escape from this awful library, packed with parents and teachers and upstanding old biddies who believe themselves the sole arbiters of what they call "Best Society," we'll meet up with Clara, and the three of us will trade in our long, demure party gowns for short, beaded dresses with rolled-down stockings. Then we'll escape out the window and make our way to a speakeasy called the Lazy Susan.

Clara's told us all about the speakeasies up in New York. The slow, flowing music. The dark secrets whispered in dark corners. The girls who dance with strangers, and drink in front of men, and speak aloud whatever thoughts come to mind without first considering propriety. Girls like the ones Mrs. Rose has known, whose lives are more than etiquette lessons and husband-hunting, and who care more for adventures than debutante gowns.

The hardest part has been keeping our plan secret. We can't risk the rest of our friends getting into trouble for our sakes. Mrs. Rose may be more forgiving than some, but she's headmistress all the same.

No one can find out. It's as simple as that.

For a few hours, while our parents and teachers think we're tucked into bed dreaming of our future mansions, the three of us will be out in the city, drinking bootleg liquor and listening to modern music and consorting with people of whom no one in this room would ever approve. And not a soul will be the wiser.

"What are you looking at?" Milly steps toward the window, peering out, but she doesn't seem to notice the motion. Perhaps it's stopped.

"Is it Clara?" I ask her. "Is it time to go?"

"Not yet. It's something about a freshman losing her diamonds, but..."

"Gertie! There you are. You need to come. Trixie stole a girl's earring, I'm sure it was her. She's been acting even stranger than usual, and..."

Clara stops talking when I turn to face her, but my smile's already grown wide.

I haven't seen her since yesterday. She was late arriving to tonight's party, after spending the Jewish Sabbath—she calls it Shabbat—with her cousins in Baltimore. That's not so long to be apart, I suppose, but every time I see Clara after any interval, it feels as though the sun is coming out again.

Before this year it was always Milly and me, but when we met Clara four months back, everything changed.

I run the orientations for new students each September. Most are freshmen, of course, but Clara entered as a senior, so Mrs. Rose arranged for her to begin orientation a day later to avoid being lumped in with the younger girls.

So Clara came alone, her smile curving under a pair of knowing dark-brown eyes and a forbidden dark-brown bob. With her equally forbidden deep-red lipstick and the soft rosy tint to her cheeks, she looked like Lillian Gish in *La Bohème*. As though a title card might pop up at any moment and tell me what she was thinking.

That day, as I explained the rules and the daily schedule and showed her the room she'd share with Trixie—right next to mine, as it happened—Clara never wiped off her lipstick or apologized for her hair. She did ask several questions about school athletics, though. When I told her I was the basketball team captain, she immediately challenged me to a game.

"Unless you don't like being unreservedly vanquished, that is," she'd said, dark eyes gleaming.

I didn't terribly mind the idea of being vanquished if Clara was going to be the one doing it, but I replied, "I should warn you. My nickname on the court is Unreserved Vanquisher."

Clara started to giggle, then straightened her smile into a pretense of competition. "Earn it, then."

We were both laughing before we'd laid a finger on the ball. I won that day, but it may have been because she let me.

On the first night Clara spent at the seminary, I learned that she was not only the daughter of a newly elected congressman, but the granddaughter of the proud owners of the best kosher grocery store in Brooklyn. I also learned that she knew a shocking number of curses, thanks to her older brothers. And that I laughed harder with her than I ever had with anyone but Milly.

Clara's lived a far more interesting life than me. So has Milly, for that matter. *Her* father's an ambassador. She's lived all over Europe. I've spent *my* whole life here in Washington, DC, with only occasional trips to Baltimore or New York or Philadelphia, always under my mother's watchful eye. Doing as I was told.

Two days after Clara's arrival, the upperclassmen returned to the seminary, with Milly coming fresh from the RMS *Mauretania*'s transatlantic crossing. By then, Clara and I were sitting side-by-side at every meal and every evening social, and word had spread about the newest member of our senior class.

The halls had filled with fresh whispers. Girls murmuring that Clara had *had* to move due to some sort of scandal at her old school. Girls muttering that her parents had paid the board a fortune to let her in, given her hair and her history. Girls complaining at full voice in my hearing that she'd already been guaranteed a spot on the basketball team when half a dozen juniors were clamoring for it.

In the end, though, when the girls actually *met* Clara, they warmed up to her quickly, and the rumors stopped. In truth, when directly confronted with her smile, her warmth, it's very nearly impossible to dislike Clara. The only two who had seemed immune were Trixie Babcock—who despised everyone—and Milly.

The first time she shook Clara's hand in the dining room, Milly wouldn't meet her eyes. Nor did she smile. All through dinner, she kept darting wary glances from Clara to me and back again. But after the dishes had been cleared and the girls had crowded into the windowless downstairs hall, where the smoke from the fires makes the whole world wonderfully strange and shadowy, Clara invited Milly to the billiards table.

I knew that night that I was watching something bloom between them. Something strong and real and entirely unexpected. Just as it had bloomed between me and each of them already.

By the end of the evening, the tension had dissolved, and we'd become a group of three.

We've stayed that way in the months since. Gray autumn afternoons feel lighter, warmer, when spent on a walk with the two most interesting people I've ever met, both of whom speak beautiful French and know how to serve tea, waltz, and curse in equal measure. Dreary Monday Bible classes take on an easy air when I'm enduring them with Milly on one side of me and Clara on the other, all of us trading furtive glances and barely suppressed giggles. Even the lectures my mother writes in her weekly letters are entertaining when I can read them aloud, imitating her very sternest tones, while Milly and Clara perch on my bed with laughter on their lips and gleams in their eyes, Clara's dark brown and Milly's light.

Some nights, when I fall asleep with Milly a few feet away and Clara on the other side of a thin white wall, those four brown eyes run in circles in my dreams. It's enough to make any girl forget she's supposed to give it all up to marry some faceless man and spend her days selecting curtain fabrics.

As I smile at Clara, she steps toward me, holding out a hand. Her dress is burgundy and falls gently to her ankles, with satin shoes to match, and her cheeks blush to nearly the same color when she spots Milly on the other side of the bookshelf. "Oh. Hello. Did you..."

"Yes." Milly nods stiffly as the clock chimes in the grand hall. "I was informing Gertie of the situation, yes."

They're being awkward with each other, almost formal, and I don't know why. It must be some joke I'm not privy to.

I straighten my spine and go along in my own overly prim voice. "Good evening, Clara. How do you do. It's so good of you to call. Do leave your card with the butler, if you please."

Clara laughs, still blushing.

Behind her, Mrs. Rose is watching us.

She's hovering in the northwest corner of the room in her sleeveless gown, the deep orchid fabric falling to her calves over plain black stockings and patent-leather heels, her gleaming yellow hair fastened with a pair of feathered combs. She's alone, as she usually is at faculty parties.

She dreads these affairs, she told me once. Then she laughed and asked me never to repeat that. It wasn't a surprise—everyone knows Mrs. Rose doesn't get along with most of the faculty, or with my classmates' parents, for that matter—but it made me smile, that she trusted me enough to share her thoughts.

I smile at her again now, wishing it were proper etiquette to wave across a room. My mother isn't far away, though, and I'd undoubtedly hear from her about my lack of refinement, and how she'd *never* have done such a thing in her day. My mother and Milly's have been fast friends since they were in school together themselves, and sometimes I wonder if my mother would've preferred Milly for a daughter. My mother argues with Milly far less often than she does with me.

"Let's, then." Milly takes my hand and leads me through the clusters of partygoers, Clara on my other side.

As we pass them, we offer silent, polite smiles to the teachers, the board members, the little groups of parents, and the maids and waiters scattered around the edges of the room with their aprons and bow ties and trays laden with carefully wrapped canapés. The faculty party is a dry, low-key, off-season affair thrown by our parents, meant to thank the teachers for instructing us this term, but truly it's an excuse to put on staid velvet and pearls and gather shoulder-to-shoulder on a Saturday night, listening to the plodding piano in the grand hall and getting scorched by the blazes in the carved-marble fireplaces.

"Miss Otis!" Mr. Farrel, our Latin teacher, stops Milly as we pass, nodding kindly at Clara and me. "I do hope you're enjoying the *Passio*."

"Oh yes, very much." Milly offers him a gracious smile. "I appreciate your lending it to me."

"I don't get a lot of girls clamoring for volumes from my shelves. Had to buy more titles in French and Italian as well as Latin solely to keep up with your demands. You know, an old friend of Miss Parker's is head of the romance languages department at Barnard. I know your heart lies in mathematics, but I think you'd find a lot to enjoy about studying in New York."

"I imagine so." Milly nods eagerly. "I didn't realize Miss Parker had been to New York."

"Oh, she hasn't, she hasn't." Mr. Farrel shifts his gaze across the room to where Miss Parker, the trigonometry teacher who always scowls when asked a question and loves to whip out her ruler to assess our skirt lengths, is sipping her punch and watching us. Her eyes look tired and watery, almost as though she's inebriated, though that's impossible. She must simply be exhausted. "But you'll soon learn how it is with old friends from finishing school. Though I don't mean to suggest that *our* esteemed seminary is merely a finishing school. You girls learn a great deal here, and some of you may well go on to further education! Why, a few of the women's colleges are nearly as good as their brother schools, and...Oh, dear, were you on your way to see Miss Baker?" He glances over at Elizabeth. "Poor girl seems to be in a state again. You'd better go and help."

"How do you do, Mr. Farrel," I chorus with Milly and Clara, each of us bobbing our heads in turn, and we walk as fast as decorum allows toward where a dozen girls have gathered by the northern wall.

Elizabeth Baker is at the center of the group, her face streaked with tears. Seminary girls lose things all the time, from eighty-nine-cent silk gloves to ruby-studded heirloom bracelets and fox-fur coats, but it's different for Elizabeth. Ever since her mother died last year, she's been clinging to what she has left of hers—mainly, her jewels. The trouble is, Elizabeth has always been forgetful.

"What size are the diamonds, exactly?" I ask, after several eager young voices have attempted to explain the situation, leaving me with a confused muddle.

"Quite small. Well, one is." Elizabeth, with her pale hair,

flushed cheeks, and a wobbling lower lip, shows me a single earring, freshly plucked from her earlobe and cradled in her palm. The diamonds are a deep blue, nearer to sapphires in color. "See here, the stone on top is tiny. The one below, a trifle larger. I was supposed to save them for the dance, and my father said if I lost any more jewelry, he'd..."

"I understand." I take Elizabeth's hand in mine gently, and fold her fingers closed over her remaining earring. "Don't worry. We'll find it."

"I'll tell you where to look." Milly tilts her head at Trixie Babcock.

Trixie doesn't see us, though. Her lips are tight under the fringe of her dark-brown bangs, and she's striding across the room toward Mrs. Rose.

As a new student, Clara got stuck sharing a room with her. Trixie has the most luxurious suite in the seminary, with its own little sitting room, but all the same, no one would consent to be her roommate.

She'd roomed with a freshman last year, and only a few days into term, Trixie told everyone the poor girl still wet the bed. It turned out she'd started the rumor because the girl refused to let Trixie have her best seal stole, even though Trixie's the richest girl at the seminary and probably has three seal stoles of her own.

"Don't worry," I assure Elizabeth as Trixie approaches our headmistress. Mrs. Rose offers her a strained smile. Even *she* can't manage with Trixie. "We'll find it before your father notices. He's not even paying attention, is he?"

We all glance at the center of the room, where Elizabeth's father is standing in a large group of men that also includes my father, Clara's, and Trixie's, plus a dozen more, all of them wearing three-piece suits with cigars bulging from the pockets.

They'd never smoke in the presence of ladies, but it's clear from the way their fingers keep reaching out to stroke their pockets that they're itching for the moment they can head down to the tobacco room and strike their matches.

Laughter arises from the group, and a man at the center— I think it's Trixie's father, but it's hard to make out at this distance—calls, "You should've been on the rifle team at Penn. Back then, the parties were jolly!"

"Those days, it was anything goes!" one of the other men adds.

"You mean anything *went!*" another cries. "Straight down the gullet!"

That man lets out a deep laugh before remembering where he is and lowering his voice.

My own father, on the outer edge of the group, coughs and closes his eyes before turning to glance at the clock in the hall. Even before he was named to the bench, he took Prohibition seriously.

Though no one else seems to. We're only a few weeks away from 1928, and the Temperance ladies love to crow about how the capital city has been dry for a decade. Yet as far as I can tell, the liquor here never stopped flowing. In alleyways, men drink grain alcohol from brown bottles, and at society dinners, bow-tied waiters pour glasses of imported champagne. The wealthy hoard bottles in their cellars, insisting it was all bought before the laws changed, and everyone—rich, poor, and in between— drinks in speakeasies across the city seven nights a week. Everyone but seminary girls.

Well. Officially.

It's true that liquor *has* penetrated the school walls. Sometimes a girl will get hold of a bottle of bathtub gin from a brother or a sweetheart and pass it around her dorm room, while a circle of us settles on the floor with our skirts tucked under our knees, trading sips from the foul-smelling bottle until we've stopped wrinkling our noses and begun laughing ourselves silly.

"You don't really think Trixie took it, do you?" asks another girl just as my mother glances up from her group of friends, stifling a yawn and trying to catch my eye. I look away quickly. "What would she do with one earring?"

"What does Trixie do with anything?" Milly shrugs.

"Never mind Trixie," I say. Trixie's indeed been known to steal things, for reasons that have never been clear to anyone except her, and Clara did notice that she's been acting strange tonight. Still, Trixie hasn't given us any reason to suspect her of stealing anything this time. "The simplest explanation is that it fell out of Elizabeth's ear, and in my experience, simple explanations most often suffice. Let's spread out, everyone. Have a close look at the rug. The blue stones should stand out easily enough."

I start toward the middle of the room, carefully turning my back on my mother and moving toward the corner where Mrs. Rose and Trixie are talking. Trixie is holding her hands out in front of her, pleading.

"It has to be tonight," Trixie says. I slow my pace, casting my eyes at the ground so they won't notice me listening. "I can't stay there, not if..."

Mrs. Rose interrupts her. "It'll be fine, Trixie."

"But what if she—"

That's all I hear before the gunshot rings out.

THE SOUND ECHOES FROM ONE SIDE OF THE NARROW ROOM TO
the other. Sluggish, as though it's dragging through water.

All around us, people have frozen, mouths dropping open.
Conversations stopped mid-word. A woman gasps into the
silence.

Milly's gone stiff, too, but Clara's eyes are darting around
the room, racing toward the windows and then coming back to
me. Following me as I run.

And I am. Running.

The sound came from the side of the building that faces the
alley. The same window I'd pressed my forehead against minutes ago.

I'm the fastest girl at the seminary. It's why I'm captain of
the basketball team. That, and because I'm the only one the
other girls will follow during drills.

Forward, back. Jump! Forward, back. Jump!

It's the drills that echo in my mind as I reach the widest
window. When I peer into the darkness, I see movement again.
Whoever's down there is running.

I stretch up onto my toes, trying to see their face.

"Get away from the windows!" a man bellows behind me.
"You! Get back!"

Someone's at my side. Clara. "Did you see anything?" she
whispers, urgent.

"I think there's a..."

Before I can say more, a hand closes on my arm above the elbow, jerking me back.

Milly. She's gotten me halfway across the room before I can even try to resist. The partygoers have huddled into little groups, as though clustering close will protect them. No one seems to know where to look or what to do.

"You heard Trixie's father," Milly murmurs in my ear. "It isn't safe, not with guns out there."

Then a glass shatters, and there's a shout, high and shrill. "This'll be something to do with *you*, and we all know it!"

More gasps fill the room, the quiet stillness broken.

Shards from a broken punch glass lie on the ground beside Miss Parker's feet, and she scowls harder than usual, swaying on her low gray heels.

She's pointing at Mrs. Rose.

"Everyone knows the sort *you* spend your time with." Miss Parker spits the words out. "It's your low-life friends out there, isn't it? Gangsters, or worse!"

That word, *gangsters*, earns more gasps, and the huddled groups burst into frantic conversation, fear dissolving into anger and blame.

All night, our teachers have been lingering in the corners of the room, talking in low voices. This party is meant to be given *by* the parents *for* the faculty, but the parents here tend to view teachers in much the way they view the aproned maids lingering around the edges of the room. They don't see Mrs. Rose as much more, either, exalted as her headmistress title must be.

She's standing with her back to the windows, only a few feet from where I was when Milly pulled me back. She's watching Miss Parker. It's the first time I've ever seen Mrs. Rose struck dumb.

No one speaks as the parents stare at her with unusually

open dislike. The teachers keep silent. Even the girls are gazing at their feet.

My own anger surges. I don't know what happened in the alley, but I know these people don't understand how vital Mrs. Rose is to the seminary. To *us*.

"I'm quite sure there's no danger," I say.

And every head in the room swivels to me.

I hadn't meant my voice to carry so far. Milly's always telling me to be cautious. That something about the way I speak tends to make people listen, whether I want them to or not.

But it's too late for that. I draw in a breath and add, "That sound was likely from a passing automobile."

I said it to calm the room, but I regret it in the same instant, because the falsehood seems to work immediately, and better than I intended. The worried creases on the adults' faces have already begun to smooth.

They don't know about the figure I saw outside, running.

They don't understand that we *all* need to get out of this library. Immediately.

Mrs. Rose steps into the center of the room. "Thank you, Miss Pound, I agree with your assessment. Let's all progress into the grand hall for a change of scenery. Lucy, if you'd be so good as to inform the kitchen, and please ask Anderson to telephone the police. An unfortunate motorist may be in need of assistance."

Lucy's already moving, her pressed apron swishing as she hurries through the door. Sensing, I suspect, as Mrs. Rose seems to, that my "assessment" was entirely incorrect, and that the urgency is far greater than either of our tones would convey.

The crowd follows Mrs. Rose out of the library, their murmurs growing louder as they cast nervous glances back toward the windows.

"Many apologies, ladies and gentlemen." Mr. Farrel clears his throat as he walks beside Miss Parker. Her lips are pressed tightly together, and shame is slowly writing its way across her wrinkled forehead. "Our good Miss Parker isn't quite herself this evening. She hopes you'll excuse her as she goes to rest until she's feeling better."

"I'll go speak to the police," my father says as he passes through, buttoning his jacket over his waistcoat. When he spots me, he leans in for a whisper. "Stay inside, Gertie. It isn't safe to go looking around tonight."

"I wasn't planning to go look around at anything," I say, though I'm longing to do precisely that.

A half-dozen men move toward the staircase to accompany my father. "Think there's any truth to it?" one of them mutters. "*Does* she associate with the criminal element?"

"With that woman, anything's possible," someone mutters in reply.

Mrs. Rose is standing opposite us in the grand hall, speaking in a low voice to one of the servants. If she heard the men talking, she doesn't give any sign of it. But then, I've never been able to tell what she's thinking.

I still try, though. Every morning, I give it my very best attempt.

I can't remember when, exactly, my visits to Mrs. Rose became a daily occurrence. At first I only went once a week. As editor of the student newspaper, I'm expected to review each edition with her before publication. We've found that it doesn't take us long to dispense with that, though, as there's only so much to say about upcoming dances, fawning reviews of National Theatre performances we've all already seen, and poetry about dandelions composed by eager freshmen.

The conversations that come after business is over are far more interesting.

Every morning, I find Mrs. Rose in the same spot, behind her desk, writing letters, while Lucy sets a fresh pot of tea by the fireplace. Mrs. Rose starts each visit by thanking her, taking off her glasses, and rubbing the bridge of her nose before turning her smile to me. The tiny lines around her eyes are always tired, but the eyes themselves are bright and quick.

When we sit by the fire together, I can talk about absolutely anything. My friends. My family. Politics, and basketball, and the past, and the future. Until I met Mrs. Rose, I never knew I had so much to say about the future.

She asks me questions, too, in her soft, easy manner, about what I dream of doing someday, should circumstances ever permit it. To hear Mrs. Rose talk, circumstances can permit quite a lot.

I've tried to tell her it isn't so simple. My future's already laid out. I'll find a husband next winter, during my debutante year. There will be engagement parties and a wedding at the National Cathedral, with red and white carnations. My mother's own wedding wasn't in the proper season for them, and for years she's told me about all the carnations *I'll* have, without once asking how I felt about carnations.

And after that... that's the trouble. I can't imagine anything after. My mother's plans stop with the carnations.

I suppose I'll use my grand education at the best girls' schools in the city to manage my household, as my mother has. To host dinners for the wives of husbands as important as my own. To send my children to the very best schools, so they can become imitations of their parents and grandparents. My son, a high-ranking government man. My daughter, a high-ranking government man's wife.

Somehow, though, when we sit before the fire, Mrs. Rose and I wind up discussing other futures. The kind that belong to other people. Girls she's known who've gone away—not for marriage, but for New York, or Paris, or Istanbul. Girls who've spent years planning not their husbands' careers, but their own.

I ask her questions, too. She answers them all.

She's shockingly young for a headmistress. That, I knew without having to ask. Decades younger than our last headmistress, and younger than most of our teachers, too. Yet she's done so much. She's read every book, seen every painting. She's been to operas in Vienna and museums in Madrid. She's sailed the Mississippi and climbed the pyramids. She married a man in Greenwich Village, lost him to a nasty flu in Portugal, and came back from grief determined to make herself into a new person. To educate girls. Good girls, with the potential to be great.

Mrs. Rose is brilliant, and handsome, and accomplished. She's everything I want to be.

And she's sworn never to marry again. She has too much to do.

If I ever said such a thing to my mother—that I don't desire to marry; that I have plans, ideas, that don't involve tying myself to some Harvard man's ambitions—she'd have me exorcised.

Most of the other girls here are a bit more like my mother. Perhaps that's why the majority of them don't quite seem to understand Mrs. Rose. Even Milly sometimes casts me skeptical looks when Mrs. Rose launches into her speeches at our weekly assemblies, sharing her perspective on literature or history or athletics while the teachers watch with fixed smiles and pursed lips.

Clara, though, beams when she sees Mrs. Rose, and the two of them have regular tennis lessons at the park a few blocks north. It's the one sport I've never quite mastered.

The last of the adults vanishes through the door, leaving the old library nearly empty. I feel a steady presence at either side, though, and I don't need to look to see that Milly and Clara hung back along with me.

"What is it that they think?" I whisper as we hover against the northern wall, farthest from the windows. "That because Mrs. Rose is a little unconventional, she must spend her days associating with... *gangsters*?"

"Miss Parker wouldn't know a gangster if one sat down in her parlor." Milly lays a soft hand on my elbow. "Are you all right?"

"Of course I'm all right." But I'm shaking. I didn't realize I was shaking.

Milly moves her hand to my back, and I lean into her steady presence. Clara turns away.

"It... truly could have been a car, couldn't it?" I ask. "That sound?"

"No." Clara shakes her head once, firmly. "It was a gun."

"You're sure?"

"I'm sure."

Clara knows a lot of things I don't. Something about being from New York. I wonder how many gunshots she's heard before tonight.

My father's safe out there, isn't he?

Certainly, he is. With so many men together, no one would dare try to harm them. Besides, a gangster would have no reason to target him in particular. No way of knowing he's a judge.

Still. I'll be glad to see him return.

"It could've happened blocks from here." Milly steps over to my other side, away from Clara. "Sound carries."

"I... I saw someone in the alley. Even before the shot."

They both turn to me sharply. "Who?" Clara asks.

"I don't know."

She's already striding back toward the windows.

"We can't!" Milly says, but Clara doesn't stop, and I'm quick on her heels. There's a frustrated sigh behind me, then Milly's rapid footsteps sound at my back.

The three of us crouch below the window and slowly rise to peer up over the sill. We can't get a good view from so far down, but there's no visible sign of movement.

Whatever was out there must be gone. Or hiding, immobile, in the darkness.

We slide back from the window, struggling to rise in our long gowns and high heels. Fortunately, there's no one here to see us except one another as we reach out, gripping hands, helping one another to our feet. We stumble to the safety of the northern wall, and I sag against the closed library door.

"Are we safe here?" Milly whispers.

"I don't know," Clara whispers back. "But it's not as if we can leave. There's a party in the next room."

"We need to get Elizabeth's earring back." I sigh. "And my mother is bound to seek me out soon to correct whatever my most recent failing may have been."

It all sounds so mundane. What if there *are* gangsters outside? Waiting, in the darkness?

That's when the *thump* sounds.

"Gertie." Milly's voice is an anxious whisper. "Get back from that door."

I leap away, and Milly steps forward, shoving the door with her shoulder.

It crashes open. And on the other side, someone topples backward.

3

"T*RIXIE?*"

Milly holds the library door wide, revealing Trixie Babcock sprawled across the floor of the anteroom that leads out to the grand hall.

She must've been pressed directly up against the door. Hoping to hear us telling secrets, no doubt. That's what Trixie does. But we don't often manage to catch her in the act.

"I hope you're having a pleasant evening, Miss Babcock." I paste on a smile that would satisfy Madame Frost, our harshest etiquette instructor.

Trixie's eyes dart behind me to where Milly and Clara are coming through the door, and she staggers backward into the corner between the library and the servants' rooms, her face blanching.

I thought Trixie would act snide, or ashamed. Instead, she looks...terrified.

Perhaps Milly was right, about her taking Elizabeth's earring. Perhaps she's afraid we've found her out. She may even feel remorseful.

It's worth a try.

"You're all right," I tell Trixie, as though I'm soothing a horse who's lost a shoe as the carriage is about to depart. I step in front of the others and clasp my hands behind my back, looking Trixie straight in the eye and flattening out my palm, where Clara will be sure to notice. I need her to stay where she can see my back, and Trixie can't. And I need to keep Trixie busy talking all the while. "If you give the earring to me, I'll take it to Elizabeth. No one else needs to know."

As I'm speaking, I move slowly to the side, closer to Trixie. She rolls her eyes. "All hail Gertie Pound, savior of crybaby little girls. Your daddy would be so proud."

"Would yours?" I ask.

Trixie's eyes cloud over, and I realize I asked the wrong question.

Behind my back, where Trixie won't see, I draw out a finger and point to my left. The answering rustle of velvet and silk tells me Clara's moving, slipping into the shadows. She excels at going unnoticed.

"Or," I say, "if you want to tell me what happened, I can help Elizabeth and the others to understand."

"Right. Everyone listens to *you*." Trixie's mouth twists into a sneer.

She's parting her lips to say more when Clara's arm slips under hers, quick fingers snatching something from the seam of Trixie's green velvet dress. Clara's finished before Trixie can even work up an indignant cry, passing a small, glittery object to Milly.

"I'll take this straight to Elizabeth." Milly darts away.

Trixie's lip quivers, as though she's unsure whether to scream or cry. It's almost enough to make me pity her.

But Elizabeth's devastation was real, too.

"Go back to your room," I tell Trixie. "You can calm down there, in private."

She glares at me again. But when her eyes shift to Clara, she shrinks away, pushing past us toward the eastern staircase.

I turn to Clara with a small smile and catch her elbow in my gloved hand.

I'm aching to get away from here. From shadowy figures

and cruel tricks and petty rivalries. All I want is to take Clara and Milly and launch a lifetime of adventures, without having to live up to anyone's absurd expectations.

But before I can tell Clara that, before I can so much as take a step, my mother swoops in front of us, and my mouth clamps firmly shut. She's dressed in a gray velvet gown with a burst of crystals at the shoulder, and she's frowning down at where my fingers still clutch Clara's elbow.

My mother says I'm too young to wear crystals. She says girls my age are meant to go unremarked upon until our debuts, and that if we *must* be noticed in the meantime, it should be in a way that does credit to our families.

My mother grew up wearing white lace dresses that trailed to the floor and hats trimmed with dead birds. She dreamed of having her own ballroom with space to fit four hundred, so she thinks that's what I dream of, too.

The world she was born into bears no resemblance to the one I inhabit. Women can vote now, and cut their hair. All the girls at school dream of being motion-picture stars. My mother has never known what *I* dream of, because she's never asked.

All the same, I let go of Clara's elbow.

"Good evening, Mrs. Pound." Clara bobs her head in the appropriate level of deference.

"How do you do, Miss Blum. Please give your mother my regards the next time you write." My mother offers Clara a smile so gracious I almost think she's happy until she turns to me, brandishing her punch glass like a weapon. "Gertrude, dear, I'm in grave need of your assistance. Mrs. Mayfield asked about that darling shop we discovered last summer at the shore, and I daresay I've forgotten several details. If you'll forgive us, Miss Blum?"

"Certainly, Mrs. Pound."

My mother nods stiffly at Clara and marches me across the crowded grand hall, where a white-haired man is bent over the piano, his eyelids dropping over his own slow, dull music, a tune that might've been popular sometime before the war.

"No need to pout," my mother murmurs. "You see these girls every day. A party is an opportunity to make connections with the women who can ensure your future. I don't need to remind you that this season will be your last before you leave school and have to make your way in the world."

I nod stiffly. It's forbidden to complain among company.

My mother seems to think the sole purpose of my education is to give me topics of conversation for Washington's annual social season: those painful months from New Year's to Easter, when the stately dinner parties and grand balls stretch into eternity, with the country's richest families swooping in to occupy their custom-built mansions just long enough to lobby congressmen and senators to support their business interests over platters of lobster à la Newburg and prewar champagne. Until the congressional session ends and they head back to Manhattan or Newport or Chicago, leaving our city to those of us who actually live here.

We reach the grandest window, where Mrs. Mayfield, Mrs. Patterson, and Mrs. Paul are sipping punch. Three grown-up versions of Trixie Babcock. Mrs. Paul is endeavoring to prevent a yawn, her cheeks hollowing out and her eyes pinching, and I manage not to laugh as my mother and I enter their circle. They're all married to government men of varying degrees of importance, and Mrs. Patterson, with her white hair tucked up neatly over her wrinkled white face, is the wife of a particularly prominent assistant cabinet secretary. She's been the city's chief society hostess for decades, with her daughter, Mrs. Mayfield, due to inherit the title, thanks to her own husband's recent assignment to the White House.

The three of them are capable of striking anyone they choose off the guest list for any dinner in the city. Mrs. Patterson could probably strike my name off Saint Peter's list itself if she so chose.

They all detest Mrs. Rose. Last Easter, I overheard Mrs. Paul telling my mother that my classmates and I would have to go to New York and Boston to find husbands if Mrs. Rose dragged the seminary down any further with her insistence on prioritizing academics over dress and deportment. The *local* families, Mrs. Paul whispered, would never let their sons marry overeducated bluestockings with loose threads trailing from their skirt hems.

I *never* want to become one of these women. So bored that I spend my time deciding when other people have made mistakes.

"How do you do, Mrs. Patterson." I hold out my hand to her first, then go around the circle, my mother's keen eyes on me all the while. If I make a single error in my words, my tone, she'll be sure to inform me in great detail later. "Mrs. Paul. Mrs. Mayfield."

"How do you do, Miss Pound." Mrs. Patterson pauses to study my ankle-length blue velvet dress, my pearl necklace, my bare face, and my pinned-up hair before giving a nod of approval. "I understand your school has a dance next week with the men of George Washington University."

"That's right, Mrs. Patterson." I smile enough to suggest that I'm delighted, but only appropriately so, at the prospect of moving sedately across a dance floor with some dull boy who expects me to blush and flirt, while Milly and Clara do the same with dull boys of their own. All under the careful gaze of three dozen chaperones suppressing yawns and fiddling with their fans.

As I go on appropriately smiling, I spot my father coming back into the room with the other men. They're laughing, accepting fresh punch glasses, and rubbing their arms against the cold outside. It's clear from their demeanors that they didn't find anything worrisome in the alley.

My smile turns genuine.

Clara was wrong. It *was* a car engine, or something like that.

That doesn't explain the running figure in the alley, though.

"Well, I certainly hope your headmistress won't be permitting any of those new dances the young people get up to." Mrs. Paul purses her lips. "*Animal* dances, that's what they call them in the papers. The foxtrot, the Charleston, the *bunny hug*..."

"I imagine not, Mrs. Paul."

She nods at me, too, no doubt pruriently envisioning all the terrible dances being played out in this very hall, and all the scandalous behavior that would be bound to follow.

But I don't care what Mrs. Paul thinks. Her nod means I've passed their test. For now.

And so I keep up my mild smile and perfect manners as I give Mrs. Mayfield the name of the store in Ocean City, and the women return to the conversation they were having before I arrived, which seems to have been about the wife of the newest Supreme Court justice and the inadequacy of her silver service.

"Beg pardon, ma'am. Ma'am," a familiar voice murmurs, and I turn, smiling, to see Mrs. Rose.

Her own smile is strained as she edges past us. Mrs. Patterson and Mrs. Paul cast long, sour looks at her back, where her dress's low neckline is draped in a Spanish-fringe shawl patterned in dark hues of purple and cobalt, accented with glimmers of gold. Mrs. Rose doesn't seem to notice.

Perhaps that's why Mrs. Paul doesn't wait until she's very far away to say, "I don't see how that woman made it to be a headmistress saying *Beg pardon* or *ma'am* in Best Society. She sounds like a common seamstress!"

Mrs. Patterson responds with a lift of the chin and tilt of the head, but Mrs. Rose has already sailed past us to greet Trixie's uncle. Mr. Damian Babcock has significantly less hair than his brother, and his face has a startling pallor and a mess of wrinkles, but he's head of the Babcock railroad company and the wealthiest man in the room, and that matters far more than his appearance.

"Pleasure to see you, as always, Damian." Mrs. Rose extends her hand in its embroidered black glove. "I hope that moment earlier didn't trouble you."

"How do you do." Mr. Babcock shakes her hand. He doesn't flinch to hear her address him by his first name, even though he's president of the seminary's board of trustees, which makes him Mrs. Rose's boss.

"I had a few questions about the budget figures you shared yesterday." Mrs. Rose gently places her full punch glass on the tray of a passing footman.

"Certainly." Mr. Babcock's smile is firm and polite. "We can discuss it on Monday. The wife would never forgive me for talking business at a party."

"Of course." Mrs. Rose's smile stays in place, but the frustration in her voice is as evident to me as I imagine it must be to Mr. Babcock.

"Gertrude, you'll want to try the punch," my mother says. "It's delicious this evening."

The punch is atrocious. I tried it earlier and couldn't manage more than a few sips, and neither could any of my friends. Only the adults are bothering with it. "Yes, Mother, I shall."

"Enjoy the remainder of your evening."

I've never been more grateful for a dismissal.

I pass the punch table at a quick pace, searching the crowd for Milly and Clara. I've made nice with my mother, and whatever was happening in the alley seems to be over, and so the three of us can finally slip away.

Once we're in our short dresses and rolled stockings, no one will take us for prim seminary girls.

"Miss Pound?" a voice calls softly behind me.

Just outside the library doors, a few feet from the piano, Mrs. Rose is calling to me.

I DIDN'T EXPECT TO FIND YOU APART FROM YOUR FRIENDS," Mrs. Rose says.

"Only for a moment." Warmth spreads across my cheeks. I'll have to keep my distance from Mrs. Patterson and her ilk or they'll say I've been using rouge.

"Well, if I can keep you from them for yet another, would you accompany me to my office?"

I try to disguise the intensity of my delight. "Why, yes, that would be lovely, if you please."

"We've certainly trained you to be quite proper, haven't we?" Mrs. Rose gives a little laugh. "Don't worry, you needn't answer that. Come, we can take the back hall."

Mrs. Rose's office is only a short distance from the library, but instead of going through the grand hall by the main staircase, she leads me past the south servants' stairs. We go through a narrow room with a sink and counter, then a door that leads to a slightly bigger, darker room, this one lined with shelves and smelling of mothballs.

"The old linen cupboard," Mrs. Rose says over her shoulder. Her golden hair is twisted into a perfect knot above the creamy skin of her neck. "Not used much since they installed the new laundry downstairs. I take it you've never been to the servants' rooms?"

"No."

"It's quite convenient if you want to get somewhere without

making conversation." She opens the next door and waves for me to walk ahead of her into the office.

It's my favorite room in the seminary. My favorite place to talk and think and dream.

But it's cold tonight, the fireplace dark. I wrap my hands over my bare arms as Mrs. Rose goes to the bureau.

"I appreciated your quick thinking back there." She opens the bureau drawer and rummages inside. "You kept your cool, and helped others do the same. Not an easy feat. But then, I've come to expect nothing less of you, Miss Pound."

I flush to my collarbone. "Thank you."

"And while it's unconnected to tonight's events, I do have something for you." Mrs. Rose draws a long, flat box wrapped in brown string from the bureau and turns, holding it out to me.

"Oh!" I'm so surprised the sound leaves my mouth before I can think of the proper phrasing. "That's to say, thank you very much, Mrs. Rose, I'm ever so grateful."

"Go on and open it here. It wouldn't do to have the other girls see. I couldn't get Christmas gifts for them all, though a few wives of board members were kind enough to bless me with such useful objects as bejeweled letter openers and hand-embroidered parasols, rather than paying me a salary comparable to what they'd expect for their husbands."

I giggle, thrilled that she trusts me enough to say something so shocking, and take the box, tucking back my hand so my gloved fingers won't touch hers. "Thank you."

It's a flat white box, the kind shop assistants use to package up clothing, and I have to remove my gloves to unwrap the string, my bare fingers fumbling. When I finally lift the lid and pull back the thin paper wrapping, I clap a gleeful hand to my chest. "Is that for *me*?"

"I've seen you admiring my shawl." Mrs. Rose watches as I

run my fingers over the Spanish fringe. "I thought you'd enjoy having one of your own."

I bite my lip. It's all I can do to keep from beaming in a way that would utterly defy decorum.

I never knew she'd noticed.

The shawl neatly folded into the box is strikingly similar to the one Mrs. Rose is wearing. When it isn't draped across her shoulders, it hangs from her bureau. All autumn, I've gazed at it during our meetings, and occasionally, when Mrs. Rose is occupied in pouring out the tea, I've risen from my seat and let my fingers trail over the silky fabric with its painted floral pattern.

"It's beautiful." I lift my gaze to meet hers, then drop it quickly.

"I'm pleased you like it." Mrs. Rose is smiling, but it's not the mild, pleasant smile she gave Trixie's uncle. This smile is warm. Real. "Mine was a gift as well, from a friend. I'd be remiss, though, if I didn't mention that there's no law requiring you to long for the things you see in shop windows."

My fingers fumble on the fringe, and it slips back into the box, flushing. "Oh, I didn't... I only liked the look of *your* shawl, that's all, I never..."

"I don't mean the shawl. Spectacular though it may be." Mrs. Rose tilts her chin to one side, eyelashes casting down toward the flat white box. "Your generation is poised to change everything. You aren't beholden to the mores of your parents. We've been through a war and an epidemic, but at last, things are changing. Drawing rooms and dinner parties don't have to be the order of the world any longer, not if you don't want them to."

I laugh. I can't imagine a world without dinner parties. "You mean... for girls? Girls like *us*?"

"You've been taught you're powerless, but the truth is quite the opposite." Mrs. Rose never takes her eyes off me. I resist the impulse to shift on my feet. "There's a reason I chose to work at girls' schools, Miss Pound. This is the one brief, shining time in your lives when you won't be surrounded by powerful men eager to throw around glittering nonsense meant to keep intelligent women from using their abilities before those abilities can become threats. Now that women—*some* women—have the vote, they're seeking new ways to limit us."

I tear my eyes away from the shawl. "What sort of ways?"

"Certain rules are so ingrained..." She pauses, turning her gaze toward the bureau, with its beautiful carved mahogany panel. "It never occurs to many to question them."

My breath catches in my throat.

Rules?

Does she know, somehow, about our plan? That Milly and Clara and I are stealing away tonight?

"Oh, I always follow the rules," I say in my most reassuring voice. "Since I was a child."

"I'm well aware." A strain creeps into Mrs. Rose's voice. "My apologies. I'm not being very direct with you, am I?"

It feels as though I'm disappointing her.

"It's strange, but..." I fix my eyes on the shawl's painted pattern. Gold and red, weaving and interlocking. "Sometimes I worry that what I want isn't what other people want."

Mrs. Rose raises her eyebrows. "Well. *That* is something to celebrate."

"Excuse me?"

"Ah. Never mind." The strain in her voice evaporates so quickly I'm not sure it was ever there. "Are you looking forward to the holiday recess?"

"Very much, thank you." It's a relief, returning to courtesy. "You're ever so kind to ask."

"No need to stand on ceremony, Miss Pound. You may speak freely."

"Then...I'm dreading it." The words fly out, but at Mrs. Rose's answering smile, I permit myself to smile, too. "Here, I have a place all my own, where other girls..."

"Look up to you," Mrs. Rose finishes.

I flush again. "At home, though, I'm a child."

"If I may offer some advice. When the strain gets to be too much, use the time to study the people around you. Detachment aids endurance, and you may learn something that'll serve you later."

"Well, if I *am* speaking freely, I'll say that I've been living with my parents for seventeen years, and all I've learned is to steer clear."

She laughs. "Then try looking at it differently. Remember, you might disagree with their decisions, but there's a reason they make the choices they do. You or I may disagree with those reasons, and one never wants to give others cause to think their background is the sole determiner of their accomplishments in any case. But one trick I use, whether I'm talking to certain board members or haggling with a shop owner over the price of, let's say, a shawl, is to forget about what *I* want and consider *their* goal. If I can discern that, I can gain a lot of useful information. That's the most important skill to master, in my view. Even more than how to do a quality cannonball serve."

I smile. Mrs. Rose is mad for tennis. "Thank you."

"Certainly. Now, your friends must be missing you."

Another dismissal. But a kind one. "Thank you for the shawl, Mrs. Rose."

"You're very welcome, Gertie."

She's never called me that before.

I want to drape my new shawl around my shoulders, but my mother would be horrified if I wore such a thing in the presence of Mrs. Patterson. For a moment, though, as I retreat back through the linen cupboard and the serving room, I picture my mother's face at the sight of me, red and gold Spanish fringe draped over my demure blue velvet, and I smile as I climb the back stairs to the third floor.

My room is directly above the old library, so it only takes me a moment to drop the gift box and shawl on top of my bed and retreat back down the main staircase. It's empty, the sounds of the party below dimmer than before. People are beginning to leave at last.

I'm halfway down the grand stairs when a familiar voice rises up.

"Gertie." Milly climbs the steps to meet me. We're alone. Or as alone as it's possible to be with a party slowly ending in the next room. "Thank heavens. I couldn't take one more second of trying to make nice with Madame Frost. She tried to get me to practice my royal curtsies in front of *everyone*."

"Preposterous. You don't need to practice. Everyone knows you already have the best curtsy in the senior class."

Milly laughs and demonstrates, bending her knees and bowing her head. Her back is perfectly straight, and her long, narrow dress clings to her curves.

I laugh, too, but the sight leaves me a little breathless. Milly curtsying, just for me.

"Did you get the earring safely back to Elizabeth?" I ask.

"I..."

"Might we leave yet?" Clara appears behind Milly on the staircase, her modest pearl necklace glowing in the lamplight.

I wonder why she and Milly didn't come out of the grand hall together. It's striking to see the two of them side by side this way, Clara's small angles next to Milly's height and curves, Milly's soft yellow curls beginning to escape from her hairpins beside Clara's shining brown bob.

"I think we can," I say, when Milly doesn't answer her. "I've satisfied my mother."

"My father left, too, with a few of the others." Clara smiles at me. It's a little strange, the way she and Milly are both keeping their eyes on me, never turning toward each other, but then, it's not *that* strange. There are still moments when I'm reminded that it was me who drew the two of them together, and that I need to be the one to keep them that way. "A lot of the girls have gone back to their rooms. It's the perfect time to slip away."

"Let's, then." Milly turns to stride up the stairs, and Clara and I quickly follow.

"Shall I fix your hair, Gertie?" Clara murmurs at my side. "I can do a braided bun that would be perfect for you."

I love the thought of her fingers plucking through my dull brown hair. "By all means. That is to say, yes, please, if you would, Miss Blum."

She laughs softly.

We stop by Clara's room for her things, then retreat to the room Milly and I share. The fire burns cheerfully in the grate, and Milly carefully arrays her cosmetics, all strictly forbidden under seminary rules, across the bare writing desk.

The clock chimes in the grand hall below, faded music echoing from the remnants of the party beneath our feet, but we ignore it all. Clara takes out a stack of pins and I relax into the sensations of her smoothing my hair into neat strands, the evening flowing out of me like water.

My mother's gloved nails digging into my arm. The fury in Trixie's eyes. The rising and falling strains in Mrs. Rose's voice. It's all in the distance now.

I'm with the two people in the world who know me best. Who never ask me to pretend.

Milly pulls the dresses she ordered for us out of the wardrobe. The shop in New York had shipped them in plain brown boxes made to look as though they held innocent sets of stockings and combinations, and we had to alter the gowns ourselves, years of domestic science classes serving us at last. Clara stitched a little wrap to go over her shoulders, and Milly adjusted her neckline in the back, but all three dresses are black, beaded, and sleeveless, and they dip well below the collarbone.

Milly ordered us beaded handbags to match, too. They're already stacked on the table, each with a lipstick and a roll of cash tucked inside. The roll in Milly's bag looks awfully large, as though she's packed up her entire term's worth of spending money, and I'm about to ask if she thinks we'll need that much when the clock chimes again and I realize it's been a full hour since we shut ourselves away from the world. The achingly slow piano music has ended, and there are soft footsteps in the hall, and softer voices. Our classmates, murmuring greetings and whispering gossip as they get ready for bed.

Milly goes out in her gold dressing gown to ensure that all the partygoers have departed and that our dorm mother, old Miss Klein, who stopped bothering to do nightly bed checks by our junior year, is fast asleep.

When she comes back, Milly walks straight over to me. "You ought to borrow my headband. With the rhinestones. It would fit perfectly over those braids."

I reach back to feel the coils Clara wound. "That sounds lovely. Thank you."

"Trixie has one like that," Clara says as Milly retrieves the headband from a drawer.

"I've never seen her wear it," Milly says.

"Half of our room is covered in finery that Trixie never wears. There's barely room for either of us to turn around. Last night she slept in our sitting room, of all things."

I laugh. "Why?"

"I have no idea. It was awful. She kept stomping around, moving those two little chairs from one end of the room to the other, as if she'd decided to redecorate in the middle of the night."

"Is *that* what that sound was?" Milly eyes the wall.

"Did you think it was a ghost?" I grin. "Clara, you do look lovely in white, but try not to go scaring Milly, please."

Clara laughs, and we finish getting ready quickly. Milly tugs on her corselet while Clara and I step into our chemises, all of us pulling on our dresses last. The current fashion dictates that dresses be designed solely for girls whose bodies run in a straight line from top to bottom, like Clara and me, though I'm too tall to have a truly fashionable figure. Milly, with her curves, has to use an arsenal of corselets and side-lacers to achieve the effect.

I drape my new shawl over my bare shoulders. Clara eyes it as she slips on the thin silver bracelet I loaned her for the night. "That looks so much like Mrs. Rose's shawl."

"She gave it to me." The words are out before I can remember Mrs. Rose's admonition not to tell anyone. But surely that rule doesn't apply to Clara and Milly. "Tonight. During the party."

"How kind of her," Clara says. "Should we check the teachers' floor?"

"I'll go," I offer.

"I can do it," Milly says.

"No, it's all right. I'll be fast."

Lights-out time has come and gone, but I wrap my dressing gown tightly over my beaded dress and creep down the hall, peering outside to get a look at the windows two levels below ours. The seminary is designed on an angle, to face Dupont Circle, giving me a good view of the opposite hall.

The faculty are all meant to be in bed by this time, but you never know. One night, when she went down for a glass of water, Clara spotted our French teacher washing out her bloomers in a basin by the window. It was after lights-out then, too.

Tonight, though, the teachers' floor is dark and quiet. Almost too quiet. It usually takes longer for the building to settle down after a party. It's fortunate for tonight's adventure, though.

I'm hurrying back to tell Milly and Clara when I remember that sound in the alley. The gunshot ringing out.

No. It wasn't a gun. It wasn't anything to be concerned about at all. I've got to stop that voice in my head telling me otherwise.

But I'm glad we won't be going down *that* alley tonight.

When I get back, Milly and Clara have tucked away all the contraband and built the blankets on the beds into careful piles. Anyone who looks in while we're gone will think Milly and I are fast asleep, with the window open to let in a bit of a breeze. Clara's already done the same to her own bed, and if Trixie carries on with sleeping in their sitting room, even she won't notice her roommate's absence. Fortunate, again.

We all fall quiet, gazing at the open window. All that's left now is the drop.

We've gone over the plan a dozen times. I'll go first, then Milly, while Clara waits at the window. If she sees anything of concern, she'll call out the signal—back in Brooklyn, she learned to do a spot-on imitation of a nightingale—and Milly and I will conceal ourselves as best we can. When Clara's quite sure it's safe, she'll follow.

The drop from our window leads to the library balcony below. From there, we'll climb down the tree that leads to P Street. If we can make it that far without being seen, we'll cross to Massachusetts Avenue and walk to Thomas Circle, where the Lazy Susan is tucked down a dark, quiet alley.

The city must have dozens of speakeasies, if not hundreds, but we've only managed to learn the names and locations of a handful, and the passwords to even fewer. Milly's brother writes her letters every week from Cambridge, and despite his repeated insistence that his little sister should never enter such a scandalous place, it seems he can't help bragging. Lately, every letter seems to describe a new speakeasy he's heard about from his friends back home.

Milly pushes the window sash higher, and a cold wind sweeps into the room, sending up flickers from the fireplace.

We all hesitate.

"We could stay here, I suppose." Clara speaks in the lowest of murmurs, reaching up to adjust her glittery headpiece. "I don't know about you, but I have a hankering for a game of Parcheesi."

The spell is broken. Milly's body rocks with silent laughter.

I grin at my friends, lift my handbag and my shoes out over the windowsill, and let them drop. They land on the flat terra-cotta balcony with muted thumps.

There's no going back.

Milly and Clara drop their shoes and bags, too, and before the fear can overtake me, I tug up the hem of my beaded skirt and swing one leg out the window. I bend my elbows, planting my fingers firmly on the ledge.

Then I drop.

5

THE COLD HITS ME FIRST, EVEN BEFORE MY FINGERS FEEL THE
strain from clinging to the ledge. My coat is sturdy wool and
trimmed in fur, but my legs are clad only in sheer stockings,
and the wind is whipping past, finding every inch of vulnerable
skin. I lower my chin into the chill as Milly clambers out awkwardly alongside me.

Crack.

The sound only lasts an instant, and my face is still clenched
against the freezing temperatures when I realize my best friend's
elbow has just slammed into my nose.

That's when the pain comes, too.

I twist into the wind and grit my teeth to quiet the scream
bubbling in my throat. *Anyone* could've heard that crack.

When I risk a glance behind me, Milly's gotten a tighter
grip on the ledge and her elbows are folded back in front of her
where they belong. *I'm* glad she didn't fall, but my throbbing
nose is less certain of its opinion. I want to rub the soreness from
it, but we're two stories off the ground and both of my hands are
busy clinging to the ledge alongside her.

I crane my neck to look down at the street below. I don't see
anyone. Haven't heard any shouts, either.

We haven't been caught. Yet.

"Watch it!" I whisper-hiss, my frozen toes digging into the
recess in the cold brick wall.

"Sorry, sorry, sorry!" Milly whisper-hisses back, her crystal headpiece still somehow pinned neatly over her hair. Milly always stands at the height of fashion, even when hanging off the side of a building. "I didn't mean to!"

Then she lets out a soft giggle. A second later, I do the same. Milly dips her chin to peer at the windows on the faculty hall and gives me a confident nod.

Time to jump.

The old library is dark and curtained, the party over and the mess tucked away, but the balcony outside it will be as hard, rough, and cold as ever. If we land wrong, we could break a kneecap or crack our heads. But now that I'm here, hanging in the wind, suddenly I'm not afraid of getting hurt. In fact, I wouldn't mind if our window ledge were a few feet higher.

We're not cloistered into our seminary any longer. Out here, the world is wide open all around us. The cold air swells with possibility.

I let go of the ledge.

I land, too quickly, on my feet, my toes in their stockings curling back to cushion the blow. Before I can straighten to my full height, a *thunk* sounds beside me, and when I turn, Milly's sprawled out on her heinie, her skirt up past her knees, her crystal headpiece flapping off her head.

I've seen Milly with no skirt or headpiece of any kind more times than I can count, but I look away to be polite, though there's no way she'll miss my silent laughter as I fluff out the fringe on my new shawl and hold out a hand to help her up. She stumbles to her feet, glaring, and snatches a fallen hairpin from the ground, thrusting it at me without a word. I keep my giggles to a minimum while I get her headpiece back in position over her curls, and we bend to retrieve our shiny shoes and beaded handbags from the gray terra-cotta floor.

Now comes the hard part. We're one level off the street, but getting down shouldn't be difficult, thanks to the sturdy oak tree. The problem is the ancient double-globe lamppost on the opposite side. We're safely in the dark here on the balcony, but that old lamp shines straight onto the tree, and it's bare in wintertime. People walk out at all hours on Dupont Circle, and there are always motorcars trundling this way and that, and sometimes horses, too. There's no telling who'll be looking skyward.

We need to get into that tree and out of it again as fast as we possibly can. Any passerby could see us skirting along the branches and call the police. Or, worse, Mrs. Rose.

A delicious mix of fear and fervor crawls down my spine as I check to make sure the sidewalk is empty before I move toward the tree. It's difficult, clambering over the wide stone railing in my short dress, and even without anyone below, I can't help but worry about displaying my bloomers and garters to the cold outdoor air.

When I reach the first branch, I perch carefully to test its weight. It holds firm, so I move on to the next branch, then the next. Forward and over, forward and over, never slowing or looking down, until the trunk is inches from my outstretched fingers.

A patch of rough bark snags my stocking, and my toes nearly slip. It's a fight to regain my balance, but soon enough I'm braced against the sturdy trunk. I can feel a small rip in my heel, and I move carefully to keep it from widening. I wish I'd thought to tuck a spare stocking into my handbag.

Milly must've. She thinks of everything.

She's coming along behind me, the lamplight playing over her round, frowning face as she creeps forward across the branch. Her lower lip is tight between her teeth, and there's worry in her bright eyes.

I reach out a hand, but before she can grasp it, her foot slips on the rough patch and she plunges straight through the barren branches, her eyes wide and desperate.

I lunge, wrapping my legs around the trunk and twisting back, shoving my arms under hers. My back screams, my stockings and skin shredding against the bark. Milly's legs churn wildly in the air, but she isn't falling anymore.

We work together, me heaving up, her pushing down in one swift motion. A moment later, we're both nestled safely amid the branches.

My breaths come out in fierce, noiseless pants. *Someone* must have seen that. Or heard it. But there's no sound from below.

We begin moving carefully down the trunk. I'm about to ask Milly about those extra stockings when the sound comes from above. I peer up through the skeletal brown leaves.

A figure is leaning out a window above us.

I keep silent and still until my eyes focus in the darkness and I recognize the oval-shaped face peering down.

It's Clara. Her short brown hair falling in a disheveled halo, her lips parting rhythmically as she makes the sound of a bird's song.

Not *a* bird. A nightingale.

My heart flies to my mouth as our eyes connect. Clara's leaning out the window on her elbows, pointing to the street.

That figure I saw, moving in the alley. Running.

What if he's here? What if he's seen us, and he—

I twist my head, and I spot them.

Two figures, crossing the circle, nearing P Street. Twenty yards away and getting closer. But neither one's running, and there's no sign of any guns.

Instead, a man ambles toward us in a raccoon-fur coat, his head tilted back in laughter, a woman's hand tucked into his arm. She's laughing, too, with a cigarette clasped easily between her fingers.

I suck in a breath. It's Mrs. Rose.

I don't recognize the man at her side. He certainly wasn't at the faculty party. An old homburg sits angled on his head, tall and straight with a wide black ribbon, like the one my father wore years ago. On this man, though, the hat doesn't look old-fashioned at all. Everything about him, in fact, seems perfectly current, from his high, sharp cheekbones and rosy peach skin to the soft, easy smile on his lips.

Mrs. Rose has never mentioned any man.

I can't think about that now. If she catches us stealing away, it won't matter who she's with, or how many hours I've spent by the fire in her office.

Leaving the seminary without a chaperone is strictly forbidden. Climbing out the window must've been so inconceivable the board didn't even bother to specify it in the rule book. If we're caught, the expulsion will be automatic and instantaneous.

I'm not sure which to dread more. The punishment, or the disappointment in Mrs. Rose's eyes.

The man leans down to say something into her ear, and she laughs again, her long, pale neck arcing in the pool of light from the streetlamp. The jewels in her ears glitter. She's wearing a plush fur stole over her coat, with the Spanish fringe of her shawl dangling loose around it.

Her laugh tonight isn't like any I've heard her utter before. Mrs. Rose is always calm. Composed. Gentle. Tonight, her laugh is open, friendly, and brash.

I never could've imagined describing Mrs. Rose as *brash*.

"Those people tonight, dear God," she's saying to the man

in the homburg, lifting the cigarette to her lips. I've never seen her smoke. Women teachers at our school aren't allowed, though Mr. Farrel smokes through every Latin lesson. I leave his classroom each morning smelling like a furnace. "Parties are the most horrendous part of this job. If I hadn't been coming out with you afterward, I'd have thrown myself into the punch bowl."

The man in the homburg laughs again and pats her hand where it's tucked into the crook of his arm. It doesn't seem to be a lingering, romantic stroke, though. More of an amused, friendly tap.

"Careful," the man says. "You'd run the risk of ruining your *spectacular* shawl."

"If needs must!" Mrs. Rose replies, her cloche hat tipping backward as she chuckles. "Sad as I'd be to part with it. Would you believe I wore it in front of those ladies tonight? Nearly gave that old Patterson biddy a heart attack."

The man laughs again. These two seem to laugh together quite a bit. "You wore a knockoff Spanish shawl in front of *Thomasina Patterson?*"

"Oh, I'm past caring what any of those women think. They wrote me off the moment I dared to suggest their school acknowledge the dawn of the twentieth century. To hear them talk, you'd think I was stalking from room to room with a pair of kitchen shears each night, bobbing their granddaughters' hair as they sleep."

I dig my fingers into the tree trunk and stretch the toes of my left leg down as the man laughs again. I want to get a better look at him. There's something about the way he and Mrs. Rose are leaning in toward each other. It's so comfortable. So familiar.

"Watch what you say," he tells Mrs. Rose. "I've seen a few

of your colleagues at the East Room around this time of night. Some may be passing us on their way out as we speak."

"Oh, no, the whole lot of them's fast asleep. You should've seen those teachers dragging themselves out of the party, nodding off on their feet. The parents, too."

"Tired from the excitement of sipping fruit punch and chatting about bonds?"

"I *wish* they'd talk about the stock market. In New York, all the party talk was about money, and I was used to it. Could chat about commodities until the cows came home. But here, no, with *these* parents, it's all who's in line for which first assistant secretaryship, and who spoke out of turn to which justice at so-and-so's dinner party, and who's building a new mansion well beyond his means, and what a *scandal* it all is." She lets out a barking laugh, and I think again of that word. *Brash.* "None of them would know scandal if it bit them in the toe! Every party here's a competition for who can make the dullest conversation."

"My dear Jessica." The man takes another puff on his cigarette. I didn't know her first name was Jessica. How did I not know that? "One would think you were new to our lovely capital."

Mrs. Rose's answering laugh is so sharp I flinch.

My foot slips. Cracked leaves crunch sharply underneath, and I have to grab the trunk to keep from falling, my gloved hand landing against it with a stinging slap.

It's the slap that makes Mrs. Rose's head jerk toward us.

I shrink into the branches, willing myself to turn the same shade of gray as her stole. The wind whips past me, but I can't shiver.

She saw us. She *must* have.

"Something wrong?" the man asks her.

I dart a glance up toward the building, but the window is empty. Clara's gone back inside.

I'm glad. When Milly and I are expelled, at least we can spare Clara the same fate.

Mrs. Rose hesitates. Finally, she turns back to the man. "No. Nothing."

"Must've been the wind. Shall I escort you to the door?"

"Better not. Lucy'll be waiting up. The dear girl never sleeps." Mrs. Rose says something more, but they've passed the corner of the building, and I can't make out the words.

Neither Milly nor I move. Not for a long, excruciating moment, and another after that.

The voices of Mrs. Rose and the man fade away to nothing. Then comes a small, faraway motion that might be the seminary's front door opening and closing, or might be nothing at all.

Finally, when it seems enough time has passed and then some, I exhale, my heart pumping fiercely.

The branch below me shudders. Milly's climbing down.

I reach out to help, and soon we're both crouched on the cold brown grass outside the dining room, past the lamplight. Clara comes quickly afterward, making the entire descent look positively easy, and the three of us duck behind the tree to brush the broken leaves off our coats, wipe away one another's lipstick smears, and strap on our shoes. Milly gives me her extra pair of stockings and holds out her coat to shield me from the street while I struggle out of my torn pair.

Her cheeks are flushed as we start down the sidewalk, heels clicking on the pavement. Clara's face is pale with fear, but she manages to smile as she loops her arm through mine, and Milly links elbows with me on the other side.

I answer with a bright smile and the startling realization that after everything—the near fall and nearer expulsion, the scrapes burning along my thighs, the lingering questions about that man and Mrs. Rose—I'm still bubbling over with delight, from my carefully perched headband to my fashionably pinched toes.

It's time to put as much space between us and the Washington Female Seminary as we can. Our night is finally beginning.

I WONDER WHAT MRS. ROSE WAS DOING OUT SO LATE," MILLY murmurs as our heels click-clack down Massachusetts Avenue. The Lazy Susan isn't far off, but the howling wind feels colder here, as though it knows we've left the seminary's protection behind. "And who was that man?"

"I don't know."

"She wasn't wearing that stole at the faculty party," Clara murmurs, darting a look at Milly as we all huddle into our short coats. "She couldn't have bought it herself, not on her salary."

"Perhaps he gave it to her." Milly taps her chin. "She may be in the market for a new husband."

I shake my head, my nose aching where it collided with Milly's elbow. "She told me widowhood suits her. Women can do much more without husbands tying them down."

"Oh." Milly's lilting words come easily. But then, most things come easily to Milly. "He must be her lover, then."

"Milly!" I gasp. "She doesn't have one of *those*!"

I wait for Clara to agree, but she only lets out a tiny hum.

"How do you know she doesn't?" Milly's tone is patient, but she quirks her eyebrows at me, the way she does when she thinks I'm being naïve.

It's what she teases me about most. Our classmates go to great pains to make sure the whole school knows how many boys write to them. Every evening in the downstairs hall, the seniors read aloud the newest letters they've gotten from freshmen and sophomores at Princeton and Yale and George Washington. Girls gather around to listen as though it's the hottest new radio play, giggling at the poorly written accounts of rugby games and fraternity pranks, and recounting stolen kisses in theater balconies, or imagined ones in more secluded spaces.

I join in sometimes, to be friendly, but most nights it's a great deal more fun to play billiards on the far side of the room. Besides, there aren't any boys I *want* to get letters from, much less kisses. Clara's never mentioned any, either.

Milly gets letters from a boy in Paris, but she never shows them to anyone, even me. Sometimes, she'll stare down at a newly received envelope with her brows creased and set it aside without opening it.

She's always been far more interested in literature, spending most of her nights burying her head in essays about socialism or novels written entirely in French. Last night she vanished for the duration of dinner, and when I asked her about it later, she told me she'd gotten so caught up in a volume on recent scientific discoveries that she hadn't even realized she was hungry until after the dessert course had been cleared away. Irene Donovan and I split her custard between us.

Milly loves to point out how unusual I am for my lack of interest in everyone's romances. For my part, though, I think it's very sensible of me.

"Mrs. Rose is our headmistress," I remind Milly. "If she had a...if there were a man in the picture, she'd lose her job."

"I'm well aware of how thoroughly you venerate her, but you can't deny that the two of them looked awfully familiar."

Milly's the star of our debate team, and she can convince just about anyone of just about anything, but not me. Not tonight. Something about the way Mrs. Rose and the man in the old-fashioned hat walked together didn't seem romantic.

But there was something else that's giving me pause. "What was it he said?" I ask. "Did he call her shawl a knockoff?"

"Well, yes." Milly nods. "Anyone could see how cheap it was. They used *paint* instead of embroidery, for heaven's sake." She glances at the matching shawl draped across my shoulders and adds, "Of course, that one looks divine on *you*. Economizing was all the rage in Paris last season, and you absolutely have the shoulders for it, besides."

The way that man spoke about the shawl... *could* it have been him who gave it to Mrs. Rose? The parents at the seminary gave her proper gifts, she said. Parasols and letter openers. This shawl, with its Spanish fringe, is pushing the boundaries of good taste, if ever so slightly.

It's something to think of. Mrs. Rose, breaking the rules. Smoking cigarettes. Going around with men.

We walk past shuttered stores, our heels ringing out in the quiet. We passed by several people a block or so after we left the seminary, but this far down the street, this late at night, no one is in view.

"I suppose you'd know," Milly says as we near a set of steps leading down from the sidewalk. "You spend more time with that woman than anyone."

"No, I don't."

A door at the bottom of the steps, on the basement level, has a drab green awning with a set of faded black letters across the front reading DUKE'S. The awning is so old and tattered I can't tell if Duke's is still in business or if that sign's been there since before Prohibition.

"You do tend to linger in her office," Clara says. We've progressed farther down Massachusetts Avenue, and the streets aren't quite as empty here. Every so often we pass a woman wrapped tightly in a shawl, or a man with his hat pulled down around his ears. No one speaks, though. Not to us, and not to each other. I don't miss the confines of the seminary, but I long for its warmth. "This morning you were in there a full hour."

"Well, we get to talking. Did you know she went to college in California? She took the train all on her own when she was barely older than us. It's so glamorous."

"Nothing's glamorous about a girl traveling alone," Milly says. "People think you're common. Men leer."

"Milly, no one's ever thought you were common in your life."

"Well. They leer all the same."

We cross Scott Circle. The brownstones fade into taller apartment buildings, and the coats on the passersby grow shabbier. A handwritten sign on a darkened grocery store window promises lard for ten cents a pound. Milly stops walking, peering down into the empty alley beside the store.

No—it's not empty. Someone's standing there.

Clara turns to me. "That shawl," she says, fingering the Spanish fringe. "It's lovely. She must be awfully fond of you."

I stop walking, too, my shoes growing tight around my toes.

If that man *did* give Mrs. Rose the shawl, what does it mean? If he's not her lover, then who is he?

Unmarried women aren't supposed to be friends with men. Headmistresses aren't supposed to so much as speak to them.

Something isn't right.

I raise my eyes from my shoes. "Where's Milly?"

Clara's eyes are still fixed on my shawl. "Down in the alley, talking to that man."

"What man?"

"The beggar. You didn't see him?"

Then I hear the voices rising from behind us. Milly's and another, low and unfamiliar.

"Grazie," the man says.

I don't know much Italian. It's enough of a struggle for me to keep up with our French and Latin classes without adding another language into the mix. Milly, though, learned Italian as a child, when she lived abroad with her parents, and it's because of her that I know *grazie* means *thank you.*

When she emerges from the alley, Milly's alone.

"Who was that?" I ask.

"A poor man who needed money." Milly shrugs, walking quickly in her narrow heels.

"And you... gave him some?"

"He needed it for his family." Milly stares at me, as though *I'm* the one speaking a foreign language.

I'm beginning to feel silly. "I didn't even see him."

"All right, well, I certainly didn't imagine him." Milly lets out a tiny laugh.

"I heard him speaking Italian with you."

"Yes. He must have trouble earning money without speaking the language." Milly shakes her head.

It's not the first time Milly's spoken Italian with a stranger. Once she ordered an entire meal for us at the Roma on F Street without my understanding a word. The waiter spoke English to me, though, when he asked if I'd like more bread.

It isn't the first time I've known her to give away money, either. Milly's always generous with beggars. Besides, she brought that awfully large roll of cash in her handbag.

Though when I glance down at the beaded bag dangling from her hand, I don't see the bulge of banknotes anymore.

"This is it," Clara murmurs after another moment.

The lamps above us have faded as we've walked on, and the whole street is draped in shadows, the apartments and passersby far behind us. I know from the street numbers that the Lazy Susan is farther up this block, but there's no indication of it here. I suppose that's to be expected. It may be the most famous speakeasy in the city, but its existence is still, officially, secret.

I do hear something, though. Heavy footsteps, shuffling toward us in the grit.

A man, from the sound of it. A large one.

At first, I worry that it's the man Milly spoke to, here to ask for more money from the rest of us, but no—this one is coming from the opposite direction. He's tall and broad, with a slow, careless gait, and it's too dark to see his face. He's at the end of the block, dressed in a heavy brown suit, and he's got something in his hand, swinging as he walks. Metal and black. The light glints off it as he passes.

A gun. He's carrying a gun.

Our adventure in the city doesn't feel exciting anymore.

The man steps away from the streetlamp, shadows falling around him. All I can make out is his silhouette, wide shoulders in a boxy brown suit jacket, his fedora soaring over his tall frame.

Just as my heart begins to race, the man turns away. Tucks the gun into his coat and rounds a corner up ahead.

He didn't see us.

I exhale.

Milly nods fast, the movement nearly imperceptible. "Let's get inside."

"Yes, please."

The block darkens as we pass into the next alley. A short man and a taller woman are standing outside a shut-tight door at the back of a drab gray concrete building halfway down, and we hurry toward them. This man is dressed in a gray flannel three-piece suit, and he looks about my father's age, with a thick pair of dark brown eyebrows.

As we stand, watching, the man bends at the waist until

his face is directly in front of the door's mail slot. His rear end stands straight up, bringing to mind a sketch of an ostrich I once saw in a book.

"That's it," Milly whispers. "The Lazy Susan. It's got to be."

Still, none of us moves any farther.

Halfway down the alley, on the other side of that door, is freedom. Tantalizing, wide-open possibility, like the drop down from the window ledge.

But the alley's so dark, and the air smells foul. Like sour food and too many people's sweat.

And we don't know what else might be out here. That hulking man, with the gun...

If we go back, we'll still have had a *taste* of freedom. Of dirty street corners and shapes lurking in the dark.

Beside me, Milly shifts her weight from one T-strap heel to the other. I'm parting my lips to suggest returning to the seminary when a new footstep sounds in the gravel at our backs.

Then another. Heavier than the first.

I look at Milly and Clara. They're both nodding rapidly.

We don't hesitate any longer.

7

W E RUSH UP BEHIND THE COUPLE AT THE SHUT-TIGHT DOOR AS the man in the gray suit straightens to his full height. The woman is younger than her companion, with dark hair that falls to her ears and a crystal headband across her forehead. Her eyebrows are largely pencil, and her ring finger is bare. Her black T-strap shoes and dark red lipstick both match Milly's perfectly.

At the sound of our clicking heels, the woman turns and looks us up and down, her lip quirking.

The door finally opens a single inch, then stops. A pair of eyes peers from the darkness behind the cracked green paint.

The man in the gray suit reaches for the knob, pulling the door open wide enough to squeeze through. The woman stops before she follows him in.

"Let these three kids in, too, won't you?" she asks the eyes in the doorway. "They're with us."

I don't let my surprise show on my face as the woman casts us one more half-smile and slips through, leaving us alone with the eyes in front of us and the darkness at our backs.

Milly, Clara, and I press forward as the gap in the door widens, shedding enough light to reveal an olive-skinned man in a plaid suit and derby hat, a cigarette hanging from the corner of his thick-lipped mouth. It's burnt nearly to the end.

I paint on my brightest smile.

"Girls." The man in the plaid suit inclines his head so slightly I'm not sure it happened at all. He pulls the cigarette from his mouth, tipping it into a corner of the doorway that's already piled high with ash. I wait for him to ask how old we are, but all he says is, "Evening."

"Wishing a very pleasant evening to you as well, sir," I say, as smoothly as if I'm in our weekly etiquette lesson with Madame Frost.

The man chuckles and gives me an elaborate bow. Milly catches on and holds out a gloved hand, and he takes it in his nicotine-stained fingers. For a moment I'm afraid he's going to kiss it and get ash all over the satin, but he stops short and lifts his head, chuckling again.

"Password?" he asks.

I freeze.

The password was in Milly's brother's letter. I know it. Or rather, I *knew* it. Before the near-fall from the tree, and that man walking arm-in-arm with Mrs. Rose, and the strange hulking shape in the dark...

It started with an *L*, didn't it? *Lavender? Lincoln?*

"Forget it." The man chuckles again and steps aside. "I ain't never seen dry squad agents look that jumpy. Have a nice night, ladies."

"We're very grateful, sir," Clara says. "Thank you ever so."

We move quickly past him, following the couple ahead down a dark hall that smells worse than the alley. I avert my eyes from the splashes of liquid in the corners and inhale through my mouth. At the top of a narrow flight of stairs, the woman takes off her coat, revealing a black velvet dress and four strands of pearls hanging to her waist. I've never seen anyone wear that many pearls at once except Milly, and she only did it on the first night Clara stole into our room after lights-out, when we all took turns dressing up like Zelda Fitzgerald and laughed ourselves silly.

Music trickles down as we steer around the fetid hallway,

climb the stairs, and pass through another door, where a thick wave of cigarette smoke overpowers the other scents.

Milly clasps my hand, her satin glove in mine. On my other side, I take Clara's hand, too, and together, we lift our chins and step through the door.

It's barely any lighter here than it was in the hall, with smoke dimming the scattered lamps. We pass our coats to a tall check girl with a deep-brown complexion and a sunny smile and wind our way through a cluster of tightly packed tables.

Ahead of us is a tiny, crowded dance floor, where men and women only inches apart step effortlessly to jaunty jazz music, many while holding a glass in one hand, liquid spilling out with each movement. Most of the tables are crowded with groups of five or six, as though the people here are determined to fill every last bit of space.

The women are all wearing low-waisted dresses that skim their knees in deep hues, like ours. Milly's dress plunges in the back, nearly to her waist, and more than one man eyes her as we steer toward an empty table. I remember what she said before, about leering.

Milly walks briskly, her chin lifted. Still, the beaded fabric of her handbag is crumpled in her clutching fingers, betraying her carefully concealed discomfort.

This room is the precise opposite of the seminary library, with its old ladies grading everyone else's decorum and men competing to out-boast one another. Here, there's no room for etiquette or excess. People have to lean in across their tables to speak, or forgo conversation altogether on the dance floor.

Somehow, Milly finds us a table. "What can I get you girls?" asks a waiter with a black bow tie, light brown skin, and slick black hair before we've properly sat down.

Nearly all the staff in the room seem to have brown skin of

various shades, though everyone seated at the cocktail tables is white, like us. In New York, Clara told me once, her school had Black students as well as white, but then, the laws are different there. Though I'm not sure why segregation laws would matter in the Lazy Susan, when its very existence is illegal.

The four men gathered onstage with horns, a piano, and a drum set all have dark brown skin, too, and the music they're playing is a far cry from the dull plodding of the white-haired man at the piano back in the grand hall. It's joyful, and vibrant, and *alive*. It makes me wish I knew how to dance to jazz music.

The waiter looks at me expectantly, and I realize I have no idea what to tell him. The only liquor I've ever had is bathtub gin, and it tasted like pine trees mixed with my mother's reducing soap.

"Three whiskey sours, if you would, please," Milly says, and the waiter's gone as quick as he came.

Milly's eyes slide past me to Clara, and the two of them hold each other's gaze. I wonder if they agreed on whiskey sours before we came. Perhaps they discussed it while I was down the hall, peering out at the teachers' windows.

My eyes roam the room, from the pair of women in a corner table each balancing a long cigarette holder in one hand and a drink in the other, to the couple checking a mink coat that must have cost five hundred dollars, to the puddles of spilled liquid making the dance floor sticky and dark.

A small smile creeps across my face. We're *here*. We made it through every door, past all that lurked in the dark city and into this intimate, interesting place, with music pouring from the stage and thin gray smoke making the world around us soft and hazy.

Clara leans toward me, her forearm brushing mine. "I recognize that fellow."

I hadn't been paying much attention to the fellows. "Which?"

"Next to the bar."

It's the man in the gray suit, with the woman in all the crystals and pearls. "Yes. He came in just ahead of us."

"I met him at a party. With my father."

The waiter deposits three mismatched glasses on our table. I sip my drink. Lemon and sweetness. A group of men with twinkling eyes at the table next to ours laughs and puffs on cigars, while the man and woman behind us watch the band and trade silent smiles.

"He's assistant secretary of something," Clara goes on. "Perhaps Commerce. Mr. Pengelley, I believe."

From all the parties my parents have dragged me to, I'd swear half the men in this city are assistant secretaries of one cabinet department or another. Still, I didn't expect to see such a high-up government man in a nightclub. No one can breathe a word about speakeasies in my father's presence, not unless we want him to launch into a grumbling lecture about vice and impropriety.

Milly stops a girl with a tray strapped around her shoulders and asks her for a cigarette and a match. The girl's red silk dress is so short we can see her knees. Milly passes the girl a few coins, and I catch a glimpse of lacy black garter under her hem. I draw in a sharp breath and look away.

The cigarette girl leaves, but before Milly can strike her match, a man in a tailored tweed suit leans over from the next table and lights it for her. Milly thanks him, and he smiles, blue eyes sparkling, before twisting back to the rest of the men at his table.

One of his friends, a man with yellow hair in a nearly identical tweed suit, glances up at a trio of very tall men who entered the room behind us, then turns and says something in a low voice that causes his whole table to erupt into raucous laughs. With his cigarette dangling from the edge of his mouth and his pomaded hair gleaming, he reminds me of the man we saw with Mrs. Rose tonight.

The yellow-haired man stands up and takes a bow as the laughter crests. "I'm saving the punch line for the Seven Seas," he says, loud enough for everyone nearby to hear. The two women from the opposite table smile at him indulgently.

"You can tell it to Victor, and Admiral Jenks!" one of his friends replies, and that makes them all laugh harder. They may well be having the most fun of anyone in the Lazy Susan.

We watch as the first man, the blue-eyed one, leans in to murmur something to one of his friends, nearly so close as to defy propriety. Though perhaps *propriety* means something different in a place like this than it does in the real world.

Milly leans in and drops her voice. "If I didn't know better, I'd think they were..."

A smile blooms on Clara's face. Her lips look nearly black in the shadowy light. A person could drown in Clara's lips.

"Well," Clara murmurs. "They say this *is* the place for that sort of thing."

Milly smiles at her. Clara smiles back, for an instant, then drops her gaze to the table.

"What sort of thing?" I ask.

Both of them glance at me. Then they lock eyes, their smiles curving.

Another joke between them I don't understand. I shift in my seat.

"You know." Milly lowers her voice so far I have to scoot in until our cheeks are touching. *"Pansies."*

I'm lost, until I take another look at the group of men. The six of them are gathered around a table that's even smaller than the others. Perhaps that's why they're all sitting so close together.

Or perhaps...

I sit back heavily in my seat and sip my drink. My thoughts are moving rapidly, and the whiskey is strong and sweet.

In August, my father insisted on bringing my mother and me to the Ambassador Theater to see a motion picture he'd read about called *Wings*. It was about two pilots in the Great War, but what I remembered most was a single, brief moment. It only appeared on the thirty-foot screen for a second or two, yet it was fixed in my memory as though I'd watched it countless times.

It was a scene in a bar, with several couples sitting at tables. A bar not so different from the Lazy Susan, come to think of it, but before that was illegal.

One of the couples was made up of two women. They both wore men's suits. One even had a man's hat. Yet their faces were soft, and their hands were clasped. As the camera swept past them, their eyes locked on one another's faces and their lips parted in rapturous, heady smiles. Then one of the women reached over to stroke the other's cheek.

I've played that moment over countless nights, lying in bed in my soft flannel nightgown, listening to Milly's even breaths across the room.

In, out. In, out.

Once, when I could hear Milly tossing in bed, struggling to fall asleep, I asked if she'd seen that picture. If she remembered that moment in it.

"I have," she'd answered immediately, rolling over in her bed to face me in mine. "And I do."

I tore my gaze from the ceiling, and our eyes met in the darkness. Just like the women in the picture.

I was seized by worry, suddenly. A fear I couldn't name. An abrupt awareness that it wasn't all right for me to be talking about this, even with Milly.

Particularly with Milly.

I drew up my blankets and rolled over to face the wall.

Perhaps that fear was unnecessary. The men beside us aren't turning away, after all.

Shouldn't they, though? It's against the law, isn't it? Being that way?

When I look up, Milly and Clara are both watching me. Milly is clenching her cocktail glass, and Clara's chin is wobbling.

I blush. "Oh."

"*Oh*, indeed." Milly laughs, and Clara's lips shift into a smile.

The waiter glides by, sweeping up our empty glasses and depositing them on a heavy black table that's already stacked high with dishes. I wait until he's gone before I speak again.

"Why are they called *pansies*?" I ask Milly.

She wrinkles her nose. "I'm not sure. Do you suppose that term's only for men?"

"Sometimes they say *gay*." Clara nods. "For women, it's *violets*."

Milly raises her eyebrows at Clara, then quickly turns back to study the tabletop.

"None of it's true, of course." Milly drops to a whisper. "Men like *that* wouldn't dare come out in society. Their families would never want to see them again. It happened to a boy my brother knew at university, and he had to move to Greece. He'd have been locked up in St. Elizabeths if it'd happened here."

"That's if he was lucky," Clara adds, so quietly I have to lean in to make out her words. "If he didn't get a beating and a prison sentence."

"They beat them at St. Elizabeths, too," Milly says.

"...Oh." I knew it was illegal, but...beatings?

St. Elizabeths used to be called the Government Hospital for the Insane, and it's still an asylum, southeast of the Capitol. It's where they send the people my father calls "criminally insane." Murderers and thieves.

The men at the next table don't look like murderers and thieves. Still, perhaps I *was* right to roll over and face the wall that night.

Then my eyes catch on a table near the stage, and I forget all about pansies and violets and the tweed-suited men.

"Look." I whip around to face my friends.

Milly sees them first. She turns her back on them, too, slower and more carefully than I did. "Hmm. Interesting."

Clara turns away. The expression on her face hasn't changed, but her fingers in their white gloves are wrapping tightly around the edge of the table.

Directly in front of the tiny stage are Damian and George Babcock. Trixie's uncle and father are hunched over a table, laughing hard at who knows what. They're both shiny-faced and smoking, and the empty glasses in front of them are clearly not their first of the evening.

Either one of them would recognize us instantly.

What are they *doing* here? I never imagined being seen by respectable people in a place like the Lazy Susan.

I long to squirm, but I've been under strict orders not to since I was barely out of diapers.

"I don't want to leave." I try to keep my voice low and serious, but it comes out a petulant whine. "Not so soon, but..."

"We're not going anywhere." Milly's breaths are steadier than mine.

"How?" I lay my hands flat on the table, trying to act calm, the way Milly is. Clara hasn't spoken since we spotted the Babcocks, but her fingers haven't loosened their grip on the table.

Milly glances at the Babcocks and taps her cigarette into our table's ashtray. "Honestly, they're both three sheets to the wind. I don't think they'll notice us."

"Are you sure?"

"Well, no, but if they *did*, odds are they'd look the other way."

Clara finally nods. "It's no better for them being seen here than it is for us."

"But what do you think would happen if..."

Before I can finish my worried question, the lights cut out. The whole room plunges into darkness.

Then a girl screams, "It's the *feds!*"

And in an instant, the whole room is moving.

8

Whistles blast through the room. A dozen of them. A hundred.

It's too dark to see. I try to stand, but I'm moving too slowly, as though swimming underwater. All around us is a pitch-black haze. The music's stopped.

"What's going on?" Clara asks at my side, her voice high. I reach, blundering through the smoke for her hand, but I can't find it in the darkness.

The whistles are buried in the sound of stamping feet. Hundreds of them. The group of men in tweed is already dashing through the haphazard arrangement of tables. "Meet at the Seas!" one of them shouts to his friends.

Then, a hand. Milly's hand, grabbing mine across the table. Holding tight.

The jazz band has vanished, leaving a single cymbal still vibrating. People are tearing toward the stage. There must be a door behind it.

It's a little exciting.

Then something knocks Milly forward into the table and our glasses topple to the side, liquid pooling with a clutter of melting ice cubes, and the excitement yields to panic.

"Now!" Milly yanks on my hand, pulling me up. My knee smashes into the table. A rush of pain shoots up my leg.

Beside me, Clara grunts. Milly has her by the hand, too. Behind us, a crash rings out.

"This way!" Milly calls. I try to step around the table as she jerks my hand again, pulling us toward the stage.

I squint into the darkness as Milly stumbles up on her heels. The world is vague and hazy, glimpses of lighted ends of cigarettes, abandoned on tables and the floor, others still clutched in hands as people down the remains of their drinks and run, empty glasses dropping wherever they land. The table behind us is on its side, crunching into broken glass as people push past it, footsteps pounding as everyone rushes in the same direction.

I clutch at Milly's fingers. It would be too easy to lose each other.

My shoes stick and skid on the wet floor. Someone bumps into me, and I fumble my grasp on Milly in the noise and the dark. Then there's another crash, the loudest yet, and Milly's fingers slip out of my grip.

My head pounds. Someone in front of me—it might be Clara, but it's too dark to tell—is bending forward, straining, heaving. She hauls something up. A table—the one that was stacked high with plates and glasses. The dishes are covering the ground now, in fragments, and among them, Milly's struggling to her feet. Clara's helping her up as people swarm around them.

I try to move toward them, but I trip and fall into a man's back. He grunts and pushes me away, and I fall forward again as someone knocks me from behind. I jerk away an instant before my palm lands on something sharp and jagged. The room is a sea of backs and legs in motion.

"Gertie!" Clara screams. *"Where are you?"*

"Here!" I try to shout, struggling to my feet, plucking the glass from my hand and tightening my fist around the thin stream of blood left behind. *"I'm here!"*

But my friends can't hear me. Can't find me. I'm alone, and it's dark, and there's nothing but pushing, shouting.

"*Get off!*" someone bellows as I finally pull myself upright. Then there's a smacking noise. A thud.

A light flashes so brilliantly I have to shut my eyes. When I open them a moment later, a man is sprawled on the floor at my feet, moaning, his tie sprung loose from his jacket and crumpled in a pool of liquid. Another man's standing over him, chest heaving.

It's one of the Babcock men. The one with hair. Trixie's father. He's rubbing his hand. The elder Mr. Babcock is at his side, eyes darting around the room.

The man on the floor is trying to get up, and the assistant secretary of something-or-other, the man who came in just ahead of us—Pengelley, that's what Clara said his name was, Mr. Pengelley—runs between the Babcocks and the stranger, throwing up his arms. "Stop it! All of you!"

I start toward them, to help somehow, but before I can close the distance another light goes off, closer than before, and I fling my arm over my eyes.

Then comes the shout—"Nobody move!"—and I see them. The dry squad. A dozen officers are charging in from the front hallway, flat black hats on their heads and guns in their hands, flashing as they point in every direction.

Shouts. Bedlam. Worse than before. Much worse. Hundreds of people, pushing, shoving, running for the stage. Shattering glass. Indecipherable screams.

The Prohibition agent who called out for no one to move is in the middle of the group, but he's not wearing a black hat or a uniform. He's bigger than the rest of the men, his shoulders wide and his chin high, and he's wearing a boxy brown suit and fedora. He's the only person in the room who isn't running.

I remember that suit and hat. It's the man we saw out on the street. Looming at the end of the block with a gun in his hand.

I try to run, but everywhere I turn, people are crushing forward. More officers rush into the room, billy sticks over their heads. Another man in a gray suit follows, a large camera in his hands.

A sharp cry rings out behind my right shoulder. The woman with the pearls.

"Bruce!" she shouts.

Mr. Pengelley is standing with his back to a wall and his hands in the air. Two officers are moving toward him, clubs raised. There's no sign of the man who was lying on the floor a moment ago, but the Babcock brothers are sprinting past us, Trixie's father stumbling and clutching at his left leg.

Will they recognize us in all this dark and chaos?

"Bruce!" the woman screams again.

I reach out. I grab her hand, tug her toward the stage.

"No!" The woman yanks out of my grip, twisting back. Behind us, a billy club crashes down, and a man cries out. I look back to see a trickle of blood on a forehead, and then a rush of it, thick and black in the low light.

I grab the woman's arm above the elbow, tighter. She looks at me for the first time, her eyes wild and wet. I can't see the Babcocks anymore.

"Hurry!" I shout. It's too noisy to hear much, but I think she understands. "Come with me!"

I drag her toward the stage. She staggers across the wooden floor. *"Bruce! BRUCE!"*

"It's too late!" I shout. "Come *on!"*

A hand closes around my other wrist, yanking so hard my shoulder twists. The hand drags me into the crush of bodies, until I'm the one being crushed. Still, I don't let go of the woman, even when I hear her screaming.

I can't breathe. I can't bear this.

That man's cry as the club crashed down.

Then I'm past the curtain. Behind the stage. Milly and Clara are there, panting, both of them trying to talk to me at once, pulling me into a stifling hug. The woman in the pearls is there, too, bent at the waist, her crystal headband gone, her hands on her knees.

She looks up long enough to nod at me.

I can't understand what Milly and Clara are saying. I don't know which of them pulled me through, and there's no time to ask. The crowd is thundering down the stairs, and we're all caught up in the rush. The screams from inside the club have been replaced by a hushed urgency, and all I can think about is not tripping in my heels as we dash into a pitch-black hall that smells of old vomit, down a set of stairs I can't see, and out into the cold, open air.

Clara and Milly are on either side of me, the three of us holding hands as we run. The mess of bodies has room to spread out at last, but no one slows. The woman in the pearls is running, too, ahead of us and around a corner, until she vanishes from sight.

The front door of the Lazy Susan is open wide as we run past. I wonder what happened to the bouncer.

We bolt for Massachusetts Avenue. Behind us, a stomach-churning boom—a gunshot? A bomb?—goes off. We cover our ears and sprint.

Patronizing an illegal establishment. My father sentences people for that. We'll be arrested *and* expelled.

We dart down one block, then another, before we start to slow down.

Are the police behind us? I can't risk looking back.

Our coats are still with the check girl. I hope she got out. The waiter, too.

Milly must be even colder than me in her backless dress. Clara notices, and she peels off the little black jacket she stitched to go over her own dress. Milly frowns, hesitating to take it, but when a group of men passes us on the opposite side of the street and one of them whistles long and low, she nods to Clara in a silent thank-you and wraps the jacket around her shoulders.

I'm trembling. We're all trembling.

"They could be following us," Milly whispers. We've shifted into a walk—anything more would draw too much attention now that we're apart from the crowd—but we're still moving faster than I've ever moved in heels. "Let's take a different route home."

"They aren't following us," Clara whispers back. "We'd know."

"What are they *thinking*, storming into a place full of government men?" Milly sounds indignant, but there's a catch in her voice. Her fear hasn't disappeared.

"Will they shut down the Lazy Susan?" I whisper as a sleek brown Ford trundles past. My nose is threatening to drip, and I inhale roughly until it stops. It's bad enough for Clara to see my chattering teeth and the goose pimples running up my arms without her seeing me sniveling, too.

"They might," Milly whispers. "It was selling liquor. Besides, you saw the sort that gathers there. Those men. That's illegal, too."

"But...will they open again?" I'd thought tonight would be our first of countless evenings at the Susan. Where I could try on being somebody else, and get it better each time. Until I knew how to act like a girl who didn't have to worry about doing the just-right thing, marrying the just-right man, living the just-right life.

That's my future. It's always been my future. But I thought I'd have some time before it came for me.

"Even if they do, we can't go back," Milly mutters. "You nearly got caught. If I hadn't pulled you away when I did, you'd be with the feds instead of with Clara and me."

"The feds aren't looking for girls like us." Clara's voice tilts up, as though she's about to laugh, or cry.

I want to lean into her. Exhale slow breaths into the crook of her arm. Take comfort in her warmth.

But we can't stop moving.

"The law only cares about men with power," Clara goes on. "Men they can make a show of."

Like that assistant secretary, Mr. Pengelley. Bruce.

I wonder who the woman in the pearls was to him. She wasn't wearing a wedding ring, but she was certainly acting like she loved him all the same.

"It doesn't matter," Milly says. "Even if they didn't arrest us, being brought home by the police would guarantee our expulsion. Worse, if the press found out. Can you imagine? A judge's daughter, caught up in a speakeasy raid? Though it'd be worst for you, Clara. Your father would never win reelection."

"He wouldn't get that far," Clara says. "If this made the papers, he'd have to resign."

"*Your* parents may not mind," I tell Milly, trying to think about something that isn't my father being in the papers for a scandal *I* caused. "They're more permissive in Europe."

"My parents wouldn't be in Europe anymore, not if this got out," Milly says. "They'd call my father back and assign him to some unimportant desk job until everyone forgot both he and I existed. He'd never forgive me. European permissiveness notwithstanding."

We all start walking faster after that.

I shiver in my borrowed stockings. I thought speakeasies were another world, a dream world, but it turns out they're only another part of the same world we live in every day.

The seminary is our real home. It's always quiet this time of night, the lights extinguished until the servants rise in the morning, and it shouldn't be difficult to steal inside without being noticed. All I want is to be back in my room, in my flannel nightgown and slippers, huddled in front of our fireplace, with Clara and Milly tucked close on either side of me. Away from all this cold and fear.

I rub my hands along my arms and drag my thin shawl around me, running my fingers over the fringe.

"Do you suppose we could slip in through the kitchen?" Clara murmurs. "I bet there are leftover canapés."

"I could do with a fruit cocktail," Milly murmurs back. "With lots of powdered sugar."

A craving for oyster toast surges on my own tongue, and I'm about to say so when we hear the voice around the corner up ahead.

We all stop at once, the click-clacking of our heels falling silent. The streetcars don't run this late, and there aren't any motorcars driving past, either. The man's voice is the only sound.

"The last of 'em got away?" he's saying. Milly, Clara, and I glance at one another and step soundlessly into the recessed doorway of a butcher shop. The shadows are deep here, and we can stay concealed as long as we need to.

Unless that man, and whomever he's talking to, come our way.

"Yeah. Queers are fast." The second man answers in a snarl. "I got that skinny one last time we hit *their* bar. Smashed his head in good. He must've sprung back up again like a damn jack-in-the-box."

"Their bars are the same way," another man says. "I heard it from Bonnard. After we shut that one down, they started again out by Navy Yard. His team's been over there looking for it every night."

"Did you see that big blond pervert in the tweed?" the first man asks. "I swear, that fairy had the damn nerve to *laugh* when he ran by us tonight. Next time, that's the one getting his damn head smashed in."

The other men chuckle.

I don't look at Milly and Clara. If I did, they'd signal for me not to do what I'm about to do.

So I keep my back to my friends as I slip off my shoes, step out of the doorway, and lean around the corner.

It's as I thought. The men talking are police officers.

They have their backs to me, the three of them, and they're climbing out of a black car. Even from behind, though, I recognize the lead Prohibition agent's brown suit and fedora.

I slink back to the butcher shop and shove on my shoes. I've got to be ready to run.

The police station is only a few blocks north of here. The agent and the black-hatted officers must be driving back from the Lazy Susan. I can't imagine why they've stopped amid the dark, empty shops and businesses of Massachusetts Avenue in the middle of the night. Until a moment later, when the sounds and smells make it clear that they're relieving themselves against the office building a few feet away.

I push past my revulsion and signal to Milly and Clara. It would be too risky to speak, or even to whisper. So we wait, tucking our icy fingers into our knocking elbows, until we hear the men climb back into their car and drive up the block, away from us.

Queer.

Fairy.

Smashed his head in good.

I can't believe I thought tonight would be an adventure. That there could be excitement, even charm, in defiance.

The three of us resume our walk without speaking. Without looking at one another.

Until finally, finally, we turn onto P Street and we can see the seminary again.

But we see the flat black hats, too.

A thick knot of police officers is surrounding the building. I don't see the man in the brown suit and fedora this time, but...

"Are they here because of the raid?" Milly murmurs. "Because of *us?*"

"There's too many," Clara whispers.

She's right. How many police officers would it take to arrest a few girls in the middle of the night? One? Perhaps two? Yet there are at least twenty coppers in front of the seminary.

And they've spotted us.

"You girls!" one of them shouts, pointing his billy stick from across the street. "Wait there!"

My breath catches in my throat.

I can move fast on the basketball court, but not on the street in my high heels with the pinching toes. Besides, Milly couldn't keep up even if we all flung off our shoes and left them behind for the police like a trio of Cinderellas.

And we aren't going anywhere unless it's together.

Milly's hand moves to catch my own, lacing her cold gloved fingers into mine. Clara slips behind us.

"What are you doing? What did you see?" the officer shouts as he gets closer, running toward us across the empty street. I'm still itching to dart away, but Milly squeezes my hand and releases it, and I find the courage I need.

I throw back my shoulders and walk toward him, forcing my chin high.

"Good evening, Officer." My heart pounds in my ears. Across the street, electric torch beams swing out, trailing across the ground. Every so often one flashes our way and catches my eyes, blinding me almost as badly as that flashbulb at the Lazy Susan. "How can we be helpful to you on this chilly night?"

The officer's face is red, his lips pulled back, but he reaches automatically to shake my outstretched hand. His eyes flick from my glittering headband to my bare arms to Clara making herself small behind my back. When Milly clears her throat, though, his gaze settles on her soft smile, and his expression relaxes.

"Evening, miss." He hastily removes his flat black hat and holds it against his chest, a mat of dishwater-colored hair falling into little curls across his forehead. "I'm afraid you girls will have to come with me. Need to ask you some questions about that dead body."

9

MILLY DOES THE TALKING AFTER THAT, WEAVING A FICTION SO fast I can barely keep up while Clara lingers behind us, studying the pavement at our feet.

We'd been up in our dorm, Milly's telling the officer, and had decided to celebrate our last week before the winter recess by dressing up like those foolish girls in the motion pictures—"*Flappers*, you know, that's what they call them. Silly little things."

We didn't realize how cold it was, Milly says, and had decided to go out for a quick walk in our costumes. We realized our mistake soon after we stepped through the door to the laundry room, and were about to go around to the front to go back inside when we spotted the bevy of police officers.

At first I don't see how he'll possibly believe this story. Then I notice the strange, high voice Milly's using, the simple words. As though she's much younger than she is, and much slower, too.

And as I watch the officer nod, I remember all over again how brilliant my best friend is. This man will never suspect we were doing anything more illicit tonight than putting on dresses that would've made my grandmother reach for her smelling salts.

"You're lucky I found you," he tells Milly, lifting his chest importantly. He isn't that much older than us, I see now. His forehead's smooth and untroubled, his eyes and skin pale. "It's no time for girls like you to be on the streets. I'll take you back to your school."

I want to stop him—like Milly said, it'll look terrible if we're brought back to the seminary by the police—but I don't know how.

Besides, there are coppers everywhere. Tall men in uniforms keep passing us as we near the front doors, their electric torches trailing along the ground. There must be three times as many here as there were at the Lazy Susan.

And, somewhere nearby, there's a body. Mrs. Rose must have offered to let the police use the seminary as a base of operations while they investigate. Still, it's unnerving to see our home surrounded like this. Invaded.

If we can avoid Mrs. Rose seeing us, we might be able to slip upstairs. The trouble is, she's bound to be close. With all this going on at her seminary, she'll have placed herself right in the middle of things. That's her way. I cast my eyes about for her Spanish-fringe shawl, but everywhere I turn there are only coppers, studying every inch of the space around us.

The young officer opens the seminary's front door and ushers us through. My heart thuds as we squeeze into the paneled foyer, but his are the only footsteps on our heels.

The entrance hall is dim, lit only by a few lamps and the fires in the grates, but it's packed with people. More than I've ever seen here, even in the daytime. There's no sign of Mrs. Rose, but police officers are at every turn. I didn't know the city had so many.

The blinds over the windows are drawn tightly shut, and a fire blazes behind the grate by the staircase. I want to move toward its warmth, but we need to go straight to the third floor. Yet the grand staircase with its marble steps and iron railings is blocked by a cluster of officers speaking in low voices with cups and saucers in their hands.

The servants, the same parlor maids and footmen who wait on us every day, are scattered around the room with trays of tea things, as though hosting a reception. Their faces are turned down, though, their black uniforms rumpled. They must've dressed in haste. Mrs. Rose would have had to call them out of bed to tend to all these guests.

Milly steps forward to say something to the young officer while I peer through the doorway to the left. It leads to our mathematics classroom, where Miss Parker spends her days glowering at us, but tonight it's dark and cold. The lone window at the end of the room faces out to Dupont Circle, and its blind is only partway drawn. Beyond it, the street is empty, the shadows shifting, ripped papers and old cigarette stubs blowing in the wind.

Except for one shadow that isn't moving at all.

I blink, my eyes focusing slowly on the shape on the far side of the street.

Someone's standing against the thick trunk of a red oak tree, the brim of a hat casting their face into darkness. They're wearing a suit, not a uniform, and leaning on something long and thin. They're looking right at the window. Through it.

Right at me.

I draw back abruptly, a fierce tension taking hold in my gut, and turn around.

The room around us is full of people, but aside from that figure across the street and the officer who led us in, no one has taken any note of the three of us.

It doesn't make sense. People *should* be taking note of us. We're breaking every dress and decorum rule in the handbook, and that's aside from the fact that we're coming in from outdoors on a bitterly cold night without coats.

And it isn't only police officers and servants filling the room. There are men in bowler hats and suits, too, men I've never seen before. And most alarmingly, there are teachers. Miss Parker is hovering silently behind a pillar off the entrance hall. Old Mr. Farrel's here, too, plopped in an armchair with a cigar burning in his hand, staring down into a glass.

We need to get upstairs. Quickly, and quietly. Before either of them sees us.

Then a sudden noise, a cry, carries out from the arched doorway that leads into the dining room. A girl in a servant's dress and cap is bent in half, sobbing. A brown-haired officer stands in front of her with his hat in his hand, running his fingers over the back of his neck, looking from side to side and back again, as if he's hoping for help to arrive.

It's Lucy, Mrs. Rose's maid. She lights the fires in our rooms every evening, too. She's our age, or perhaps a year or two older, with pale freckled skin and auburn hair that's wound up in a tight bun. She always has a warm smile for Milly and me. Once, I spotted her slipping an extra cup of tea to a homesick freshman after curfew. I couldn't hear what Lucy said to the girl, but it made her laugh for the first time in days.

I don't want to know what could make Lucy cry the way she's crying now.

Milly, still draped in Clara's jacket, turns back to the young officer who escorted us inside. "Pardon me. Did you say there had been a... an accident?"

"I didn't say accident, Miss Otis." He clasps his flat black hat in front of him. His hair grease glimmers in the firelight. Milly must have told him her name when I wasn't listening. "Now, you girls'd better go on up to bed and stay there. Someone'll be around to question you in the morning."

He hurries toward the front door. The coppers at the bottom of the grand staircase step aside to let us by with a few glances at our legs that earn them a glare from Milly.

It's no use being quiet as we climb past the landing to the third floor. The voices in the front room will cover our footsteps. I'm leading the way, with Milly and Clara behind me, when I notice there are sounds coming from above, too.

Feet, scurrying. Voices, echoing. Not the full-throated conversations of the police officers in the entrance hall, but hushed murmurs of girls who should be asleep at this time of night.

And at the top of the steps, Trixie's crouched behind the railing. Her pale pink skin is scrunched in frustration, her lips pressed tight. A fashionable blue-and-silver-embroidered scarf is tied over her silvery yellow hair. I wonder what she'd think if she knew her father and her uncle were brawling with strangers at a speakeasy an hour ago.

"You're awfully dudded up, Miss Pound." Trixie raises her eyebrows, fingernails drumming on the thick oak banister. "Night on the town?"

"Good evening, Miss Babcock." I hold back a hand to warn Milly and Clara not to come yet. If Trixie sees them, she'll wonder why they're in short dresses, too. "You're up late."

She doesn't answer. There are tears in her eyes. Real tears.

Trixie? *Crying?*

"Trixie?" I kneel. This isn't her. "Are you hurt? What's happening?"

"You didn't hear?"

"Hear what?"

"I was sure they'd have told *you* first." She shrugs one shoulder and sniffs hard. "Your beloved Mrs. Rose is dead."

THE WASHINGTON EVENING STAR

Sunday, December 11, 1927

SUDDEN DEATH OF HEADMISTRESS LINKED TO ILLEGAL LIQUOR TRADE

The body of 35-year-old Mrs. Jessica Blackwell Rose was discovered early Sunday morning in her office at the Washington Female Seminary, a girls' school located on Dupont Circle. City police and federal Prohibition agents reported that no blood was found at the scene, where her body lay on the floor of her office clad in a nightgown, but that they found numerous bottles containing grain alcohol of the sort commonly mixed with kerosene and other poisons by federal officials as a deterrence to prevent illegal drinking. Her death was therefore ruled an accidental poisoning following the illegal consumption of liquor.

"There were at least a half dozen bottles, and footprints on the rug that appeared to be from a man's shoe," said Prohibition Bureau Agent Samuel Perkins.

Women teachers at the Washington Female Seminary are not permitted to fraternize with men, and men are not allowed in the residential quarters.

The morning following Mrs. Rose's death, a note was received at the *Evening Star* office signed by an anonymous writer claiming to be a student at the seminary. The girl wrote that Mrs. Rose had, some days prior to her death, invited the girl into her office and offered her a glass of gin, stating that Mrs. Rose had obtained it from a bootlegger with whom she had previously done business. The author of the note stated that she refused the offer.

Agent Perkins reported that federal authorities would investigate the allegations of bootlegging and the provision of alcohol to underage girls, and that further inquiries would be conducted until additional

(Continued on Page 2, Column 8.)

10

I'VE READ THE ARTICLE A DOZEN TIMES. IT'S HARDER TO MAKE out now that the paper is five days old, and crumpled from when one of the cooks accidentally tossed it in the bin with the vegetable scraps.

I've since taken to hiding it in a trunk under a stack of summer clothes, so Milly and I are free to pore over it as often as necessary. Though I've only seen Milly read it once, the day it came out, when we studied it together, gazing long and hard at the single grainy photograph.

She insists I keep it tucked under the tablecloth when I bring it to the dining hall now. Folded back, so the picture won't show.

"I've been through every trunk and I can't find that bracelet." Irene Donovan dabs at her lips with a napkin and sets her spoon neatly beside her dish of stewed tomatoes, nearly knocking over the vase of mistletoe and lilies. Floral arrangements have flooded the entire building. When our last headmistress, Miss Thurman, died two years ago of a heart ailment, there were so many flowers our mathematics classroom smelled like gardenias for a week, sending Miss Parker into constant bouts of sneezing. "Could I borrow your other black hat for tomorrow, Milly? My best one has that silk bow. I can't wear it for a funeral."

"Certainly." Milly sets her teacup on her saucer soundlessly. Rattling of saucers in the dining hall is strictly forbidden, though there's no one here to enforce that rule. Or to stop me from reading a newspaper under the table during luncheon.

Two days after Mrs. Rose's death, we were shepherded into the entrance hall to find Damian Babcock standing in the same place where Mrs. Rose had delivered speeches during our assemblies, and we sat in silence as he explained what the board had decided to do with us.

We were supposed to have another week of classes, followed by four days of examinations. Then, the term was set to end with our final basketball game and the winter dance with George Washington University.

Nearly all of it was canceled. There would be no classes, no game, no dance. Our examinations would be moved up by a week. Once we'd finished them, Mr. Babcock told us, we were free to leave the seminary.

He made no mention of next term.

Our last examinations finished this morning. By this time tomorrow, the seminary will be empty. Many of the younger girls have left already, departing in their family cars or taking taxis to the train station, their parents having decided that examinations paled in importance compared to being associated with the site of a scandalous woman's scandalous death.

Most of the seniors stayed. None of us studied for our examinations, not even Milly, but we sat for them, all the same.

We still intend to graduate. Though no one's said anything about that, either.

I run my fingers along the fringe of my shawl and turn back to the article. It takes up the entire bottom half of the front page. The photograph is hard to make out, like newspaper photographs always are, but a moment of study is enough to reveal Mrs. Rose, dead on the floor of her office, bottles strewn around her on the pale carpet. Her face is stark white, and so is her nightgown, but her eyes are dark.

"Translation," Milly whispered that first dark afternoon as we leaned over the article by candlelight, reading the quotes from Agent Samuel Perkins again and again. "She drank, entertained a man, and died. Vice leads to vice, children, you've been warned."

"Why do they keep talking about her wearing a nightgown?" My fingers had gripped the thin newsprint hard enough to tear. "It was late! Of course she'd changed out of her day clothes. She always reads and writes letters in her office late into the night. She told me so!"

"She must've neglected to tell the Prohibition Bureau her evening routines."

I wanted to go on arguing, but the trouble was, I couldn't see any other explanation, either. Mrs. Rose was young and healthy.

It simply doesn't seem right to me. That she and that man... that they...

She was a headmistress. A *scholar*. She'd told me in no uncertain terms that she didn't plan to marry again.

Besides, I've read about the poisoned liquor before, and the newspapers always said it was only done to the cheapest, foulest kinds of alcohol. If Mrs. Rose did drink, I couldn't imagine her drinking *that*.

As for the "anonymous note" the paper had supposedly received, it had to be a fabrication. Mrs. Rose, offering a girl gin? In her *office*? How absurd.

There was another article on page two of that same day's paper. On the very same sheet of newsprint, in fact. This one had a photograph, too, of several men's backs turned to run. Only one face was clear, caught in the blinding flashbulb—that of Assistant Commerce Secretary Bruce Pengelley. The article said he'd been arrested during a speakeasy raid, along with several of the club's employees, but that his "female companion" had escaped. There was no mention of the Babcocks.

At the very edge of the photograph was a blurry white fragment of what I strongly suspected was my elbow. Had I stepped an inch to the right, *my* face might've made the paper.

I can't believe we did that. Climbed out the window. Walked through the city in the middle of the night, alone. We broke every rule, purely because we found it fun.

We could've gotten caught. We could've wound up *dead*.

Mrs. Rose did.

"Gertie." Milly raises her voice. It's evident this isn't the first time she's tried to get me to look up from the paper, but her eyes are clear and patient as they meet mine. "Did you decide on a dress for tomorrow?"

I blink at her. On Milly's other side, Irene is watching me, her plate and teacup empty.

I shiver, rubbing my arms with my hands. It's always cold in the dining room.

"Tomorrow?" Then I remember. The funeral. Yes. "Oh. My black crepe."

"Did you remember to hang it separately in the wardrobe?" Milly stirs the remains of her tea casually, but I know her well enough to recognize the exasperation in her eyes.

"I…may have forgotten." I smooth out the newspaper across my knees. It's sure to leave smudges on my pale purple day dress.

"Oh no." Irene frowns. "The maids will have packed it away in the trunks. It'll be creased by tomorrow."

"Don't worry, Gertie, I'll speak to them." Milly's being so kind I can't bring myself to tell her I don't care about trunks or dresses. "I'm sure someone can find it."

"It's all right." I draw my hand out from under the table. My fingers are smudged, too. "I'll go as soon as I've finished my tea."

"Good morning." Dorothy Bradley, one of the other seniors, gives us a weak smile as she enters the dining room and drops into the empty seat next to mine. Clara slips through the door behind her. Milly turns quickly back to her teacup, edging her chair closer to mine. "That is, I should say... I suppose it isn't a *good* morning, given that tomorrow, we're... But I don't know quite how to..."

"Don't worry." I force a weak smile of my own and pat Dorothy's elbow. "No one knows what to say the day before a funeral."

"My parents didn't like her." Dorothy mumbles the words, though we already know. Dorothy's mother only invited Mrs. Rose to their August barbecue after a third of their original guest list came down with a summer flu. It was all anyone talked about for weeks. "But she was always kind to me."

Clara settles into the last seat at the table, on the other side of Dorothy, and touches Dorothy's other arm lightly. She's wearing a soft gray dress with a white feathered brooch, and a few wisps of dark hair have escaped their clips to delicately frame her chin. With Clara here, it feels as though the sun has finally risen.

I shift my gaze back to my plate. I shouldn't think things like that. Not after what those police officers said about the men at the Lazy Susan.

Besides, I don't have any right to think warm thoughts of any kind. Mrs. Rose is dead.

"It's all right," Clara's telling Dorothy. "We all know how parents can be."

"My mother thinks the seminary will shut down for good," Irene murmurs. "With all the... the rumors."

Everyone knew she came from nothing, I heard a sophomore murmur yesterday in this very dining room. *Her parents were bohemians. She only got the headmistress job because the board was desperate after Miss Thurman died. They'd never have given it to someone so ill-bred under normal circumstances. It's no surprise she turned out to be a criminal.*

It's absurd, all of it. Drinking *is* against the law, I suppose, but there's no proof Mrs. Rose was drunk. She wasn't when we saw her with that man.

Though she *was* laughing quite a lot. And I don't know how else to explain the bottles, or the man's shoe prints.

We heard the man in the homburg offer to walk her to the door. We heard her tell him no. But I suppose she could've changed her mind later.

"Where would your parents send you?" Clara is asking Irene.

"Perhaps the Chevy Chase school. What about you, Gertie?"

"I don't know." I can't stand to think about the seminary closing. It's our home, and Mrs. Rose's, too. Her *last* home. "Clara, do you..."

"I'm not sure, either." Clara gazes from Irene to Milly and finally to me. "My father said something about a college in New Rochelle."

"That's...in New York, isn't it?"

Clara nods. "Just outside the city."

"Oh." I drop my eyes to my teacup.

Clara can't leave me. Leave *us.*

"I should go speak to the maids." I push back my chair, its legs groaning as they scrape along the black walnut floor. "If you'll excuse me."

They all do. Clara moves into my vacant seat and murmurs something to Milly as the others lean in for more gossip.

I gather up my newspaper and escape to the entrance hall.

It's easier to breathe here, despite the flowers crowding every corner, and I pause after shutting the door behind me. The windows are still fastened tightly, the blinds drawn, an old-fashioned mourning custom that's strangely soothing. Only a thin ray of morning sunlight illuminates the gleaming white pillar that stands between me and the grand staircase.

I should go up to my room. Instead, I linger in the stillness.

Five days have passed since Mrs. Rose died. One floor above where I'm standing.

Rumors are useless. What we need are *answers*.

"Make sure you tell the police chief," a girl is saying at the other end of the entrance hall. "My mother thinks..."

"Thank you," a man interrupts, and I straighten. His voice doesn't sound like any of our male teachers, but I know I've heard it before. "I'll be sure to pass that on."

The entrance hall isn't large, and when I peer out from behind the pillar I can see them, standing by the fireplace in front of an enormous vase of lilies. Trixie Babcock, hovering by the mantel, arms crossed over her chest.

That's a surprise in itself. Trixie moved out of the seminary the morning after Mrs. Rose's death, bright and early, as if examinations were worthless and she couldn't wait to be free of us all.

But even more of a shock is the man standing across from her, tall and wide-shouldered, in a brown three-piece suit. He has thinning light-brown hair and a pleasant, slightly strained smile across his face.

He's holding a fedora in his hands.

11

I HAVEN'T SEEN THE LEAD PROHIBITION AGENT SINCE THAT NIGHT, but I recognize him instantly.

Plenty of police officers have come through the seminary, and federal dry agents, too. That first morning, the seminary was crawling with them. While we went to church to pray for Mrs. Rose, they tore through the entire building. We returned to find the servants busily putting things back to rights, their black uniforms still rumpled.

The dry squad men spent the day searching Mrs. Rose's office, collecting all the bottles on the carpet and searching the drawers and cabinets for more. The agent with the fedora wasn't among them, though. I've been keeping a careful watch.

Will he remember me from the Lazy Susan? And Milly and Clara, too?

"Don't worry, we're going to have all of you girls out this afternoon, Miss Babcock," the agent is telling Trixie. "Your teachers, too."

"Oh?" Trixie doesn't sound remotely worried. "I thought the seminary wasn't closing until tomorrow."

"Your uncle's arranged for things to finish up earlier. Our men need to take a more thorough look around the place, and we don't want to bother you girls, of course. Someone should be making an official announcement soon."

"Of course." Trixie smiles brightly. It's strange to think of how crushed she'd seemed that night when she told me about Mrs. Rose's death. It was almost as though she'd cared about another human being. There's no trace of such compassion in her face today. "Thank you very much, Agent Perkins."

"Thank *you*, Miss Babcock."

Perkins. Most of the newspaper's quotes were from an Agent Samuel Perkins.

Why was the man who led the raid on the Lazy Susan giving quotes to the papers about Mrs. Rose's death? Why is he here now, talking to *Trixie*?

And do we truly have to leave *today*? We were supposed to have one more night together.

I duck back behind the pillar so I'll be out of sight as Agent Perkins moves to the front door to leave. But I don't hear it open. I suppose he means to stay and search once we're gone.

I'm not ready to go. Leaving this place feels like leaving Mrs. Rose's memory behind.

I wish I'd known, that night at the faculty party, that it would be my last visit with her. I've worn the shawl she gave me every day since, its fringe constantly tickling my elbows.

I wish I could go back and sip tea with her again. Talk about the future. Though I can barely think past the funeral tomorrow.

It's hard to think about much at all, in fact. Perhaps that's why, though my mind never forms any kind of plan, my legs begin carrying me up to the second floor. To Mrs. Rose's office.

I don't need to go through the servants' rooms this time. There's no one in sight. I simply cross the landing and come face-to-face with the heavy oak door.

I twist the knob, and I'm there. I'm in the room where she died.

I hadn't thought of her office that way before. In my mind, this was always where she'd *lived*. Where she'd worked. Warm and welcoming and solid, with her desk rising up under the big window. The soft chairs by the fire where we'd sat for tea. Her bedroom only steps away...

It's not that room any longer. The room where I'm standing now is cold, and dark, and horrible.

Mrs. Rose's beautiful old Oriental rug is covered in ripped papers, and furniture has been shoved carelessly around. The chair that used to stand by the fireplace where she liked to sip her tea is lying on its side, stained with ash from the coals still scattered across the hearth.

Yet I don't see any bottles. They must have been dumped in a field somewhere. That's what Prohibition agents do with confiscated liquor in newsreels—shatter the bottles on rocks so the alcohol spills out into the grass, then fling the broken bottles into the gutters.

This was a mistake. I shouldn't be here.

She's not here. It doesn't feel as though she ever could have been.

Though it still smells much as I remember it smelling on those long, quiet mornings. Of smoke, and ink, and something else, warm and rich and not so easily defined.

I shut my eyes and grope behind me for the doorknob. My hand lands on something sharp. For a brief, frightening moment, I think again of those broken bottles in the newsreels, but when I turn, it's only the door to the linen cupboard Mrs. Rose led me through the night of the party.

There's a discoloration in the wood that I didn't notice that night. Though as I look closer, I see that it isn't discoloration at all. Small fragments of the wood are chipped and splintered by the doorknob, as though someone sawed at it with a knife. A tiny piece of wood protrudes from the edge of the door, too, directly above the keyhole.

When I twist the knob, the door opens easily enough. It

isn't locked. I don't remember Mrs. Rose unlocking it the night of the party, either. She must have only locked it when she'd gone to bed for the night.

I'm staring down at the chipped wood, trying to make sense of it, when I spot the shadow by my feet. Its shape is odd. Crooked.

It isn't a shadow at all, I see, as I peer closer. It's a dark line on the floor, protruding from under a shut cabinet door. A piece of yarn, or a string, perhaps.

I sink down, balancing on my toes to examine it. I know these threads. It's part of the fringe on my shawl. Or, rather, a shawl much like mine.

The pattern on mine is gold and red, where Mrs. Rose's shawl had violets and deep blues. The fringe on both, though, was a pale yellowish brown. Precisely like the fringe I'm looking at now. A piece of her shawl's fringe must have fallen off and gotten stuck under the door.

When I grip the fringe in my fingers and give it a tug, though, a bigger piece of fabric comes into view.

I recognize the painted pattern at once. This isn't a lone piece of fallen fringe. Mrs. Rose's entire, intact shawl is here, puddled in the cabinet.

Something of hers. As fresh as the last day she wore it.

I open the cabinet and lift the shawl, the silk pooling in my hands. I step back into the office, holding the shawl out toward the winter light filtering in from the window.

This belonged to her. It's cool against my skin, but it's easy to imagine the warmth it must've held when it wound around Mrs. Rose's neck.

I could take this with me. No one would have to know where I'd found it.

My eyes linger on the painted flowers, my fingers running

over the cool fabric. The pattern has more red in it than I remember, deep rust-colored patches, and it must've been painted by hand, because the color's run a bit. Streaked, as though the painter was in a hurry.

Drops of that same rust color appear here and there, too. Flecks, spreading out and breaking off under my fingers.

I drop the shawl and kick it away from me, clutching my chest to keep from shrieking. Those flecks aren't paint at all.

They're blood. *Her* blood.

12

W E HAVE TO BURN IT."

Clara's voice falters on every word, but it trembles hardest on *burn*.

Mrs. Rose's shawl is heaped in the middle of the room I share with Milly. The three of us are perched around it in an uneven circle on the rug—Milly with her legs tucked neatly underneath her on one side of me, and Clara hovering uncertainly on the other. We all try to avert our eyes, but it keeps drawing us in, like a bloody magnet.

"We can't burn it," I say. "It's evidence. We have to give it to the police."

It's the third time I've said that. Yet I haven't moved to do anything about it.

I can't rise from my place on the floor. I can't fathom touching that thing again.

I can hardly believe I brought it here. It felt like a fever dream. Balling the stained shawl into my fist. Charging through the servants' rooms, around the corner, and up the stairs. Pounding in my heels as I stormed into my room to find Milly collecting her hat and gloves from a shelf, staring at me with her lips parted in worry, then begging me to tell her what was wrong.

When I found I couldn't speak, she ran next door to get Clara. Only when they were both there, speaking to me in soft, pleading voices, was I able to calm my racing heartbeat enough to tell them what happened.

While they laid the shawl on the floor and bent over to study it, I shut my eyes tight, and I thought it through.

From the newspaper photo, we know Mrs. Rose's body was in her office, lying face down. Her head was near the fireplace, and her feet were angled toward the linen closet. And I know from my visit this afternoon that the door to that closet had been hacked at with a sharp object.

My mind is still racing now, but I've only been able to come to one conclusion:

Mrs. Rose didn't die from accidentally drinking poisoned liquor. Mrs. Rose was strangled, with her own shawl.

The murderer must have exited the same way he'd come in—through the linen cupboard—and dropped the shawl on his way. Perhaps he'd even left it there on purpose. He was in a hurry, and may have meant to hide the murder weapon, but without time to do it properly, he simply shoved it in a cabinet and ran. He was smart enough not to get caught, but when someone's running, and frightened, mistakes are bound to happen.

"What I don't understand," Milly says, her eyes landing on the shawl before darting away again, "is why there's blood on it. The article said they didn't find any blood."

"That's true." I shut my eyes again, thinking. "It could be *his* blood. The killer's. They didn't find blood on *her*, but if she fought back...if they struggled..."

I can't help picturing it. Tears spring to my eyes, but I can't get overwhelmed. I need to *think*.

"It doesn't seem likely that some strange man burst into this building in the middle of the night to murder a woman he didn't know." The tremors in Clara's voice are growing smoother. "Her room is on the second floor. If I was going to break into a building and kill someone, I don't think I'd bother climbing the stairs."

"You think she was killed by someone who lives *here*?" Milly asks. "One of the teachers? Or the servants?"

"Or the girls?" Clara sighs and shakes her head. "You're right. It's preposterous."

"Besides," Milly adds, leaning back against the side of my bed, her dark wool dress already covered in fibers from the woven Turkish rug, "everyone knows murders are done for money. Mrs. Rose probably made pennies working here. Preposterous, indeed."

"You *don't* think she was murdered?" I ask.

"Oh, I think she was murdered. I simply think it's a preposterous murder, start to finish."

I give Milly a smile, because I know my Milly. She's trying to coax one out of me. To make me feel less awful.

Yet I can't imagine finding anything funny. Not today.

Most of the girls have left by now. Our room is nearly empty, except for our hats and coats and handbags. The announcement was made in the dining hall, not long after I left. We've all been instructed to leave the seminary this afternoon. Cars and train tickets have been ordered. Our trunks have already been sent on, Milly's and mine to my parents' house in Georgetown, where she always stays between terms, and Clara's to the Capitol Hill hotel where she's staying with her father until the congressional recess. The three of us are all supposed to be downstairs soon.

"Strange that you were the one to find that shawl." Milly taps her chin. "I wonder how many coppers must've walked right past it. It's not a strong indication of their detective skills that Gertie's better at their job than they are."

"We saw Mrs. Rose wearing it before she died," Clara says. "Perhaps only *minutes* before."

"It could've been stained already," Milly says. "From an accident, or..."

Clara shakes her head. "She wouldn't have worn it out with a stain. Perhaps she cut herself after she got home, and bled on it. She could've left it in the linen cupboard for maids to clean in the morning."

"But Gertie found it on the floor," Milly points out. "She wouldn't have thrown it down like that. She was always courteous to the servants. Besides, if she'd had a cut, the doctors would've seen it."

"There are so many parts of this that I don't understand." My frustration is mounting. "Like that figure we saw through the window after we came back that night—the one watching from the trees. I keep thinking *that* person could have had something to do with this. Unless it was a plainclothes detective, I suppose..."

Milly arches her eyebrows. "What figure?"

"Standing on the edge of the circle under the red oak. Leaning on something, like a cane, and looking through the window at us. You didn't see?"

"I don't remember." Clara frowns. "That whole night feels like it was so long ago."

I didn't realize I was the only one who saw the figure through the window.

If I *did* see a figure. If my memory isn't getting muddled.

"Well, if she was murdered, we almost certainly saw the man who did it." Milly folds her arms across her chest. "He walked her home that night. You're right, Gertie, we have to go tell the police so they can find him before he does it to someone else."

I shake my head. "Mrs. Rose seemed to trust that man."

"She wouldn't be the first person to trust someone she shouldn't," Clara says.

We all fall quiet for a moment.

"Well, the police will be sure to investigate anyone else who might've had a problem with Mrs. Rose," Milly finally says. "There were plenty of those."

"No one had a big enough problem with her to do *this*," I say.

Milly only looks at me. She doesn't want to tell me I'm naïve, but she's thinking it. Again.

I sigh. "Mrs. Rose was controversial, certainly. Too modern for a lot of people. That might've been enough to cause a few arguments, but not a murder."

Milly shrugs. "Perhaps. It's always possible a stranger *did* break into the seminary, come to the second floor, and hack through her door."

"That gunshot during the faculty party," Clara says. "That could be connected, too."

I nod. "We should go to the police right away."

"We can't go to the *police*." Clara's grown angry suddenly, her forehead creasing. "They'll want to know where we were when we saw him. If they know we were stealing away, they'll be sure to tell the seminary, and our families. We'll be expelled. My parents would send me away from the city for good."

My heart starts to race again. "To New Rochelle?"

"All I know is, I couldn't stay here."

If Clara left—if I couldn't see her every day . . .

It would feel like another death.

"My parents might have me come back to Brussels, if I were expelled." Milly holds out her hands, palms up. "Or if the seminary shuts down."

A third death, then. I swallow, hard.

"All right." I don't want to lie, but I don't know what else to do. Besides, it doesn't matter what we tell the police, as long as it starts them on the path to finding out what truly happened to Mrs. Rose. "We'll tell the police we saw him out the window. And that Milly and I were alone, since you were supposed to be in your room, Clara. Just the two of us should go."

"Perhaps we can find Byron," Milly says. "I doubt he's at the station at this time of day, but it's possible."

I raise my eyebrows. "Byron?"

Color creeps into her cheeks. "Remember when we were coming back from the Lazy Susan? That young copper who led us inside?"

"Yes." I glance at Clara, but she's staring down at her hands.

"Well." Milly's voice would sound smooth and even to anyone else, but I can hear the slight embarrassed edge to it. "We've…gotten to know each other some. His name is Byron."

I drop my eyes to my hands, too. "I see."

"No, no, it isn't like that. Not that he wouldn't want it to be." Milly sighs. "I've simply…It's been difficult these past few days. I've…seen him a few times, that's all. To take my mind off things. You understand."

I don't. But I don't tell her that. "You think we should go and tell this *Byron* the whole story?"

"Well." Her cheeks darken from pink to red. "Perhaps not. There's bound to be another officer here in the building."

"As long as it's not Agent Perkins," I say. "We can't run the risk that he'd recognize us from the Lazy Susan."

"We can put on our hats and coats before we go looking," Milly says. "Just in case. The hats will hide our hair, and the coats will hide our bodies, and as for our faces…well, we were wearing makeup that night. That might be enough to keep us from being recognized."

"It might." I nod. The truth is, I'm eager to forget about

Milly stealing away to meet up with this Byron fellow. To forget the image of Mrs. Rose trying to fight off a murderer, too. To forget everything except what *we* can do. "We'll find an officer, give him the shawl, and tell him about the man in the homburg. The police will find him, ask him if he saw anything of importance that night, and…"

That's when I realize why this feels like such a wonderful idea.

If we're right—and if this makes it into the newspapers…

It could change the way people remember Mrs. Rose. It could make them treat her memory with respect.

Perhaps it's not too late to help her after all.

"This could do it," I say softly, smoothing my skirt across my knees. "It could put to rest all these rumors. About men, and bootlegging, and whatever else occurs to Miss Parker and Mrs. Patterson and the rest of them."

Clara raises her eyebrows. "You're saying that if someone broke in and attacked Mrs. Rose, *that's* better for her reputation?"

Milly nods, her eyes locked on my face. "If the alternative is that she sexed and drank herself to death, then yes. Murder is better."

I smile a genuine smile.

"It would be in the papers for sure." I climb to my feet. "They *love* a good murder."

I grab an extra hat from my shelf, turn it upside down, and drop the shawl inside.

"Let's go." I extend a hand to help Milly up. "Before I lose my nerve."

13

MILLY LOANED ME A COAT, SINCE I LOST MY BEST ONE AT THE Lazy Susan, and by the time the two of us have reached the entrance hall, the seminary is nearly empty. A few girls are calling out to one another, bidding farewell. Clara has already retreated to her empty room.

We don't find any police officers in the entrance hall. I peek outside, but no one's there. Anderson sees me looking, and politely informs me that the car that'll take Milly and me to my parents' house will be here soon, and that we should gather up the last of our things.

Milly and I trade glances. We're running out of time.

"Perhaps they're upstairs," she mutters to me when we're a safe distance away from Anderson. "Let's check Mrs. Rose's office."

It's the last place I want to go, but Milly's right as usual, so we turn to the stairs.

When we reach the landing, the heavy oak door to Mrs. Rose's office is wide open, and there's a man inside. Agent Perkins. He's left his fedora perched on the tip of Mrs. Rose's desk as he opens and closes drawers, slipping things into his pockets.

The back of my neck crawls. I imagine he's only conducting police business, but I hate seeing him paw through her things.

I glance at Milly. She nods. There's no sign of any other officers here, and we don't have time to search the entire building. We'll have to speak to Agent Perkins and hope our hats and coats and bare faces are enough to keep him from realizing we were in the same dim, smoky room he was six nights ago.

"Pardon me?" Milly calls into the room. "Might you have a moment?"

Agent Perkins whirls around, but when he sees us, he smiles and strides out onto the landing. "Certainly, certainly. Anything for seminary girls. How do you do. I'm Agent Perkins."

Milly and I bow our heads.

"How do you do. I'm Millicent Otis."

"I'm Gertrude Pound. How do you do."

He bows to each of us. The well-spoken gentleman in front of me is a sharp contrast to the man we saw commanding a heavily armed squadron before urinating in the street. "What can I do for you, Miss Otis, Miss Pound?"

The formality of the introductions makes me feel self-conscious about the hat tucked under my arm with the bloody shawl inside. Still, I want to keep this conversation as short as possible. The less time Agent Perkins spends looking at our faces, the better.

I open the hat, reach inside, and pull out the shawl. "I found this today. In the linen closet, just through that door."

Agent Perkins raises his eyebrows again and takes the shawl from my hands. "How pretty. I'm afraid I'm not informed enough to offer an opinion on ladies' fashions, unfortunately."

Is that some kind of joke?

"There's blood on it," I say. "I believe this shawl was used to murder Mrs. Rose."

His eyes widen, his smile fading. "Please, tell me more, Miss Pound."

I tell him every detail. About finding the shawl, and the noise in the alley during the faculty party, and the figure I saw lurking out the window. Milly tells him about the man we saw walking arm-in-arm with Mrs. Rose, giving a detailed description of his homburg and his raccoon coat. Agent Perkins listens closely, nodding and looking each of us in the eyes with a piercing gaze.

"Where did you say you were when you saw Mrs. Rose with this man?" he asks when we've finished.

"At our dorm room window," Milly lies smoothly while I cast my eyes down. I'd resolved to be dishonest about this, but I don't like it. And given how closely Agent Perkins keeps looking at us both, I wonder if our efforts at concealment may not have been enough. "It overlooks P Street, and has a partial view of Dupont Circle."

"And you think this man murdered your teacher?"

"Headmistress," I say, just as Milly says, "Yes."

"I think someone used that shawl to strangle her," I say. "And before that, they struggled, and she fought back hard enough to draw blood. It's his blood that's on the shawl."

"You think that, do you?" Agent Perkins is still unfailingly polite, but I don't sense that he's taking my opinion entirely seriously.

"You must've heard about the gunshot during the faculty party," I say. "It was reported to the police."

"Yes." He nods, absently setting the bloody shawl down on a polished wood end table on the landing. "I'm not sure how much experience you have with automobiles, but they can make remarkable sounds. Not unlike the gunshots you might read about in pulp magazines. It has to do with what's called an engine. That's a part of the car that you can't see, but it does make noise from time to time."

I force myself to draw a breath. This certainly isn't the first time a man has spoken to me as though I'm an uneducated child, but it might be the most important one. "Surely you noticed the damage to the closet door."

"Oh yes." He glances back into Mrs. Rose's room as though it's an afterthought. "Thank you for noting that, Miss Pound."

"And there's clearly blood on that shawl."

Agent Perkins lowers his eyes then, but he isn't looking at the shawl piled on the end table. He's peering down at my hands where they're clasped in front of me. Madame Frost always said clasping was the best thing to do with hands during a conversation held while standing up, if there was no teacup or saucer that needed holding, but I wish now that I was wearing gloves.

"We'll take a close look at that shawl back at the station." Agent Perkins raises his gaze to my face. "If you don't mind my asking, Miss Pound, have you had any recent injuries? Any cuts on your fingers, perhaps? Or have you, Miss Otis?"

I smile. It's the only method I can think of to contain my anger. "No, Agent Perkins, I haven't."

"Nor have I," Milly says. "And neither Miss Pound's father, nor mine, will appreciate hearing that you suggested we'd fabricated evidence of a crime."

Agent Perkins' smile doesn't waver. "I'd never dream of suggesting anything of the sort. There's no need to trouble the honorable Judge Pound or the good Ambassador Otis with such a trivial matter. Particularly if you're able to tell me more about this man you saw with your teacher that night, and how, precisely, you managed to get such a good look at him from a third-story window."

My heart drops to my feet.

He knows who our fathers are.

He knows we're lying.

Did he see us at the speakeasy? Is he threatening us?

"I have reason to believe," Agent Perkins goes on, as though he hasn't noticed my faltering smile—though I'm sure he did— "that your teacher was involved with some people who've been known to violate the law, and if you saw her with a man the night she died, then that's a man I'd very much like to speak with. I don't suppose either of them mentioned this man's name?"

"We couldn't hear what they were saying," Milly lies smoothly. "We were too far away."

I wonder if she's as frightened as I am. I don't dare look at her.

"That's unfortunate." Agent Perkins retrieves Mrs. Rose's shawl from the table and bunches it between his hands. I wish he wouldn't touch it that way. It isn't *his*. "And the other girl you're friends with—Miss Blum, isn't it? It was awfully nice of your Mrs. Rose to let her in. I imagine they don't allow many Jewish girls in your school. Did Miss Blum see this mysterious man, too?"

He says Clara's name like it's another threat. I swallow and shake my head again.

How does he know we're friends with her? How does he know so much about us *all*?

"I suppose you'd like to clear your teacher's name?" Perkins is still fingering the shawl. "Better for you girls if she's a victim, rather than being involved with anything unseemly?"

"We're telling you the truth." Milly folds her arms across her chest.

I don't say anything. We haven't told him the *entire* truth, and I'm fairly certain he knows that.

"Well, it's good to have met you both." Agent Perkins bows again. "Next time I'm in your father's courtroom, Miss Pound, I'll be sure to tell him I had the pleasure of making your acquaintance. And I'd recommend being careful how far you lean out of windows in the future."

14

Milly and I can't speak as we walk away. We can't risk Agent Perkins overhearing.

I'm too furious to speak in any case. The *nerve* of that man!

Yet I'm frightened, too. He might indeed have recognized us from the Lazy Susan, and he definitely seems to know my father.

My father would never permit me to return to a school that had allowed me to escape to a speakeasy. Or to associate with friends who'd done the same.

Clara was right to be wary of the police.

Milly and I emerge into the grand hall to find it empty. The piano that's used for our dance classes and parties is pushed into a corner, and there's no sign of anyone. Until Clara emerges from the north corridor, smiling at us.

That's strange. Only a moment ago she was in her room, getting ready to leave. The north corridor doesn't lead to anything but our art history classroom on one side and Mrs. Rose's bedroom on the other, with her office a short distance away.

"How did it go?" Clara whispers as she reaches us.

I glance over my shoulder. We should be far enough away now.

"Terribly," I whisper. "What are you doing over here?"

"I felt bad for not going with you to talk to the police, so I went into Mrs. Rose's room. I wanted to see if she truly had liquor bottles, but I didn't see any."

"The police already cleared those out." I shake my head. "Of her office, too."

Milly glances down the hall. "We shouldn't be talking here."

She leads us back down the northern corridor and into the dim, wood-paneled art history classroom, where we've spent countless hours studying books of Renaissance paintings and memorizing lists of sculptors, the better to make conversation at future dinner parties. Milly shuts the door. "That Agent Perkins isn't someone we can trust."

Clara sighs. "Well, they tend not to be."

"That's true. He's a Prohibition agent, after all." I nod. I'd been thinking of Perkins as a police officer, but he isn't one, not really. "All those dry squad men are on the take. My father says the speakeasies bribe the squads so they can keep operating. The only bars that get raided are the ones that don't make their payments."

Milly frowns. "Do you think what happened to Mrs. Rose had something to do with what happened at the Lazy Susan?"

"I don't know." But it's still so clear in my mind. The bow-tied waiters. The cigarette girls in their red dresses. The government men lining the bar. "The Lazy Susan could've afforded bribes. Besides, don't speakeasies have other ways to keep raids from happening? Signs to warn customers the police are coming? Trapdoors to hide the liquor?"

I look at Clara for confirmation. She only shrugs. "In motion pictures, they do. What did Perkins say, exactly?"

As Milly tells Clara about our conversation with Perkins, I shut my eyes again, trying to think it through.

Perkins only seemed interested in hearing about the man in the homburg. He didn't give any sign that he cared about the broken wood on the closet door, and he barely glanced at the blood on the shawl. In fact, he seemed to think I'd bled on it *myself.* All to clear Mrs. Rose's name.

And I *do* want to clear Mrs. Rose's name. She wasn't giving liquor to her students or running around with bootleggers. She was far too smart for any of that.

More than smart. She was *brilliant*. She was everything I wanted to be.

Yet it seems I can't trust the police to prove that.

"We need to do this ourselves," I say, when Milly's finished explaining. "The police don't seem to have any intention of investigating the real evidence, not even when we've handed it to them."

"They might." But Milly sounds uncertain. "He said he'd take that shawl to the station."

"Well, if they find the murderer, then lovely." I shake my head. "But do *you* think that they will?"

Milly shakes her head. "I think Agent Perkins saw us as a pair of useless, dim-witted girls with useless, dim-witted theories we must've read in pulp magazines. And I imagine his fellow officers would think the same."

"Then we should ask some questions ourselves," Clara says. "Talk to people who knew Mrs. Rose. They might know who that man was."

"And we should look into the seminary's finances," Milly adds. "Murders are always about money. If anyone picked up a single newspaper, they'd see that."

"Finances..." As I echo Milly, something occurs to me. A moment from the faculty party, not long after the gun went off outside. "Mrs. Rose was trying to talk to Damian Babcock. She wanted to discuss the seminary budget, but he said his wife wouldn't allow him to talk money at a party."

Milly's eyes light up. "That might be it! Perhaps...perhaps Mr. Babcock stole from the seminary, and she found out?"

"You think *Trixie's uncle* murdered Mrs. Rose?" Clara doesn't hide her skepticism. "How *old* must that man be?

Besides, the Babcocks have plenty of money from their railroad business, as Trixie's always telling everyone."

"Having money doesn't mean you don't need more of it," Milly says.

A burst of voices rings up from the floor below. More girls bidding one another goodbye.

"We need to talk to whomever we can before we leave." Clara's already moving toward the classroom door. "Let's see who we can find."

We head for the northern stairs and nearly walk into Lucy. She's climbing up with a bucket of coals in her hand, her face drawn and tight. When she sees us, though, she puts on a smile quickly. "Oh, did you need something, Miss Pound, Miss Otis, Miss Blum?"

We aren't meant to use the servant stairs. We have no acceptable explanation for being on the second floor at all. But I don't think Lucy will turn us over to anyone.

"How are you, Lucy?" I ask.

Her smile remains sunny. "Very well, thank you, miss."

I shake my head. "It's all right. None of us are truly well at the moment."

"I suppose that's true, miss. I..." Lucy bites her lip, the bucket sagging in her hand, as though it's suddenly grown much more burdensome.

Clara steps forward and takes the bucket from her hand. From the way her shoulders bend, it must be awfully heavy, yet Lucy didn't even appear to be straining.

"Thank you, miss." Lucy sinks down onto the step, her pristine white apron spreading across her lap. I sit down beside her, with Milly at my feet. I've never done anything like this before, and it feels both terribly informal and entirely appropriate.

"I'm so sorry about Mrs. Rose," I say. "It must be awfully difficult for you."

Lucy doesn't meet my gaze. "Thank you, miss."

"Will you come to the funeral tomorrow?" Clara asks, setting down the bucket and taking a seat beside us.

Lucy shakes her head. "I prefer to stay back, miss. I don't want to remember her that way. I...It was me who found her that night. I heard a strange noise, like someone falling, or—or I thought I did, I suppose, and I went down to see what it was, and..."

Milly and Clara draw back, their lips forming into surprised Os, but I nod. I thought it must have been Lucy, given the weight of her sobs that night. "I'm so sorry," I say again.

"The police were quite kind." She reaches into her apron pocket and withdraws a small object, holding it out to me. "They even let me keep this after I found it with her. I did think it was strange she had it. Mrs. Rose doesn't smoke." Lucy draws in a breath, lets out a *mmm* sound. "*Didn't* smoke."

It's a matchbook. Plain black, and worn, as though it had been carried around for a good while in a series of pockets. Faded wide letters across the front cover spell out DUKE'S.

I glance at Milly, and she gives me an imperceptible nod in return. Mrs. Rose *did* smoke. We saw her do it. Yet Lucy doesn't seem to know.

"That was in her office?" Milly asks.

"It was." Lucy drops her eyes to the floor. "On the carpet. The policeman said it wasn't important, so I could keep it to remember her. Only, I've found I'd rather remember her as she was, and not...You can have it, if you like."

"I understand." I press the matchbook into my palm. "Thank you, Lucy."

The clock chimes in the grand hall behind us.

"Oh!" Lucy straightens, startled. "I'm so sorry. You three have missed your tea, and all on my account."

"Oh, no, we didn't want—" Milly tries to say, but Lucy's already standing, the bucket in her hand.

"There's a second tea, for the faculty, in the old library," she says, sweeping her arm for us to follow her. "Miss Klein and Mr. Peck left this morning, so we only have two teachers left. There'll be plenty extra."

None of us have the heart to resist. Lucy leads us through the grand hall where the clock is still echoing, past the silent grand piano, and into the library, which somehow feels even stuffier than it did the night of the faculty party, despite the winter sun shining through the windows.

The room is empty except for a frowning Miss Parker. She's wearing a dress I've seen her in a hundred times before, an ankle-length deep-blue velveteen number that was last in style during the Great War, if it ever was. I have no idea how old Miss Parker is, with her upturned nose, olive skin, and wrinkles fading in around her eyes, but she's got to be older than my mother if she's retained that ancient wardrobe.

Lucy slips away wordlessly, leaving us alone with her.

"Girls?" Miss Parker's tone makes it quite evident that she can't imagine why we're here. Fortunately, etiquette doesn't permit her to ask. "How do you do. Won't you come in and take a seat."

When Clara reaches out to shake her hand with a smile, Miss Parker returns it after only a second's hesitation. No one, not even the most disagreeable teacher, can resist Clara's smile.

"It's a pleasure to see you, Miss Parker." Clara's voice is sweet as honey as we all take seats around the table where the tea things are set out. Lucy was right about the food. There's a stack of cakes high enough to feed ten Miss Parkers. "The three of us were talking about how much we all, well... It's been a challenging few days."

"Indeed." Miss Parker nods. "It must be difficult for you girls. Mrs. Rose was only at the seminary a short time, but you may have already gotten accustomed to her, to some degree."

Her words hit like a slap. The light, easy kind of slap, that isn't meant to hurt, but stings around the edges all the same.

Clara and I exchange a glance, but Milly gives Miss Parker a quizzical lift of her eyebrows. "May I be frank, Miss Parker?"

The teacher's eyes widen. "By all means, Miss Otis."

"Well... it's only that it all feels a bit strange. The mourning, that is. The fanfare." Milly tugs on her wool skirt in a feigned display of discomfort, though it was tailored to her exact measurements by her personal seamstress. "I hate to speak ill of the dead, but... I never *entirely* trusted Mrs. Rose."

Clara shifts in her seat, but Miss Parker's eyes light up. I see what Milly's doing. It might very well work, too, as much as I dislike lying.

Assuming Milly *is* lying.

Miss Parker pours tea neatly into four cups. "*Trust* is an interesting word to use with regard to your late headmistress. Again, with all respect to her memory... more than a few of the faculty preferred our old ways."

"When Miss Thurman was headmistress?" Milly asks.

"To be honest with you, Miss Otis, there had been discussions about, shall we say... whether Mrs. Rose might not have been more content at another school. One that *needed* changing. Here at Washington Female, we educate the daughters of the very best families, and they've always done quite well with our traditions."

"Forgive me," Clara says, "but which traditions are those?"

"My apologies, Miss Blum. This must all be quite befuddling

to you, having only arrived this year." Miss Parker smiles indulgently at Clara. "I'm referring to certain...standards we once had. Dances, for one thing. Mrs. Rose limited the schedule to allow for only two dances each term so the girls could focus on their studies. I told her dances are far more important than studies! How are you all meant to learn how to act around young men when you never get to *see* any young men? Why, when I was in school, we had a dance every Saturday."

Her eyes have gone dreamy. We need to pull her back to the present day.

"Are there any other old standards you missed?" I ask. "Apart from the dances?"

"Naturally." Miss Parker nods with great importance. "Starting with faculty decorum and presentation. Miss Thurman always said that at a girls' school, we must *all* be beyond reproach. We're bringing up the young ladies who will lead the women of their generation, and it was up to us to set a proper example."

I reach for my tea. Mrs. Rose taught me that trick once. *Teacups make superb camouflage,* she'd told me. *Take a sip anytime you need to stop yourself from saying what you're thinking.*

"Mrs. Rose was particularly interested in relaxing standards," Miss Parker goes on. "Before she got here, all skirts were required to reach the ankle."

Milly nods gravely at my side. Miss Parker loved the old ankle rule, because it didn't require her to take out the measuring stick. Our freshman year, if she caught so much as a glimpse of a girl's stocking, she'd order her back to change. Dorothy Bradley missed nearly half of our first year of mathematics thanks to that rule, and only Miss Parker never realized it was by design.

"She sought to allow nonsense like bobbed hair, too." Miss

Parker scowls. "We told her the next thing, girls would be showing up with bare legs and painted faces!"

Miss Parker clutches a hand to her chest, but her cheeks are pink and eager.

"Though I should say, Miss Blum," she adds after a moment, "your hair is growing out quite nicely."

"Thank you, Miss Parker." Clara's smile never falters.

"You and the other teachers have always presented us with an excellent example of..." I sip my tea while I try to think of how to say it. A scent of smoke wafts in, more than just the fire in the grate, but I don't let my nose wrinkle. "Decorum."

"Thank you, Miss Pound, I'm pleased to hear that." Miss Parker doesn't seem to notice that I'm being insincere. I thought it would be obvious, as I've never been good at lying. Or maybe it's that I haven't often tried. "Yet it isn't only the teachers who must demonstrate decorum. The administration has an even greater obligation."

"Telling the girls about Jessica's Saturday nights?" I recognize the booming voice immediately, but the smoky smell would've given away Mr. Farrel's identity without it.

Saturday nights, he said.

Mrs. Rose died on a Saturday night.

"Good afternoon, Mr. Farrel," Miss Parker says.

Milly, Clara, and I wait as Mr. Farrel strolls over from the doorway and stubs his cigar in an ashtray. "Hello, girls."

Students don't speak unless spoken to, but now that we've been given license, we respond promptly.

"Good afternoon, Mr. Farrel."

"Good afternoon, Mr. Farrel."

"Good afternoon, Mr. Farrel."

"Same to you, same to you." Mr. Farrel shakes our hands and takes an empty armchair without waiting to be invited.

His gray suit is as crumpled as it always is on school days. For the first time, I wonder how many sets of clothing our teachers own. "Appreciate the visit. We don't get many girls coming to join us for tea."

"It's a pleasure," Milly lies. "May I make an inquiry, please?"

"You may, Miss Otis," Miss Parker says.

"Thank you. It's something I've been wondering about."

While Milly pauses, trying to formulate her question, Mr. Farrel grabs a cake off the top of the stack, still holding his teacup. I pretend to look at Milly, too, but hold my head at a slight enough angle that I can see him set the cake on his plate, then reach into his coat pocket for something before he turns back around and takes a sip of tea.

Only when I see Miss Parker giving him a glare that isn't as subtle as she probably intends am I truly certain that Mr. Farrel has poured something into his teacup. He must carry a flask in his coat.

I try to catch Milly's eye, to see if she noticed, but she's concentrating on Miss Parker. Clara is, too.

"I wondered if Mrs. Rose ever mentioned having any difficulties?" Milly asks her. "Of the...financial sort?"

Milly bites her lip as soon as she's stopped speaking. That isn't a question she should've asked over tea, not in those words. It's as though she's forgotten we aren't at a school debate, where the goal is to catch the opponent off their guard.

Miss Parker purses her lips in disapproval, but Mr. Farrel barks out a laugh.

"A rather gauche question, Miss Otis," he offers. "I ought to have a word with you about your cheek, but as class is not in session at the moment, I'll merely answer in the affirmative. The board barely pays any of us enough to scrape out a living. Why, I myself get a pittance. Scarcely more than she received, and I've been teaching since before she was born! I'd certainly say *that's* a difficulty of the financial sort!"

"Pardon me, but what were you saying a moment ago, Mr. Farrel?" I lift my teacup, only to find it empty. I pretend to sip anyway. "You mentioned Saturday nights? Is there someone Mrs. Rose is known to see on Saturdays?"

"Was," Mr. Farrel says.

I lower my empty cup. "I beg your pardon?"

"*Was* known to see. You asked if there was someone Mrs. Rose *is* known to see. Forgive me, I'm cursed as a teacher of languages to correct my students even beyond the boundaries of the classroom."

"Oh." I keep my smile carefully fixed to my lips. "Thank you, sir."

"Now, you were asking about the antics of your late head-mistress. Too young for her job, that's all it was. With age comes wisdom, and that's where your Mrs. Rose was lacking. No fault of her own, that, but they didn't have to name her head-mistress. In any case, yes, on Saturdays, she'd slip out the back door and go out on the town. No one knew precisely where, or with whom, but, well. After what's happened, we have to assume the worst."

"Oh."

My smile evaporates as I try to picture it. Mrs. Rose, stealing out the back door. Spending her evenings with men like the one in the old-fashioned hat.

It happened. We *saw* it happen.

All those mornings by the fire, sipping tea. She'd told me about her life. Or rather, I thought she had. I thought Miss Parker and the people like her, the ones who loved to talk about Mrs. Rose's scandalous connections, were liars and fools.

Perhaps *I* was the fool.

Besides, if Mrs. Rose was going out night after night, she'd have encountered all sorts of people. Her killer could be *anyone*.

"I brought it up to her a time or two," Mr. Farrel goes on. "I was worried you girls would notice. Start to get ideas."

"Did anyone ever tell the board?" Milly asks. "Call for her to be fired?"

Miss Parker and Mr. Farrel glance at each other. Then Miss Parker fixes her eyes on the table, and Mr. Farrel turns back to Milly and shakes his head.

"No, no, nothing like that." Mr. Farrel lifts his palms, as though to show he'd given up on Mrs. Rose long ago. "But I must say, I never thought it would lead her to an early grave. I suppose it serves as a sufficient warning to you lot, though."

"*Mr.* Farrel." Miss Parker's voice is low. She lays an admonishing hand on his open palm. Lets it linger there.

Then she sees me looking and snatches it back.

I drop my eyes, as though I didn't notice.

But...that movement was too easy. Too familiar. And Miss Parker looked far too guilty afterward.

That's how I know she's touched Mr. Farrel's hand many times before.

My breath catches in my throat, but I don't let out a sound.

Two unmarried teachers caught having a love affair would be as bad for them as being seen stealing out the window would've been for us.

It's automatic grounds for dismissal, without references. They'd never be able to teach again, here or anywhere.

I will the flush to leave my cheeks. This isn't the time to be naïve.

But now I know why they never reported Mrs. Rose to the board. Miss Parker and Mr. Farrel have something to hide, too.

What was it that man in the homburg said?

I've seen a few of your colleagues at the East Room around this time of night. Some may be passing us on their way out as we speak. I bet the East Room is another speakeasy. How many of our teachers drink, like Mr. Farrel? How many of them break curfew? None of them are married, per the rules, but how many are *truly* celibate, the way we're all supposed to remain until our wedding nights?

I don't dare look at either of my friends. They'll know not to let on that they've noticed. Not when Mr. Farrel seems poised to reveal something of true significance.

"No harm in these girls learning one last lesson from that woman," he tells Miss Parker. He doesn't give any sign that he's aware of what she inadvertently revealed. "I know some of you liked Mrs. Rose, perhaps even looked up to her, but there's still time to get back on the right path. You see what happens when you get involved with liquor and men."

I want to splutter out a reply—that he's certainly not one to talk about liquor *or* love affairs—but Miss Parker leaps in.

"That's *enough*, Mr. Farrel." She holds her teacup squarely in front of her face, as though considering whether to fling it at him.

"What was that about men, Mr. Farrel?" I ask. "Was there a particular man who..."

"My *dear* Miss Parker, I think I've earned the right to be frank with my students." Mr. Farrel coolly sips his tea and turns to shout down the hall, "Delicious as usual, Lucy."

No reply comes.

"Mr. Farrel," I ask again, though Milly's trying to catch my eye. We must be getting very short on time. "Was there a particular man who..."

"This city is full of men, girls, and you can do one better than your old headmistress and keep away from them. You want to keep your reputations intact, and more besides!"

"Mr. Farrel!" Miss Parker is on her feet. "You should retire to your room."

"Now listen here, Grace, there's no need to..."

"Girls!" Miss Parker's voice is so loud and sharp Milly flinches beside me. I'm so shocked he used her first name that I very nearly laugh. "I'm terribly sorry, but we'll have to leave you to enjoy your tea. Mr. Farrel needs to rest."

"Certainly," Milly says. "It was lovely to see you both."

Miss Parker swoops toward the door. "Likewise, of course."

Voices echo up from below as we make our way down the stairs. Anderson is showing the last few girls out into taxis. He tuts at our lateness as we join our place in line.

How many of the adults we've been taught to look up to have secrets to keep?

And do any have secrets they'd kill to protect?

15

THE FUNERAL IS NEVER-ENDING.

I wish I could melt into my seat between Milly and my mother. Disappear into the pew's felt cushion. Instead, I sit as I've been taught. Back straight, shoulders set, eyes dry. Crying in public is forbidden. Besides, I've cried enough in private.

"Mrs. Jessica Blackwell Rose was dear to many of you," Reverend Fuller drones from his pulpit. He drones everything, whether at a wedding or a funeral or a Sunday sermon. "Her loss will be felt for years to come, but she will live on in your hearts and in the kingdom of heaven. Please rise for a hymn of mourning."

As everyone climbs to their feet, I turn back to where Clara and her father are standing on the opposite side of the aisle. They'll leave this afternoon, after the funeral, for Shabbat and the start of Chanukah in Baltimore, but they'll be back by Monday morning.

I lean over far enough to catch Clara's eye. She catches mine in response, and a tiny bit of warmth flows into me. I don't realize I'm smiling, though, for anyone to see, until a forearm knocks into mine.

Milly. Her plain black crepe dress stretches from well above her collarbone to her ankles. The mirror opposite of the beaded, backless dress she wore to the Lazy Susan. Her face is turned forward toward the pastor, but the meaning of her arm pressing into mine is clear. No smiling at funerals.

I straighten my back, and the line of my lips, too. Milly's right. Again.

Mrs. Rose's family must be here somewhere, after all. The processional was short. Only the clergy and the pallbearers with their black armbands reading GARRETT'S FUNERAL HOME stitched in thin white letters.

She never mentioned her family, aside from her late husband. Surely, though, she had parents and brothers and sisters and all the rest. They're probably up at the front of the church, concealed from view behind all the wide-brimmed black hats.

This church is only a few blocks from the seminary. It's the same one Milly and I and all the Episcopal girls attend each Sunday during the term, but it feels strikingly unfamiliar this morning.

It isn't Sunday. We aren't supposed to be here.

This isn't supposed to be happening.

I distract myself by returning to my search of the hymn-singing crowd for the man we saw with Mrs. Rose that night. I've been looking for him since before the service began, without success. With his sharp cheekbones and rosy skin, he should've been easy to identify even without his hat.

I don't see him anywhere, but at the far end of Clara's pew, another man I don't recognize stands in stiff silence. His eyes are dry, but his face is tanned and freckled, and he's wearing a faded brown-and-white-striped knit tie. That homemade tie, paired with his rumpled dark gray suit, stand out in the church full of men in gleaming, freshly pressed silk ties and black suits straight from the Palais Royal department store. He isn't young—about Mrs. Rose's age, perhaps—yet his tie has the look of something his mother may have knitted for him years ago. The only thing about him that looks new is the sturdy brown cane laid across the empty stretch of pew beside him, separating him from the other mourners.

It must be something, to come to a funeral alone.

Yet it's inappropriate to stare, and more inappropriate still to wonder, so I tear my eyes off the lonely man and continue my search.

I recognize most of the other nearby faces. Two rows of servants who've been at our seminary much longer than I have are sitting near the back. Nearly all of my classmates are here, and their parents, too. Elizabeth Baker and Helen Anthony are behind us, wearing their finest black dresses and gloves, heads bent over hymnals, no diamonds in sight. Trixie Babcock is in the first row, wearing a black velvet hat and an elegant, tailored black dress, undoubtedly the most expensive of any girl's here.

She's dabbing at her eyes with a delicate embroidered handkerchief. It's no surprise to see Trixie sitting up front, putting on an ostentatious display of mourning. Her mother, at her side, is dabbing at her eyes, too. Her father and sisters are bent over their hymnals, and her uncle looks even paler than the last time I saw him.

Perhaps I was wrong to leave the Babcocks to their fate that night at the Lazy Susan. I did it to keep our secret, but Trixie's uncle is an old, frail man. He could've been hurt.

Though perhaps everyone in this room is keeping secrets of their own.

When the service ends, we file into the cold hall next to the sanctuary for tea. I look around for a receiving line with Mrs. Rose's family, but all I see are waiters in tuxedos holding trays of canapés.

The adults step toward the fireplace, exchanging polite coughs and subtle glances at one another's carefully pressed funeral clothes. My classmates keep to the other side of the room, their faces turned down.

"Isn't it so terrible?" I hear my mother asking someone as she reaches for a lobster sandwich. "What an awful scandal. Not appropriate to discuss here, though, of course."

Over the murmuring crowd, I hear a snippet of a conversation about the chief justice and a dinner party, and I remember how Mrs. Rose described seminary parties to the man in the homburg that night.

It's all who's in line for which first assistant secretaryship, and who spoke out of turn to which justice at so-and-so's dinner party...

Her voice plays in my mind, so sharp, so alive, and an ache swells in my chest. As though a part of me's gone missing.

Clara falls into step beside Milly and me, and we move wordlessly to join a cluster of seminary girls.

"The dance was meant to be tonight," one of the juniors murmurs.

"Hush," another replies. "It isn't right to talk about dances here."

"Mrs. Rose hated dances," a sophomore adds. "She said girls would make more use of geometry than waltzes."

"*I'm* rubbish at both," the first girl says, and no one seems able to decide whether it's safe to laugh.

"Here, Gertie," Milly says.

I expect her to put another warning hand on my arm, but this time, she's passing me a handkerchief. A tear seems to be slipping down my nose. I dab at it hastily, but more tears are already springing free.

"It's all right," Milly whispers, and I turn my face to the wall, sucking in breaths of air to steady myself. "We can pretend we're discussing someone's dreadful choice of funeral attire. I'll say we saw an old man with the gall to wear plus fours."

That image, of a white-haired man standing solemnly at a funeral in knickers tied below the knee, makes me laugh. A genuine snort that turns into a sniffle. It's enough to help me pull myself together.

I lay a hand on Milly's elbow. She must sense my silent gratitude, because she lays a soft hand on top of mine.

I gulp down the last of my sobs and dab at the damp spots on my face.

"Can you believe how Mr. Farrel acted yesterday?" Clara whispers. She's trying to distract me, and I'm glad. "That man is absurd."

"I can believe it, actually," Milly says. "He's never been one for *decorum*, as Miss Parker would say. She must loathe having to spend time with him."

"I imagine it's quite the opposite." I force a tiny smile. "You saw how she touched him."

"I only saw him pouring gin into his teacup. He always thinks he's being so discreet." Milly lets out a small laugh. Then, when she sees my face, she stops. "Wait. What do you mean?"

"The way they argued?" I remind her. "The way she put her hand on his to stop him talking? The way he used her first *name*? They're courting. In secret."

"You're sure?" Milly glances behind her, as though Mr. Farrel and Miss Parker might be canoodling across the room as we speak.

"I don't think it's true." Clara's voice has gone sharp, her eyes flinty. "We shouldn't make assumptions about what's happening between people based on a single touch."

Milly glances at Clara, but she doesn't say any more.

"Well, that's their business," I say uncertainly, wondering what I could've done to make Clara so angry so fast. "What matters is, we know that Mrs. Rose usually went out on Saturdays. Perhaps the man we saw her with was a regular companion."

"Perhaps," Milly says. "Yet, as the teachers didn't know *where* she went when she left the seminary, I'm not sure how much help that is in finding him now."

"They definitely thought she was up to no good." I drop my voice to an even lower whisper. "Could she have been going to speakeasies?"

"Seems too pedestrian for Mrs. Rose." The anger in Clara's eyes is already dimming. "I can't picture her at the Lazy Susan."

I couldn't, either, until I heard what Mr. Farrel said. Now, I'm not so sure.

"Someone needs to find out what truly happened." Milly takes her handkerchief back and slips it into her handbag. "The rumors are only getting wilder. If more papers start to pick them up, our parents will worry. They already think this will make it harder for us to get married."

I roll my eyes. "I don't *want* to get married."

Milly glances over her shoulder. "Please don't tell anyone that."

"I'm not stupid."

"I know you're not." She takes my gloved hands in hers, the silks sliding. "Listen. Last night, I overheard your mother saying the committee's debating whether the seminary should reopen for the new term at all. They're going to decide in the next two weeks. Before New Year's."

I close my eyes. I can't look at my friends.

"They're waiting to decide," Milly goes on. "Out of respect, but..."

"There's nothing *respectful* about any of this."

"You're right." There are dark circles under Milly's soft brown eyes. "Let's wait until a few days after the funeral—out of *true* respect—and go to see Damian Babcock. Perhaps we can get some information on those budget numbers Mrs. Rose was asking him about."

I raise my eyebrows. "It isn't appropriate for us to pay a social call to a man."

"We can visit his wife, then. She may know something, and he might be there, too."

"How are you going to ask either of them anything? You know talking about money is never permitted."

"I'll find a way."

I look toward Clara to see if she's as skeptical as I am, but she's staring at the floor, at our low-heeled black shoes. Three pairs of toes pointing in to make a neat little triangle. She still won't meet my gaze.

I wish I understood what was happening inside Clara's head. Instead, I lift my gaze to take stock of what's happening outside our little circle.

Groups of girls are scattered around the room, speaking in low voices and trading occasional smiles. Parents are stifling their yawns and taking long sips from their teacups. My mother is talking with Mrs. Paul and Mrs. Mayfield. Trixie is alone by the refreshments table, staring down into a bowl of iced tea. Her uncle is on the opposite side of the room, holding his top hat and murmuring to his wife, the white-haired, kind-faced Penelope Babcock.

And the man in the knit tie. He's stepping out through a side door, leaning on his cane.

Something about the movement, the posture, makes me think again of the figure I saw through the window that night. Watching the seminary from a perch across the street. That figure had leaned on something, too.

Could it have been the same man?

He's already left the church. I may never see him again, not unless I go after him.

But I can't leave this room. It's packed with people, and

all of us have been trained since birth never to leave a funeral before the primary mourners depart.

Yet that's precisely what I do.

There's no time to explain. I step away from Milly and Clara, laying a finger to my lips in a silent request for secrecy as they look at me in surprise, and go straight after the man in the knit tie, slipping through the funeral crowd in my black dress, moving smoothly enough not to cause a stir.

When I push open the same side door he disappeared through, I catch a glimpse of him. He's got a derby cap on his head. He doesn't glance to the left or right, focusing solely on the path ahead of him.

I long for my coat as I step out into the street, tugging on the ends of my black gloves. I could catch up to him easily if I ran, but that wouldn't be appropriate, so I keep to a steady walk, my hat tilted down as though I'm any other girl out for a morning stroll.

A flash of movement catches my eye. The man in the knit tie has picked up his pace and is cutting across the road ahead of a trundling streetcar. The driver rings a bell at him in reprimand, but he doesn't look back. He barely seems aware of the world around him at all.

Still, I keep well behind him, gathering my heavy skirt in a gloved hand. I succeed in reaching the opposite sidewalk without ruining my dress, but by then I've lost sight of him and have to pick up speed until I'm dangerously close to a trot.

I finally pause beside a wrought-iron railing to search the sidewalk until I spot the man's derby cap up ahead, showing no sign of slowing.

He doesn't pause, not for blocks. They must be looking for me at the funeral by now. My classmates. My parents. What will they do when they realize I've left the building? Will people think it's because I don't care about Mrs. Rose?

I should've taken a second to tell Milly and Clara what I was doing, at least, so they could make something up for the others.

But I *need* to know who this man was to Mrs. Rose. If he could possibly have had some connection to her death.

Finally, on Desales Street, he slows. I'm forced to slow down, too, but he gives no indication that he knows I'm following him. He turns toward a dark door set into a long yellow brick wall with a round awning stretched over it and disappears inside when I'm still halfway down the block. I slow my pace until I can read the sign printed over it: HOTEL GRAFTON—MEN'S ENTRANCE.

When I reach the door, there's a heavy sound coming from the other side of it. A thick echo. The sound of weeping.

Is it the man from the funeral? He disappeared through that door only moments ago.

He must've known Mrs. Rose, somehow. Yet he didn't speak to a single person at her funeral.

If he's weeping, is it out of grief? Or something darker?

And what was Mrs. Rose doing, associating with strange men?

Whatever happened to her, someone's got to find the answers. Before anyone else gets hurt.

16

We have our lines prepared when we arrive at Damian and Penelope Babcock's Georgetown home two days later. Three stories of red brick and gleaming windows tower over us, with broad white columns lining the front porch on either side. When the butler opens the door and sees the three of us on the doorstep, he silently extends a gloved left hand, an empty silver tray perched on top.

Milly draws her card out first and drops it on the tray. Her favorite green velvet-and-lace hat is pulled down low over her eyebrows, so she has to hold her chin high and her eyes cast down, like a queen.

Clara and I quickly follow. My card is unglazed white bristol board, with MISS GERTRUDE POUND neatly engraved with shaded block letters, and our address printed in the lower right corner with smaller type. I've never paid a formal call during the afternoon visiting hour without my mother, but I hold up my chin just as Milly does, determined to act as though I belong.

"Is Mrs. Babcock at home?" I ask the butler, phrasing the question exactly as Madame Frost instructed us.

He steps back inside, silently holding the door open, which means she is. We follow him past a rack stacked neatly with umbrellas and into the cavernous house, past a fountain with carved stone cherubs dancing under a stream of water.

Damian and Penelope Babcock don't have children. They've kept this entire home for themselves, and it has a desolate chill, like a monastery, or a museum. A place where no one could truly live. Certainly not a child.

Milly enters first, chin high, and Clara and I follow. We'll only have twenty minutes of visiting time before propriety requires us to leave, so debate-champion Milly will lead the questioning of Penelope Babcock, while Clara and I commit her answers to memory. Should Damian Babcock be here as well, Milly will focus her questions on him instead.

Yet when the butler leads us through the dark-wood-paneled foyer with its gold-leaf trim and announces, "Miss Pound, Miss Otis, and Miss Blum," as stiffly as if he were bringing us in to meet the queen of England, I can already see several pairs of high-heeled feet in the drawing room, and know our visit isn't going to go as planned.

The three of us linger in the hall for the designated half-minute to allow the drawing room occupants to ready themselves, and when we finally step inside, only Madame Frost's training prevents me from gasping audibly.

Trixie is here.

The room is packed with her family, in fact. Her mother, Alice Babcock, is sitting on a sofa beside Penelope, wearing a slim tea dress trimmed in black and silver and a pinched smile. On the opposite side of the room are Trixie's three sisters—the youngest couldn't be more than seven, but she's nonetheless sitting silently, her back straight and her pale blue dress pressed as neatly as both of the Mrs. Babcocks'—and Trixie herself.

Penelope Babcock stands first, and the three of us take turns stepping up to shake her hand. She's wearing a sage-green dress that's meant to look simple but probably cost fifty dollars. Her smile appears genuine, but her eyes are tired. Exhausted, no doubt, from hosting Trixie and all those little sisters.

Alice Babcock and the younger girls give us gracious,

insincere smiles, but Trixie shoots daggers with her eyes. At each of us, but at Clara most of all. I wonder if there was some roommate altercation that I haven't heard about.

"Such a lovely surprise to have you girls pay us a visit," Trixie's mother says after we sit down. Two maids in silver-gray taffeta dresses with organdy collars and aprons scurry through the room, ensuring everyone has teacups and saucers.

"How fortunate for us to have visited at the same time, Mrs. Babcock," Clara says, seeming oblivious to Trixie's glares.

"Ours is an extended visit," Alice Babcock says. "Mr. and Mrs. Babcock have been kind enough to permit us to stay with them until our new home is ready."

Penelope Babcock's smile grows. "It's a blessing. The children are dear, and Alice is such a help to me. Even George, so busy at the bank, you know, takes the time to bring us tea in the mornings."

"How lovely." Clara's own smile is warm as she turns to Trixie's younger sisters, all lined up on the smallest sofa. "I'm sure you girls enjoy spending time with your aunt and uncle."

"Yes, Miss Blum," says the oldest, who looks about twelve. She and the younger girls are each holding their cups with their little fingers curled, exactly the way Trixie's mother is holding hers. An *affectation*, my mother calls that finger curl. A hallmark of false elegance. Not something the "truly cultured" need bother with.

"Tell me, Miss Otis, are you coming out next season?" Penelope Babcock asks Milly with a polite tilt to her head. "Trixie's ever so excited for her debut."

Trixie appears anything but excited. She's barely spoken, and her little finger isn't raised to quite the level of her sisters'. She must not think us worthy of a full curl.

"I'm not certain, Mrs. Babcock," Milly answers. I try to

imagine what's happening inside her head as she works out ways to shift this discussion from debutante balls to the seminary's finances in front of Trixie's entire family. I don't see how it's possible. "I may be overseas for the winter."

Is Milly lying? She hasn't said anything to me about going abroad. She isn't generally eager to see her parents any time of year.

Milly's father, Ambassador Otis, has always believed first and foremost in his own importance, and he makes it clear that he expects everyone else to feel the same way. He's spent his career steaming from city to city and country to country, taking one exalted government position after another, without ever adjusting his estimation of his own inherent value, or considering his family's actual needs. And as for her mother, while Mrs. Otis has always made sure Milly and her brother were outfitted in the latest fashions, she prefers to spend her time attending glittering parties and impressing glittering people.

"Perhaps you'll be invited to debut in Europe." Alice Babcock's expression shifts into a sparkle. "Imagine, being presented to the king and queen! Well, the balls here will be lovely, too. My own was at the very height of the season in New York. I remember my gown, pure white net and the most exquisite antique lace..."

I try to picture being presented into official Washington society, forced to make pleasant conversation while waltzing around a ballroom with a dozen different men. My mother used to talk dreamily about my debut, until a few years ago when it became clear that I'd inherited my father's height and will inevitably tower over all the other girls during the procession. Now, coming out is simply a task I have to get through. Like everything else.

"Why are you *here?*" Trixie asks abruptly when her mother's story peters off.

Everyone in the room goes stiff. "Beatrice!" her mother hisses.

"My father and I were so grateful for the invitation to your Christmas ball, Mrs. Babcock," Clara says swiftly, as though Trixie's outburst didn't happen. "How wonderful, that your new home will be ready so soon!"

"We'll be very pleased to receive you." Alice Babcock turns to Clara, but her smile, still pleasant, no longer reaches her eyes. "We're putting on the final touches this week."

"It'll be the event of the year. No one will have ever seen anything so grand, not in all the city." The fresh warmth in Penelope Babcock's voice reminds me of my own grandmother. She died when I was ten, but she loved nothing more than talking about balls. She made them sound so marvelous that it wasn't until I was thirteen and attended my first real ball that I realized her enamored memories may not have been entirely trustworthy. "It'll be the most lavish ball anyone can remember, and their new house will be the talk of Washington once people get a look at all its marvels!"

The younger Mrs. Babcock purses her lips. "Yes, it'll be marvelous, indeed."

"When do we get to move?" the youngest girl interrupts. "I'm tired of having everything in boxes."

The twelve-year-old knocks an admonishing patent-leather shoe into her sister's.

"The morning of the ball, as we've discussed." Alice Babcock doesn't look at any of her children as she speaks. She must save all her own admonishments for Trixie. "Now, Miss Pound, if I may ask *you...*"

But her unasked question dies in the air as the front door opens and raised voices blow into the drawing room.

"Have someone take care of it," a man is saying.

"I understood *you'd* take care of it," another replies. "Garrett keeps calling and I don't...Ah."

The two men come into view just outside the drawing room. Trixie's father shoves his hat into the hands of the white-tied butler, but his eyes stay fixed straight ahead as he marches past the drawing room and into the hall.

"That Mr. Babcock," Penelope says with a smile. "So absorbed in his work he doesn't even notice visitors."

Or his own children, apparently.

"Hello, there, ladies." Trixie's uncle moves more slowly, stepping into the drawing room before handing his hat to the butler. "Thank you, Richardson."

Damian Babcock's friendly smile glides over the room, but the look in his eyes is a hundred miles away as he bends to shake hands with each of us. His face is still quite pale, and his palms are marked with age spots, but his handshake is firm and easy.

I can't shake the memory of them at the Lazy Susan. Damian Babcock, president of our board, railroad tycoon, one of the richest men in the city. George Babcock, vice president of a bank. Both of them standing over a cowering man, bleeding on the floor. In a speakeasy, of all places.

"As much joy as it brings me to see you ladies, I hope you'll forgive me if I continue my conversation with my brother." Damian Babcock grins, as though he's a jolly old uncle to us all. A hefty, winking, white-cheeked man who could never pose a threat. Though given that he's currently battling a railroad strike, some of his employees may feel differently. "Matter of business, you'll understand. Quite dull to such lovely company as we have assembled here."

"Of course." Penelope nods.

These are the sort of men we're taught to admire. If we're lucky, we'll get to marry others like them one day.

I wonder how many families are as full of hypocrites as the Babcocks.

With one more brief smile, Trixie's uncle vanishes down the hall. He says something to the other Mr. Babcock, but I can't discern the words.

I try to catch Milly's eye, but she's watching Penelope.

We don't have much time.

"Pardon me, Mrs. Babcock," I say before either of the two Mrs. Babcocks in the room can launch into another polite question. "May I inquire as to the bathroom?"

Alice Babcock's eyebrows knit severely across her forehead. I can already hear the story she'll share later when it's time to gossip with her friends. *That Gertrude Pound, you know, parents are ever so respectable, father's a judge, attends the same finishing school where we send our Trixie, but would you believe she asked about the* bathroom*!*

But Trixie's aunt gives me a sympathetic smile. "Certainly, Miss Pound. Richardson can show you the way."

"Thank you, Mrs. Babcock."

I don't look at Milly or Clara, but I can feel their eyes on me. This wasn't part of our plan. I'm not following the rules, of etiquette or otherwise.

The two maids in their silver taffeta move soundlessly across the foyer as I pass through, eyes averted, bundles of linen stacked neatly in their arms. The butler, Richardson, sees me right away. "Yes, miss?"

If I'm going to be dishonest, I should at least strive to be consistent. "Could you direct me to the bathroom, please?"

"Yes, miss." He nods to the door at the end of the hall. To my relief, he then immediately turns away.

He doesn't give any sign of doubting me. But then, why should he? Why should anyone? I've been trustworthy and proper all my life.

No one's watching as I slip past a dim, empty dining room, then a kitchen where a silent cook in a black dress and apron stirs a pot on the stove. I haven't seen Damian Babcock yet, but when I do, I'll find a way to ask him some *real* questions.

I slip from room to room, not crouching, or hiding, or making any attempt to keep from being seen. Still, in this house full of people, no one takes notice of me.

Perhaps I'll succeed. Find something truly useful. Milly will be astonished.

Then I realize I'm not alone after all.

"I need to tell you something." Trixie's whisper comes so suddenly over my shoulder, only my pinching shoes prevent me from leaping into the air.

I turn, furious to have been interrupted just when I was getting somewhere, to see that her eyes are wide, her face white.

I'm angry. *She's* terrified.

We're in a narrow hallway lined with enormous cabinets. A pantry, I suppose, though I don't know why a house for one couple needs a pantry big enough to supply a state dinner.

"Tell me what?" I say. Or perhaps I snap it. It's difficult not to snap with Trixie.

The color returns to her cheeks, and she crosses her arms over her chest. "Why *are* you here?"

"I beg your pardon?"

"Stop it." Trixie steps so close our lips could touch. She's nearly as tall as I am, and her arms are shaking under her thin blue dress with its delicate white polka dots. "I know this is all an act. You'd never come to *my* house on a *social* call."

I can't let Trixie get in my way. I take a long, low breath.

"I'm surprised at you, Miss Babcock. If your mother or your aunt heard you speaking that way, you'd find yourself in serious trouble."

"*You're* the one in trouble. That's what I'm trying to—"

"Go *away*, Trixie."

As soon as the words leave my mouth, I wish I'd held them back. I'm *never* rude. I didn't realize I knew *how* to be rude. But Trixie... she's just so...

"Miss Babcock." I should apologize, truly, yet I find I can't. "What was it you came to tell me?"

But Trixie's already striding away, her chin lifted so high I half expect her to topple backward.

I've lost track of where I'm meant to find the bathroom, and I'm turning to search when I hear another voice. One that makes me forget all about my ill-advised snapping.

"...don't see why you insist on having it this year," a man is saying on the other side of a thin wall. It's Damian Babcock, I believe, except he doesn't sound like a jolly old uncle now. More like an impatient man who's used to getting precisely what he demands.

George Babcock answers him, but his voice is too low for me to make out. I step back until I'm nearly up against the wall, then edge toward the cracked-open door so I can peer inside.

The two men are in a study, like my father's but larger, with an enormous oak desk in the center and two walls taken up entirely by bookcases. They're standing in front of one, examining the books with their backs to me.

"Take it up with Alice if you object," the younger Mr. Babcock is saying.

"Perhaps I will." Damian lays his hand flat against the wall beside the bookcase. It doesn't look like a very comfortable way to stand. "Perhaps, while I'm at it, I'll tell her what you got up to last Saturday evening."

"Go ahead," George says. "The first thing she'll do is tell Penelope."

"I can handle my wife." Damian steps back. Just beside the point on the wall where he'd pressed, the bookshelf moves. The wall behind it is swinging toward him, but neither man looks alarmed. "Can you handle yours?"

My mouth drops open as they both disappear into the opening in the wall, their voices falling into indistinguishable murmurs.

Just as I'm trying to edge closer, they step back out again. Damian is holding a tall bottle full of brown liquid, and George has two glass tumblers full of ice.

Damian Babcock has a false wall in his study. To store *liquor*. And *ice*. That space behind the false wall has an *icebox*.

"You nearly got us both tossed in a paddy wagon," Damian says as he pours the drinks. "*My* name could've been dragged in the papers, and that's the last thing I need during this godforsaken strike. You know well that the only reason it didn't happen is because *I* took care of it."

"Yet you remind me every day. Well, despite that great hardship, the size of your wallet doesn't seem lessened. You could even afford to keep the girls' school operating, if you cared to bother."

"I know how to manage *my* funds."

"You're telling me I don't?"

"I'm telling you to stop borrowing from those fellows in New York, and pay Garrett before he badgers my secretary with more—"

"Miss?"

The voice at my back is so sudden I nearly jump again. It's quiet and polite, though, which means it isn't Trixie.

I turn to see the taffeta-clad maid who handed me my teacup earlier, smiling. Her brown hair is fashionably bobbed under her white cap, and she's perhaps two or three years older than I am. "May I provide some assistance?"

It's obvious I'm eavesdropping. There's no use hiding it, and the only excuse I can think of is quite flimsy. I'll simply have to decide to trust this girl.

I lower my voice to a conspiratorial whisper, tilting my head toward the study with the two Babcock men inside. I need her to come away thinking I'm idly curious and nothing more. "I was looking for the bathroom, and I became distracted by the... Well."

"Ah. I understand." The girl smiles again. She knows exactly what I'm talking about, clearly. "The lavatory is this way."

She leads me back through the pantry. Once we've left the study in the distance, I whisper, "I'm surprised a family like the Babcocks would have such a... closet."

I tried to be vague, so the girl wouldn't feel that she had to confess anything to me, but she doesn't hesitate.

"Oh, that's only the *upstairs* supply," she whispers. "There's far more in the basement. We have to restock this one from it every morning."

I smile knowingly. It's surprisingly easy to play along. As though I'm no different from any other gossiping seminary girl. "All left over from when it was legal, I'm sure."

"Oh, no, miss." The girl is giggling. I giggle, too, hoping it'll encourage her to go on. "They ran through the old stash long ago. Now they have a man who brings it fresh each week! Used to be a right handsome fellow, but these days it's a new one, with oily hair. I have to let him in at the back door. He smells of shoe polish." She wrinkles her nose and giggles again.

The Babcocks have their own personal bootlegger. Who makes *home deliveries*. As though he's the milkman.

The newsreels are full of stories about gang wars in New York and Chicago. Bootleggers shooting one another on the streets. Innocent people getting hurt, too.

Meanwhile, Mrs. Rose is being held up as some sort of fallen woman for dying with a half dozen bottles on her carpet.

But the friendly maid is smiling, as though it's all very funny, so I try to match her tone. "It must cost them a fortune!"

"Oh, there's plenty where that came from. Though you wouldn't know it to hear them talk. Why, they won't even lend money to their own family, and you can probably guess what that means for us..." The girl's smile fades. She's gone too far, and she knows it. "That is...pardon me, miss, the lavatory's right here."

She ushers me into a narrow room with a gleaming white washstand, a fresh bar of soap, a stiff, clean towel, and a half-empty bottle of Fowler's Solution sitting along the rim. The mirror is polished to a bright shine, and even the toilet looks strangely opulent.

Everything inside this house feels over-the-top, off-kilter. I can't wait to get away.

"Thank you," I tell the girl. "So sorry to trouble you."

"No trouble at all, miss." The color in her cheeks rises again. "We don't get much friendly conversation around here, if you understand me. Good day to you, miss."

17

"I‍t didn't go well, then?" I ask.

Clara firmly shakes her head. We're in my room a few blocks away, sitting on the floor in the dark. My parents have already gone to bed, and they think we've done the same. Only our butler, Norris, is still moving around downstairs, putting out the fires and shutting off the lights. It's the first opportunity the three of us have had to talk in private since we left the Babcock home, thanks to my mother's insistence on dinner protocols and my father's sincerely held belief that everyone shares his devotion to certain evening radio programs.

"As soon as I said the word *budget*, Trixie's mother had a coughing fit," Milly says. "She's probably allergic to talking about money. Though not to spending it, obviously."

"That's why we had to make our apologies and leave as soon as you came back," Clara explains. Her father had a late dinner with some of his allies in Congress, and he asked her to collect her things from their hotel and spend the night here, so my parents could look after her. We haven't discussed yet where she's going to sleep, but my bed is certainly big enough to share.

"It was just as well," Milly adds. "By then I'd hit the limit for how long I could spend in that house without sniping at anyone. Though it sounds as if you did that for us all."

I bite back a smile. I've already told them about my run-in with Trixie and all the rest. "I did think it was interesting that Trixie's uncle was so worried about getting found out for being at the Lazy Susan during the raid. I don't see why he went there at all if he was that concerned."

"Particularly given that the Babcocks have their own private family bootlegger," Clara points out.

"Secrets." Milly nods. "Like Miss Parker and Mr. Farrel's affair. Everybody has something to hide."

"Except us." I shift, my bare legs growing cold against the rug. We all took off our dinner dresses and stockings once we came upstairs. I feel strangely exposed wearing my dressing gown in front of Clara now that we're not in the seminary anymore. All three of us have gotten dressed and undressed together plenty of times before tonight, but it's different here, somehow. "None of us have ever had any secrets. At least, up until that night."

Milly glances at Clara, then looks down. Clara notices and avoids her gaze.

"What?" I say.

No one answers. Clara looks away. Milly shakes her head.

I don't like this. "Is there something you two aren't telling me?"

"Of course not," Clara says quickly. "Although—well, Gertie, I do think Milly might not have been willing to tell you *quite* how loudly you snore. I could hear you through the *wall*."

I laugh, affronted and a little stunned. "Truly?"

Milly drops her head, snorting out a laugh of her own. "I'm sorry. It's true."

"You've kept this from me for *years!*"

All three of us are laughing hard enough to risk waking someone up.

I shake my head after a moment. We've got to focus. "Well," I say, forcing my breaths to even out, "it's clear *she* had secrets. Mrs. Rose, I mean. *That's* what we need to figure out."

"All right." Milly nods, her expression growing somber. "We need to start by finding the man in the homburg."

"How?" Clara asks. "It was so dark when we saw him, and we don't even know his name."

"I'd know him if I saw him again." I nod firmly. "I'm certain I would."

"Then we need to go to the only other place we know for sure he's been," Milly says. "The East Room."

This time, we get ready in the dark. Norris has long since gone up to bed, but nonetheless, we can't risk attracting attention. Milly ducks out of the room to find dresses for us while Clara winds my hair into a coil.

"I'm a little nervous about going to another speakeasy," I admit. I try to keep my voice light, but it's hard not to let my memory slip back to the Lazy Susan. The sound of that billy club cracking on the man's head. The sight of the blood oozing. "And that time, we didn't have to worry about my parents seeing us stealing away. Plus, we weren't looking for a murderer."

"At least this time we won't need to go through the window." Clara's voice comes close to my ear. "Besides, we should be fairly safe in such a big group. At a speakeasy, there won't be space to get murdered."

I freeze, horrified. Then I start laughing. Clara's always the one who can make me grin.

She smooths a new strand of hair, her finger grazing the nape of my neck. The light touch makes me shiver.

We're sitting on my bed, still in our dressing gowns. When I turn, I see that hers is dipping open in the front, a tiny line of bare skin revealed between the layers of thick silk.

I draw in a breath. "Clara, would you...that is, have you ever..."

The door opens silently before I can finish, Milly slipping back into the room. I twist back around so fast my hair pulls tight in Clara's hand, nearly making me cry out.

I truly don't know how I would've finished the question I started asking Clara. I only know that I wish I could've heard her answer.

She finishes my hair, and the three of us change quickly. I keep my eyes firmly fixed to the floor until we're all in our dresses. Milly and I pull on the same black beaded dresses we wore to the Lazy Susan, but Clara's is packed away, so Milly brought out a dress I've never seen before—silvery and slippery, with metal embroidery around the hem. It doesn't quite fit Clara, but after she applies a few clever stitches, it's close enough.

Remembering Milly's trouble with her backless dress, I insist on loaning her the shawl Mrs. Rose gave me. I've taken to wearing it every day, and it's strange to part with it, even for a night. Milly doesn't look entirely comfortable in it—bothered, perhaps, that it's not at her usual standard of fashion—but when she sees me eyeing it, she only gives me a quick thank-you before wrapping her gray fur stole across it. When she pulls her black cloche over her yellow curls, she looks so much like a young Mrs. Rose that I have to turn away.

She'd pored through her brother's old letters this afternoon, and found one that described a friend's visit to the East Room. It's one of the bigger bars, he'd noted, almost as big as the Lazy Susan, and took its name from the White House only a few blocks away.

Our escape attempt is a success. There's no one to notice us creeping down the stairs and through the kitchen, and soon we're out the back door, tiptoeing down the path through our tiny yard and around to the street, until we find a shadowy place to don our shoes.

We only have to walk one block before Clara finds us a taxi. It's my first time taking one after dark, and though the cabbie is unfailingly polite, with lots of tips of his hat, it feels wrong being in a car with a strange man at night.

Soon we're stepping out into the mouth of another dark alley, this one off Nineteenth Street and Pennsylvania Avenue. Tomorrow, Milly and I are meeting my mother and Mrs. Mayfield for luncheon at a prim tearoom on this very block, but tonight we hurry into the alley, folding our coats and wraps tight around our short dresses.

"If we find him, I'll do the talking," Milly whispers as we approach the door. This time, the mail slot is at eye level. Light shines faintly around the edges of the door.

What if there's another raid? If tonight ends with my parents getting a phone call from the police, would they ever let me see Clara and Milly again?

Milly knocks on the door four times, with a pause between the third and fourth rap. That's the signal, according to her brother. Still, the apprehension runs through all of us until a narrow piece of wood behind the mail slot slides open, revealing that it doesn't appear to be intended for mail deliveries at all. A pair of eyes stares through at us, the shadows around them so dark all we can see is a few tiny glimmers.

"We've come for the tea party," Milly tells the eyes.

They squint back at her, flicking to the sides to take in Clara and me. Then they disappear. For an instant I'm sure the wooden cover is going to slide into place and that'll be that, but then the door opens a crack.

"You members?" asks a bouncer with an enormous brown suit, close-cropped hair, and ruddy white skin.

"Not yet," Milly says. "How much?"

"Two. Each."

Milly reaches into her handbag and produces six dollar bills. I've never carried that much money with me at once, but then, I'm not Milly.

The man inspects them and nods, opening the door all the way. "Third faucet."

Milly steps past the bouncer, her stole whipping past him in a blur of soft gray fur, with Clara and me right on her heels.

Inside, the room is narrow, dark, and mostly empty. Tables and chairs are scattered around, with a few men and women sitting at them. There's no music, and little conversation. The three of us stand out far too much. I try to catch Milly's eye—this place is too quiet and sparsely populated to be of any use to us, and it certainly wasn't worth six dollars to enter—but she's walking briskly past the tables and toward the back of the room, where a door with the words MEN'S LAVATORY carved across it is set into the wall.

I lock eyes with Clara. She looks as confused as I do. When Milly throws open the door to the men's bathroom, I blush harder than I've ever blushed. *"Milly!"*

But she's already strutting past grimy urinals toward a row of sinks that's even grimier. She leans out, grabs the third faucet—which looks slightly shinier, slightly less filthy, than the rest of the room—and twists it straight down.

And the wall opens up, revealing a dark hallway on the other side.

I come very close to laughing. I wonder if the same builders who created the secret compartment in Damian Babcock's study worked on the East Room, too.

The short hall is empty, quiet, and dank. The three of us walk down it until we reach a second door, and when Milly opens that one, we step through into heat and music and laughter.

The East Room is smaller, darker, and louder than the Lazy Susan. There's no sign of a hat check girl, but the jazz tune playing is infectious. The room is packed with dancers, stepping and twirling with abandon. The freedom on display is frightening, after what happened at the Lazy Susan, but the longer I watch, the more exhilarated I feel.

"Wonder why Miss Tankel never taught us that one," Clara murmurs in my ear.

Half the people here seem to be laughing as they twirl around the floor, arms and legs and hips all moving to the music. The dancers' skin colors range from white to brown to black, and if there are any government men among the crowd, they don't look it. The men's suits are patterned and their eyes are sparkling, and the girls in their beaded and spangled dresses smile up at them with lips parted, as though perpetually ready to be kissed. The frantic happiness filling the room is enough to make me want to dance myself, even though all my previous dance instruction has consisted of waltzes and minuets taught by our stiff-necked instructor Miss Tankel.

The Lazy Susan was nothing like this. It was a place to see people, or, perhaps more importantly, to *be* seen. The East Room is a place to let go.

"Pardon me, girls," a voice says, and a yellow-headed waitress slides between Clara and me, a tray expertly balanced above all our heads, with a half-dozen mismatched glasses of dark brown liquid perched on top. She looks five or six years older than us, and she's wearing a black dress not so different from mine, but with tacked-on spangles instead of stitched-on beads. We watch as she dodges between two exuberantly dancing couples and arrives at a table full of men, where she passes out the drinks so fast I expect them to splash out across the table. Instead, the drinks stay intact, and the men thank her with big smiles and tinkling coins that disappear into the tiny bag she's somehow carrying, too.

"Another for me, kitten?" a man at the next table calls.

"Not if you ask like that, Mickey," the waitress calls back. Everyone within a three-table radius laughs, Mickey louder than anyone. "Try a *please* next time."

"Please, Bridget, baby, *please!*" Mickey cries, falling down at the girl's feet and getting grit all over the knees of his green-and-blue-striped suit. The others laugh even harder. Bridget laughs, too, and steps away from him, the tray still perfectly poised in her hands.

"Her." I twist around to my friends. Clara's watching the dancers quick-step across the floor, and Milly's eyes are drifting from table to table. "We need to talk to that waitress. I bet she knows everybody in this place. If she saw Mrs. Rose in here, she could tell us who she came with."

"We need to sit down first," Milly says.

She leads us through the cluster of tables to an empty one, her head lifted at exactly the same angle it was when we walked into the Babcock home, as though she's queen of the speakeasy. Clara takes off her coat and drapes it over her arm. We pass Bridget, who's somehow already got a fresh tray of drinks, but before Clara and I can join Milly at the table she's found, a man with a bow tie and brown hair slicked to a fierce shine steps out from the crowd of dancers, grabs Clara's hand, and whisks her into the throng.

I go to snatch her back, but she's already vanished into the sea of beaded black dresses and double-breasted suits. Just as the worry in my chest threatens to break out into a shout, I spot her.

She's doing the Charleston. She's smiling, and laughing, and toe-tapping perfectly in time to the music with the bow-tied man.

And she looks like she's *enjoying* it.

"Aw, don't look so sad, doll," a man to my left cries, reaching for my hand. "Let's hit the floor with 'em!"

I smile politely. "Thank you ever so, but I'm afraid I have two left feet."

The man lets out a guffaw, but before he can argue, a girl in a spangled red dress catches his eye and an instant later he's whirling off onto the dance floor with her.

I fight over to where Milly's sitting at the table, a glass in her hand. She's watching the still-dancing, still-laughing Clara, too. The man in the bow tie has draped her coat over his shoulder as they quick-step on.

"Well," I say, as I throw my own coat heavily across the empty third chair.

"Well," Milly agrees stiffly.

The man in the bow tie says something that causes Clara to tip her head back and let out a peal of laughter, her beaded headband glinting in the faint light.

"What can I getcha, sugar?" a voice asks.

I wrench my eyes away to see Bridget smiling down at me, her empty tray perched on her hip.

I have to put Clara and Mr. Bow Tie out of my mind. This is our chance. I turn to see if Milly wants to ask the questions, like we'd planned, but she's still scowling at the dance floor.

"Could we have two whiskey sours, please?" I ask. Bridget nods. I've seen enough to know she's about to disappear and do it fast, so I quickly add, "And...did a lady by the name of Jessica Rose ever come in here?"

Bridget's smile doesn't budge. "Can't say I recall that name, sugar. Be right back with your drinks."

I sigh once Bridget's gone. "So much for that."

"We need to ask the men." Milly hasn't taken her eyes off Clara. "Mrs. Rose wouldn't have been going around telling her name to the waitresses, but if she was here, the men will remember."

Will they?

I picture Mrs. Rose's silvery hair. Her intelligent smile. The way she walked across a room as though she was its sole possessor.

I suppose Milly's right. The men *would* remember.

Yet I can't picture Mrs. Rose in a place like this. Twisting that grimy faucet. Dancing with men like these. Smiling up at them, like the other women here.

That wasn't *her*. Not the version of her I knew.

I wish I'd known every version of Mrs. Rose. She might not have been the headmistress everyone wanted her to be, but she was *ours*. Until some murderer took her from us.

I straighten, lifting my chin like Milly's. "Where do we start?"

Milly eyes a pair of smoking men dressed in cheap gray flannel suits. "I suppose we simply...get up and ask them?"

But neither of us moves.

"Whiskey sour for you, sugar." Bridget sets a glass in front of me. "Special for another first-timer."

"How'd you know it's my first time?"

"Never seen you here before." Bridget smiles at me and then Milly. "Or your friend, either. I always keep an eye out for the new girls, so they don't get into any trouble."

"Like what?" I ask.

"Like him," Bridget says, but she laughs as she points at one of the gray-suited men. He's arrived at our table, one hand holding his hat against his chest, the other stretched out toward Milly. He's in his twenties, perhaps.

"You girls friends of Bridget's?" he asks. "'Cause any friend of hers is a friend of mine."

"Let 'em drink in peace, Roger." Bridget swats the man on the shoulder.

I haven't been around men much. Finishing school is odd that way. We spend all our time preparing for marriage, but our only opportunities for meeting marrying-age men are at the painful dances in our grand hall, rotating around a dull wood floor to dull music, clasping hands with duller boys who sweat into their shirt collars and try to look down our dresses.

Milly, though, smiles and holds out her hand as if she's used to meeting boys all the time. Which I suppose she is. There are those mysterious letters from Paris, after all.

Still, I've never seen her act this way, and I'm not sure I like it.

"Bridget's quite nice, and you don't seem half bad yourself," Milly purrs up at him.

"I'll leave you to it!" Bridget whisks her tray away.

The man, Roger, slides into Clara's empty seat, and as he turns his gleaming smile toward me, I make my choice.

Milly can have him. I'm going after Bridget.

I steer my eyes from where Clara's now dancing with an altogether different fellow and wind through the tables.

It's not that I'd have preferred a raid, but at least at the Lazy Susan, there was none of *this*.

Dancing with strange men. Speaking in breathy little tones that make their lips curl up.

I don't want to do any of that. I don't see why *anyone* would.

What was Milly writing to that boy in Paris about, anyway? Why didn't she ever show me any of his letters?

I push all that to the back of my mind and find Bridget at the bar, stacking a fresh round of drinks onto her tray. "Well, hello, sugar! Need something?"

The drinks she's hauling need to get to a table, and it's clear from the state of her dress and the freshness of her smile that Bridget needs every tip she's due. So I get straight to it.

"There's a man we're looking for," I say. "I don't know his name, but he's quite handsome, and talks as if he's quite smart, too. He has a raccoon coat."

Bridget smiles, two dimples shining. "You just described half the men in this place, sugar."

I smile back. "He wears a homburg. Looks as though it should be all old and fuddy-duddy, but on this fellow it's positively debonair."

"Oh, you mean Victor!" Bridget laughs. "Shoulda said so!"

"You know him?" My heart pounds. I can't wait to tell Milly and Clara I actually got something right.

Victor. I've heard that name. Where have I heard that name?

"Is he here tonight?" I ask her.

"Haven't seen him, sugar."

I don't let my disappointment show. "Do you know where we could find him?"

"He's only about the easiest man to find in the city." Bridget spins the tray in her hands until she's got the half-dozen brimming glasses perfectly balanced. "Just head to the Capitol. Trust me, everyone at the Capitol knows Victor. Now sorry, sugar, but I've got some thirsty folks waiting."

"Of course. Thank you so much. Here, my apologies, I forgot to tip you earlier."

I fish two quarters out of my purse, and Bridget takes them without even having to adjust her tray.

"By the way, watch out for your girl," she adds. I turn back to the table, thinking she means Milly, but she's nodding toward Clara. "That fella she's dancing with is bad news. Acts like he's on the up and up, but everybody around here knows better."

"All right. Thank you again."

I'm not sorry to have an excuse to pull Clara away from the dance floor.

I weave my way through the dancers, which isn't easy. Everyone's moving so fast, I keep having to jump out of the way of stepping heels. A man in a pink-striped tie tries to grab my hand and pull me in to dance with him, and I laugh apologetically and draw away.

He frowns, and my heart speeds up again. Dancing is fine for those who enjoy it, I suppose, but is every girl truly expected to dance with every man who wants her to?

The band slides into a waltz as I reach Clara. Her new dance partner is looping his hand around the curve of her back as I tap her on the shoulder.

Clara turns, and when she sees it's me, her face transforms. She was smiling already, a thin smile that didn't reach her deep brown eyes, but a fresh sparkle is forming there, and a dimple flashes by her chin.

"Gertie!" She turns away from the man and throws both arms around my neck. I let out a surprised little laugh. The man's arm stays firmly affixed to her back, though she's trying to politely pull away. "Henry, this is my dearest friend, Gertie."

Henry's gaze slides over where Clara's face is pressed to mine. She called me her dearest friend. "How do you do, Gertie."

"How do you do."

"Henry and I were discussing mutual acquaintances," Clara says, arms still clinging around my neck. I never want her to let go.

It occurs to me, suddenly, that I *do* want to dance tonight. But not with Henry, or Roger, or the man in the pink-striped tie, or any of these other men I've never seen before and hope to never see again.

I want to dance with *her*. I want her arms to cling around my neck while we spin across the floor. I want her to giggle up at *me*, the way all these girls around us are giggling up at all these men.

Dancing with a girl isn't against any rules. I strongly suspect, though, that *wanting* to dance with a girl—wanting her to cling to me, wanting us both to leave all the men behind—is against every rule I've ever been taught.

I may have had too much whiskey.

"I'm afraid I don't know that other girl you were asking about." Henry hasn't taken his hand off Clara. "A flower name, wasn't it?"

"Jessica Rose," I say, and Henry's dark eyes meet mine.

"Yeah. Can't say that rings a bell. Gertie, would you care to take this dance with my friend Tony? I was about to show Clara my waltz. I'm not so shabby a dancer, wouldn't you say?"

"I would." Clara laughs. "Gertie, was there something you were going to tell me?"

I can't very well tell her what Bridget said in front of Henry, so I improvise. "Milly says we have to go."

"It's too early!" Henry steps in closer. "Tell you what, Gertie, you and your friend head on out. I'll make sure Clara gets home safe."

I want to take off my high heel and drive it into his eye.

But Clara laughs and presses her palms against Henry's

chest. It looks as though she's flirting, and it makes my stomach churn, until I realize she's trying to put space between them. It doesn't work. "Rules are rules, I'm afraid. We're meant to be tucked into bed by eleven."

Now he's the one scowling. "Funny. You don't look like a nun."

Clara turns to her side, angling him back with her shoulder, and reaches out to grasp my hand. Her palm is slick with sweat. She's still smiling, but there's a hint of fear in her eyes.

I don't pause to think about propriety. I simply reach up to where his arm is still on Clara's back, grab his wrist, and peel it away, exactly as if I were on the basketball court prying a ball away from the opposing team, without worrying about fouls.

"Hey!" Henry's voice is sharp enough to make my blood pump faster. When several nearby dancers look up, though, he turns it into a joke, lifting his empty hands and backing away. "Right, right, everything's jake. Forgot I promised that other doll a waltz, better see where she got off to…"

"You do that," I tell him, pulling Clara by the hand and hoping the doll in question doesn't object to Henry's company nearly as much as we do.

I don't bother being polite anymore as I lead Clara through the dance floor, dodging couples when I can and pushing them aside when I can't. I want to feel triumphant, but I can't manage it.

Soon we're back at the table with Milly and Roger. He's leaning in to whisper something in her ear, and she's laughing, and his arm is draped around the back of her chair, and I want to kick him in his gray-flanneled kneecap.

Milly looks up at Clara and me, our sweaty hands still clasped. Her smile drops.

"We need to go," I say.

"It's early!" Roger booms as I pass Milly her black cloche. "You girls sit here with us. We'll get some more chairs. Hey, Bridget, could we get some more—"

"No need to bother poor Bridget." Milly smiles as she lifts Roger's arm from her chair and retrieves her coat. "Gertie's right, we've got to be going. Thank you ever so much for the lovely conversation."

"Aw, well." Roger scrambles to his feet. "I'll get you girls a taxi."

"We can manage," I tell him. All I want is to get as far away from this place as possible.

Milly lets Roger help her into her coat, and he tries to follow us out before Milly whispers something in his ear that makes him stop and blush all the way out to his extremely round ears.

"Next time, then," he says.

"Sure thing, fella." Milly wiggles her fingers at him as we leave, and I hope we'll come across a dirty can out in the alley, because I need to smash something.

We leave through the grimy bathroom and the nearly empty restaurant at the front, pass the silent bouncer, and emerge into the foul-smelling alley. I walk faster, ahead of my friends, the images playing through my mind.

Clara, whirling across the dance floor with Mr. Bow Tie. Milly, whispering in Roger's ear.

Victor. Why does that name sound so familiar? Why can't I remember?

"Gertie." Milly's voice behind me is only a murmur, but when I don't slow down, she raises it. "Gertie!"

"Yes?" I work to keep my voice perfectly pleasant, in case Milly and Clara actually thought any of that was fun. A few people are coming toward us from the opposite end of the alley, women in short dresses and a man in a peacoat, all of them heading toward the East Room.

"We should find a taxi," I say, without looking back. "My parents could've noticed we're gone."

"Roger didn't know anything about Mrs. Rose," Milly murmurs as she catches up to me. "But he used to go to the Lazy Susan, and *he* heard it was raided because of that government man we saw there, Mr. Pengelley. Apparently, he had a lot of enemies who wanted him out of his job, and if the rumors are true, the whole raid was a pretext so they could arrest *him*. It worked, too. He's about to plead guilty and resign."

"That's very interesting," I say.

Thank you ever so for the lovely conversation, Milly said to him.

Did she truly have to say that? Did propriety require her to go *that* far?

I speed up again, leaving Milly and Clara behind me. The two of them are walking with several feet of empty space between them and their heads bent to face the pavement, and I'm moving faster yet when a shout rises up from the far end of the alley.

No, not a shout. A roar. Full of violence and fury.

When I turn back, I see him. The roaring man. He's enormous, with a wide chest and shoulders, dressed in a heavy olive-green plaid jacket and cap-toe boots. His skin is pink, almost ruddy, under his black felt hat.

It's his hands that capture my attention, though. They're enormous. Out of proportion with his already massive frame. Even at this distance, I can see the thickness of his wrists and fingers, the heavy weight of them dangling from his sleeves.

He's still shouting. The same word, again and again. It's not a word I've ever heard before. "Stregoneria! Stregoneria! Stregoneria!"

He's looking straight at Milly. Crouching, as though to run.

The street is nearly deserted. If that man wanted to hurt us...

"Run." Clara grabs Milly's elbow. "Run!"

The three of us bolt out of the alley and down the street just as the man lunges forward.

18

"BUT WHAT DID HE *WANT*?" I ASK AGAIN.

My heart hasn't stopped hammering since last night, when that man on the street shouted at Milly. We'd run at top speed for three blocks before we realized he wasn't behind us anymore. Then Clara waved down a taxi and we all clambered inside, casting anxious looks back at the empty street behind us.

Milly and Clara only talked about how lucky we were to get away from him, but what I want to know is *why*.

What was he doing there? Why was he shouting at *us*?

We were all so shaken up that the three of us piled together into my bed to sleep, yet I couldn't shut my eyes. After an hour of listening to Milly's and Clara's soft, sleepy breaths on either side of me, I gave up and slipped downstairs into my father's library. I wanted to find that word the man had shouted again and again. *Stregoneria.* I had to go through three different dictionaries, until there it was.

It's an Italian word for a dark kind of magic. Witchcraft.

I sat in my father's chair for another hour, thinking, until I could only come to one conclusion.

The man was looking at Milly when he said it.

She was wearing my shawl. The shawl that's nearly the twin of the one Mrs. Rose wore the night she died.

From the back, with that shawl, her yellow curls, her gray fur stole, and her black hat, Milly must've looked much like Mrs. Rose did that night.

Black magic, indeed.

Could *he* have been the man who killed Mrs. Rose? Strangled her with those big hands?

When he saw Milly, did he think Mrs. Rose had come back to haunt him?

I wish she could. He'd deserve it, a thousand times over.

I can't bring myself to tell Milly and Clara. It sounds preposterous. Impossible. Witches, and ghosts, and theories based on nothing except my own imagination.

Yet I can't stop thinking about it, either.

"He didn't want anything," Clara says, biting into a chestnut. A vendor was selling them a block down from the House Office Building by the Capitol.

Just head to the Capitol, Bridget said last night. *Trust me, everyone at the Capitol knows Victor.*

"He was a mean drunk shouting in the street," Clara goes on. "He probably didn't even notice us. We're the ones who overreacted. Though I do wish it weren't always *quite* so exciting, leaving speakeasies."

It's a cold morning, and the frost is clinging to our eyelashes, the wind chapping our cheeks. Clara recommended afternoon tea dresses for visiting the Capitol, so Milly's wearing green wool tweed and Clara's in polka-dot crepe. I'm in deep brown, with the shawl draped around my shoulders providing the only color. Our stockings barely protect us against the chill, and we're walking as fast as propriety allows as we munch our chestnuts.

"I *would* like to try walking out of one, instead of running for our lives," Milly says.

"I'm sure most of the time, leaving a place like that is quite simple." I try to sound as amused and breezy as the two of them as our heels clack along the sidewalk. The House building's main entrance is a hundred yards ahead up a wide set of steps, a heavy brown door set into gray-tinged white marble. Men in three-piece suits and wide-brimmed hats are streaming through it, their workday beginning. There are a few women hurrying into the mix, too, wearing suits and coats and low-heeled shoes of their own. No tea dresses or polka dots in sight.

"You've done it plenty of times in New York, haven't you, Clara? Without having to...flee in terror?"

"Naturally." Clara nods. She was the one who thought we should get here early this morning, when we could blend in amid all the hubbub. Her father's already in his office, tucked into one of the far corners of the building, and Clara's confident we won't run into him. He always arrives early during the session, and never emerges until dinnertime, unless he has to go to the Capitol building for a vote.

"How, precisely, are we meant to find this Victor fellow?" Milly asks.

The crowd around us is thickening, footsteps pounding on every bit of sidewalk. A few men glance at us, then quickly look away again. A beggar sits beside a gray wall, a sign propped up beside him reading WAR VETERAN, and Milly drops several dollars into the hat at his side.

"He must work in one of the offices," I say.

"A murderer, working for Congress." Milly keeps her voice low, but she tosses her fur wrap over her shoulder carelessly. "I suppose that's no real shock."

"He may not be the murderer," I mutter.

"If you say so." Milly tries to shrug, but her shoulders are stiff. I don't blame her for being nervous.

"Which office is Victor's?" Clara asks me.

"Bridget didn't say, but she made it sound as though he'd be easy to find. Everyone at the Capitol knows him, she said."

"She said *everyone*?" Clara stops walking abruptly. Several men step around her as she veers off the pathway toward a bench, and Milly and I hurry to follow. "She used *that* word?"

"I think so?"

Clara shakes her head. "Let's finish our chestnuts here."

Two men in three-piece suits are seated on the bench, smoking, but when they see us they stand up with gallant sweeps of their arms.

"Thank you ever so." Clara smooths her skirt and lowers herself onto the empty seat. I drop down next to her, with Milly on my other side.

"What's this about?" Milly asks. She's the only one of us who didn't buy any chestnuts, and she's eyeing the bag in Clara's hand as though she's regretting that fact.

"He must be..." Clara's speaking so quietly I have to lean in to hear. It reminds me of the way that man, Henry, leaned in to whisper to her last night. None of us has said a word about Henry or Roger or any of those other boys since we left the East Room, and I'm not sorry about that. "I can't believe I didn't realize..."

"Say what you mean, please," Milly says.

Clara eyes the flowing crowd around us and lowers her voice even more. "The *Capitol bootlegger.*"

Milly goes rigid. "Mrs. Rose would *never.* She'd have been sacked in a second."

"Not if no one knew," Clara says.

"What are you talking about?" I pull my hat lower over my eyes and twist around to make sure none of the men walking by will see my face. Madame Frost would probably say it's against etiquette for girls to sit on a bench outside Congress, whispering. For that matter, she'd most certainly forbid eating chestnuts in public. "There couldn't be a bootlegger selling *inside* the Capitol. He'd be caught in an instant."

"There is, actually. It's sort of an open secret on the Hill. My father was talking about it with some of the others when he thought I wasn't close enough to hear. There's a man who works out of a basement office in the House building."

"They let him have an *office?*" I nearly laugh. It sounds like something out of a Charlie Chaplin picture.

"Well, it's more of a storeroom, but he has a key, and a desk." Clara smiles lightly. "A lot of congressmen do business with him."

"And *this* man... was Mrs. Rose's friend?" It's coming more naturally, I realize. Speaking about her in past tense.

"I heard them use those exact words. *Everyone at the Capitol knows Victor.*"

"A code." Milly's eyes darken. "Like the password to get into a speakeasy."

But if Clara's right, the man we've come to see is a dangerous criminal.

Everything I know about bootleggers comes from the papers and the pictures. Bootleggers make their living flouting one law, so they have no reason to bother with the others. In Chicago and New York and Los Angeles, there seem to be shootings every day, with one gang of bootleggers fighting another, and innocent people dying in the crossfire.

A man who'd willingly join such a profession certainly wouldn't have any qualms about strangling a woman. Particularly in a room full of liquor bottles in the middle of the night.

Even if, only hours earlier, he'd pretended to be her friend.

I gaze up at the heavy brown door. It was frightening enough to think we were coming to find a potential murderer. But a bootlegger, too?

The crowd of men flowing inside in their matching three-piece suits is growing smaller. If we wait much longer, it'll be even harder to blend in. If we ever truly could.

I don't want to think about this any longer. If we don't go inside that building and find Victor right this minute, I'll be too afraid to try.

I spring to my feet. Milly and Clara stand up, too, startled.

"We've got to go inside," I say. "Now. This man's the best chance we've got to find out what happened.

Milly's eyes are wide. "We can't just go say hello to a..."

"You can stay out here, if you want to," I tell her. "But it's the Capitol. There are people everywhere. Police, too. We'll be safe inside."

"The storeroom would be in one of the far corners," Clara muses. "The southeast, most likely. It's the least traveled."

"Gertie." Milly lowers her voice to a hiss. "The man's a *bootlegger*. And probably a murderer."

The crowd around us is growing thin. I shrug. Milly's right, but... "He's still our best chance."

Finally, Milly groans, laying a hand on the side of her neck and rubbing at her shoulder. "One of us should at least wait outside his door. To listen, in case there's trouble."

"I'll do it," Clara says immediately.

Milly frowns. "I think it should be me."

"You're going to be the one asking the questions, aren't you?" Clara says. "Besides, I'm used to darting all over the tennis court. I can run for help fast if I need to."

I can do that, too, I want to say, but Clara turns to the door as though the matter is settled and marches us through what's left of the crowd. The men still moving through the lobby doff their hats to us as we pass, and we lift our chins and our smiles and stride to the wide marble hallway as though we belong here.

We take a narrow staircase down one level. The walls

around us are dark, the electric lights barely illuminated this early in the day. The cacophony of last night at the East Room feels like a century ago as we steer down basement halls full of shut doors and scurrying suited men, footsteps echoing from every side. A bored-looking police officer strides through, his eye twitching as he absently tips his black cap at us and continues toward the doors.

"It'll be somewhere near here..." Clara murmurs as she leads us down the darkest corridor. "I hope."

"It looks deserted," Milly says, as we pass an open doorway with a dark, windowless room on the other side.

"I suppose these basement corridors *are* a tad desolate," Clara whispers. "I think we're close, though."

All I see is more dark, empty doorways. When we turn the next corner, though, a door is opening, and a man emerges from it.

This man is a good deal older than the man we saw with Mrs. Rose, and he's got a package tucked under his arm. A long package, wrapped in brown paper. Clearly meant to conceal a bottle, and not doing it terribly well.

My friends and I glance at one another as the man vanishes down another hallway. He certainly *could* be a congressman. Or a congressman's aide.

Why is the dry squad leading raids on places like the Lazy Susan when they could simply raid the Capitol itself?

Well, at least we can be reasonably certain we've found the right place.

Clara retreats to a shadowy spot on the opposite side of the hall where she'll be safely out of sight. Milly and I wait until the man with the brown-wrapped package has turned the far corner before approaching the door. He's left it ajar.

I have no idea what to expect on the other side. A bouncer? A jazz band?

But all we see when Milly pushes open the door is a handsome man in a three-piece suit, his face mere inches from ours, reaching out for the doorknob to push it closed.

A homburg dangles from his hand.

19

I STOP BREATHING. IT'S AS THOUGH I'M BACK IN THE TREE, AND he's on the darkened street with Mrs. Rose on his arm again, laughing and warm.

The man is startled, too, his eyes going wide. He doesn't appear to recognize us, though. The surprise on his face gives no hint that he has any idea who we are or why we're here.

His face, with its sharp cheekbones and rose-tinted skin, is far too young to belong to a member of Congress, and his suit, though the same style as those of the other men streaming through this morning, is newer. Brighter.

He's too slim to be the figure I saw watching the seminary through the window that night. His suit is too narrow, and he's far too tall. I couldn't have made that determination when I'd only seen him from above, but now that we're face-to-face, it's clear that even with an overcoat, even if he stooped, the figure lurking outside the window couldn't have been him.

"Well, hello." The surprise in the man's eyes has already turned into light. He's good at this. "Must say, I don't often get to welcome a pair of pretty girls to this office, but what a delight. My, what a spectacular shawl, did you know that's my absolute favorite style? Please, do step inside and tell me what I might be able to do for you two."

My *spectacular shawl*, he called it. The same way he did that night. With her.

We wait until he's closed the door behind us and gestured pleasantly to a set of chairs. Milly and I sit down cautiously, tucking our hats and handbags into our laps. The room is small, dark, and windowless, but the chairs are covered in worn, soft cushions. The only other furniture is a weathered old desk and a tall, heavy bureau along the back wall, its doors shut tight. That must be where he keeps the booze.

I wonder where he keeps the gun. Bootleggers always carry guns in the pictures.

The door is already closed behind us. If this man wanted to kill us, he could do it anytime. We'd be powerless against any kind of serious weaponry, and there's nothing Clara could do to protect us from out in the hallway.

I keep my hands neatly folded in my lap, but it takes everything in me not to grip the edge of my chair.

I wait for Milly to speak, but she's staring silently around the room, so I decide to start the questioning. As strange as this place is, this man, this Victor, with his worn old furniture and bright new suit, doesn't feel entirely like a stranger.

Mrs. Rose knew him. He may be a dangerous criminal, but she placed her hand into the crook of his arm all the same. She laughed with him. She told him things she'd never told me.

He *knew* her. In a way I never did.

I reach up to run my fingers along the fringe of my shawl.

"We're students of Mrs. Rose," I tell him. "That is…we were."

The surprise flashes back into his eyes. This time, it doesn't fade. "Jessica?"

"We saw you with her," I tell him. "The night she died. We know you were there."

This isn't what we'd meant to say, not at all. Milly had spun out a plan for us first thing this morning, a complicated story that maintained our innocence, and most of all, our ignorance.

Victor was a dangerous man, she'd said again and again. We shouldn't let him realize what we know.

Now, though, Milly is silent, her cheeks white.

I have to keep going. This might be our only chance to talk to the man who was with Mrs. Rose that night. Besides, the damage is already done.

"We were stealing away from the seminary," I tell him, my heart racing in my chest. "We were up in a tree, and we saw you and Mrs. Rose walking back. Our teachers told us she went out every Saturday, and we were wondering if you...if you knew anything. About how she died."

Victor stares at me. He hasn't budged the whole time I've been talking, but now he shakes his head, slowly, and lays his hands on the table in front of him. His skin is fair, his palms calloused. "That's...Good heavens. That's not at all what I thought you were going to...a *tree*, did you say?"

He reaches for a cup on his desk. I lean away, thinking he's offering us the same poisoned liquor Mrs. Rose was supposed to have died from drinking, but the brown liquid inside smells exactly like my father's favorite coffee. Victor takes a long drink and sets the cup back down on the bare desk, where a ring has formed from other mornings and other coffees.

"Who did you think we were?" It's the first time Milly's spoken. She's gripping the arms of her chair tightly.

"Well. You could be anyone, I suppose. A few of my clients do send their girls down to place orders for them." Victor stretches back in his chair, combing a hand over his carefully slicked black hair, then lays both hands on the desk again.

Something about him reminds me of the table full of men who sat next to us at the Lazy Susan that night. Perhaps it's the scent of pomade.

"But then, you could also have been friends of some people who don't much care for me," he goes on. "They've never sent society girls to collect, but I wouldn't put it past them."

"Are there a lot of people who don't care for you?" Milly asks.

"We can't all be as popular as you." Victor smiles at her, and Milly's eyes grow even wider. "Miss... I'm sorry, I didn't get your names?"

His courteousness automatically triggers my own. "Miss Pound, sir. I apologize, we ought to have introduced ourselves."

"How do you do, Miss Pound. Please, call me Victor."

It's terribly inappropriate for him to give us his first name and nothing more. He's at least a decade older than we are, but even if we were the same age, we'd still be expected to call him Mr. Last Name.

"How do you do," I say.

"I imagine you were quite close to Jessica, if you've gone to the trouble of coming to find me here." His eyes fix on me. "It must have been difficult for you. Losing her."

Tears threaten. Only a tap at my arm keeps them from brimming to the surface. Milly, her ever-useful elbow knocking gently into mine.

Careful, Gertie. Her voice might as well be ringing in my head. *He's charming. Too charming.*

She's right. We already know this man was the last person with Mrs. Rose before her death, and we also know he was likely the cause of it.

"I'm surprised at your question, though." Victor folds his hands neatly on his desk. "You must've read the same papers I did. Their analysis seemed quite conclusive."

"Yes." Milly glances pointedly at the bureau behind Victor's desk. "It did."

He raises an unfazed eyebrow. "I didn't catch your name, Miss?"

"Smith." Milly folds her hands in her lap.

"Miss Smith." He nods. "And your friend waiting in the hall, is she also a Miss Smith today?"

Milly makes a tiny, outraged sound in the back of her throat.

"In any case, Miss Smith," Victor says smoothly, "I assume that, as a fellow student of Mrs. Rose, you're as devastated by her loss as Miss Pound."

"Obviously." Indignation creeps into Milly's voice.

"When we'd walk to the pictures on Saturdays, Jessica would tell me stories about her students. She thought the world of you all."

Victor smiles at us. His smile is a treasure, all softness and warmth.

Perhaps that's how he succeeds in his business—he gets people to trust him. Perhaps that's what he did to Mrs. Rose.

"Did she tell you about the gunshot that night?" I ask him.

His smile fades slightly. "Did you say a *gunshot*?"

"During the faculty party."

"She said something about a car backfiring." His eyes have gone hazy. Remembering, perhaps. Then he shakes his head. "Nothing about a gun. She abhorred weapons, as do I."

Milly snorts.

Victor turns his attention her way, a half-smile returning to his face. "Something on your mind, Miss Smith?"

"Only that people like you aren't exactly known to stay away from guns."

"Our lovely capital isn't Chicago, Miss Smith. There's no gang warfare here. We've been fortunate in that regard."

"Do you know anything about someone watching the

seminary later that night, after her death?" I ask him. "From across the street, in Dupont Circle?"

Another shake of his head. "Afraid I don't, Miss Pound. I'd left the neighborhood by then."

"Did she ever mention anything to you about her finances?" Milly asks.

Victor raises his eyebrows. "That isn't where our conversations tended to focus."

"Did she say if she had a will?"

"Never came up. I'd be surprised, though. Not many unmarried women have them. Or unmarried men, for that matter."

Milly leans forward, her eyes fixed on his face. "Where were you when she died?"

Victor holds Milly's gaze with his warm brown eyes, his hands still flat on the table in front of him. "I can't recall."

"You can't recall where you were when your supposed friend *died*?" Milly's poised on the edge of her chair, as though she's about to leap to her feet. Her fear seems to have transitioned into wrath.

"Jessica was indeed my friend, and I didn't bring about her death, Miss Smith. But no, I'm afraid I don't recall the specifics of that evening after she and I said our goodbyes." Victor doesn't move. "To be honest, if I did, I don't know why I'd be eager to share that information with you girls. Or why you're sitting in my office to begin with."

"Pardon me," I say. "Though you may not choose to share it with us, you *would* need to share it with the police, should they ask."

"The police ask me questions with some frequency, as you can probably imagine, given the circumstances in which you've found me. I'll note, incidentally, that that must've taken some ingenuity on your part. Jessica would've been proud."

The tears are threatening again. Until I'm distracted by Milly leaping to her feet.

"Stop that," she orders.

Victor rises from his seat as well, holding his hands out in front of him. Not a threatening gesture. A chivalrous one. "Stop what, if I may?"

"Stop trying to make us think you're...that you're not—"

"Not what, Miss Smith?"

"You act *ever* so polite, ever so much a gentleman, but we *know*." Milly's shaking. "We *know* you..."

"Easy." I lay a hand on Milly's shoulder. She's trembling through her wool coat. "Easy, now."

"We *saw* you that night," Milly tells him. "With *her*."

Victor's face still doesn't change. "Yes. In a tree, your friend said. And may I ask what such nice young ladies as yourselves were doing out so late, and in such an unexpected spot?"

"We went to the Lazy Susan." Milly's breathing hard. I've never seen her like this. Never. "We were coming out the window and we *saw* you."

When Milly says the name of the speakeasy, there's a shift in Victor's eyes. It's small, but it's there.

He's thinking. Calculating.

Still, his tight gaze on Milly never wavers.

"Listen to your friend, Miss Smith," he says coolly, and I realize I'd nearly forgotten to be afraid of him. "It isn't wise to go around accusing people of murder. Not this early in the morning."

Milly's arm tenses. I'm truly afraid she's going to strike him.

I have to say something, *do* something, to ease the tension and fear that's grown so thick so fast.

"We aren't accusing you of anything, sir." I try to think of what Milly might say if she were my usual calm, thoughtful

Milly. "But if I may point out, we've been very direct with you about Mrs. Rose, and I can't say you've offered us the same."

Victor nods slowly. "Very well, then, Miss Pound. I would argue that I've in fact answered a good many of your questions, out of goodwill to your former headmistress, but I'll be direct with you again. Jessica Rose was my dear friend, and I'm grieving her death more than words can adequately express."

"We didn't see you at the funeral." I keep my hand on Milly's arm. She's still breathing hard.

"That's true. I wasn't there. As I've mentioned, there are some people in this city who don't care for me much, and a good number of them were likely in that church alongside you."

"Forgive me if those words don't seem like an adequate expression of grief," Milly says.

"How about these, then." Victor turns back to her. The resolute look on his face never changes. "I agree with you that the newspaper account of Jessica's death didn't seem plausible. I've thought about it a great deal, as much as you girls have, if you can believe that, and I've come to suspect that her death was brought about by a hired man. A professional. There was a party at your school that night, as you've mentioned. It would've been the perfect opportunity for such a person to slip inside."

I stare at him. Is that possible?

Could this Victor, this bootlegger, have thought about Mrs. Rose's death as much as we have? And could he be right?

Could we have been so focused on finding *him* that we missed someone else? Someone who was right in front of us that night?

"Nevertheless," he goes on, his voice soothingly steady and rhythmic, "I fully expect the police to question me in the next few days, given that *they're* claiming she died by drink. Which can't possibly be the truth, by the way. Jessica could never abide the taste of alcohol, even my best, and some of what I have is very good indeed. You girls ought to follow her example and stay away from it. It's a nasty business, what it can do to people. In more ways than one."

If what he's saying is true…

It could have been the man with the big hands. Someone could've hired him to kill Mrs. Rose. *Anyone* could've.

Including Victor. He's charming and intelligent enough to say something like this to throw us off our guard.

We were right to be afraid of him.

"In any case," Victor goes on, "what the police know is anybody's guess. Whether they care what truly happened is unclear, and whether they're capable of discovering it, even less. All of which is a far greater dishonor to Jessica Rose's memory than my appearance, or lack thereof, at a religious service which she would certainly not have chosen for herself, and which I imagine functioned primarily as a social opportunity for people of your parents' ilk. If anyone asked me, *those* are the people the police should be talking to. Yet no one is likely to ask me *that*. Aside, I suppose, from you."

He directs the last word to me.

"Sir," I say.

"Victor, please."

"I know this may seem like an odd question, but did Mrs. Rose ever…" I struggle to form the words. "That is, did you and she…"

He gives me a new, gentle smile, and his lips are parting to form an answer I'm not sure I want to hear when two sharp knocks come at the door behind us.

"Ah. It's my turn to apologize, Miss Pound. Business beckons."

He crosses to the door, opens it a crack, and speaks to

someone on the other side. Then he turns back to us. "You may want to go straight to the west stairs. My associate has agreed to wait around the corner."

"Certainly." I haven't learned the etiquette for this situation, so I fumble for a guess. "We're grateful for your time, Victor."

"Of course. I'd say to come again, but…I'm not sure that's a good idea."

Milly and I move fast, hats and handbags clutched in front of us, coats wrapped tight around our middles.

I turn to look for Clara as we emerge from the office, but what I see makes me stop mid-stride.

I grab Milly's arm. We can't stumble. Can't draw attention.

But it's too late. Clara's moving toward us quickly, a dark warning in her eyes. She's seen him, too. Which means he's almost certainly seen her.

We were wrong to think the danger would be inside Victor's office. It's out here, in the hall.

Where the man who shouted at us in the alley last night, the man with the big hands, is standing only a few feet away. Looking straight at us.

20

I can outrun him. I'm sure I can. Maybe Clara could, too. But Milly can't.

That's the calculation running through my head as I stare at the man in the corridor. He's wearing the same olive-green jacket he had on last night, but his stare isn't fixed on Milly this time.

This time, he's looking at me.

My chest heaves. Perhaps I can distract him long enough for the others to get away.

Before I can think of a way, though, the man with the big hands takes a step toward us, and I give up planning. I grab Milly and Clara by the elbows, shoving them ahead of me to the west stairs. Then, we run.

Our heels clatter on the stone steps, hats and bags held tight against our chests. I don't dare look back until we've reached the ground floor.

When I do, there's no sign of anyone in an olive-green jacket.

Still, I slow down only by a fraction as we enter the building's lobby. I steer Milly and Clara out the door, and then I break into a run once we reach the sidewalk.

"Gertie." Clara's voice is at my shoulder. "Slow down. People are looking."

I glance back. Clara's right there, with Milly a few paces behind us, her face bright red. There's still no sign of the man.

I slow down.

"How long was he in the hall with you?" I ask.

Clara shakes her head. "I didn't see him at all until you were coming out of Victor's office."

I take Milly's arm. She's safe now—but anything could've happened.

How long was he outside Victor's door? Was he listening to us?

"Gertie." Milly tightens her grip on my arm. "You're shaking."

"You recognized him, didn't you? The man who shouted at you last night?"

"I didn't get a good look then." Milly eyes me. We're a block from the House Office Building, surrounded by people, and I allow us to slow to a brisk walk. We move three abreast down the frost-covered sidewalk, earning pointed looks from men in suits and women in fur collars, all of them forced to step around us. "You're sure it was the same man?"

"*Yes.* You didn't see him last night, either, Clara?"

Clara shakes her head. "I didn't want to look. I could *hear* him clearly enough, though."

"It *was* the same man. You believe me, right?"

"Of course we believe you," Clara says, glancing at Milly.

"Well, I don't know what to make of *that* man," Milly says. "But we're quite fortunate to have gotten away from Victor. You heard what he said about having enemies."

"The dry squad doesn't seem to have caught him yet," Clara points out.

"He must bribe them, I suppose," I say.

"Obviously," Milly says. "Which means he could've bribed them over something else, too."

"We shouldn't talk about this out in the open," Clara murmurs as a woman in a black seal coat passes us with a stern look.

"You're right," I say. "Let's go to your hotel, Clara. It's closest."

Milly shakes her head. "We can't. We have that luncheon with your mother and Mrs. Mayfield."

I'd forgotten. Even though my mother lectured me for a full ten minutes this morning on the importance of making the pleasantest possible conversation today. Mrs. Mayfield's husband works in the White House, after all, and he was recently named to the seminary's board, too. "*No*. I can't see my mother right now."

"After lunch, we can go to the library," Milly goes on, ignoring my protest. "We may find something helpful in the old newspapers about the finances of the seminary, or about Mrs. Rose being hired there. Or, better yet, about Victor. Arrest records, or anything else. It could all be connected."

"Gertie?" Clara asks suddenly. "What happened to your shawl?"

"What?"

I touch my neck. Then I reach around to the back of my coat.

Frantically, I undo the buttons, feeling around my collar. Did it slip down into my dress?

No. It's gone.

The Spanish fringe shawl Mrs. Rose gave me. I must've dropped it when we were running.

How could I do that? What's *wrong* with me?

"We can go back," Clara says. "We'll help look. It's probably not far, and…"

"No." I pick up my pace. I'm not going anywhere near that man with the big hands again, and I don't want Milly or Clara near him, either. "It's fine."

"We should get a taxi," Milly says. "I'm sorry about your shawl, Gertie."

"You don't need to be sorry."

"All right. Then could you... slow down? A little?"

I stop. Beside me, Milly is breathing hard. On my other side, Clara's watching with concern in her eyes.

"Sorry," I say. "Sorry. Sorry. Yes, let's get a taxi, please."

From the moment the driver drops Milly and me off at the dim little tearoom on Pennsylvania Avenue, crammed with narrow tables and rickety chairs and ladies with pale, lined faces talking loudly to be heard over other ladies with pale, lined faces, it's all I can do to meet the bare minimum of civility.

Mrs. Mayfield gives me polite smiles as she, Milly, and my mother discuss department store fashions and Mr. Lindbergh's handsomest features. Just as I fear I might fall asleep over my bowl of clam broth, the conversation moves on to the Babcocks' ball.

"Velvet would've been the traditional choice," my mother is telling Mrs. Mayfield, "but for Gertrude's gown we've ordered taffeta for the trim. What color is your gown, Milly?"

"I'm afraid I can't recall, Mrs. Pound. It's still with the dressmaker."

"It's so lovely to have a ball to look forward to, and in only a few days!" Mrs. Mayfield crows. "Alice said Secretary Davis will be in attendance. Will your friend Miss Blum and her father be coming?"

"I'm afraid the congressman will be out of town," my mother says. "The ball is on a Saturday. The family is Jewish, you know."

"Actually, they've decided to stay in the city," Milly tells her. "They'll come to the ball after sunset."

"Naturally!" Mrs. Mayfield sounds happier talking about

the ball than if she were talking about her children's births. "The ball won't start until half past nine at the earliest. In New York, no one would turn up until nearly eleven. We went to so many beautiful balls there, didn't we, Edna? And your mother as well, Milly. The three of us were written up in the papers all the time. About our dresses, you know, and the names on our dance cards. They always filled up well in advance."

"Secretary Davis might run for Senate," Milly puts in. "It'll be an opportunity for the president to name someone to the cabinet who'll take a more progressive stance on immigration."

"An excellent point, Millicent." My mother smiles at her and turns to Mrs. Mayfield. "Did you know Miss Otis is the top student in her class? Please, Milly, do tell us where your mother found you this darling dress. Or was it part of the wardrobe she had made for you in Paris? Remind me of your shop's name, please?"

Milly gamely tells my mother and Mrs. Mayfield everything they want to know about her French dressmaker, and goes on to carry enough conversation for both of us as the lunch proceeds.

Thanks to seventeen years of repeated lessons, I'm able to produce smiles at the right moments, and take appropriately sized forkfuls of cold roast beef with spiced tomato jelly and mashed turnips while I ignore my mother's nudges under the table. Through it all, my thoughts never stop racing.

Victor walked Mrs. Rose back to the seminary that night. They said goodbye, and she went inside. The next person to see her was Lucy, who found her in her office, already dead.

No. No, it was the killer who saw her next.

What was Mrs. Rose doing, spending time with someone like Victor? A liar and a criminal, who wouldn't even tell us where he was when she died?

She always talked about following her own path. Resisting

the restrictions of society. She never said it meant associating with people like *him*.

He did seem kind, though.

"Why, hello!" my mother cries, sharply enough to interrupt my stream of doubt. "What a pleasure."

I look up to see Mrs. Patterson, the grand society matron who's also Mrs. Mayfield's mother, standing above our table, wearing a mink muff and an expression laden with disdain.

"A pleasure, I'm sure, Mrs. Pound." Mrs. Patterson eyes each of us at the table in turn, her gaze settling last and longest on me and my untouched plate of chocolate rice pudding with cream. "Mrs. Paul and I were just finishing our own luncheon. Did you find the oysters uncharacteristically terrible?"

"No, I'm afraid I had the broiled striped bass," my mother says, in the tone a person might use to apologize for causing the Great War.

I can see why Mrs. Rose enjoyed Victor's company. Still, even if he weren't the sort of man who could stomach murder, he could have hired someone else to do it. Perhaps that man with the big hands came to his office to collect payment.

"Gertie agrees," Milly says, and it's clear that I've missed some crucial part of the conversation. Though I can't imagine that anything said in this tearoom could be considered crucial. "Isn't that right?"

"Of course," I say, hoping I sound agreeable.

"In that case, we'll look forward to seeing you at Alice's ball." Mrs. Mayfield nods importantly from across the table. "A much more proper venue for girls your age than these...What did you say they were called, Mother?"

"*Whoopee* parties." Mrs. Patterson sniffs. "That's what the officer called it when he took all those young people down to the station. I don't know how they thought anyone was meant to sleep while they were carrying on into all hours of the night. Parents were away on a trip, they told me when I called. I suppose they don't realize children need proper supervision."

"Right you are, Mrs. Patterson." My mother sniffs, too. "I always know what the girls under my charge are up to."

I want to snort with laughter. My mother would fling herself off the Connecticut Avenue Bridge into Rock Creek a hundred feet below if she knew what we were up to last night while under her charge.

"Well, they won't be up to that *school* for long," Mrs. Patterson says. "They'll shut it down, surely, after what that girl did. Has Mr. Babcock made the announcement yet?"

"I'm not certain." My mother glances at me. "There's some time still. The girls' new term doesn't start until the middle of January."

That's not true. Milly overheard my parents say the board would decide by New Year's. Less than two weeks away.

My mother's lying. Because she knows *I'm* listening.

"I'll have a word with Penelope." Mrs. Patterson sniffs. "They should announce it immediately. No sense ruining these girls' reputations any further than they already have."

My mother only smiles at her. As everyone says their goodbyes, I fight not to let my panic show.

They *can't* close the seminary. Mrs. Patterson and my mother and the others, they think they're so important, but they can't—they wouldn't truly do this to...

Milly lays a hand on my arm. Her eyes bore into mine. *Breathe*, she mouths.

I do. I breathe.

I *need* to think clearly. I need to put this together, all of these pieces, and do it fast. I *need* to find out what truly happened to Mrs. Rose in time to stop the seminary from closing for good.

When I look up again, Mrs. Patterson is gone, and Mrs. Mayfield is preparing to take her leave as well. She and my mother settle up the bill, and moments later we're outside, blinking into the winter sun as people hurry past us. It must have rained while we were inside, because the sidewalks are wet and dirty from shoes scuffing into puddles. A pair of police officers in flat black hats are standing in the street out front, sweeping out their arms in an attempt to direct traffic while horns honk from every side. One of the policemen tips his hat in my mother's direction, and she nods back, always the gracious judge's wife.

"Milly, you go on home," my mother says. "I'll hire you a taxi."

"That isn't necessary, Mrs. Pound, but thank you. Gertie and I are going to stop by the library."

"No, no." My mother lifts her hand, and a taxi slows to the curb right away. "I need Gertie to accompany me. I'm gravely behind on my Christmas shopping."

I stare at her. "Mother, please. Milly and I need to..."

"I'm afraid I must insist. Have a lovely afternoon, Milly." My mother lifts Milly's hand, helping her into the taxi so there's no room for further argument, and steers me away, lowering her voice to a strong whisper. "*If* you hope to return to that school next term and graduate, should there *be* a school to return to, you'll need to learn how to shop for your own family one day."

It's a punishment, I realize, as she turns on her heel and strides pointedly toward F Street. For staying quiet during luncheon. Now I'll have to endure this, too.

It takes hours. I could be at the library with Milly, uncovering vital facts about what happened to Mrs. Rose. Instead I'm trotting along on my mother's heels from one shop to another, forced to form opinions on pocket watch accessories and chair cushions and pencil boxes. We finish on F Street and move down Connecticut Avenue, nearly bumping into a man with a cane, where we head into yet more shops, each dimmer and duller than the last.

Every store is crowded with women in dark fur coats and low-heeled lace-up boots, standing shoulder-to-shoulder and greeting one another with uninterested "How do you dos," alongside assistants carefully wrapping up rayon kimonos and rubberized silk tea aprons, bathrobes and ribbons and parasols.

Finally, my mother seems to feel I've been punished enough.

"Why don't you take a taxi home with these." She passes me the parcel of cigarettes a shopkeeper has wrapped up in brown paper and twine. The rest of our purchases are being delivered to our house. "I'll finish at the stationer's and return home right before your father. Check in with Sarah on the dinner preparations, please, and make sure everything is ready for him."

"Yes, Mother."

She disappears into another shop as I trudge toward the corner with the parcel. When I raise my hand to catch the attention of a taxi trundling by, a voice calls over my shoulder.

The stranger with the cane is shouting my name.

21

Miss Pound! Miss Pound, isn't it? Gertrude Pound?"

The man with the cane isn't *quite* a stranger, I realize as I turn. We've never met, but I've seen him before. At Mrs. Rose's funeral, sitting alone, wearing the knit tie. I followed him to a hotel that day, not far from here, in fact. I listened to him weep on the other side of the lobby door.

He's wearing that very knit tie now. The same rumpled suit he wore that day, too, with the same derby hat. One of his hands grips the cane, and the other is pressed against his vest pocket.

Anyone could be watching us. I have no choice but to defer to etiquette.

"How do you do," I say, with a small bob of my head.

"Ah, yes, I thought it was you." The man speaks oddly. As though he's from far away. Out in the country, perhaps. "I heard one of the other girls say your name at the funeral. I remembered it from her letters."

"Whose letters?"

"Hers. Jess...Mrs. Rose's."

Mrs. Rose sent this man letters? About *me*? "What sort of —"

His head jerks up suddenly, his eyes fixing at a point over my left shoulder. "Is anyone following you?"

I whip around, drawing stares from several passersby, but all I see are women in day dresses and wool coats, carrying packages. Men in three-piece suits and bowler hats, too, smoking pipes and cigarettes.

I search each of their faces, looking for *that* man. The one with the big hands who was watching us outside Victor's office. Who screamed at Milly when she was wearing my shawl.

Could *he* have followed me from the Capitol? Through lunch in the tearoom? In and out of shops with my mother?

The streets are crowded thickly with cars, horns blaring, tires churning in the damp streets. The police officers have given up on directing traffic and are chatting with a pair of girls in squirrel-fur coats.

I turn back to the man from the funeral. If he's trying to frighten me, I can't let him know it's working.

I lift my chin and fold my hands behind me. "Certainly not."

The man squints over my shoulder again, but he must not see anything, either, because he shifts his gaze back to my face. "I'm staying in the Hotel Grafton."

He waves to the yellow brick building down the block. I nod, as though this is new information. As though I didn't follow him there myself, lurking in the shadows.

"I spotted you from the window," he says. Only now do I notice the pain in the man's soft blue eyes. Grief, or guilt? Both? Neither? "I came down, but you were with your mother, and I was worried that... It's not important. Miss Pound, I need your help. We have to find out what truly happened to Mrs. Rose."

Staring is forbidden, but I do it anyway.

"I'm not sure what you mean, Mr.....?"

His eyes dart down the street behind me. "Could we go into that shop? I could buy you a cup of coffee."

"I'd prefer to speak here."

The man nods, gesturing down to his rumpled suit. "I know I don't fit in with your sort. We can meet somewhere else, if you want. Wherever you'd be comfortable. Perhaps you could come for lunch."

"And when I come to the Hotel Grafton for this lunch, whom am I to ask for?"

He darts his eyes behind me again. "I'm registered as Mr. A. Frances."

"Is that your name?"

He doesn't answer. Again.

I don't trust this man. Yet he may know something of value.

"I'm sure Mrs. Rose was important to you." He rubs his chin and sighs. This Mr. Frances, or whatever his name might be, is clearly no gentleman. My mother would be furious to see me talking to a man who'd openly rub his chin on the street. "She was to me, too, and the police can't...*won't*...well, either they don't know how to find out the truth or they simply don't intend to do so, but the result's the same. I want to see justice done for her."

"Mr. Frances, I can assure you, the police *are* investigating. I've spoken to them myself."

"Have you?" Mr. Frances raises his eyebrows. "The detectives interviewed you?"

"I talked to a Prohibition agent."

The man sighs. "The feds don't care about justice. Only finding bootleggers, so they can get a bigger cut of the profits. Did you tell them anything?"

"Mr. Frances." Anger creeps into my nervousness. "I don't make a habit of telling strangers details of my private conversations. I really ought to be going."

He nods. "You're right to be cautious. Mrs. Rose remarked on that. She said you were very intelligent, and very cautious. Almost to a fault."

"Oh." I pause. "Was there...anything else she said?"

"Oh, dear, there you are." My mother's hand is on my arm, but she looks mildly alarmed instead of angry. "If you'll excuse us, please, my daughter has an urgent matter to attend to."

Mr. Frances, or whatever his name is, lifts his hat an inch off his head and doesn't say anything more. My mother propels me to the corner faster than I've ever seen her move before.

"I'm putting you in a taxi myself." My mother raises her hand, and a cab slows instantly. "I know you've been taught to be courteous to everyone, but when you're approached by a man like *that*, you have to consider safety as well as propriety. This city is going to be ruined if men like him are permitted this close to the good shops. I do hope you didn't give him any money. It only encourages them."

I don't argue. The cabbie steps out to open the door, and my mother hands him a quarter and tells him our address. "Take her straight there, if you would, please. Don't stop."

"Yes, ma'am." He lifts his hat to my mother, exactly the way Mr. Frances did.

A streetcar trundles past, with a young boy hanging off the back whistling a jaunty tune I don't recognize. Footsteps scud along the sidewalk behind me as I climb into the taxi, the parcel of cigarettes on the seat beside me, but when I turn, I don't see anyone out the window but a few laborers. That man, this so-called Mr. Frances, has been putting ideas into my head, about being followed.

Even so, he may well have truly known Mrs. Rose. If he received letters from her, they must have been close.

I don't trust him, but it might be wise to speak to him again. Somewhere out in the open and far away from my mother.

I can go to that hotel and ask for him, but on my terms, with a plan in place. A list of information to obtain.

Starting with where this Mr. Frances was on the night of Mrs. Rose's death. And what she wrote him in those letters.

I press my forehead to the window of the taxi, trying to think of how I'll phrase my first question, and that's when I spot it. A drab, tattered green awning over an old basement restaurant. The same awning I passed with Milly and Clara on our way to the Lazy Susan. Faded black letters, spelling DUKE'S.

The matchbook. The one Lucy showed us. The one she found next to Mrs. Rose's body. It was from Duke's.

I should have thought of it days ago.

What does it mean, though? If it means anything at all?

Mrs. Rose could, I suppose, have gone to Duke's herself and taken a matchbook, but I doubt it. It was too close to the seminary, and it doesn't look respectable. She'd have risked being seen entering by a board member, or one of the faculty.

The matchbook *might* have belonged to her killer, though. He could've dropped it in his haste to leave, just as he dropped the bloodstained shawl.

The idea churns my stomach. But I can't let that stop me from thinking it through.

By the time the driver drops me off at our front door, darkness has swathed our block, and electric streetlamps offer up the only pools of light. Footsteps echo on the wet sidewalk behind me. But then, in a city, there will always be someone walking nearby.

I want to talk to Milly. I need her to help me make sense of everything that's happened. But there's no light on in her room, and the downstairs parlor looks dark and empty, too. She must still be at the library.

As I cross the sidewalk to our front steps, I see one of my mother's packages, small and narrow, that's already arrived. The delivery boy left it perched on the railing. Strange—Norris would have answered the door if the boy had knocked. When I mount the top step, I reach over to collect the package.

That's when I see that it isn't a package at all. It's a shawl.

My shawl, that I lost this morning. It's hanging from the railing, with a scrap of paper tucked into a fold.

No...no, the shawl is *tied* around the railing. In a knot.

If someone found it, why would they return it to me *this* way? And how would they know where I live?

My fingers fumble as I struggle with the knot, and I have to peel off my gloves, despite the chill. The knot is tight, the fabric wrapped around the old wooden railing several times. Something seems to be holding it in place. A hard, metallic shape at the center of the fabric.

A nail.

I can see it, as I fold back the fabric layers. The light is dim, but it's enough to see the old, sharp metal, coated with rust and something else. Something dark.

My foot slips on the icy step and I fight to catch myself before I can fall, my heart thudding in my chest.

Someone's stabbed my shawl through with a rusted, bloody nail and left it here for me to find.

22

$W_{\mathrm{E'RE\ WATCHING\ YOU."}}$

Clara drops the note into her lap as if it's bitten her. She stares at the pile of torn brown paper I used to conceal the stained, crumpled shawl—the paper that had previously been so carefully wrapped around my mother's cigarette parcel.

Clara's cheeks stretch in horror. It's a wonder she managed to read those scrawled words aloud. "Who *did* this?"

"I don't know." I'm trembling. I've been trembling ever since I frantically unwound the shawl, the nail, and the scrawled note. I left the cigarettes in an untidy pile on the porch, where they're sure to infuriate my mother, and ran to Wisconsin Avenue just in time to catch the streetcar.

I couldn't go into my house. I couldn't devise thoughtful questions for Sarah about the night's menu, or put on a dinner dress and make polite conversation over pot roast, or gather in the sitting room afterward, listening to the plodding orchestra music of my father's favorite radio program.

I needed to talk to someone, and since I had no idea which library Milly might have gone to, I've come to Clara's hotel on Capitol Hill.

It's brand-new, the entire first floor smelling of cigars. I worked to steady my hands as I found my way through the gleaming limestone lobby to the front desk and asked for Clara Blum. The clerk called up to her, and when she emerged from the elevator a moment later, still wearing the same polka-dot dress she'd worn to the Capitol this morning, the sight of her sent me close to tears.

I never knew it was possible to need someone this badly. The very sight of Clara made the blood in my ears stop rushing, the panic in my chest fade into a steady heartbeat.

I can't do this alone. With Clara, though, it might be possible. *Anything* might be possible when I'm with her.

She saw my stricken face and steered me without speaking to this quiet corner of the lobby, waving away a waiter who tried to approach, and sat me down across from her in a pair of low chairs by a brick fireplace.

The fire's warm, but I'm still shivering.

She shoves the scrap of paper with the scrawled note into the brown-wrapped package, and I notice for the first time that she's trembling, too. "Don't ever look at that again, Gertie."

"It's a message, isn't it? Someone left it there to scare us, but I don't know who. We *need* to know who."

Clara grabs my clenched hand, pressing it between her palms. I'm so stunned by the gesture that I fall silent and let my hand open under her careful fingers.

"Listen to me." She stares into my eyes, and I listen more intently than I've ever listened to anything in my life. Her voice drops to a whisper. "You need to be more careful. Someone *killed* a woman. They could do it again."

I nod, trying to catch my breath. "Someone wants to stop us from asking questions."

"Not *us*. That was *your* shawl. *Your* house. The message was for *you*."

A message from a murderer.

Victor?

He noticed my shawl this morning. He could have stolen it

and brought it to me as a threat. But how would he have known where I lived?

Then I remember. I gave him my name. Only my last name, but it might have been enough. Milly was right to call herself Miss Smith.

"We shouldn't discuss this here." Clara releases my hand. "Can you walk?"

I nod. It's strange how much clearer my thoughts are, now that she's here. "I'm also at risk of being terribly late for dinner. Why don't you come home with me? Milly should be there, too."

Clara nods and takes my arm, her fingers light around my elbow. I want to sag against her, but I stay upright as she steers us down the hall.

I reach up to run my fingers along the fringe of my shawl. Yet it isn't there. It's wrapped in the crumpled brown paper still clutched in my hands.

My spectacular shawl.

We get back on the streetcar. I'm running out of coins, so Clara pays our fares back to Georgetown. As we sit in silence, the brown wrinkled package held tightly in my lap, I want to tell Clara so much. About Mr. Frances. About how frightened I've been. Clara's staring at her knees, as though there's a lot she's thinking about, too.

"Clara." I reach into her lap, take her hand. A woman across the aisle holding a bag full of groceries catches my eye and smiles. I give her a small, polite smile back. "It's all right."

Clara shakes her head. "It's not."

"It's..." But I can't argue. "You're right. It's not."

"I feel *terrible* about what happened." Clara's voice is choked. As though she might cry right here on the streetcar, surrounded by government men with their heads in their newspapers and women in day dresses and maids' uniforms. "I miss her so much. Every day. I didn't know I'd feel so..."

"I know. I miss Mrs. Rose, too."

Clara meets my gaze, almost as though she's surprised. Then she sniffs. "The last time I talked to her, we argued. Though it was the same disagreement we always had."

I'd never really thought about Clara and Mrs. Rose having arguments. Or even conversations. But then, they had all those private tennis lessons. Mrs. Rose was a tennis champion in her youth, and some of the students paid her for private instruction, Clara most often of anyone.

I wonder if their conversations went the same way my own talks with Mrs. Rose tended to go. "Was your argument about your future?" I ask her.

"No, it was more about...the past. And the present, I suppose."

"The past? Did she tell you about taking the train by herself to California for college?"

"No. We mostly discussed... *my* past."

"What past?" I furrow my eyebrows and lower my voice. "Oh. Did she find out you used to go to speakeasies in New York?"

Clara hesitates, lowering her voice, too, before she gives me a small smile of her own. "I...never went to any speakeasies in New York."

"What?" I blink at her, sure I misunderstood. "But you planned our entire venture to the Lazy Susan. You know all the dances. You used to go all the time."

"I...may have given that impression, but I'm not quite as...Well." Clara stares down at our clasped hands. "At my old school, the girls used to teach one another the dances during recess, for a lark. Some of them used to go out. My mother was far too adept, though, at keeping our doors locked after dark. The truth is, I never went *anywhere* except school, the store, and our apartment."

I can't believe it. "Not *once?*"

"I couldn't have. Not without waking up my parents, or my aunt and uncle, or my brothers, and..."

I don't smile, but I want to. "Why didn't you say so?"

"I wanted you and Milly to think...well..." Clara tucks a curl behind her ear. She looks younger than usual. "That I was interesting, I suppose."

"Clara." Now I do smile. "You're *devastatingly* interesting."

"You're kind, Gertie." She smiles down at our hands. My palm feels suddenly warm against hers, despite the chill. It's very fortunate that no one ever thinks to look askance at two girls holding hands, because at this moment, it *feels* as though we're breaching the rules of propriety. "You've always been so kind to me."

I smile down, too.

"What was your argument with Mrs. Rose about, then?" I finally ask. "If it wasn't about that?"

"It was about..." Clara draws in a breath, as though she's about to say something. Then she lifts her face, casts her gaze around the bus, and exhales, slowly. "My hair. I wanted to get it cut again. She told me the board of directors and their wives would never forgive her."

"That counts as a fight?"

"Well. Perhaps not."

We don't talk any more after that. We sit quietly, hands folded together, listening to the groans of the car as it lurches.

We arrive home as Sarah is announcing dinner. My mother purses her lips to see me coming in so late and not yet dressed for the meal, and I imagine there's a lot she'd like to say about the way I left the cigarettes piled on the porch, too. But when she sees Clara with me, she puts on a smile and welcomes us both, and we go in to greet my father in the drawing room. Milly's there, too, looking smart in a maroon tea gown with a black pattern around the trim and tilting her head in surprise to see me coming in with Clara.

I dash up the stairs to put the wrinkled parcel in my room. All I want is to get Milly and Clara alone where we can talk through everything that's happened. But first we have to dispense with the pot roast, and my father's terrible jokes, and my mother's stories about all the rude people we encountered during our shopping trip. When she announces that a strange man accosted me in the street, everyone looks at me suddenly, but all I can do is murmur that he didn't seem dangerous. Fortunately, my parents don't ask any further questions.

During the after-dinner radio program, Clara calls her father's office and easily gets his permission to spend another night here. He's working on some important legislation, it seems, and is glad for her to be with friends. I doubt he'd be quite as glad if he knew what we've truly been up to.

When the three of us finally retreat to my room, my thoughts buzz, trying to make sense of everything that's happened since we first showed up on Damian and Penelope Babcock's doorstep.

"Mr. Frances hardly seems trustworthy," Clara says when I've finished telling them the full story. "Stopping you in the middle of the street like that."

"Did you learn anything at the library?" I ask Milly. "You must've been there all afternoon."

She shakes her head. "The librarian was very kind, but she wasn't able to find anything of use. We found Mrs. Rose's birth announcement and her wedding announcement, and the notice about her being named headmistress, but there was nothing about her salary or her finances. Nothing we didn't already know. All it said was that she went to college in California and did postgraduate studies in New York, and that she'd lost her husband to cholera. I tried to find the husband's death announcement, in case it included anything about his will, but he died overseas, and the library doesn't have the foreign papers. I wound up reading long, dull volumes about estate law for hours while she searched, until I finally asked her to give up."

"We need more information." I shake my head. "We're close to something important. I can feel it, like an itch."

They both raise their eyebrows. "An itch?" Milly says.

"You know what I mean." I stand up and cross the room to my wardrobe, reaching up again to stroke the fringe of my absent shawl, then lowering my hand in frustration. "It could've been Victor who stole my shawl. It was gone by the time we left the House building."

"Of *course* it was Victor." Milly stands up, too, leaving Clara alone on the rug. "It was *all* Victor. But we need proof before we can go to the police again and tell them what we know. Then we can be witnesses in his trial, if it comes to that."

I try to imagine the look on my mother's face if I told her I was a witness in a murder trial. She'd sooner see me dance the Charleston in a hundred speakeasies.

"Then let's get proof." Clara's rising, too. "Get him to incriminate himself."

"We already tried talking to him," I remind her. "The more questions we asked, the more adamant he grew that he *didn't* do it."

"That's because we spoke to him in his office," Milly says. "Men are at their most powerful in their own offices."

We're standing close together now, all of us, talking in low voices. The room is dark enough for it all to feel conspiratorial and strange, and a little exciting, too, despite everything.

"You're right." Clara's eyes dart to Milly. "We should try to catch him off guard. Somewhere he won't be expecting a confrontation."

I shut my eyes. I need to make sense of what's going on with Victor. I need to *think*.

That's when I finally know where I heard the name Victor before.

I'm saving the punch line for the Seven Seas, a man's voice says in my memory. A man at the table next to ours. In the Lazy Susan.

You can tell it to Victor, and Admiral Jenks! another man replies.

I can't *believe* it took me this long to remember.

"The Seven Seas," I say, opening my eyes.

Two faces turn to me, heads tilted. "I beg your pardon?" Milly says.

"Remember those fellows at the table next to us at the Lazy Susan? They said something about Victor. And the Seven Seas, and an Admiral Jenks. They made it sound like Victor and Admiral Jenks were *sure* to be at the Seven Seas. It must be another speakeasy, right? It certainly sounds like the name of a bar."

Milly draws in a sharp breath that makes it clear she does, in fact, remember. But she shakes her head. "There must be three hundred men named Victor in this city."

"Probably, but...did Victor remind you of *those* men, at all? With his fine suit, and the way he'd styled his hair?"

Milly tosses her braid over her shoulder angrily. I furrow my eyebrows at her in confusion. "The city is full of men in fine suits and pomade, too."

"Admiral Jenks," I repeat. "If the Seven Seas is a speakeasy, could that be the password?"

"It's not a password, it's a statue." Clara's eyes light up with sudden recognition. "Down past Capitol Hill, near the Navy Yard. My cousin and I went past the old statue of Admiral Jenkins a dozen times delivering gift baskets for the sailors for one of my aunt's charity projects. The Seven Seas must be close by."

"Do you think it's a bar for..." I swallow. "For men like... those? Gay people?"

"No." Milly shakes her head vigorously. "We can't go to that kind of place."

"If they were talking about the same Victor..." Clara nods again. "It's worth trying."

"What? *No!*" All at once, Milly seems truly furious, and I can't understand why. "You're both being daft! It's not going to be the same Victor. Besides, you heard what those coppers said about going to *their* bars and smashing *their* heads. Anyone who sets foot in one of those places could be arrested on morals charges!"

"They wouldn't arrest *us*," I say. "We're girls."

"You'd be surprised what they can arrest girls for," Clara says, dropping her gaze to the rug.

"Well..." I look down, too. "*Do* you think the bar could be for women as well? What did you say they're called? *Violets?*"

"I'll tell you what we should do," Milly says. "Go to that hotel and see that man. Mr. Frances. He might know something important."

"It's far too late to go to a hotel tonight." I shake my head. "They'd never let us in. You were right, Milly, we should try to speak to Victor again. He's our best lead."

"*Think*, Gertie." Milly comes to stand in front of me, edging out Clara, and takes my wrists in her hands. Her skin is warm and soft. "Last night you were terrified of breaking the rules. Tonight you want to go to a bar full of... *queers*?"

The word is harsh and hateful in my ears.

Is *that* what Milly's upset about?

That she disapproves of those kinds of men? *Despises* them?

Those kinds of women, too?

The idea lands in my stomach with a sickening thud, and I turn, wrenching my hands out of Milly's grip.

I can't look at her.

"All we want is to find out what truly happened." Clara's voice is startlingly calm. I don't know how. "We'll leave at the first sign of trouble, Milly."

"You won't find anything *but* trouble in a place like that!"

I look up to see Clara laying a soft hand on Milly's forearm. Milly jerks away.

Are those *tears* in Milly's eyes?

"You two do what you want." She lifts her chin, as though she's wearing her best hat. Then she turns and flings open the door, lowering her voice to a harsh whisper. "*I'm* going to bed."

CLARA AND I MOVE BRISKLY THROUGH THE DARK. THE SIDEWALKS are nearly empty, and the quiet is grim and cold. The few people we encounter are moving just as swiftly and wordlessly through the streets as we are.

Milly's absence stabs at me, the wound as fresh as when she first strode out of my room. For the hour that followed, as Clara and I carefully applied lipstick and rouge and rolled down our stockings, we cast constant glances at the door to see if Milly would change her mind.

But I don't know if it's possible to change a mind to that degree.

I know Milly isn't unusual, to feel the way she does about people like that. I heard Perkins and his copper friends.

I don't know why it hurts so much more to hear it from Milly.

Milly, who's slept in the bed beside mine for three and a half years. Milly, from whom I've never kept a single secret.

She had a point, though. It *is* an enormous risk to take, stealing away again, and to a place like *this*. I can't think about what it could do to my father's career, or Congressman Blum's, if we were caught.

But it's a relief to have Clara with me. To slip through the darkened streets side by side, just us two.

Though that makes me feel guilty, too. Being glad to be alone with Clara, and sad to be without Milly, all at the same time.

Clara flags down a taxi on Wisconsin Avenue. We're quiet during the ride, sitting on opposite sides of the wide leather seat. This would be the perfect opportunity to ask what *she* thinks about what Milly said, but I find I can't. Some crucial balance between the three of us has been knocked off-kilter without my noticing until it was too late, and it's only tilting further. I fear it might topple off entirely.

It's a long ride across the city, past the White House and the Capitol, and when the driver finally lets us out, there's no clear indication of where we should go. The streets this close to the Navy Yard don't have alleys. Men in sailor uniforms are everywhere, and girls in furs and heels and cloche hats, too, laughing uproariously at whatever the sailors have just said.

"Hey there, kittens!" one sailor calls when he sees Clara and me. "You looking for somebody?"

I glance at Clara. She shrugs. It's worth a try.

I approach the man so I won't have to shout. He grins at me under his sailor's cap. "Do you know a place called the..." I frown, as though I can't remember the bar's name. It's meant to stay secret, after all. "There's a number in the name, I believe. Six? Seven?"

"I know another one you'll like better, doll. Come along. You and your friend."

He doesn't know the Seven Seas, that much is obvious. "Thank you ever so, but we have to be going."

Clara and I cross the street, dodging cars and military vehicles, and walk two more blocks. The crowds are growing thinner. Finally, we reach the statue of Admiral Jenkins, perched on a high pedestal in an old-fashioned military jacket with thick whiskers and a pair of binoculars in his hand.

I look around on the ground foolishly, as though there might be a trapdoor, until Clara touches my shoulder. "Look."

I follow her gaze to the building across the street.

The Seven Seas isn't like Duke's, with its clearly labeled awning. Here, there's just a gray cement munitions warehouse. Letters are scratched into the base of the wall with what looks to have been a chunk of charcoal, barely visible in the light from a distant streetlamp.

7S.

Clara and I lock eyes and nod.

We cross the street, step around the corner past the scrawled letters, and find ourselves in a tiny entryway, facing a greasy door. The sidewalk is deserted.

I can't imagine that there's a bar here. Or anything else, for that matter.

Until we hear a single set of heavy footsteps on the same path we just took, growing louder. Moving toward us.

It's quite dark. Quite empty. And Clara and I are quite alone.

What if Mr. Frances was right, and someone *is* following me? What if it's the same person who left that bloody shawl at the door for me to find?

Clara presses her hand into my shoulder, pushing me back against the gray cement wall, so abruptly I stumble.

I start to speak, to ask her what's happening, what we should do, but she touches my face in a silent command. Then she opens her handbag and withdraws a long, thin object. I recognize it from advertisements in the back of my father's magazines.

Clara carries a *switchblade*. In her *handbag*.

She turns toward the sidewalk and takes a step. Then another. When she steps out of our little entryway and dips out of sight, I stop breathing.

A long, terrible moment passes.

Then a figure walks past. A tall young man, in a Navy uniform. He doesn't look at us. He doesn't even seem to *notice* us.

Clara steps back into the entryway beside me, folding the switchblade and tucking it into her handbag.

I exhale, wondering what else I didn't know about Clara.

I turn back to the door set into the gray concrete wall. The top half is glass, painted black, with an iron screen that's painted black as well. The handle is rusted, with an even rustier padlock below, and neither appears to have been touched in years. A sign screwed into the door below the window, worn and covered in old brown stains, reads DANGER 6000 VOLTS.

A disguise. Like the bookcase in Damian Babcock's study.

Could *this* be a place where those sorts of men gather to drink? And... what else? Dance? Together?

Those sorts of women, too?

I want to see it. To be admitted into whatever's on the other side of this door.

Clara shifts, looking out into the street. No one seems to be paying us any attention.

I knock on the door. I don't know how many times to knock, or what I'll say if it opens, but I do it anyway.

There's no response.

I knock again. Still nothing.

Clara tilts her head for me to follow her. I do, stepping out into the street, where we can see the girls and sailors laughing together, a small crowd of them gathered on the next block up. Clara tries to lead me in their direction, but I plant my feet on the sidewalk beside the little entryway.

"I'm not sure," Clara murmurs. "It seems to truly be a munitions warehouse."

"But it might *not* be. I don't want to give up when we've barely..."

I stop talking as two uniformed sailors walk by. They're both young, with dark, searching eyes, and the close-trimmed haircuts all sailors have. Neither one is smiling.

They slow down, eyeing Clara and me. They glance back at the warehouse door quickly. Then they walk on, as though they'd meant to pass it all along.

"This isn't the place for us," Clara says when they're out of earshot.

"We don't know that! Perhaps those two could have gotten us in. Like that woman who told the bouncer to let us into the Lazy Susan."

"This is different."

"It might *not* be."

"I don't think..."

Over her shoulder, I see another man approaching the rusted door. Clara and I step back deeper into the shadows.

This man isn't in a Navy uniform. He's in a tweed three-piece suit and a top hat, and he's older than the sailors. In his thirties, perhaps. He has a kind look about him as he walks up to the door, glances over his shoulder, and knocks twice.

Twice. That's it. *I* knocked three times.

There's no time to consider it any longer. We might not get another chance.

I check to make sure no one's watching, then stride up to the man in the top hat. He hears me coming—it isn't possible to stride silently in heels—and his face shifts into an open smile.

Behind him, the door stays shut tight.

"Well, hello there." He gives me an elaborate bow and steps back from the door, then back again, until we're several yards away. The sidewalk is empty except for us. Clara's hanging well back.

I point to the door. "Could you get us in there? Me and my friend?"

"In *there*?" The man looks at the door as though he's never seen it before. "Why, this is a munitions warehouse. But if you and your friend are looking for somewhere interesting to visit, I know an excellent spot a block or so from here."

He's putting on an act. He'll probably try to lead Clara and me to some other speakeasy, so we won't suspect anything. "No, thank you. I need to get into the Seven Seas."

The man's eyes widen, but only for an instant before his smile returns. "Ah yes. It's three blocks south, by the river. You'll want to take South Capitol Street."

He's lying. My certainty helps me square my shoulders. "Did you ever meet a man called Victor?"

His face doesn't change. "I'm afraid not. I really have to be..."

"Please, we need to find him. It's urgent."

"I see." The man's smile doesn't change, but his gloved fingers are curling in and out of fists at his sides. "I wish I could be of assistance, but I'm afraid I need to hurry on."

It isn't safe to linger here, not for either of us. I have to make this quick.

"Surely you know him." I try my hardest to sound breezy and charming, like Bridget, the waitress at the East Room. "Everyone at the Capitol knows Victor."

The man stops smiling. "Well, we're far from the Capitol here, and it's too late to be doing business."

I nod, still breezy, but inside, I'm lighting up. This man wouldn't be talking about business if he didn't know Victor was a bootlegger. Even if we can't get into the Seven Seas, I might be able to get some actual information here.

"I'm not here to do business," I say. "I only want to speak to Victor. Please. If you can get us in, I'll find him myself, and I won't bother you anymore."

The man shakes his head. "How old are you, anyway?"

I want to kick something. "Sir, *please*..."

"All right." He huffs out a breath, as if he wants to kick something, too. "Tell you what. Go on down to the river. I'll have him meet you there."

My eyes widen. "Truly?"

"Truly. What name shall I give him?"

I pause. "Smith. He'll know who it is if you tell him Miss Smith."

"Very well, Miss Smith. Go on ahead now."

"Thank you ever so, Mr...." He turns back to the door without answering, but I'm certain he heard.

I take Clara's arm and start walking south. When I glance back, the man in the top hat is watching us.

We keep to an even pace, as though we're any two girls out for a night of fun in the Navy Yard, until we reach a group of laughing sailors and girls farther down. Neither of us speaks until the crowd has grown thick and drunk enough for Clara and me to slip through unnoticed.

"If that man had been an agent..." She shakes her head, slowing her pace.

"He wasn't," I murmur. "He knew Victor. He's helping us."

"I don't know about this." Clara slows her steps, though we're barely more than a block from the Seven Seas.

"Victor's one of them," I murmur. "This proves it, doesn't it? He's a...you know."

"It doesn't *prove* anything. But...perhaps."

"Do you think Mrs. Rose knew?"

Clara sighs. "I've been wondering that, too."

"Have you?"

Clara gazes off into the distance. We're surrounded by people, but no one's paying the slightest attention to us. It's as though we have our own little island in the middle of the city.

"Clara...it seems as though you know a lot about...well. *Them.*"

Her gaze cuts down to her shoes. "I don't."

"You knew about those men at the Lazy Susan."

"That was only a guess."

"You said the word was *violets* for women. How did you know that?"

She glances up at me, quickly, then looks away again. "You want to talk about that now? *Here?*"

"Yes." I want to talk about it so badly. Anywhere at all.

"Someone could hear."

"No one's listening. *Please.*"

I step toward the concrete wall and turn to face Clara, and to my surprise, she's looking right back at me. She's opening her mouth to speak when something behind her catches my eye.

A block north of us. At the far end of the concrete building that houses the Seven Seas. A door has just swung open.

I spring off the wall and grab Clara's wrist as a figure in a three-piece suit emerges and starts moving up the street at a startling speed.

Victor's tearing away from us as fast as he can, clutching his homburg to his head.

24

I TUG CLARA THROUGH THE CROWD AND EMERGE TO THE NORTH, our heels clicking on the pavement as Victor breaks into a sprint.

I want to shout after him, to cry his name at the top of my lungs, but I don't. Names are precious here.

Besides, Victor knows we're chasing after him. It's obvious from the way his shoulders hunch forward, as though he's trying to make himself smaller, even as he runs. He's trying to get away from us. Desperately.

But Clara and I can run, too.

The crowd thins the farther north we get. Heads turn to watch as Clara and I rush past in our dresses and heels, but the faces look amused, not concerned. It's all a game to them. Another strange bit of amusement late at night in the nation's capital.

Yet it's not a game to Victor. He's running as though his life is at stake. He seems to have left the bar without his coat, too. He must be freezing.

What does he think we're here to do? Arrest him?

Just as that thought occurs to me, Victor's pace starts to slow, and a moment later, I see why. Across the street, a car has pulled up to the curb, and a pair of flat black hats is emerging from it.

Victor stops running altogether and turns back to face Clara and me, smiling broadly.

"Hello there, Miss Pound! So sorry, I must not have heard

you calling." He holds out his empty, ungloved hands and begins walking back into the crowd, leaving us no choice but to walk alongside him. He turns to Clara. "Pleasure to meet you officially, Miss Smith. I seem to recall you lurking in the shadows outside my office this morning. What can I do for you girls tonight?"

"We had another question or two to ask you," I say.

"Ah. Does your father know you're out here?"

"There's a lot I don't tell my father."

"Oh? It's the same for me." Victor glances behind us. The coppers are still on the opposite side of the street, talking to some of the Navy men. They don't seem to have taken any particular note of us. "Do you like coffee, Miss Smith?"

"I beg your pardon?"

"There's an Automat that's open late. It would be my pleasure to treat you both."

He's trying to steer us away from the Seven Seas. To take control, exactly as he did in his office this morning.

But a conversation over coffee isn't such a bad idea. We'll be able to hear one another more easily in an Automat than we would inside a speakeasy, anyway.

I lift my chin, like Milly. I'll let him think he's in charge, but tonight, I'll be the one deciding where it goes from here. I'll do as Mrs. Rose advised me. Forget what *I'm* feeling and try to understand what *he* truly thinks, underneath all the charm and falsehoods. "You're very kind. Yes, we do like coffee."

Ten minutes later, we've left the coppers far behind and the three of us are in a sparsely populated little neighborhood south of the Capitol, gathered in a sticky booth with cups of steaming coffee in front of us. Clara's beside me, next to a window that's in need of several washings, with Victor opposite. The Automat is nearly empty aside from us, with only a few old men sleeping in the corner booths and a woman in a wide-brimmed hat alone by the counter.

"I'm surprised to see you out at the nightclubs, after your previous experience," Victor says after he takes his first sip. "I can't imagine what made you come all the way over here."

"We heard some men talking about it at the Lazy Susan." I'm endeavoring to tell the truth as much as possible, in case it makes Victor willing to do the same. "We wondered what the Seven Seas was like. If Mrs. Rose ever came here."

Victor chuckles. "No, I can't say Jessica ever ventured out to the Seas."

"Where did you usually see her, then?" I lean across the table, arms bending at the elbows. My etiquette is a far cry from Trixie's sisters sitting with their fingers held just so around their teacups, and I don't care. "According to our teachers, she went out to speakeasies every week, and lied about it afterward."

"I never saw Jessica at any bar." Victor looks me straight in the eye. "As for lying, well...personally, I've never felt that truth had to be strictly adhered to, in a moral sense. There are situations in which it's kinder to all involved to do otherwise."

Clara bites her lip.

"But I think I can tell you what you want to know." Victor stretches one arm across the empty seat next to him and lays his other hand flat on the table. He's keeping his hands visible, I realize suddenly. He did that in his office, too. He's trying to reassure us. Show us that there's no reason to be afraid of him. "I met Jessica the summer before last. I was still making house calls then, and I used to go to the movies alone in the evenings, to relax. I was in a theater watching some ridiculous gangster picture and I heard a woman's voice, laughing at all the same parts I was. Mind you, no one else in that theater was laughing at all—most were cowering under their seats, actually—and I thought to myself, I've *got* to meet that woman. Lo and behold, coming out of the theater, I spotted her, a dazzling gem in a room full of dull old rocks, and I asked if she'd like to join me for a cup of coffee."

"Just as you asked us," Clara says. Her bare hands are folded on the table, too. She must've tucked her gloves away.

"Just so." Victor nods. "We spent two hours tearing that picture to shreds. Longer than the picture'd lasted. Neither of us was in any hurry to get back to work, so we kept chatting. She told me she'd moved down from New York and didn't know a lot of people here. We made a plan to go to the pictures again the following week, and afterward, we got coffee and ripped that one apart, too. The next thing I knew, I had a new best friend."

It all sounds so utterly charming. I find myself wanting to reach for Clara's hand, to give it a squeeze. But I don't. There's nothing wrong with girls holding hands, but here, tonight, somehow, it feels as though there is.

"One night, she spotted a shawl in a shop window," Victor goes on. "A quaint little thing, fake Spanish fringe, handpainted silk instead of embroidery—well, you're familiar with it. Jessica told me how much she missed shopping in New York, since all the clothes here are knockoffs, and the next week I went back to that shop and bought that shawl, and I presented it to her with great fanfare. I meant it as a joke, but she wore that shawl every single time I saw her after that."

His mouth turns down, and I find I'm on the verge of tears.

No. No, I need to keep steady. This could all be part of Victor's act.

But the more I can get him to say, the more likely he is to reveal something he *doesn't* mean to.

"She got me a shawl just like it," I say.

Victor nods. "You had it on this morning. For a second,

when you first came in, I thought...Well. It was kind of her, to give you that. But then, Jessica could be very kind when she cared about someone."

If he's the one who nailed the shawl to my railing this afternoon, he's a terribly gifted actor. But then, he'd have to be, to have escaped detection for so long.

"Tell me." Victor smooths his silk tie, "what is it you're trying to do here, Miss Pound? Truly. If you have a police escort hiding somewhere, now's the time for them to appear. I'm at your mercy."

"We don't have any kind of escort. We want to know what happened to her. That's all it is."

Victor studies me across the table for a moment, eyebrows knitting together. Slowly, he nods.

"Well, best of luck with that." Victor exhales, drops his eyes to the table, then looks up at me again with another tiny nod. As though he's coming to a decision. "You said you saw us coming back that night. Did *you* notice anything out of the ordinary?"

"I don't know what *ordinary* would've looked like. We'd never been outside after lights-out."

"Lights-out. How very sweet." He rubs his eyes again. "Well...*I* saw something, as it happens."

My heart leaps. "That night?"

"After I left Jessica at your school, yes." He wraps both hands tight around his coffee cup. "Miss Pound, Miss Smith, I do believe that you're here because you truly cared about Jessica. I did as well. So may I have your word, please, that what I tell you tonight, you'll keep in confidence?"

"Yes." I sit up straight, eager.

"Yes." Clara looks Victor in the eye.

"All right." He nods again. "I walked with Jessica to the end of the block, at the corner of P Street, on the circle. She wouldn't let me come any closer to your school than that. Worried her maid, Lucy, might see me and be scandalized. I turned around to cross back into the circle, but a movement caught my eye. A man was leaving the delivery alley that runs along the east side of the school."

The alley where we heard the gunshot.

I work to keep my breathing even. "What kind of man?"

"He was tall, with a dark coat and a dark hat pulled down low. Honestly, it could've been anyone, but it seemed late for a delivery to come. I only saw him for a moment, and then he was out of sight again. I doubt I'd have thought anything of it, except..."

"What?" My heart is pounding. "Except what?"

"He seemed a bit... familiar. As though I'd met him before." Victor shrugs. "But then, I've met a lot of people."

"If he was leaving, he couldn't have been the one who did it," Clara puts in. "Mrs. Rose had only just gone inside. She was still alive."

"That's true." Victor shrugs again. "So it's probably nothing."

"Did you see his hands?" I ask.

"What?" He blinks at me.

"The man's hands. Did you notice anything unusual about them?"

"I... don't recall his hands in particular." Victor tilts his head at me curiously. "He might've had them in his coat pockets."

"Oh."

"There was something else, too." Victor strokes his chin. "I've asked around a bit about what happened that night at the Lazy Susan. It isn't typical for a raid to happen quite that way, in a place like that."

"We'd heard." Clara taps a finger against the back of her other hand. Her skin is pale and smooth, despite the cold.

"Those places pay bribes to keep that from happening, don't they?"

"Yes, and the Lazy Susan was paying the most of anyplace. When the dry squads raid a bar like that, the agents generally don't want to antagonize the clientele. A lot of those customers are government men, which makes them the agents' bosses. The dry squad might arrest the owner, perhaps a bartender or two, but they'd let the customers leave without all the theatrics."

"We heard it might have had something to do with a particular government man who was at the Lazy Susan that night," Clara says. "A cabinet undersecretary."

"That's possible." Victor shrugs again. "I also heard it might be connected with some shady business up on K Street. Someone who made an arrangement with the feds to get them a bigger payout than their usual weekly fee."

"Could…" I frown, trying to think it through. All those black hats in the Lazy Susan. That fedora. While back at the seminary, Mrs. Rose was lying on her office floor. "Could the *police* have had something to do with what happened to her?"

"I don't know what any Prohibition agents would have stood to gain from the death of a respectable headmistress." Victor offers me a tight smile. "Something else was odd, though. That photograph in the *Star*. I've been paying attention to this industry for a number of years, and I've never seen a photograph from a raid show up in the paper. It's simply too much hassle. Cameras are heavy, the glass plates they use to capture the images are heavy, and the whole set is expensive and liable to break in a chaotic scene like that. Most reporters wouldn't risk bringing a camera in to shoot a raid. At most they could get one image, perhaps two, and there's no guarantee that what they got would be usable. I've got a friend who works at the *Star*, so I may ask her about it."

"Could the police have arranged for a reporter to come?" I ask, thinking of Bruce Pengelley. "If they wanted to make an example of someone?"

"Certainly." But Victor doesn't look convinced. "The Lazy Susan has reopened, by the way. I imagine they've doubled their payments. They won't want to be raided again after they went to the trouble of buying new glassware."

Victor smiles, but he doesn't look amused.

We're all quiet for a moment.

"You're aware that none of this matters, I'm sure," he says then.

"What?" I forget to hide my surprise.

He stirs his coffee, eyes fixed on the stained tabletop. "It won't bring her back."

I've never been punched in the stomach, but I've seen it happen in motion pictures. This is what I suspect it would feel like. As though all the air in me has been wiped out with one blow. Then I remember to look at Victor, to see what *he's* feeling.

What I see is pain.

His head is low, his shoulders hunched. His entire upper body crumpled. His teeth are digging into his bottom lip, but his chin is quivering.

This is a man who makes his living selling illegal liquor to the very people who passed the laws banning it. Then, at night, he crosses town to visit a place that's breaking even more laws, simply by existing. So much so that when he heard we'd come to see him, he sprinted out the back door.

So much of Victor's time is spent lying. Keeping himself protected.

He's good at that. Making people trust him is his life's work.

Is he on the verge of crying because he misses his friend? Or because he killed her?

Is this all a performance for our benefit?

"What's it like in there?" I tilt my head back in the direction of the Seven Seas.

"Where? Oh." He shrugs. "Like any other bar."

"Is it?"

"Heightened risk of arrest aside."

"But it's got to *feel* different inside, doesn't it? It's for people like...like..."

Victor cocks his head at me. "Why are you so interested, Miss Pound?"

I flush. "It's part of our investigation. Into what happened to Mrs. Rose."

"Is it?"

I glance at Clara. She's studying the tabletop, but her cheeks are flushed, too.

Victor sees me looking at her, but he doesn't remark on it. When I turn back to him, though, there's something new in his eyes. Some understanding that wasn't there before.

"Well." Victor pushes his coffee away. "I suppose it *is* always different. Being around people who understand you."

He stands up. Clara and I scramble to our feet, too.

"If you ladies would be good enough to excuse me."

I wait for Victor to say more. To tell us why he needs to leave. To tell us what he's holding back. But all he does is nod, button his jacket, and walk out the door, dropping his homburg neatly onto his head.

"Slow down." Clara's footsteps pound behind me on the pavement. "Wait, please!"

I slow down. Clara doesn't ask me for much.

We've left the Automat far behind. The block we're on,

southeast of the Capitol, is dark and empty. A few stores, boarded up for the night. Office buildings, warehouses, but no homes. No signs of life.

My trepidation returns. Anyone could be lurking in these shadows.

But when I turn back and see Clara's eyes on my face, the fear slips away.

We duck into the shelter of a shop entrance with a faded advertisement for sewing machines tucked into its window frame and a handwritten *VACANT* sign tacked to the door. The wind has picked up, but it doesn't reach us here. A private sanctuary, just for us, protected from eyes and ears and cold.

My hand searches for Clara's under our heavy coats. When I find it, and clasp it, she steps in closer.

My mind is racing. I'm thinking about Victor, and that man in the top hat, and the Seven Seas. And that hospital where they send people like them. St. Elizabeths.

I'm thinking about the rules. About what happened to Mrs. Rose when she tried breaking them.

"We can't go to the police." Clara's eyes dart into a shadowy corner at the back of our little shelter. "We don't have any new evidence."

"I know." I step in closer, until my coat is flush with hers. She doesn't pull away.

"And whatever we do, we can't tell them about that place," she goes on. Our faces are so close. "The Seven Seas. The people who go there, they... they *need* it, they..."

"I know," I say again. "I know they do."

And neither of us says any more after that, because I'm reaching out. I'm cradling her neck, gently. And then I'm breaking the biggest rule I know.

I'm kissing her.

It's so fast. So fast, I don't know it's happening until it is.

Soft pressure. A light touch. A closeness that I never understood before.

Our bodies tilt together. She's so warm. I want her heat to be *our* heat.

I don't want anything about this to ever end.

But she's already moving away. Pushing me back, her spine curling under her coat, under my hands.

Clara looks horrified. I *horrify* her.

She turns, eyes darting toward the street.

"Clara…"

But she's gone. She's running, away from me, down this block and then the next.

I want to pound my fists against the wall, the sidewalk, the littered cigarette butts, the broken glass kicked into the corners. But I can't.

And I'm alone now, listening to the shadows whisper.

25

"Gertie. Wake up."

It's my mother.

She knows. Somehow. She *knows*.

Where I was last night. What I did with Clara in that darkened storefront.

She *knows*.

Then I open my eyes, and it's not my mother above me at all. It's Milly, her arms crossed.

"Oh." I sit up, my mind scrambling to make sense of this.

I'm at home. In my room. Alone. Or I *was* alone, before Milly came in.

And Milly can't find out what happened last night, either.

My panic thrums higher.

Clara must've gone back to her hotel. Though I can't imagine what she told her father, much less the man at the front desk, coming in after midnight wearing lipstick and rouge.

Smudged lipstick. My own was smudged, anyway, when I looked in the bathroom mirror after I got home.

It was the first time I'd seen myself the way I am now. Perhaps the way I've always been.

A violet.

"It's ten in the morning." Milly unfolds her arms. "I told your mother you weren't feeling well, so she let you miss breakfast, but she's threatening to call Dr. Garrison if you don't get up."

I struggle to lift my shoulders. My thin white nightgown is

rumpled, my hair tangled into knots. I pull the blanket up to my neck, suddenly modest, despite having shared a room with Milly for four years.

She, as usual, looks perfect, her yellow hair swept off her face with gleaming gold clips, her deep gray day dress freshly pressed and clinging to her hips.

I remember what she said as though it was only seconds ago.

Queers. Pronounced as if she was talking about something so revolting it hurt her to speak the word.

"Get up," she says now, but she says it gently. "Make yourself presentable."

My parents would be too devasted to even look at me if they knew. I could be sent away to St. Elizabeths. Have my head smashed by coppers like Perkins and his friends.

But right now, I'm most worried about Clara.

Did she *want* to kiss me back? I thought she did, then, but what do *I* know about kissing?

What if she thinks I'm depraved? What if she refuses to ever speak to me again?

"I'm sorry about last night." My words come automatically. Any time I make Milly angry, I'm always sorry. Even when she's the one who was wrong.

"Yes, well, I see that you survived the night." Milly shrugs. "As did Clara, it seems, given that she's downstairs."

I'm so stunned I let the blanket fall to my waist. "She's *what?*"

"She's having tea with your mother. Alma came up to announce her, so I told her I'd wake you up. I'll go down first, and you can come when you're dressed."

Clara's having tea with my *mother?*

Surely she wouldn't tell her. No. I don't need to worry, not even in my muddled brain, about Clara telling my mother.

But there *is* one person she might tell. Particularly if she *does* think I'm depraved.

I can't let Clara talk to Milly. I have to be there, too. All the time, from now on. I can't ever leave the two of them alone.

"Could you wait here for a minute, please?" I shove my way out of bed, ignoring the creased sheets, and go straight to my wardrobe. I yank the first day dress I see, a shapeless stretch of dull brown wool, off its hanger, and pull a chemise out of a drawer. "I'll walk downstairs with you."

I slip into the corner behind the wardrobe before I pull the nightgown over my head.

I wish I could tell her everything. Milly's always the one who reassures me that I did the right thing, and helps me understand why. Yet I can't tell her this. Even if she didn't object herself, and she obviously does, it wouldn't be right to tell her without asking Clara first.

And I can't ask her. Not after the way she ran off last night. As though I'd hurt her.

"Did you...learn anything?" Milly asks from the other side of the room. She doesn't sound angry anymore. She sounds sad. Perhaps even lonely. "Last night?"

I step into my chemise, then struggle to pull the dress over my head. It itches. "Yes, actually. We spoke with Victor for some time."

As I fight with the dress, I summarize our conversation for Milly. She doesn't ask as many questions as I'd expect. Milly's never this quiet.

I'm still behind the wardrobe, wrestling with the knots in my hair and trying to explain what Victor said about the difficulty of taking photographs in a speakeasy, when a knock comes at my bedroom door.

"I'll get that," Milly says. Before I can call out for her not to open the door, I hear it swing on its hinges.

"Hi," Milly murmurs.

"Hello." The answering voice, equally soft, is Clara's. "I'm sorry. I wanted to make sure Gertie got home all right."

I give up on my hair and step out into the room.

Clara looks perfect. Even more so than usual. She's wearing a burnt-orange crepe de chine dress that makes her face as bright and warm as the winter sun, and her short hair hangs in fresh waves around her chin, as though she had it styled this very morning. She's wearing lipstick, too, her mouth wavering between a smile and a thin, tight line. "Good morning, Gertie."

"Good morning." I can't help patting my own hair. It feels fully matted to my head.

Milly steps forward, until all three of us are clustered awkwardly by the wardrobe. No one seems to know quite what to say.

It's Milly who breaks the impasse.

"As I see it, we have two priorities, given that your chat with Victor failed to yield a confession." She folds her arms over her chest again. "That man who spoke to Gertie on the street yesterday, Mr. Frances, clearly knows something. We need to find out what. But even more importantly, we need to find evidence against Victor that we can turn over to the police before he kills again."

She's still certain Victor's the murderer, then. Whereas I'm not certain of anything at all. "Did you have particular evidence in mind?" I ask her.

Milly nods firmly. "A man like him is bound to have been arrested at least once, and the library will have a record of it. If we can prove to Agent Perkins that the man we saw with Mrs.

Rose the night she died is a prior convict, that should be enough to get him to take us seriously."

I nod. "But Victor never told us his last name. How are we going to find out if he's been arrested?"

Milly grimaces. "It might take all day to search through the records, but if I find something, it'll be worth it."

"All right. Then Clara and I can go to the Hotel Grafton and try to speak with this Mr. Frances."

I realize, though, as soon as I've said it, that Clara probably doesn't want to go anywhere with me at all. Much less alone.

"That is..." I don't look at Clara. I can't. "Milly, one of us should accompany you to the library to help with all that reading. I'll go to the hotel, and Clara, you can—"

Milly shakes her head, eyes widening. "No, no, you two should go together. Mr. Frances could turn out to be dangerous."

"But..."

Before I can finish my protest, though, Milly and Clara are already moving away, gathering up handbags and putting on hats.

Clara never looks at me. There's no way to know what she's thinking.

Before I can think of a way to stop what's happening we're all in the kitchen, lying to my mother about our plans. It's funny. All this time, I thought lying to my parents was one of the worst available sins, and now I'm doing it every day.

"Shopping?" My mother purses her lips. She's been conferring with Sarah about the dinner menu, and while Sarah greeted me with a kind nod, my mother only sighed to see me enter. "Again?"

"It's for my sake, really." Clara gives her most winsome smile. "I've put off buying a gift for my father's dearest friend. Milly and Gertie offered to help me make a selection."

That earns an answering smile from my mother. "All right, then, girls. You might as well go out. I'll be away this afternoon, calling on some of the board members' wives. They'll be deciding about whether to reopen your seminary shortly."

We stiffen, but all we can do is nod and step out the front door.

Milly leaves us at the corner, heading to the library at a fast clip. Already I'm alone with Clara, walking to catch the streetcar.

I should apologize. Tell her I was wrong to do what I did. Swear never to attempt it again. But we're surrounded by people here on the sidewalk, and as adept as I've grown at lying, I can't bear the thought of pretending to atone for something I don't regret in the slightest.

So I stay quiet as we climb onto the car and find seats together, right behind the driver. Clara stays quiet, too. And we remain that way until the car reaches DeSales Street, the bustle of Connecticut Avenue and its downtown shoppers sweeping up around us as we climb off. I hope my still-matted hair isn't visible under my hat.

A bellhop opens the door to us at the ladies' entrance and shows us to the front desk. "We've come to see Mr. A. Frances," I tell the clerk, realizing only then that I've been so preoccupied I didn't even consider whether it was wise to ask to see a potential murderer.

The clerk, a man with pale hair that smells of cigar smoke, scratches his chin. "Mr. Frances is out."

"Oh." I glance at Clara. We hadn't considered this possibility. "Do you know when he'll be back?"

"I'm afraid not, miss."

"Does he go out often?" I'd gotten the impression that Mr.

Frances spent most of his time inside this hotel, but the truth may be more complex.

"Most days, I suppose." The clerk turns down toward his desk, boredom in his voice.

"Do you know where to?"

"I'm afraid I don't, miss. Would you like to leave him a message?"

"Yes, please." Clara leans toward the clerk, smiling. He looks up, flushes, and smiles back. "Could you tell him we'll meet him at the hotel restaurant tomorrow at noon?"

"I'd be happy to, miss." The clerk swallows. "What names shall I leave?"

"Miss Smith." Clara glances at me. "And...Miss Smith. We're sisters, you see."

I work not to giggle. The clerk nods earnestly, writing it all down on his notepad. "Yes, Miss Smith. I'll give him the message."

"Thank you," Clara says, before taking me by the elbow and pulling me back toward the door. My giggles threaten to escape before we've even made it outside.

There's another streetcar right out front, and we step onto it without bothering to check where it's going, stepping politely past women with children at their feet and men with newspapers in their hands until we find seats in the back. A woman with a shopping bag full of celery and potatoes slides over so the two of us can sit together, and we thank her, giggling all the while.

It feels so good to laugh. After everything that's happened, all the fear, all the worry. It's astonishing to experience something like release.

Still, when I turn to face Clara as the streetcar bumps, her softly curled hair rising and falling, I can't help remembering the horror on her face last night.

"I'm sorry." The words fall out of me, my cheeks flaming crimson. "I shouldn't have...You ran off last night, and, and I'm sure you didn't mean to...didn't *want* to..."

Clara glances at the woman holding the bag of vegetables. She's staring out the window, her wide-brimmed hat concealing most of her face. There's no indication that she's paying attention to us, or that anyone else is, either. I suppose everyone has enough troubles of their own.

"It's not that I didn't..." Clara blinks, pressing two fingers between her eyebrows. "It's difficult to explain."

"I'd like to listen. If you'd try." I place a light hand on her arm. A test.

"I..." Clara doesn't pull away. Not yet. The streetcar slows to a stop, and the woman with the shopping bag climbs out of her seat and steps off onto the pavement. When she's gone and we're alone at the back of the streetcar, Clara turns to face me. "Could I tell you why I had to leave my old school? The real reason?"

"I thought you came to the city to be with your father."

She drops her gaze to the floor of the streetcar, her not-quite-shoulder-length curls casting downward.

"No one was supposed to know." Her eyes are dark, deep brown pools. "I came so it would stay secret."

"So what would?"

"That I'm..." She glances around again, holding her hands out in front of her, palms up, as though she's lifting a heavy object by herself. "*This* way."

Oh.

She already knew.

Before last night. Clara knew.

For me, that night—that kiss—was a revelation. But for Clara...

"I saw a play last year, in New York." She swallows. "That's where I learned about violets. It was about a girl who...She was in love with...Well."

I shake my head, stuttering. "That...that can't be."

A *play*? About girls falling in love with other girls?

Girls *can* fall in love with other girls?

"It's true." Clara swallows again. "It was called *The Captive*. One girl in it sent the other girl violets. There were women in the audience who must have seen it before, because they came to watch it with violets pinned to their dresses. It was...it was so lovely."

I want to go to that theater. I want to be surrounded by women like those. Women like *me*.

I want to be with other people who know about this. Who understand.

"But..." Clara drops her head again. "The girl I went to see the play with. Rachel. She was my best friend. She...Last spring, we..."

Ah. "You and her."

Clara doesn't answer.

I turn to gaze out the window. The sidewalk is littered with ashes and sandwich wrappers.

"We never talked about it," Clara murmurs, staring down at her hands. "It only...happened. Then it happened again. It was good, for a while, and...I suppose it doesn't matter. Anyway, at first we were careful. Then, later, we forgot."

And I remember what Clara said before. About having to leave.

I want to put my arms around her. Keep her safe. Instead I take her hand and squeeze it softly.

Clara shakes her head, tucking a curl behind her ear. "The principal saw us. In the stairwell."

Clara kissed a girl at *school*? "What happened?"

"I wanted to lie. Tell him he'd misunderstood. He'd have believed us, too, I really think he would, or at least he would've pretended to. He didn't want to catch us doing it any more than we wanted to get caught. The trouble was, Rachel panicked. She told him it was all my fault—that it had only happened that one time, and I'd tricked her into it."

"What?" Fury blooms in my chest. The crowd on the streetcar is growing thinner, and I'm glad, because I feel very much like shouting. "She said *what*?"

"So he told our parents, and we were expelled. In the end." Clara shrugs, though it certainly must have been the worst thing that's ever happened to her. "Rachel's parents tried to have me arrested."

"Arrested?"

She nods, rapidly. "That's why I never want to see another copper as long as I live."

I picture police officers storming into a Brooklyn apartment, batons raised. Clara's face, pale with terror, her thin arms raised to defend herself. "What did they do?"

She shrugs again. "I was working at the grocery store with my mother—I worked there every day, since I couldn't go to school—and they...they came in. They must have known the two of us were working alone that day, somehow. Three of them, these three huge men, walked in, and they sort of...they sort of *winked* at me. Then went over to talk to my mother. I could see how scared she was, but I couldn't hear what they said. But my father was upstairs, and he'd seen them coming. He came down and paid them to go away. It wasn't enough to *keep* them away, though. They're still paying, my parents." Her eyes drop to the ground. "We've had to borrow money, but if my father doesn't start earning more, they might have to sell the store."

My mind is spinning. All this for a kiss in a stairwell. "Did *everyone* find out?"

"No. My parents managed to keep it quiet. If Mrs. Rose hadn't let me come to the seminary for free, though, I might not have been able to finish school at all. She was the only headmistress they could find who'd even *consider* taking me. It's hard enough to find a school that'll take Jewish girls, but with this on top of it, well... If the seminary doesn't reopen, I don't know what I'll do."

I squeeze her hand again. "What did your parents say? At first?"

She pulls her hand from mine and wraps her arms around her chest. "Nothing. They didn't say a word after the principal left. They only cried. And cried, and cried."

Hearing her say that makes me want to cry, too.

"Then they went into their room, and I couldn't hear anything," she goes on. "It was strange. They were so quiet. They didn't even talk to my aunts and uncles, and they talk to them about *everything*. But they didn't want a soul knowing about me. I wasn't allowed to tell my brothers, either. I had to be so careful, pretending I was still going to school every day, until they got the story around that I was moving down here to be near my father."

I try to breathe, when I want to cry.

Clara's parents know. They were devastated. She had to leave her home and find a new school.

It was *terrible*.

Today, her life looks normal. Classes, and parties, and basketball games. She isn't walking around with her face cast down, a scarlet badge splashed across her dress.

Yet perhaps that's how she feels inside.

Is that how I'm supposed to feel, too?

"I overheard the police talking to my father right before we moved, when he was delivering a payment." Clara slips down into her seat. The rest of the bus's remaining passengers are all up front, near the driver. Beyond the windows, the scenery's turned green and brown. We've left the drab gray structures of the city far to our south, and most of the people, too. "They told him to be careful, or I'd end up like those boys in Chicago."

"What boys?" At first, I picture Al Capone and the gangsters the papers are always writing about. But when Clara doesn't answer, I understand.

Those boys.

A few summers ago, every newspaper headline for weeks was about a boy who'd died in Chicago. At first, all I knew was that he was my own age. Fourteen. His name was Bobby.

Then, slowly, the story of what had happened to Bobby became clearer. He'd been murdered, with a chisel, by two older boys. Though they weren't so far off from the age I am now, come to think of it. Their names were Leopold and Loeb, and the headlines said they'd spent months planning the perfect crime. The whole country was chanting for their execution, but their lawyer convinced the judge to sentence them to life in prison instead.

Everyone knew something was wrong with them. *Very* wrong. They were strange boys, both of them, and together they were even stranger.

The papers were vague about just *what* was wrong with them, but I heard enough adults talking to figure it out. The two older boys were, well. *Together.* Like Clara and that girl, Rachel.

And the way the papers wrote about them—the way people talked about them...

They all seemed to think the one thing inevitably led to the other.

Those sorts are all criminals. Barely human. They did

unspeakable, unnatural things with each other, and it was only to be expected that they'd commit another unspeakable, unnatural act.

That's got to be why Milly's so convinced Mrs. Rose's death was Victor's doing. For all that she doesn't want to say it out loud.

Murder's only one more unnatural behavior, after all. The two might as well go hand in hand.

26

End of the line," the driver booms from the front of the streetcar. The last few passengers up front are already climbing off.

"Oh." I blink out the window. "I'm sorry. I didn't realize... Where are we?"

Clara lets out a tiny laugh. "I don't know."

We climb down out of the car. According to the street sign, we're still on Connecticut Avenue, but we seem to have come awfully far north. There are no houses here. On one side, there's a little station waiting room, where we'll be able to catch another streetcar back into the city soon enough, but otherwise, we're surrounded by trees. A few are evergreens, but most stand bare and starkly brown in the cold.

"Look." Clara points to a footbridge. "There's a lake."

The streetcar trundles off to the car barn. The rest of the passengers have vanished. We're still in the city, or close to it, at least, but for a moment, it's as though Clara and I are all alone in the world.

We glance at each other, wordlessly, and set out toward the little footbridge.

A stream runs underneath it. On the other side there are more trees and a dirt path. A sign at the far end of the bridge reads CHEVY CHASE LAKE.

"Oh, I recognize this." I smile at Clara as we step off the bridge and follow the path deeper into the trees. It feels as though we've only come a few steps, but already we can barely see the station house behind us. "I haven't been for years, but in the summer, there's dancing and ice cream and a merry-go-round, and when the lake freezes over, there's skating."

"And right now, there's neither," Clara says as the lake comes into view. Cold, like the air, but not frozen yet. "It's ours."

She's right. There's no one in sight.

I reach out and take her hand again, my white glove sliding into her white glove, kidskin against suede.

We walk on, both of us smiling now.

"Do you miss your family back home?" I ask.

"Every day. But it's almost as though I've found a new family here."

She tilts her head at me. I meet it with a head tilt of my own.

"My mother seemed to think I'd be in grave danger here," Clara says. Our hands swing as we walk. "She didn't know there would be a murder at my finishing school, of course, not when I first left. But we didn't know this city at all, and she worried. She's the one who bought me the knife and taught me how to use it. So I could take care of myself if I had to."

"Then she hasn't... refused to speak to you, or anything like that."

"No." Her smile fades. "Not like Rachel."

Perhaps *Rachel's* the one walking around in scarlet. "What happened to her?"

"I don't know. Her parents sent her away."

"Where?"

"A hospital. No one would tell me where, but I can guess what it's like. Cold and dark. They'll do everything they can to change her into someone different. I was angry with her for what she did, at first, but now... I wouldn't wish that on anyone."

Like St. Elizabeths. I wonder if they beat people at Rachel's hospital, too.

"It can happen," Clara says, after a quiet moment. "You need to know that. It's my greatest fear. That happening again."

"Oh." I swallow. If she's trying to frighten me, it's working. "Is that…Is that why you ran away last night?"

She nods. "After I got back to my hotel, all I could do was lie on my bed, staring at the ceiling, until I stopped shaking. I lay there for hours, thinking about what happened with Rachel. And…about you."

I forget to breathe. "Oh?"

"I never thought I could feel that way about anyone again." She takes in a deep breath. "And…how I could never forgive myself if it happened to you, too."

I loop my gloved fingers through hers. I exhale, holding her gaze in mine. "Did Mrs. Rose know?"

Clara nods again, dropping her eyes to the path at our feet. "She told my parents she'd keep it secret. They thought that meant she'd fix it."

"Fix what?"

"Me, I guess." Clara tries to smile, but it's more of a wince. "But that's not what happened. She never told me I had to change."

Warmth surges in my chest.

"When we talked, every week over tennis, she was always after me to be more open." Clara gazes up into the trees ahead. "She said I had to learn how to trust people. As though trusting Rachel isn't exactly what caused all my problems."

I want Clara to trust *me*. Suddenly, I want it more than I ever knew.

But…if the police found out Mrs. Rose knew Clara's secret, they'd never believe she'd chosen to keep it quiet out of the goodness of her heart. They'd assume Clara saw Mrs. Rose as a threat.

They'd remember the boys in Chicago. They'd think Clara's no different.

And now, they'd think the same about me.

"Does anyone else know?" I ask.

"My old principal. My parents. Rachel's parents. Mrs. Rose." She pauses, drawing in a breath. "And...Trixie."

I stop walking. *"Trixie?"*

"You know how she listens at doors. The day before the faculty party, Mrs. Rose and I were talking in her office, and when I came out, Trixie was on the other side. It was clear she'd heard everything. She just stood there, staring at me in utter horror, as though I was about to come at her with a knife right in the middle of the hall. If she told anyone..."

She trails off without saying more, but I know what she means.

Clara's life would be ruined for good. Trixie could make sure that happened, if she chose. It would get *her* plenty of attention, telling a secret like that.

That's why Trixie does so much of what she does, after all. To make people notice her.

Yet she hasn't breathed a word. If she had, I'd have heard for certain.

I raise my eyes to meet Clara's. Hers are clear and open.

"Thank you for telling me," I say.

"Thank you for listening." She reaches out. She cups my cheek in her gloved hand. My stomach flips, then flips again. "Mrs. Rose was right, you know."

"About what?"

"Trusting people. I haven't wanted to, for so long, but...I think I'm starting to again."

I take in a breath. Let it out. The trees are close around us, the branches darkening the sky, even though it's still morning.

"I trust you," I tell her. "Entirely."

"Gertie." Clara pauses. "There's something I should... It's only that I don't know quite how to say it."

"You don't have to. If you don't want to. Last night, I wanted to apologize, but I couldn't find you, and then..."

That's as far as I get before she kisses me again.

I step in close, dropping my hand to her waist. The layers of fabric between us allow just a hint of the shape of her body underneath, pressed against mine from mouths to hips.

It's such a new, raw feeling. As though I've spent all my days in darkness, without knowing sunlight was a possibility.

I should think about what this means. Whether it's right or wrong. What would happen if we got caught, the way she did before.

But I don't. I can't think about anything but the way this feels. Perhaps I even relish it, a little.

It's like Mrs. Rose said. When I told her that what I wanted wasn't what other people did.

Well. That *is something to celebrate.*

~⁓€27⤳~

Take your coat, miss?" asks a harried bellhop as I step from DeSales Street into the gleaming tiled lobby with Milly and Clara on my heels. Clara wanted to have one of us keep watch outside, the way we did at the Capitol, but I insisted we stay together. I remember all too well how it felt, coming face-to-face with that man outside Victor's office and knowing he'd been out in that hallway with Clara, alone. Mr. Frances didn't strike the same level of fear in me, but it's clear he's hiding *something*.

"Yes, please," I tell the bellhop. "We've come to dine with Mr. A. Frances."

He helps us out of our coats and points through a tall door, propped open to reveal a glossy restaurant. Downtown Washington has a great many new hotels, all eager to promote their luxury, but the Hotel Grafton seems more opulent than most, with gray tapestry brick covering its exterior and terrazzo floors inside. It's fortunate that we came in tea dresses, mine a deep blue wool with gold buttons and handmade lace.

But I wonder if there's been some mistake. I don't see how a man who dresses and speaks like Mr. Frances could afford to stay in a place like this.

"Mr. Frances is by the bar," the bellhop says. "Shall I escort you?"

"No, thank you." I drop three coins into his red-gloved hand and we start forward.

After Clara and I got back from the lake yesterday, flushed

with our new secret, we spent hours huddled with Milly, deliberating over how we'd conduct today's interview, and trying to pretend nothing strange was going on while Milly kept shooting curious glances at Clara and me. Our plan for luncheon is to ask our most important questions and listen carefully to what Mr. Frances tells us. Then, after we say goodbye, we'll each take up a discreet position outside the hotel and watch to see if he goes anywhere. If he does, we'll follow.

Only one man is sitting near the shining wood-paneled hotel bar as we step through. He's still wearing the rumpled gray suit and knit tie, and his carved wooden cane is propped up at his side. I wonder if Mr. Frances owns any other clothes.

He sees me looking and nods before climbing out of his seat and coming toward us. I watch him, carefully, for any signs of whether he could be a murderer.

The trouble is, I don't think murderers usually do give signs.

But most of the restaurant's tables are occupied, and a half dozen waiters are moving among them with trays of steak and potatoes and carafes full of coffee. We should be safe enough among so many people, regardless of what this Mr. Frances might be hiding.

He grips his cane in his left hand and extends his right. "So *you're* the one calling yourself Miss Smith. I'd wondered."

He shouldn't offer his hand. When a gentleman meets a lady, *she* should be the one to offer her hand, and then only if they've been previously introduced.

Mr. Frances must live outside the city. Quite far outside. With his clothing and his manners, I'm surprised he's permitted even to dine at the hotel. Yet when he turns and says, without raising his voice, "Beg pardon, Danny, if you would, please?" a passing man in a tuxedo stops right away and bows deeply.

"Yes, Mr. Frances. Right this way, ladies."

To my astonishment, the waiter leads us to the brightest, grandest table, in front of the hotel's most prominent plate glass window, with a glimmering chandelier directly over our heads. Women in tea dresses far more expensive than mine glance at us from nearby tables, then turn away, eyebrows raised. Some distant voice, probably my mother's, mutters in my mind that it isn't decent for unmarried girls to share a restaurant table with a man.

The waiter pulls out our chairs, bends so Mr. Frances can speak into his ear, then straightens. "I'll return in a moment with the first course, Mr. Frances."

"I hope you don't mind that I ordered," he says when the waiter is gone. "I eat all my meals here, so I'm intimately familiar with the menu's strengths and weaknesses. Do you all enjoy oysters?"

Milly and I nod, but Clara shakes her head. Mr. Frances lifts one finger, and in an instant, the waiter, Danny, is back. Mr. Frances murmurs something more to him, and he's gone just as quickly.

"There are a few topics I'd like to discuss." Mr. Frances isn't wearing gloves, and his hands are thick with calluses. Nothing about him matches this hotel, or the waiter's deferential bow, or the oysters that apparently will be arriving very soon. "But first, I probably ought to tell you who I am."

A tea tray appears. Danny sets out saucers, cups, a bowl of sugar cubes, and a pot, then pours.

I take a long sip of my tea before responding. "Please do, Mr. Frances."

"All right." He waits until Danny's gone, then folds his hands neatly beside his teacup. "I should start by saying that my name isn't Frances. I'm Richard Rose. Your headmistress was my wife."

THE TABLE FALLS SILENT.

Tea churns in my stomach. Under the table, I clench the fabric of my wool skirt, waiting for this man to apologize for making such an inappropriate joke.

He doesn't.

"Mrs. Rose was a widow," Clara says slowly, as though perhaps he doesn't know that. I want to take her hand—I need something to keep me grounded, something that makes sense—but I don't feel steady, and I'm not sure I can move without knocking over a teacup, if not the entire table.

"That's what she told everyone." The man across the table is calm. He dabs at his lip with a napkin. Stirs his tea. "We both decided that was the best choice."

"Cholera." I remember now. "Milly, you read in the paper that Mrs. Rose's husband died of cholera. She'd told me it was influenza."

The man nods. "We also considered a streetcar accident, but she thought it might raise too many questions."

She said she was a widow. She said that to *me*.

If this man is telling the truth... He *can't* be, but if he is...

Mrs. Rose lied.

How could she? *Why* would she?

"You committed fraud, then," Milly says. "The pair of you."

"We didn't do anything illegal. No one was harmed, and we didn't make any money from it. Not directly."

Anything's preferable to divorce, my mother's voice says in my head.

Divorce is the worst scandal there is, for a woman. It would be better to never marry altogether. When my mother was a girl, everyone envied Consuelo Vanderbilt for her beauty, her wealth, and her marriage to a British duke, but we aren't even allowed to mention her name now that she's been divorced and remarried to a Frenchman.

If Mrs. Rose and her husband—impossible as it is to fathom that this strange man, in his rumpled suit in this glamorous hotel, could have ever been married to our headmistress—had wished to end their marriage, a legal divorce would've been a far greater humiliation than allegations of drinking, or even bootlegging. When it became publicly known, and divorces always did, Mrs. Rose would never again be invited to balls or parties. She'd certainly never find work as a teacher, let alone a headmistress. Nor would she be able to enter into any other profession in good society. Perhaps she could've been a shop-girl, if she kept her head down, and her employer didn't find out.

But Mrs. Rose was meant to be a leader. *Our* leader.

It would indeed have been better for her to present herself as a widow. To form a life for herself, alone. To break yet another set of rules.

"The police don't know who you are, do they?" I ask.

"That's right." The man gives me a small smile. "Jessica said you were the brightest student she'd ever taught, Miss Pound."

I have no reason to believe anything this man says. Still, a warm glow burns inside me.

But it's the second time he's used Mrs. Rose's first name.

Gentleman or otherwise, no man would call her that unless he'd known her very well indeed.

"You sat in the back at the funeral," Clara says. "Mrs. Rose didn't appear to have any family there at all."

"Oh, she did. Her family situation isn't what you think, Miss...I don't believe I got your name?"

Clara pauses, considering. "Miss Blum."

"Ah, yes, I recall young Miss Blum from her letters, too." He smiles fondly.

My shock at his revelation is shifting back to apprehension. This man is very likely a liar, and quite possibly a murderer.

I glance at Milly. Should one of us go find the police and tell them to come question this man?

Danny arrives with a tray and begins setting out plates. Oysters, and olives, and a bowl of broth for Clara. The smells are strong and savory.

"There's no use keeping secrets anymore," the man says, though I notice he waits until Danny's gone before he does. "We only kept it quiet on her account. She was the one whose career was at stake. Mine is less risky."

"If you'll forgive us, all this secrecy, whether past or present, doesn't exactly give us much reason to believe you," Milly says, her smooth, polite tone nearly covering the harshness of her words. "But we're trying to find out everything we can about our former headmistress, particularly regarding what might have led to her death. If it's true that you're her husband, could you tell us about any financial troubles she might have been having?"

He wrinkles his nose. "I never did care much about finances. Jessica and I started out with very little. We were young when we married, and her parents had been freethinkers. Unusual for their time, or any time. They traveled often.

Had no interest in money. Wouldn't fit in at all with your set." He nods toward the chandelier over our heads. "They died in a carriage accident when she was a child, and she was sent to stay with an uncle and his wife. Thought they were doing charity, taking in an orphan from the poorer branch of the family. They used what little her parents had left her to send her away to boarding school. That got them out of having to raise her. She went from traveling the world with her parents to dark rooms in New England, learning German and Greek and how to do the right kind of curtsy."

"Mrs. Rose loved school." I've barely nibbled my oysters, but I can't let this stand. This man couldn't have *truly* known Mrs. Rose. "She told me so."

"Yes, she found a new family there to replace the one she'd lost. It's why she went into teaching. Every time she visited her aunt and uncle, they reminded her what good people they were for taking her in, then ignored her until she went back again. You can see why she preferred the one over the other."

"When did she meet you, then?" Milly asks. I try to catch her eye, to see if she believes any of this, but her gaze is fixed firmly on the man's face.

"After college. She'd paid her own way there. Not easy for a girl, especially then, and she had to take in so much sewing she barely managed to sleep. But her uncle wasn't about to pay for her—he called college for women a ridiculous indulgence— and by then, they'd spent her inheritance. She always excelled at tennis, though. After her first year at Berkeley, she'd won so often a patron covered her expenses, and she wound up graduating near the top of her class and moved to New York for graduate school. That's where we met."

"You're from New York?" I file away all this information to think about later, should there be any possibility it's true. Mrs.

Rose told me she went away to college on her own, but she'd never said anything about working as a seamstress, or visiting her few remaining relatives. Only for them to tell her she was beneath them.

"Kentucky," the man says. "Coal country. I learned my way around New York, but I never bothered with the clothes or the talk. Mrs. Rose bought me a suit for our wedding, but it got to be my only one, and you can see what's become of it. At home, I don't have much need for suits, but in a place like this, it's expected."

"If you're from Kentucky, what were you doing in New York?" Milly asks.

"I was never fit for the mines or the military, thanks to this leg—polio, had it when I was five—so I left. Stowed away on trains until the line ended at Penn Station." Behind him, out on the street, cars speed by. A streetcar trundles. A woman pauses to glance in the window. The man across the table is so caught up in his story, he doesn't notice any of it. "I didn't have anything to do there or any money to do it with, so I started drawing in charcoals on the street to pass the time. The next thing I knew, a gentleman stopped and offered to buy me a canvas so I could do one for him. Another gentleman saw and did the same, then another, until I could afford to buy paint. I started getting commissions, and someone even rented me an apartment to work in, in Greenwich Village. After that, they started inviting me to parties. Those were the worst part of the whole business, but it was how I sold my work, and it was at one of them that I met Jessica. Then I met her again the next day, and the day after that. Neither of us had ever fallen in love before, and it happened so fast we didn't even know what it was until we'd decided to marry."

A whirlwind romance. Like in a novel, or a play.

But then, novels and plays are full of murders, too. Desdemona and Othello had once been very much in love.

"But things changed?" I ask.

"We thought it would work itself out, like magic. Turns out, there's no such thing." He pauses as Danny arrives to take our plates and returns seconds later with the next course, a fillet of bass with asparagus in hollandaise sauce. I doubt he ate like this when he lived in coal country. If there's truth to his story, that is. "Her aunt and uncle cut off contact when we announced our plan to marry. Never consented to meet me. They wanted her to marry someone like them, you understand. Didn't approve of a penniless artist from the sticks."

I glance at Clara, but her eyes are startlingly wide. She's hanging on his every word.

"Jessica and I laughed about it," he goes on. "Seemed romantic at the time, until reality proved otherwise. We knew within a year that marriage didn't suit either of us. Besides, she dreamed of running a school for girls. As for me, well, I wanted to create art, but I found I didn't want to do it in a city. I wanted to be where there were real colors to see, sounds to hear."

If he's making this up, he's doing very well. It all sounds terribly real.

"Where do you live now?" Clara asks him.

"A farm up in Pennsylvania. Cows and chickens, and me and my art. That's how I like it. Not Jessica, though. She craved being around people, and she couldn't have found work out there in any case. In the end, she presented herself as a widow. It suited me, anyway, to retreat from the world."

"To pretend to be dead?" Milly asks.

"To fade away, that's all. I'd been selling my paintings under a different name as it was. Still do."

"A. Frances?" I ask.

"No." He smiles. "That was a name she came up with, so we could write to each other without anyone thinking we were up to no good. She addresses my letters to A. Frances, to look as though she's writing to an aunt. I write my replies to Cousin Joan."

"You must have sold quite a lot of paintings," Milly says, gazing around at the restaurant's polished brass.

"Can't say I keep track." He slices into his asparagus with a spotless hotel knife. "For a while, I was barely getting by. Then the art world fashions changed, and suddenly my style of painting was *the* style. Jessica found an agent to handle the sales and accounting and all that. She knows I'm useless when it comes to money. Growing up with none will do that. When she moved down here, she reconciled with her uncle, and he set her up with a financial adviser in town."

"Did you ever come here to visit her?" I ask him.

"She visited me. We spent most holidays at the farm."

Mrs. Rose would've been ruined if any of this ever got out. Yet she went to the farm anyway. She went to the pictures with Victor, she smoked cigarettes on the street...

Who *was* Mrs. Rose? Truly?

It would all be easier to comprehend if this man turned out to be a liar.

"You didn't speak to anyone at the funeral." I try to make my words sound like observations, not accusations. "You didn't deliver a eulogy."

"I learned about her death, and the funeral, from the newspaper." He shakes his head. "I don't know who made the arrangements. Her uncle and his wife, I suppose. They still think I'm dead, and they wouldn't have recognized me anyway, given that we never met. As far as they're concerned, I was a mistake Jessica made for a few years, nothing more. I'd have been wiped from their memories altogether if it weren't for her name. They'd have happily gone on calling her Miss Blackwell if they could."

How convenient, for this man, that no one knows he's alive. It means we have no way to confirm his story.

But fictional or otherwise, there's only one reason he'd be telling us this. The same reason he stopped me on the street.

There's something he wants from us. From *me*.

"Why are you telling us all this?" I try to keep my face completely neutral, as though I'm merely curious.

"Jessica thought a lot of you." He smiles at me. "Smart, loyal Gertie. That's what she called you."

I order my cheeks not to flush. "I'm afraid I don't think that's a sufficient reason, Mr. Frances."

He raises his eyebrows. "She felt sorry for you, you know. You wanted to learn so much about her life. Asked her question after question. She hated that she couldn't tell you the truth. She wanted you to see how complicated things were in the real world. I think she'd have wanted me to tell you that, after everything."

He shrugs.

Shrugging isn't something a gentleman should do, not in a place like this. But then, this man isn't a gentleman. He seems to have no interest in society.

I've never known anyone like him.

"And I was hoping you could help me get some answers." He sets down his knife and fork and folds his hands in front of him, looking from Milly to Clara to me. I sit up straight, pushing my musings away, as his voice drops nearly to a whisper. "My wife was...Her death was..." He swallows. "It was no accidental poisoning. She deserves *true* justice."

"What makes you think we can help with that?" Milly asks.

"Well, the police are no use. When I went to the station and tried to ask the man at the desk for information, he laughed. Then I gave him twenty dollars, and he told me she died of drink."

"How do you know she didn't?" Clara asks him. "You read what the papers said."

"She'd never have touched that stuff. We were both tee-totalers."

I keep my face impassive. Some instinct tells me not to let this man know that Victor told us the same thing about Mrs. Rose and alcohol. "Because of Prohibition?"

"By choice. Prohibition's a violation of individual liberty, Jessica always said. But that man at the police station wouldn't listen to a word I had to say about any of it. I can't get in to see Damian Babcock, either. You three girls are the first people I've found in this city who'll talk to me."

"Mr. Babcock and Mrs. Rose didn't get along," Milly says. "I doubt he's as interested in justice for her as you are."

"He didn't want to hire her." The man nods. "But your school needed someone fast, and when she came down from New York, she sweet-talked him into giving her a try. Jessica can talk just about anybody into just about anything."

The knife slips out of his grasp, skitters across the plate. A passing waiter, not Danny, swoops in and sets it to rights.

"Could," the man corrects himself, raising his napkin to his face.

Is he *crying*?

Well. That doesn't prove him innocent.

"Why haven't you told the police who you are?" I ask him.

"You can guess the answer to that. If word got out that Jessica was still married, your sort would see that as a disgrace, and that's the last thing she wanted. I've got to do what I can

252

not to tarnish her memory any further. I trust *you* girls, but I certainly don't trust that man at the police desk, or the feds with their schemes."

"Then why are you still here, in the city?" I ask him. "Why not go back to your farm and your chickens?"

"I can't *leave.*" His lips part. It's the first time he's seemed at all surprised since we sat down. "This city is where *she* was. I can't…I can't…"

I nod. I understand.

He *can't* leave. Can't do anything. Can't go anywhere, without her.

He moves his fork through the air over his plate. My own fish and vegetables are mostly gone, but the man calling himself Richard Rose hasn't eaten since we sat down.

"Do you know a man named Victor?" I ask him after a moment of quiet.

"Jessica mentioned a Victor King. A friend."

I don't look at Milly, but I can envision her eyes alighting at this revelation of Victor's last name. "Were she and Mr. King…"

"Intimate? No."

I blush. "How can you be sure?"

"Several reasons."

I sit forward, keeping my face a mask. Does this man know the truth about Victor?

"The foremost being," he goes on, "that she and I never kept secrets from each other."

Yet it seems Mrs. Rose kept quite a lot of secrets from the rest of us.

"Do you consider Mr. King a suspect in her death?" I ask him.

"No." The word is short, but he makes it even shorter. "She trusted him. She wasn't someone who trusted easily."

Clara shifts in her seat.

"You said you aren't interested in financial matters." Milly taps her spoon against her plate. "Yet you also mentioned that Mrs. Rose's uncle connected her with a bank account, is that right? Shouldn't you have a shared account, as a married couple? Or wouldn't you have needed to give her permission to open a separate one?"

"Her family doesn't know I'm alive, so her uncle's consent was enough. She has a separate account. That is, *had*." The man rubs his temple. His food's growing colder on the plate in front of him. "Most of the money I earned went there, through some other account she had set up under a different name, of course. She didn't want it, but I sent it anyway. Your school barely paid her a salary."

"But her uncle must've known the money was yours," Milly says.

He shakes his head. "I use a different name, and it all goes through my agent. I don't know where she told them the money came from, or if they even realized she had any. Her uncle had a man to sort out the details. All very tactfully handled."

Milly frowns, clearly unsatisfied with this answer.

It's not entirely satisfying to me, either. This man isn't offering proof of this complicated arrangement. Or of anything else.

Perhaps Milly's been right all this time to concentrate her questions on money.

"It sounds as though you three are conducting your own investigation," the man says. "I'd wondered if we might come to a sort of agreement."

I glance at Milly again, then at Clara, but they're both looking to me. Waiting for an answer.

"What kind of agreement?" I ask him.

"We all want the same thing." He opens his hands, displaying his empty palms. "To see the person who…who did this, brought to justice. Perhaps, I thought, we could work together. But only if we can trust one another, and I'm not certain that's the case. It seems as though you came here today to interview a suspect, not meet with an ally."

I don't allow my face to change.

But he's right, of course. We came here to see a potential murderer. We still can't be sure he isn't one.

"I suppose I can understand that." He nods. "Someone very dangerous is out there. Jessica—Mrs. Rose—wouldn't want anything to happen to you girls. You're right to be cautious."

"Thank you," Clara murmurs softly at my side.

I can't shut my eyes here, not without drawing attention, but I wish I could. I need to make sense of all this.

This man has money. That's clear from the hotel, and the food, and the waiters' knowledge of exactly how well he tips.

If he's telling the truth, then quite a lot of money has been sitting, unused, in Mrs. Rose's private account.

Enough to justify murder?

It would have to have been someone close to her. Close enough to know the details of her finances, and how to get to them.

Victor said he and Mrs. Rose never talked about things like that. He could have been lying. But several of the things he told us have turned out to be true.

What could connect this to the seminary's finances, though? That discussion Mrs. Rose wanted to have with Damian Babcock the night she died?

I can't get all the pieces to fit together. Yet there's one thing I do know.

If Mrs. Rose was murdered over money—her own, her husband's, or the seminary's—then that means she didn't die from poisoned liquor, or some other scandal.

If we can *prove* that, her reputation might be cleared. The seminary's, too.

But the board is voting on whether to reopen in the next few days. Could we find a way to prove this before then? We're not even privy to our own families' budgets and bank statements, let alone Mrs. Rose's or the seminary's.

"Hope you've enjoyed your meal, girls." The man lowers his silver beside his plate of uneaten food. "Now, may I ask if you'll share with me what you've learned? Perhaps together, we can find some answers."

I glance at Milly and Clara. "We'll discuss it."

"Thank you." He stands, and we do the same. "I'll be in my room."

"It was good to meet you, Mr. Rose." Clara holds out her hand. "I'm very sorry for your loss."

The man clasps her hand in his. "You are the first person to say that to me, Miss Blum. Thank you. And to all of you, I'm very, very sorry for yours."

29

As soon as we leave the restaurant, Milly, Clara, and I scatter to opposite corners of the street. If one of us sees him leaving the hotel, we'll signal to the others, then follow.

He told us so much, without proving a word of it. It's up to us to figure out if there's truth to his story.

And so, when I spot a carved wooden cane passing by the propped-open hotel door from my perch at the northern end of the block, I call out our signal—a low, unladylike whistle—and start out after him.

We've already caught him in one lie. He said he was going to his room.

What else is he hiding?

I peer out from under my hat brim until I'm sure I see his knit tie and rumpled suit, then take careful, casual steps in his wake. I want to dash after him so he can't escape my sight, but I can't risk him seeing. Besides, I shouldn't draw attention to myself. In my black coat and dark, plain cloche, I could be any of a hundred women out on Connecticut Avenue this afternoon.

He isn't moving particularly fast, though, and when I step out onto the street, he's only half a block ahead of me. When he turns, I have to dart behind a tree to avoid being spotted. After that I stay farther back, mirroring his slow, even pace.

Then a streetcar slows to a stop in front of him, and he climbs on, his hand firm on the pole.

When the car speeds up again, I'm sure to lose him. Even if

I could run as fast as the streetcar, I certainly wouldn't go unnoticed chasing after it.

I face the street with a feigned casual expression, as if I'm merely out Christmas shopping, and lift my hand.

A taxi pulls over. The driver steps down to help me into the back, the brass buttons on his uniform gleaming in the afternoon sun. His accent is faintly Irish. "Where to, miss?"

"Could you possibly, ah..." I don't know how to say this. "Follow that streetcar up ahead?"

The driver turns back, his hat tilting up. He's about my age, his skin red from the cold. "Sorry, miss, not sure I quite heard?"

"That streetcar, please. I'm trying to follow to...to see where a certain rider is headed."

The driver chuckles. "That's what I thought you said. All right, then, miss, off we go."

He turns on the motor and swerves back into traffic. It's busy at this time of day, and several automobiles are close behind us. One of them honks for my driver to move faster, but he stays behind the streetcar, just as I asked.

"You going to tell me when you see your fellow get off, miss?" he asks, twisting so I can hear him over the wind.

"Yes."

"You'll have time to pay before you go running after him?"

I take two coins out of my handbag and drop them into his outstretched palm. "Will that do?"

"Yes, it will, miss." The streetcar speeds up, and we do, too, the driver smiling with my coins in his pocket.

The streetcar stops at the next block, and we stop, too. Another honk sounds behind us as cars swerve around the taxi. I watch the people descending from the car closely, but the man I'm looking for isn't among them.

We carry on like that for several blocks, stopping to watch

the people get on and off, climbing steadily north. Soon we're leaving the office buildings of downtown behind, nearing the outskirts of the city. If this keeps up, we'll be back at Chevy Chase Lake. We're already almost to the Connecticut Avenue Bridge, with its alarming lion statues at each end and the huge, gaping arches underneath.

The streetcar stops again, and us with it. The taxi driver turns back, probably to demand more payment for coming out this far, but as I'm preparing to argue that the coins I gave him should've been more than sufficient, I spot the carved wooden cane descending from the streetcar's platform.

"There!" I cry, jumping up and fumbling for the door handle. "That's him!"

"*That* fellow?" The taxi driver doesn't sound impressed.

"Help me, please, the door is sticking—"

He takes his time, climbing down from his seat in the front and whistling a little tune as he unlatches the back door for me. "Wish I had dames chasing me down in streetcars," he mutters.

I pretend not to have heard. "Thank you ever so."

The man is far ahead already, walking with his cane out in front of him, and I set after him, mirroring his pace.

Can't draw attention. Can't draw attention.

He crosses the next block and turns down a dirt path lined with trees to one side and a bare, narrow road to the other. Surely he hasn't come all this way to take a walk in a country lane?

There aren't enough people here for me to be inconspicuous. If he looks back, he'll spot me for sure. Fortunately, he doesn't seem to be taking much note of anything as he marches on.

There's no wind here, no voices, no traffic. Only birds and the rustles of dead leaves. The houses are spread far apart, not connected to one another like they are in my neighborhood, and they're set back from the street, with wide expanses of brown lawn out front.

I haven't seen a soul aside from this man since the taxi left ten minutes ago, yet it doesn't feel like we're alone here, either. And I'm getting that feeling again. As though someone's watching me.

I check the houses I pass for curtains stirring in the windows. There's nothing.

But the man ahead is slowing down. Pausing at an iron gate set into a long stone retaining wall. I stop walking as he opens the iron gate and steps inside, climbing the small slope of the cemetery path.

I can't bring myself to watch as he slowly ascends the hill to his wife's grave.

There's a tree near the iron gate, thick enough to conceal me from view, and I drop down against it, tucking my coat under me and crossing my legs with my knees bent so my stockings won't rip on the dead grass.

It's astonishingly quiet. The wind never does pick up. And so all I can hear as I wait under the tree's branches is a chirping cardinal, a brush of leaves, and Mr. Rose's voice, weeping.

I hear her voice before I hear her footsteps.

"It's me." Milly speaks softly. Even in a far-off cemetery, with darkness starting to fall, the sound coming out of nowhere doesn't frighten me. I know my Milly. Even when she doesn't sound quite like herself. "Is he still here?"

I shake my head. "He left a few minutes ago. I stuck to the shadows so he wouldn't see me."

Milly glances toward the road. "You're sure?"

I nod.

"Good." Now she sounds like Milly. Confident. Unafraid. "May I join you under your tree?"

I nod, and she smooths out her fur-trimmed Paris-made coat to sit on the grass.

"How did you find me?" I ask.

"I certainly wasn't going to let you run off alone after a potential murderer. I had Clara stay and keep watch in case he doubled back, and I got a taxi. I tried to follow yours, but my driver wasn't as adept. Fortunately, it wasn't difficult to deduce that Mr. Frances would have come this way."

"You don't think Mr. Rose is his real name, then?"

"To be honest..." Milly shrugs. "He struck me as entirely believable. Particularly given that you've followed him *here*, of all places. The trouble is there's no way to prove a word of what he says."

"I was thinking exactly the same."

"She did the right thing, though, separating from him. No one wants to go to a school run by some bohemian artist's wife, rich or otherwise."

It sounds harsh, but Milly's right.

What kind of person *was* Mrs. Rose? She lied about being widowed. She hid her friendship with Victor. And we still don't know why she died surrounded by liquor bottles, even though two men who know her far better than I did have both insisted she didn't drink.

Did Mrs. Rose change who she was, who she wanted to be, simply so she could pretend to belong in a place like the Washington Female Seminary?

Or was it the seminary that failed *her*? Should we have found a way to make it the sort of place where she wouldn't have had to hide?

I'm not sure that's possible. Isn't that's why places like the Seven Seas exist? So everyone can have a place to belong?

"Do you think Mr. Rose killed his wife?" I ask Milly after a moment.

"No." Her answer comes quick and easy. "Victor did that."

I nod. "I thought you'd have gone straight to the library, now that you know his last name."

Milly stretches back, staring up into the branches above us. They're bare and spidery. "All I know about Victor is that he's a liar, and the worst kind. The sort who makes you like him, then twists his lies around until you look like a fool for listening."

I don't respond. Milly's description of Victor sounds strikingly familiar.

A moment later, I realize why: Her words could just as easily apply to her own father.

"All he cares about is money," she goes on, and again, the parallels make me want to squirm. "Men like that are all the same. Always looking for their next opportunity to grow richer than they already are."

Victor's raccoon coat certainly didn't come cheap. I nod. "You think he stood to profit from Mrs. Rose's death?"

"I'm certain of it. She might have been a pathway for him to wealthier clientele. Like that man who provides the Babcocks with their personal supply. They're bound to pay *him* quite handsomely. A job like that might be a significant raise for your buddy Victor."

I don't know what to make of her calling Victor my *buddy*. "He did say he used to make house calls."

"Perhaps he and Mrs. Rose had some kind of arrangement, then, and it went wrong. And she wound up dead." Milly shrugs again. "The police will work out the details once we tell them about Victor."

"Will they get it right, though? Mr. Rose didn't seem to think much of their abilities."

Milly's lips form an uncertain line. I don't think she likes the idea of leaving this all up to the police any more than I do.

I don't want to see Victor arrested simply for the sake of *someone* paying the price for Mrs. Rose's murder. I want the *right* person to wind up behind bars.

Still, Victor could've told us some of what he did to throw us off track. Mr. Rose was right. We need to be careful whom we trust.

"His name isn't Victor King," Milly says after a moment.

I blink over at her. "Sorry?"

"That's not his real name. The librarian helped me find some arrest records yesterday, for bootlegging, but they weren't for Victor King. They were for a Johannes Viktor Koning. I didn't know for sure if there was a connection, but after this, it's got to be him. Too many of the details match. The address was only a block from the House Office Building, and the physical description was right. And *Koning* means *king* in Dutch."

I shake my head. "That doesn't sound like conclusive proof to me."

"Well, in addition..." Milly gives me a tentative smile. "Remember Byron? That young copper who brought us back to the seminary that night?"

"Yes."

"Well. I saw him again this morning. It was all so rushed, there was no time to tell you about it before we had to go meet Mr. Frances."

"Oh."

"And I've learned a few things. Including that Victor's been known to use a number of different aliases, and that the police know exactly who he is. They've been looking for an opportunity to arrest him again."

"For Mrs. Rose's murder?"

"Byron said they'd be happy to arrest him for pretty much

anything. They know he's ... Well. Gay. Only that's not the word they use."

I wrench my eyes back to Milly's face. "I'm surprised to hear you use it. After what you said the other night."

"Oh." Milly cuts her eyes to the grass at our feet. "I ... I'm sorry."

I don't answer her. I don't want to think about that at the moment. "What else did this Byron say?"

"That Victor used to know a fancy lawyer who got him out of prison last time, but the lawyer's skipped town. The next time they bring Victor in, they don't intend to let him out."

I shake my head. "It doesn't sound like they're interested in justice."

"I agree. But unfortunately for them, Victor took off."

I straighten up, rigid. "What do you mean?"

"Byron told me the Prohibition Bureau found Victor's office in the Capitol and went to arrest him, but the whole place was cleared out. His apartment, too. It looks like he's left the city."

My mouth drops open. I can't believe Milly didn't tell me all this the instant she learned it. "What does this mean?"

"That he killed her, obviously. He's guilty of murder, and he's trying to run."

Milly's face is so calm, so relaxed. I don't understand it. "I simply don't see how you can be so sure of that."

"Isn't it you who always says simple explanations most often suffice? He was *there* that night. He's the only one who we know for sure was with Mrs. Rose, because we *saw* him. With our own eyes."

I shake my head. "That's not *proof*."

"We aren't detectives, Gertie. We can't always be the ones to find rock-solid physical evidence, but that doesn't mean our conclusions can't be the right ones." Milly leans back, staring up into the trees. "Besides, Victor's a businessman who's used to operating outside the law, and in the end, everything comes down to money. That's what my father always says, and he should know, given how fixated he is on ours."

I turn to face her. I'm startled at this new route in the conversation, but at the same time, I'm not.

Milly never talks about her family's money. The Otises have been rich for generations, but they don't brag about it the way the Babcocks do. Yet now, it seems, there's something Milly wants to say. Something she wants me to ask.

"I didn't realize your father was so fixated on money," I say, struggling not to squirm at my own disingenuousness.

"Not as much as he should be, in my opinion. Not that he's ever interested in hearing *that*. I've tried to tell him not to rely so much on investments. Should the stock market ever turn, we'll be down to nothing."

Milly's the only girl I know who reads the parts of the newspaper that deal with banks and stocks. She'd like to work in bonds, she told me once, if such a thing were allowed for girls.

"Let's hope that never happens, then," I say. "And you can keep going on all those family trips to Paris in the summers."

"Did I give the impression that we take *family* trips?" Milly laughs again, sharply. "No, no. This year, my parents *brought* us to Paris, then left my brother and me to find our own amusement while they went off on a private tour of the Riviera. My brother sampled French wines, and I sampled French boys, and we both spent much of the summer vomiting in French gutters."

She ends this speech on a very high pitch, but I don't think she's joking. We've both read enough novels under the covers to know what it means when girls suddenly find themselves vomiting.

"Which French boys?" I ask her.

"Oh…" She sighs. "Just Pierre. He was the son of a count. Of course France doesn't have those anymore, but everyone knows who's descended from whom. It's all a lie. Like the rest."

I nod slowly. "Is Pierre the one who writes you letters?"

"No, that's Jean-Luc." She smiles, not as brightly as before. "Jean-Luc's a nice boy, as it turned out. Pierre never wrote to me. Not after… Well."

I'm fairly certain she wants me to ask this, too. "After… the vomiting?"

Milly shrugs. "After I told him, Pierre proved himself to be *not* a nice boy."

I glance around once more, confirming that we're entirely alone as I count out the months in my head. "Milly, did you… were you…"

Alone or otherwise, I can't bring myself to say the word *pregnant*. I'm already blushing at the thought of it.

"No! No, as it turned out. Ha!" Milly lets out another laugh. Her face has gone white. If I took her hand, I'd feel her pulse racing, I'm sure of it. But I don't think she wants to be touched at the moment. "I thought I was, though. For much of the summer. That was the last I saw of Pierre, naturally. The morning after I told him, he departed for Madrid. Didn't so much as leave a note. I should never have expected more from a count's son. Next, I'll try a duke's!"

Now I do take her hand. "Did you tell anyone else?"

"No. Never. I was ashamed. Isn't that funny? Being ashamed over such a trifling bit of nonsense?"

"It isn't trifling. Or nonsense." I stare into Milly's face. She won't look at me. "I wish you'd told me."

All this time, she's been keeping it secret, that she was with this French boy. This horrible boy who treated her like nothing. She must have thought I would judge her for it.

Me. Her best friend.

Me, who cares for her more than anything in the world.

But then. I haven't told Milly my new secret, either. She's telling me her hardest thing, and I can't tell her mine.

Now I'm the one who feels ashamed.

"Anyway. I've made mistakes, and I've paid the price." Milly scrubs at her cheeks. "So no, I don't see any harm in some admitted criminal going off to jail. And that's why—as sorry as I am for you, because I know how much you miss Mrs. Rose—well, I can't say that I feel the same. If she chose to spend her time with someone like Victor King, or whatever his name is, then...it's very unfortunate what happened to her, but it may also have been inevitable. She made mistakes, too."

I draw back. "You're not saying she *deserved* to..."

"Certainly not." Milly brushes at her cheeks again. "But you heard what her husband said. Mrs. Rose thought she could flout the rules. Be whoever she wanted. Be ever so kind and helpful to girls like *you*, and Clara, so much so that you want to go on helping her even after she's gone—yet she insisted *we* had to follow the rules. And all the while, she was stealing away every night herself. Lying to everyone, without remorse. Now, with her death, she might have destroyed the seminary. The one place where girls like us could truly *be*."

Now we're both crying.

I put my arms around Milly. I draw her to me, trying to feel her heartbeat beneath thick layers of coats and scarves.

I hold her, like I've held her so many times before. Yet there's something new about it, too.

"We have to get back there," Milly says into my wool-clad shoulder. She turns until her face is angled toward mine, her breath and her voice tickling my ear. "We can't let them take it from us."

I nod. My face is warm in her soft fur collar, and my chest

feels strangely warm, too. "I hate to think of it standing there forever, cold and empty."

Her arm tightens around my waist. "We're supposed to be there. Together."

I nod again into the softness.

Mrs. Rose *did* make mistakes. She chose the wrong associates. Perhaps she even played favorites with us girls.

Perhaps I've been wrong, all this time, aspiring to be like her.

And perhaps it's because I'm so focused on Mrs. Rose's mistakes, and my own, that when I draw back again and meet Milly's soft, warm gaze, I nearly lose all propriety and restraint, and I very, very nearly give in to my sudden, all-consuming desire to bring my lips crashing down onto hers.

30

I'm DIZZY ALL AFTERNOON. OFF-BALANCE. THE WORLD IS TILTING on its axis, but only I can feel it.

It's no better by the following day, when my mother brings both Milly and me on her final shopping excursion of the year. All morning long, and over lunch, too, as my mother and Milly sit at the table politely discussing ball preparations and the dressmaker's schedule, I don't look up. I can barely muster an appropriate thank-you for Sarah when she takes my barely touched plate of pickled lamb tongue sandwich and sliced bananas with cream back to the kitchen.

"We should go see Damian Babcock at the railroad company this afternoon," Milly whispers when my mother steps away. "It'll be his last day at work before Christmas. Without his family around, we might be able to get some information about Mrs. Rose's finances."

I nod. It's a good idea. But I can't look her in the eye.

What does it mean, that I wanted to kiss her yesterday?

That I still want to kiss her now?

What does it mean for Clara and me? And what would it mean if Milly somehow found out?

I remember, all too well, what she said about Victor. About people like him.

People like *me*.

"All right." I nod again without looking up.

"I've already called Clara. She's meeting us here."

Now I do look up. With alarm. "When?"

"In a few minutes." Milly frowns at me. "Is something wrong?"

Everything's wrong.

I can't see Milly and Clara *together.* How will I look at either one of them without breaking into pieces?

"It's fine." I nod again. "Everything's fine."

Surely Milly can see that nothing's fine at all. She knows me as well as I know her. But she nods, too.

When Clara arrives shortly afterward, I'm sure, for an instant, that she'll see it on my face. But all she does is smile, her eyes lighting up when they land on me.

I feel like the worst kind of traitor. Yet I find myself answering her glittering gaze with a smile of my own.

Is it possible to feel the same way about two different people at the same time? Two *girls*?

We take the streetcar downtown. Milly and Clara talk about the ball, about dresses and orchestras, and I shut my eyes, trying not to look at either of them.

Trying to make sense of all the pieces. Yet I can't get them to fit together no matter how hard I try.

The shawl tied to my door rail. The *other* shawl, bloodied and thrust into a cabinet in a linen closet.

The raid on the Lazy Susan, with the photographer's bulbs flashing. The matchbook. The bottles on the floor.

We're close. I can feel it, like another itch. But there's a piece missing, and I can't make sense of the whole without it. I'm no closer to putting it all together than I was yesterday in the cemetery, listening to Mr. Rose's sobs.

I need help from someone who knew Mrs. Rose better than I did. Someone who knows this city, too. Understands how it works. The corners I've never been to.

"We need to see Victor again," I mutter to Milly and Clara as we climb out of the streetcar down the block from the railroad company's office building.

They both turn to stare at me, quizzically. I force myself to look back. To act normal. There's still a murderer out there. And if the seminary doesn't reopen, I might not get to be with Milly *or* Clara again.

"Victor left the city," Milly says.

"He might have," I say. "Or he might be well hidden."

"You think you can find him when the coppers can't?"

"Perhaps. They don't know about the Seven Seas. If they did, they'd have shut it down."

"You want to go to the Seven Seas *again*?" Clara's voice is heavy with concern.

"It's the perfect place for him to stay concealed."

"Well, we can't," Milly says. "We're going to see Mr. Babock, and after that we need to get home to meet the dressmaker."

"And I have to go get ready for Shabbat Chanukah," Clara adds. "My father's expecting me."

"Right." I'd forgotten. We won't see Clara again until the ball tomorrow night.

I want to take her hand. To press it and hold her close.

But Milly would see.

It's cold and gray, and all three of us shiver in our day dresses as we walk, passing businessmen and shoppers, government workers and laborers. Everyone moving fast, heads bent against the chill.

"Which building is it?" Clara asks.

"Number twelve-thirteen," Milly tells her. "On the next block."

"Then...is that him? Up ahead?"

I look up just in time to see for myself. Damian Babcock, wrapped in a thick black coat, is climbing into the back of a taxi, shutting the door behind him. I nearly call out after him, but it's already too late.

"We have to get another taxi, fast." I stand up on my toes, waving my arm. "We can follow him."

But there aren't any other taxis. The street is packed with cars, but not a single taxi sign. There no streetcars in sight, either.

I adjust my handbag, poised to run, but Milly lays a hand on my arm. "We can't go running in the *street*. Someone might see."

"But..." Mr. Babcock's taxi is already turning the corner, vanishing. It's too late to dash after him. "He might not come back today, and tomorrow's Christmas Eve. We won't have another chance."

"We can wait here and see," Milly says. "In that Automat across the street. Take turns keeping eyes on the building."

"I'm afraid I can't." Clara looks at her watch. "I have to go meet my father soon."

It feels as though we're giving up, but there's nothing to do except nod.

Clara goes to catch a streetcar back to her hotel, and Milly and I cross at the intersection. The sidewalks are growing even more crowded with shoppers, forcing us to step around them, and Milly loses her footing on a wet patch. "Oh!"

I grab her arm before she can topple into the crowd. "Are you all right?"

"It's these ridiculous shoes." Milly scuffs her black patent leather Mary Janes against the pavement. "I..."

Then Milly stops, her eyes latching on to something in the alley to our right. I turn to look, too.

The man's big hands are clasped in front of him, his

ungloved fingers rubbing together. As if he's washing them without water.

His felt hat is low over his eyes, his olive-green jacket pulling tight across his shoulders. He's turned to study the brick wall beside him, but there's no question that it's the same man.

He must sense us looking, because he peers up from under his hat. His gaze meets mine, and for an instant, I stare straight into his eyes. They're brown, and focused, full of intent. Wide with fear, too.

I wonder how long he's been following us. He must've thought there was no chance we'd ever spot him.

Is this how he looked when he strangled Mrs. Rose? Did she look him in the eye, just as I'm doing now? When his thick fingers wrapped around her shawl...

I'm shuddering so fiercely I nearly lose my balance.

The man takes a step toward us. His big hands reach out, and I can picture it, so clearly. Him reaching for my neck. The sensation of his fingers closing around it. Tightening. The breath slowly seeping out of me. Like hers did.

Then he turns away. Slips into the crowd, so fast it's as though he vanished.

I can't let him vanish. Not again. He's not a ghost. He's real, and I'm not letting him go.

"Gertie!"

By the time I realize Milly's calling me, I'm already running.

31

I TURN THE CORNER INTO THE ALLEY, ELBOWING THROUGH THE crowd, boots slamming into the pavement.

I see him. He didn't vanish, not truly. Not yet.

The man's charging down the short alley at breathtaking speed, but I'm right in his wake. He sprints straight out into the street, in the path of two cars, without looking up. One swerves to avoid him.

"Gertie!" I'm about to cross the street after him when Milly grabs my arm again. I snatch it away. She's out of breath from chasing after me. "What's going on?"

I have to wait until there are no cars before I can cross, and by then the man has gotten farther ahead, already approaching the end of the next block. I take off, stumbling over a glass bottle half-full of brown liquid lying in the street.

When I look up again, he's gone.

"What are you *doing*?" Milly's at my elbow again, panting.

"Where did he go?!"

"I don't know. I suppose into one of those stores? Or he turned onto Eighteenth? What are you—"

I break back into a run.

"Gertie!" Milly's voice is a hiss at my back. "Stop! You can't!"

But I can't wait. I *need* to catch up to that man. I need to understand where he fits in with all of this.

I take the corner onto Eighteenth Street at full speed, as though I'm running down the basketball court, and come very close to barreling into two white-haired women. They're both dressed in mink, and they both shriek at our near-collision.

"Beg your pardon!" I say, too loud, and skitter past them. The man's up ahead, on the opposite side of N Street.

I run, not bothering to wait for cars anymore. I'm fast enough to pass them anyway. I've left Milly somewhere far behind.

The man never looks back.

He turns again, but this time I don't take my eyes off him as he veers onto Massachusetts Avenue, cutting across the street into traffic. The streetcar is coming, and a half dozen motorcars at a fast clip, too, and I'm forced to dodge honking horns and squealing tires until I see the man descend a set of steps leading belowground. A faded green awning comes into view.

He's gone down the steps into Duke's.

The street clears and I run across, stumbling over another discarded bottle. When I arrive, there are voices murmuring below.

I slow down enough to catch my breath and listen. I didn't see anyone else go down the steps to Duke's. Whoever's speaking must've already been down there.

I step around the low concrete barrier to peer under the awning. The man with the big hands has taken off his hat, revealing the back of a round, bald head. I can't get close enough to see who he's talking to.

"All of them?" asks the person I can't see. It's a man's voice, but I don't recognize it. "You're certain they didn't see you?"

There's an answering murmur in a thick Italian accent, too low and heavy for me to understand. Then the first voice speaks again.

"And you're ready for your trip?"

"No!" Now the man with the big hands is speaking clearly, loudly. "I told you, I need more."

The first man answers, too low for me to make out the words, but the other man's voice rises in response.

"When?" He's growing angry. There's another pause. More inaudible murmurs. Then, "Fine. Two o'clock tomorrow. I will be here again."

A hand lands on my arm. I manage not to scream.

"What is *wrong* with you?" Milly's finally caught up to me, flushed and out of breath, her lips so close to my ear that her voice covers up anything more the men might be saying. "What are we *doing* here?"

I hold a finger to my lips, but the voices don't come again.

I take Milly's elbow—gently, not at all the way she grabbed me—and steer her to the end of the block, still keeping Duke's in sight.

"That was him," I murmur.

"That was *who*?"

"The man who shouted at you that night outside the East Room." I stare hard at the awning. We're alone in this stretch of sidewalk, but on a busy morning like this, we won't be for long. "The man who was lurking outside Victor's office. He had something to do with Mrs. Rose's death. At least…I *think* he did."

"*What?*" Milly's eyes have begun to blaze. "You can't just run out into the street after some man! You could've been hit by a car, or…or he could've done something to hurt you!"

"But he didn't. Milly, do you think…"

A dramatically loud throat-clearing behind us forces us both to turn around.

The two mink-coated women I nearly crashed into a moment

ago are standing in front of Milly and me with coordinated frowns, and it's only now that I recognize them as Mrs. Patterson and Mrs. Paul. Both of whom are staring at me as though I'm a dirty coffee cup at the bottom of a pristine white sink.

Milly's angry flush transforms into a smile, and she bobs a tiny curtsy. "How do you do, Mrs. Patterson. Mrs. Paul."

"How do you do," I echo automatically, though it sounds hollow and absurd in my own ears.

We can't stand here exchanging pleasantries. The instant that man emerges from those steps, I have to tear off after him, or risk losing him forever.

I can't let that happen. Not when we're this close.

Those *hands*. I can't stop picturing those enormous hands. Winding that shawl around Mrs. Rose's throat.

He must have known her. Or worked for someone who did.

"Cold day, isn't it?" Milly asks with a perfectly polite air about her, as though we couldn't be more delighted to be stuck talking to these two old ninnies. She holds out a hand to shake, and I mimic her, mutely.

How can I find out who that man is? How can I get proof of what he's done?

"Indeed," Mrs. Paul says. She's taller than Mrs. Patterson by a half-inch or so, the result of her low, fashionable heels. Though I'm taller than them both. "You're Ambassador Otis's girl."

"Yes, Mrs. Paul."

"Millicent."

"Yes, indeed."

"And you." Mrs. Patterson bores her eyes into me. "You'll remember us, of course, Miss Pound. Well-bred girls always do."

I couldn't possibly be less interested in what "well-bred" girls do.

"Of *course.*" The words come out too fast, my impatience clearly audible, and I remember the word I once applied in my own mind to Mrs. Rose. *Brash.*

The men must have gone inside Duke's. The restaurant might as well be a hole in the ground that's swallowed them up.

Can I get in, too? But I don't know the password, or the correct number of knocks.

I could hide until the man leaves, then follow him. A murderer is bound to do something criminal if he thinks no one's watching. If I see him do it, I could go to the police. They could make the arrest, and he could tell the police who hired him, and both of them could go to jail.

That would be justice for Mrs. Rose. It wouldn't bring her back, but it would be something.

"Your mother is one of the most gracious ladies in this city," Mrs. Paul informs me. It's growing colder out, and she sniffs against the chill. "I'll be certain to tell her I saw you here."

"Thank you, ma'am," I say, my words running together, years of lessons on proper enunciation lost to me.

What will my mother do when Mrs. Paul tells her about this?

Do I care?

My fingers are going frigid inside my kidskin gloves. I wrap my arms around my chest and rub them.

"I'm surprised to hear you thank me for *that,*" Mrs. Paul says.

"Yes, ma'am."

What if he spots me when he comes out? He could start chasing me, instead of the other way around. My top speed may not be enough to save me.

I slide my hands into my coat pockets. Some vague instinctual memory tells me that reaching into one's pockets while greeting an older lady on the street is bound to be against etiquette, though I've never actually heard it stated as such.

"Gertrude, your mother has certainly told you that one of the fundamental rules of good breeding is to greet your elders by name," Mrs. Paul goes on. "You needn't call either of us *ma'am*. It's Mrs. Patterson and Mrs. Paul, thank you."

Milly steps in.

"Please, forgive us, Mrs. Patterson, Mrs. Paul," she says swiftly, in a voice containing a quantity of desperation noticeable only to me. "I was escorting Miss Pound to Dr. Garrison's office. As you can see, she's not herself this morning. I suspect it's the weather, but best to be safe, you know."

"Seems like more than weather to me." Mrs. Paul looks down her nose at me, which can't be easy given that I'm a full three inches taller. "She very nearly knocked us off our feet, and you both know better than to call attention to yourselves in public."

My gloved fingers brush the edge of a piece of notepaper, folded neatly in half.

I didn't put any papers in my coat pocket.

"You're right, of course," Milly tells them as my heartbeat quickens. "I hope you'll accept my apologies, but I really must get Miss Pound to Dr. Garrison."

"You ought to have taken a taxi, and brought Mrs. Pound's maid along," Mrs. Patterson says. I crane my neck around her, but I still don't see anyone climbing the steps out of Duke's. "With your mother abroad, Miss Otis, I shall need to speak with Mrs. Pound about this as well. I'll call on her in advance of Mrs. Babcock's Christmas Eve party. It wouldn't be an appropriate conversation for a ballroom."

"We understand, Mrs. Patterson." Milly nods her head so deeply it's almost a bow. "Goodbye."

As she drags me away, I yank the paper out of my pocket and uncrease it, my fingers trembling.

The script is neat, the ink so fresh it's spread across the paper. The handwriting matches the note I found stabbed through with a nail, tied to my shawl on the railing:

Stop. Or you'll get what she did.

32

I STUMBLE DOWN A BLOCK, THEN ANOTHER. MILLY TROTS AFTER me with frantic footsteps. She won't risk speaking aloud, not when there's a chance Mrs. Paul or Mrs. Patterson might hear.

Finally, when we reach the streetcar line, I stop running and thrust the note into Milly's hands.

"What is it?" She reads it quickly, then looks up with alarm on her face. "Where did you get this?"

"*He* put it in my pocket." I raise my hand, but the car isn't in sight. This isn't an official stop, but the driver might slow down if he sees me. I turn and start walking toward the nearest stop, though, another block south, just in case.

I have to go talk to Victor. Another piece of this puzzle is still out there, and I'm certain he's the one who can help me find it.

"The man who did it," I say, when Milly still looks confused. "The one who killed her. We *have* to find Victor."

"How? Wait—what do you mean, the man who did it?"

"He must've slipped the note in there before we saw him. He's been watching us. *Following* us." I shake my head. I can't think about that part, not now. I have to think about what's coming next. "We've got to go."

"Where? This streetcar'll be heading east."

"East is where we need to go. To the Navy Yard. The Seven Seas."

"*That* place again? It's too dangerous!"

"Everywhere is dangerous." We haven't reached the stop yet, but the streetcar is coming into view. "Milly. He put that *in my pocket.* Come with me, we'll be safer together."

"We'll be safer *at your house.*"

The streetcar's almost here. The driver's slowing down, but not enough to come to a full stop. "I'm serious. Come on."

"I'm serious, too. Your mother expects you home to meet the dressmaker, and with the ball tomorrow—"

"Who cares about the ball?" I'm very close to shouting, but the streetcar covers the sound of my voice. And anyway, there are more important things to worry about. "We're *close.* I can feel it. Soon we'll know what really happened to her!"

"Is she all you care about? She's dead. She doesn't need you anymore. We *do*!"

The car screeches past us. I reach out and grab a pole, hoisting myself up onto the ledge. "Come on!"

"I said I was serious."

"Come *on*!"

But it's too late. The car's speeding up. Without Milly.

She shouts something more, but it's lost to the screeching of the wheels.

My heart is still hammering in my chest when I step off by the Navy Yard. The streets are quieter in daylight, with men in uniforms walking soberly and with intent, and women in neat suits and day dresses vanishing into offices.

I find the Seven Seas easily enough, but it looks different. The rusted handle is still there, with the stained DANGER 6000 VOLTS sign, but the painted glass on the top half of the door is shattered, with jagged edges, and the padlock is gone.

Have the police discovered the Seven Seas after all?

I glance over both shoulders. There's no one here but me. A gust of cold wind howls past.

I knock on the lower part of the door, two times, like the man in the top hat did that night. No response.

I draw in a breath and twist the handle, my soft leather gloves digging into the rusted metal.

The door opens soundlessly, dust blowing into my face. I manage not to cough as I peer into the darkness. The temperature is barely warmer than the outside air. I glance back, listening, but there's no sound behind me, and no light ahead.

I square my shoulders. I'm wearing my blue plaid coat over my dress. I look terribly young, terribly innocent. Perhaps that will protect me.

I need to find Victor. I need him to be here.

I need to see what's in this place, too. I know it won't be like that theater Clara went to, full of women with violets pinned to their dresses, but it could still be the kind of place where people like us belong.

I start forward, feeling along the wall for a light switch.

"You've got the wrong place."

The voice is a man's, low and gruff. Scratchy, like a match being struck.

I lift my chin, the brim of my hat soaring. "I've come to inquire about Mr. Victor King."

"Never heard of him." It's a new voice that answers. Pitched higher, but not by much.

The door swings shut behind me. My breath hitches, but I don't flinch.

"I beg your pardon," I say. "I meant Mr. Johannes Viktor Koning."

In another room, barely visible through a crack in a door ahead, a bulb flickers on. The light it casts is orange and faint, but it's enough for me to get a glimpse of the space around me. It's some kind of entryway, empty of furniture, with only a few feet of distance from wall to wall. No one else is in the room with me, but on the other side of the thin wall, I can hear motion. The door to the outside must have been blown shut by the wind. No one is close enough to have closed it.

The higher voice speaks again through the crack in the door. "You a fed?"

The first voice, the gruff one, answers. "She's a baby."

I seize on his words. "I'm only seventeen. I'm not with the police, I promise you."

A pause. A long silence.

Low voices sound behind the door. The two men who spoke, and a third, too.

"They screwed up the lock," I hear. There's a muttered curse in response. Then more murmurs I can't make out.

Finally, a man steps through to face me, closing the door behind him, and I draw in a breath as my eyes strain to adjust to the low light emanating from the broken glass door at my back.

It's the man I spoke to outside that night. He was wearing a top hat then. Today he's dressed in another three-piece suit, his head bare. His graying hair is slick and perfectly even, his tie is neat blue silk, and his watch chain is tucked and shined. The folded silk handkerchief in his jacket pocket is stark white and freshly pressed.

He's indistinguishable from the men we saw streaming into the House Office Building. For all I know, he could be one of those very men.

"Hello again." The man's as polite and well spoken as he

was before, but without the theatricality. "Miss Smith, if I recall correctly?"

I don't blink. "That's right."

"Once again, you've come where you're not wanted."

I do blink this time, but I lift my chin higher than before. "I need to find Mr. King. I knew his friend, Jessica Rose. She was headmistress at my school."

The man considers this, then nods. "I heard what happened to her. It's too bad. But we can't help you here."

I bite my lip. "The police..."

"Yes, we know all about the police." The man crosses his arms, his fingers rubbing the fine fabric of his jacket, as if itching for a cigar. "They were kind enough to pay us a visit the same night you did. As you can see, we haven't had time to redecorate."

What? The police raided the Seven Seas *that night*?

Was it...It couldn't have been *because* of us. It's a coincidence, it has to be.

"You need to leave." The man's arms are still folded tight.

"Did Mr. King, or Mr. Koning, come here the Saturday before last? Around ten thirty?"

He sighs. "What if he did?"

"It would mean he has an alibi for Mrs. Rose's death." My words flow out in a rush. "If someone saw him here—you, or one of your...friends. You could tell the police that. You could keep Victor from getting arrested!"

The man watches me say all this, his eyebrows raised. "You finished?"

I shift my weight from one foot to the other. I want to wrap my coat tighter, bury myself in it. I can't see anything beyond the door behind him. Only that faint outline of orange light.

This man doesn't think I belong here.

Would he think differently if he knew what happened between me and Clara?

But it's not as though I can tell him. I don't know the code for this.

He looks down at me, his gaze hard. A long, quiet moment passes between us.

"Look." He sighs finally, and drops his arms. "Maybe he *did* come here. Maybe he came that night, and every other night, too. Maybe all of us did."

My heart lifts. "That's perfect! If you could only tell—"

"Tell *who*?" He shakes his head. "How old did you say you are?"

"Seventeen," I mutter. I might as well have said *five*.

"All right, well, Victor doesn't want us telling anybody anything, and you better not think for one more second you're gonna tell anybody a damn thing, either. I guess I felt sorry for you. Coming all the way here, thinking it'll help."

"But..." My stomach drops. I don't even flinch at the curse. "The police are looking for him. He's your friend, isn't he?"

"And the last thing he'd want is anybody else going down with him. Which is what'll happen if any of us talks to the feds. You included."

The man's language doesn't match his neat, government-man appearance. Looking at him, it feels as though my own father is standing here, cursing and talking about the *feds*. "But he could be charged with *murder*."

"Yeah, and if he'd still been here Tuesday night instead of out chatting with you and your girlfriend at that Automat, he'd be dead."

I freeze. "What do you mean?"

"Those copper friends of yours?"

"I don't have any copper friends."

"The fellows who got here right after you and him disappeared." The man never takes his eyes off my face. "The ones who busted down our door. Claimed they were looking for a couple of girls in fancy dresses. Finishing school girls, with no business in a place like this. Said they were in danger from us perverts. Then they started swinging their clubs every which way. Everybody who didn't make it out the side door got a nice crack to the head. Two guys are still in the hospital. The coppers got out fine, though. One of 'em had a twitch in his eye. Sound like anybody you know?"

I don't move. The police officer at the Capitol that morning. The one who tipped his hat at us.

His eye twitched.

Was that same officer one of the pair we saw outside the tearoom, directing traffic? Or perhaps just pretending to?

What about the officers we saw on the street with Victor near the Navy Yard? Was one of them the same man?

Did he follow us from the Capitol? All day? All *night*?

If Milly was right, that the police had been looking for Victor... If that officer saw us talking to him, and followed us all the way to the Seven Seas...

They probably thought it would be safer to arrest Victor here. If they did it at the Capitol, it might cause a scene. Risk his clients in Congress being exposed. The powerful men whose safety, whose reputations the police deemed worthy of protection.

I drop my face into my hands. How many people must've been at the Seven Seas that night? How many were beaten? Arrested?

People just trying to live their lives. Be who they are.

People like me.

"We didn't have anything to do with that," I say, too loud. "We had no idea!"

"All I know is, our floors were bloody five minutes after you and Victor and that little friend of yours left." The man sighs. "But to be honest with you, kid, it doesn't matter either way anymore. *Now* would you leave, please?"

I don't want to leave.

I want to know what it is about the Seven Seas that makes men like him come back to it again and again, despite all the reasons not to.

"What's on the other side of that wall?" I ask.

The man steps to the side, blocking my view of the crack in the doorway. "Nothing."

"Could I just see?"

"There's nothing left."

"But... you and your friends. *You're* still here."

The man shrugs. "Where else is there to go?"

33

I TRUDGE DOWN THE SIDEWALK, MY BOOTS LEADEN. A TAXI DOOR slams in the distance, but I don't look up. It isn't late, but twilight is already falling, and the clouds overhead are thick and heavy.

I've come home. I need to go straight up to Milly. To apologize for running off and frightening her, and to tell her what I learned at the Seven Seas, too.

I climb onto the porch, slide my key into the lock, and push the door open.

"Milly?" I shut the door behind me. A quiet moment passes. "Mother?"

No answer.

"Norris? Alma?"

I step carefully into the dark house. There's no fire in the grate.

"Milly?" I call again.

My mother could've gone shopping. Perhaps she brought Milly along. But surely Norris and Alma would have stayed behind.

Something doesn't feel right.

Then a sound comes at the front window. A footstep, on the porch.

Good. Someone's returning home. Milly, I hope.

I peel back a corner of the curtain on the window beside the front door, but I only see a shadow, small and dark, moving quickly toward the door.

The tail of a coat, perhaps? Could it be Norris? He usually comes in the back door.

But...no. I remember now.

Tomorrow's Christmas Eve. That's why the house is so dark and empty. My mother always gives the servants three days off over Christmas. The dressmaker will be here before long, but for now, I'm alone, aside from this new arrival.

I wait for the sound of a key in the lock. It doesn't come.

There are more footsteps, though, on the other side of the door. Crunching noises in the dead leaves.

That's strange. Whoever's come home should have let themselves in by now. Unless it's a visitor—but surely a visitor would've knocked. The door is locked, and...

Wait.

The key's still in my hand.

I came in, I shut the door, I went to look for Milly...

I didn't lock the door behind me.

Heart pounding, I step back into the front hall, careful not to let my heels click.

Someone's out there.

Our front door is solid oak. The only opening is the mail slot, set at the level of my waist, its silver plate hanging loose at the back.

And someone's on the other side.

There's a sound, small and metallic. I drop my eyes to the shiny brass knob.

It's moving. Twisting.

Without thinking, I throw myself against the door, all my weight slamming into it.

There's no way whoever's out there didn't notice that.

But they can't see me. They don't know I'm a frightened girl in a day dress and stockings.

Let them think I'm a huge, threatening ogre, poised to hurl them off my porch.

I wait for the sound of retreating footsteps, but all I can hear is the wind, rustling the bare branches of the elm by the front walk.

The man with the big hands. He must've followed me again, so he can do exactly what he threatened in his note. Kill me, the way he killed Mrs. Rose.

Once he gets through this door...do I stand any chance against him at all?

She didn't.

Hours could pass before anyone comes home and finds me. It would be long over by then.

Who *would* find me? My mother? Milly?

What if he came after them next?

A long, quiet moment passes. There's an instant, horrifying and heart-twisting, when I think I hear movement on the other side of the door, and that it's the end. He'll throw his weight against the door, the same way I did, and it'll smash open, and he'll be here.

But just as quickly, the sound stops.

Then there's a sharp clatter. The silver plate of the mail slot slamming open. I arch back so it won't strike me.

A wide, flat envelope slides through. It drifts to the ground, settling onto the toes of my black boots.

Then come the footsteps. Loud at first, then growing fainter.

He's leaving. Or pretending to.

I think. I pray. I want to go back to the window to look, but I can't leave the door unguarded.

After a brief moment, I draw back long enough to shove my

key in the lock. I twist it fast, the bolt sliding into place. Then I run to the back door and make sure it's locked, too.

Finally, I return to the front door and sink to the floor, my back braced against the door, my heart pounding in my chest harder than it's ever pounded.

The envelope is thin. There couldn't be more than a single sheet of paper inside. My fingers jerk as I tear at the seal, ripping the brown paper in half as I struggle to get it open.

It isn't paper inside. It's a photograph. Glossy. The kind a government photographer used last year when he made my father's portrait.

This image is more difficult to make out. Much of it is black, shot inside a dark room. Still, I recognize it right away.

It's the photograph from the newspaper. The article about the raid at the Lazy Susan. Most of the page is taken up by men's backs, fleeing. Bruce Pengelley, former assistant commerce secretary, is right at the center, his eyes wide in the blinding flashbulb as he turns around to look. Another man's face nearby is blurred with frantic motion, his dark hair blowing as he tries to get away.

But the photograph that appeared in the newspaper must have been cut to fit the space. This version is wider. The newspaper version showed only my elbow.

This one shows my face.

I'm turned slightly away from the camera, but I show up even clearer than Mr. Pengelley. My eyes, wide. My mouth, open to shout.

I try to breathe, and find that I can't.

My mother could've been the one to find this photograph. Or, worse, my father.

Whoever that was on the other side of that door...

They've sent me another message. Another threat, like the

shawl on my doorstep and the note in my pocket. But now they have my face.

Someone wants me gone.

My bedroom door bursts open while Viola, the dressmaker's assistant, is on her knees with her mouth full of pins, tucking up the hem of my gown.

"Gertie!" Milly's still wearing her hat and coat. "I've been searching the entire city—!"

Milly stops when she registers Viola's presence at my feet, her chest heaving. I've never seen her like this.

"I'm so sorry," I say, but it's difficult to convey how sorry I truly am when I have to stay ramrod still for Viola. My new dress for the Christmas Eve ball is thick velvet and lipstick red, with silk trim and red beads covering the full skirt, running up to the square neck of the bodice. "It was thoughtless of me to leave you the way I did. I wanted to come look for you, but when my mother got home from the market she wouldn't allow me to—"

"Thoughtless?" Milly lets out a tiny, hysterical laugh. "I was sure something had happened to you. I was..."

Viola carefully extracts the pins from her mouth. "Good evening, Miss Otis."

"Yes. My apologies. Good evening." Milly shuts her eyes. When she opens them, she's herself again, or nearly. "I beg your pardon for interrupting. It's lovely to see you, Viola. When you're through here, Miss Pound, if I could have a brief word, please."

"I'm all done, miss." Viola climbs to her feet. "Miss Pound, if you'll leave the dress with me I'll have it back first thing."

"Thank you, Viola."

She unzips the dress and I step out of it, shivering in my pink silk slip and stockings. "Thank you, miss."

Viola's gone in a bustle of beads and velvet.

"Is my mother home?" I need to tell Milly everything, but I'm wearing my shiny black satin heels, the ones with the studded rhinestones, and I stumble as I try to reach the bed. I can't stretch far enough to retrieve the photograph from where I stuffed it into my handbag. "I need to tell you—"

"No. I need to tell *you*." Milly strides in front of me and grabs me roughly by my bare shoulders. She's clutching something small and white between her fingers. "*Never* do that again! Do you understand me? *Never!*"

Blood rushes through me, fury churning inside my head. *I'm* the one who was nearly strangled in my own front hall, and *Milly's* shouting? "What?"

"I thought I'd find you *dead*! You *can't* scare me like that, Gertie, never, ever, *ever!*"

Now I see what she's holding. It's the scrap of paper I found in my pocket. I must have dropped it when I ran to catch the streetcar.

Stop. Or you'll get what she did.

"I'm sorry," I say, the words thoroughly inadequate in the face of Milly's rage. "I didn't think..."

"You *never* think. Unless you're thinking too much, about the *wrong* things." Milly's eyes are ablaze, her voice so close to shouting I'm afraid my mother will hear. "You've got to stop this before you ruin everything. Don't you *see*? You've got it all wrong. You don't care about anything, or any*one*!"

"That's not true!" Now I'm nearly shouting, too.

I *do* care. I *do*. But I don't know how to tell her that. She's still holding me by the shoulders, crushing me in her grip, and I want to shake her, make her understand—

And then she's crushing me to her, and she's kissing me.

And it's everything.

It's everything I've ever wanted. Everything I never *knew* I wanted.

We could've done this so many times. We could've done this *so long ago.*

She's always been there, Milly has. My Milly.

I never knew how much I needed her. How much I wanted this.

I break away long enough to press my lips to her ear. I murmur her name against her cheek, the brim of her hat.

And she springs back, eyes going wide, chest heaving. My slip is sweaty in the heat from the fire, clinging to me like a second skin.

Only then do I think of Clara.

Clara, who isn't here. Who has no idea.

Who trusted me.

Oh, *God.*

And then the door behind Milly swings open, revealing my mother standing on the threshold.

34

W HY IS THERE SHOUTING IN HERE?"

My mother purses her lips. Impossibly stiff. I feel impossibly stiff, too.

Milly steps back. Puts more space between our bodies.

I force myself to breathe. My mother is staring at us. No one speaks.

I long for my dressing gown. For any clothing at all, to cover my sweaty slip.

But I lift my chin high, as though I'm wearing Milly's best hat.

"Hello, Mother," I say. "You'll be pleased to hear that my gown for the ball is coming along splendidly."

"Miss Otis, could I trespass upon your kindness by asking for your assistance with the groceries in the kitchen? With Sarah away, I fear I may have purchased too much bread. I never have been good at those sorts of estimations."

My mother smiles, but there's ice on her lips.

"Certainly, Mrs. Pound." Milly doesn't look at me. She steps past my mother, and a moment later we can both hear her climbing down the stairs.

"Gertrude." My mother's smile may be ice, but her voice is fire. "I know you don't always take your responsibilities to this family as seriously as you ought to, but the tale I heard at the market today is by far the worst report I've received of your behavior yet. Making a *scene* like that! The way you spoke to Mrs. Patterson on the *street!*"

Fear rises in my chest, crowding out the relief that she didn't see us.

This morning, I didn't have the strength left to care about Mrs. Patterson. Now, alone in my bedroom with my mother and her icy gaze, it's all unbearably real.

"I'm sorry, Mother." It's what she expects me to say. I've spent the last seventeen years learning what I'm expected to say, and saying it with precision. "I behaved irresponsibly."

"*Irresponsibly* does not begin to describe your actions. Mrs. Mayfield has suggested, more than once, that I send you to Lincoln Hall in Boston, so you'd be away from all those new influences at the seminary. That's quite something, coming from her. I always declined, knowing you preferred to stay with your friends. But you never started acting this way until *she* got involved."

I drop my chin until my gaze is level with my mother's, a thin sheen of sweat growing on my palms. "I'm not sure what you mean."

But I am.

She's talking about Mrs. Rose.

"You're losing sight of what's important. As a part of this family, you're allotted a certain amount of forgiveness by the people who matter, but one more outburst like this and you'll have no chance of an important marriage."

My mother's threats mean so much to her. Yet I'm even less interested in finding an important husband than I was two weeks ago.

However. She didn't mention Boston by accident.

She can't send me away from Milly and Clara.

She *can't*.

"Your invitation to the Babcocks' ball tomorrow will stand." My mother crosses her arms in front of her. Resolute. "I made sure of that. Still, I imagine this story will follow you for years, no matter what any of us does."

"All I did was run a short distance. No one was harmed."

Her eyes light up with anger. I've never seen her like this. Not even when my aunt told her she was planning to marry that stockbroker in New York who'd been divorced twice. "You have no need to run *anywhere*. I have half a mind to forbid your playing sports, if this is what you do with the skills you're acquiring."

"Mother! That isn't—"

"I meant what I said, Gertrude."

She *interrupted* me.

My mother's never interrupted anyone in her life.

"More is at stake than you seem to realize." She steps toward me, fists clenched, fury dripping from her every word. I've never been this frightened of my mother. "Your *entire* future depends on what the people in that ballroom tomorrow night think of you."

I remember that afternoon at the Babcock house. Watching Trixie and her family, and wondering how many families were as hypocritical as theirs. How many built their lives around presenting one face to the world and another to their mirrors.

My mother doesn't have any more interest in what's going on inside my head than Mrs. Patterson and Mrs. Paul and Mrs. Babcock do. All any of them care about is the face I display.

"I understand," I say.

"I'm not certain you do. But you will." My mother nods firmly. "You'll be on your best behavior tomorrow night. I want to see you smiling at the right people. Talking to the right people. Saying the right things. There will be no slipping away with your friends, or making scenes of any kind."

"Mother—"

"I've had a miraculous stroke of luck. I just spoke with Mrs. Lindner on the telephone, from Lincoln Hall. She was good enough to consider our application quickly, given the circumstances, and she's made an exception. Miss Otis can assist you in packing your things, with Alma away for the holiday."

At the sound of Milly's name, I feel again the press of her lips on mine. It makes my head spin, my mother's words difficult to decipher. "My things?"

"Only enough for the interview. Well, that is to say, the interview's a formality, as she's already determined to accept you. We'll leave for Boston the day after tomorrow on the sleeper and arrive just in time to meet with her. You'll get a chance to see your new dormitory while we're there, too, before we come back here for New Year's."

The words are starting to penetrate my understanding.

New dormitory.

Boston.

Day after tomorrow.

"I'm not moving to Boston." I can't calculate my words. Not with the imprint of Milly's body still warm against mine. "I have to stay here. In the city. With my . . ."

I can't say *friends.*

Will Milly *want* to be friends with me when she finds out about Clara?

Will *Clara* want that?

"No. You can't stay in Washington. You've had far too many . . ." My mother's eyes linger on my slip. "*Influences* here."

She shuts her eyes for an instant, tapping a high-heeled foot. I do that, too. Close my eyes when I'm thinking hard. Coming to conclusions.

I swallow. Whatever she's going to say next, I know it isn't going to be good.

"Come to think of it, never mind about returning for New Year's." She opens her eyes. They're bright. And I know I was right to be worried. "I'll adjust our train tickets to have us both stay in Boston until your new term starts. Go ahead and dress for dinner, now. Your father will be home soon, and our family will look the part, if no more."

35

THE WASHINGTON HERALD

Saturday, December 24, 1927

DRY SQUAD NABS BOOTLEGGER FOR HEADMISTRESS MURDER AND CRIMINAL THIEVERY RING AT CAPITOL

Victor King, aged 29, was apprehended in Virginia last night by federal Prohibition agents on several liquor and morals charges. King had been long sought by law enforcement, having been rumored to sell liquor to government men at the U.S. Capitol and to frequent illegal establishments associated with degenerate behavior.

A search of a basement storage room in the House Office Building in which King was alleged to keep liquor uncovered a knife that police said was used to break into the office of Mrs. Jessica Rose, former headmistress of the Washington Female Seminary. In light of this new evidence, Mrs. Rose's death, previously considered the result of accidental poisoning, is now being investigated as a murder, with King as a suspect. Additional evidence incriminating King in Mrs. Rose's death and in other crimes was found as well, police reported.

"King and Rose were partners in a large bootleg-ging operation, which included providing liquor to the girls in her care," said Prohibition Bureau Agent Sam-uel Perkins. "King appears to have killed his own part-ner in their so-called business. He believed her to be cheating him out of earnings that were rightfully his, and her death was the unfortunate result. Such things are to be expected when dealing with degenerates and criminals."

I DROP THE PAPER BACK ONTO THE BREAKFAST TABLE. I'VE READ the article more times than I can count, but the same words keep swimming through my head.

Cheating. Bootlegging. Criminals.

Morals charges.

Milly talked about *morals charges*, too.

It's done. Victor killed Mrs. Rose. It's right there, in black and white.

It's over.

There's something deeply wrong with Victor King. He seemed charming, even kind, but on the inside, his soul must have been scarred and twisted. Dangerous.

I suppose I'm twisted on the inside, too.

I lay my head down on the table. I can do that. I'm alone in the house this morning, with my mother out at the market and my father away at his club.

Milly is . . . I have no idea where Milly is. She told my mother she was dining out last night, with a family friend, and wouldn't be back until late. This morning, she was gone before I was out of bed.

The empty house was useful. It meant that as soon as I

picked up the paper and read that article for the first time, I could search through my father's library without being seen.

I couldn't find anything in his law books about *morals charges*, but I looked up *degenerate* in the dictionary. That definition led me to look up *perversion*, which led me to *aberrant*, which led me to a word I'd never seen before.

Homosexuality.

The papers never print that word. But I suppose people who aren't naïve seminary girls already know what they mean by *degenerate*.

They mean *me*.

And Victor. And Clara, too, and all those men at the Seven Seas.

And, I suppose, Milly. If a single kiss is sufficient sin.

It didn't feel like some trifling matter. Not when it was happening. Not in the hours since, either.

She kissed *me*. And it certainly seemed as though she did it because she wanted to. It seemed as though she *had* to.

I still feel breathless, remembering.

Yet... I remember what she said about Victor, too. About men like him.

I don't understand it.

I need to talk to Clara. She's the only one who could help me make sense of all this. But the ball isn't for hours yet, and there's no way to reach her before then.

Besides, I shouldn't tell her what happened between Milly and me. She might despise us both. Or only me.

Am I meant to choose between them?

I could never. I wouldn't know where to begin.

I drop my chin and breathe in, heavy, my breath fogging the freshly shined surface of the kitchen table.

I'm a liar now. I have secrets. Too many. Like Mrs. Rose did.

My face is still pressed against the wood surface when the knock comes at the front door.

I jerk up in my seat, panic overtaking me. Then I listen again. The knocking is soft. Ladylike.

And yesterday's intruder didn't knock at all.

Yet when I cross into the front hallway and look out to see Trixie Babcock waiting on the front step in her finest mink coat with dark circles under her eyes, my relief is mild at best.

What's *she* doing here?

I open the door, painting on a civil expression. The neighbors could be watching. "Miss Babcock. So good of you to call."

"Such a pleasure to see you, Miss Pound. Is Miss Otis here as well?"

"I'm afraid not."

"My mother asked me to send her regards."

We could've gone on that way, saying nonsense about nothing in our sweetest Madame Frost–approved voices, but when I close the door behind Trixie and she realizes we're alone, her light smile shifts into a hard, pinched look.

I drop my smile, too. "What are you doing here?"

"I need to tell you something."

She used those same words that day at her house. *I need to tell you something.* "I suppose we should sit, then."

We perch on armchairs in the living room. There's no one to take her coat or serve us tea. No mothers to check our posture. Still, we both fold our hands neatly, automatically, on our laps.

"You saw the papers," Trixie begins.

"I did."

"You know they've arrested some bootlegger."

"Yes."

"And we both know they've got the wrong man."

The last person I expected to say that was *Trixie*. "I'm sure I don't know what you mean."

"I *told* them." Trixie's eyes are growing red. Until that night at the seminary, the night Mrs. Rose died, I'd never seen her cry. Wouldn't have thought she knew how. "From the very beginning. No one listened."

"I'm afraid you aren't making sense, Miss Babcock."

"I *saw* them." Trixie lifts her hands and holds them there, palms up, quivering. As though she's shaking a melon. "With my *own eyes*."

A chill forms inside me. "Who did you see?"

"First I heard her talking about it, with—with Mrs. Rose. Then I *saw* her, with..." She casts her eyes down to her hands. "Promise you won't think less of me? I didn't mean to look, I swear it."

For once, my curiosity outweighs my dislike. "I promise to listen."

"It was on Friday. The day before the faculty party. They were in *your* room." Trixie's mouth twists into an ugly, slanted shape. "I didn't mean to go that way. I was following her. Mrs. Rose. I needed to ask her about...But she went into your room, and then she sort of—she jumped, and came right back out again."

All of this was well before the murder. I want to ask a hundred questions, but I only nod. "What happened?"

"Her face had gone white, like she was shocked at whatever she'd seen. So I stole up behind her and peeked into your room, and that was when I saw. *You* weren't there, but *they* were... together. Their *mouths* were *together*."

I wait for her to explain more, but it's clear that she's waiting, too. For me to understand.

Then I do.

"Who?" My heart's thumping hard and fast. "*Whose* mouths were together?"

"They stopped right away. They'd seen Mrs. Rose. They knew they'd been caught."

"Trixie, who are you *talking* about?"

"Quit it with that naïve act." Trixie rolls her eyes, but her face is flushed bright pink. "You know it was your two little friends. My roommate and yours. Clara and Milly."

36

Fortunately, they didn't see *me*." Trixie hiccups. A tear drips along the side of her nose. "Still, I made sure I was never alone with Clara after that. I slept in the sitting room that night, and I left for my uncle's as soon as I could."

Her words register dully in my mind.

They *couldn't* have.

They couldn't have been lying to me all this time.

"I've always detested Clara." Trixie rubs a gloved finger under her nose. "Her family isn't anyone at all. It's not that they're Jewish. I'm not like *those* girls, the ones who went around saying the seminary only let her in because her father's in Congress. Though those girls *were* right. Her father's the reason they're permitted at our ball, too. It's a matter of what people would think, my mother says."

"That's awful." I shake my head. I can't think about the rest of it, not yet. "To say she wouldn't be allowed because of who she is?"

"You think *your* mother would have her over otherwise?" Trixie rolls her eyes. "I'm sure your father stands to benefit. He'd like to serve on a federal bench someday, no doubt. Clara's father could help him there."

I hate everything about this. Including the possibility that Trixie's right.

"I never understood why she chose to spend all her time with *you* two when she was *my* roommate." Trixie sniffs. "Now I see. Her sort can sense people like them. She used you to get to Milly."

It's nonsense. I *want* to think it's nonsense.

But...

How many times did it happen? How long did they keep it secret?

"This is absurd." But I'm trembling.

"I tried to warn you." Trixie spreads her palms wide. "When you came to call on us. I meant to stay with you that afternoon, because I knew *you* didn't have anything to do with it. You're not like *them*. But you were so rude to me, I didn't bother warning you in the end."

She's right.

If I hadn't acted the way I did when she approached me that afternoon, I could've found out so much sooner. Everything would've been different.

"I was afraid they'd found out, somehow. That I'd seen them." She shudders. "I thought they'd come to my uncle's to... *do* something to me. Like they did to her."

I shake my head. "Do what?"

"You know very well what." Trixie gazes at me as though she's never seen anyone so stupid. "Mrs. Rose wasn't involved in any criminal bootlegging scheme. That wasn't like her at all. No, no, *they* did it. Those two... those *perverts* who used to be our *roommates*!"

I wait for Trixie to start smirking, the way she always does after she's said some terrible falsehood.

It doesn't happen.

"Trixie," I say slowly. "Milly and Clara aren't *murderers*."

"They've fooled you, too." Another tear slips down Trixie's cheek, mixing with the dribble from her nose. "You didn't see them that day. They were *furious* she'd caught them. Probably decided to kill her then and there!"

"You can't expect me to believe this." I fold my hands tight in my lap so Trixie won't see them shaking.

"You know what those people are like. It's a *sin*, and they don't even care. Those boys in the papers? From Chicago? They don't understand normal morality. They'll do *anything* to keep from getting caught. Besides, Milly had plenty of money to hire a killer. Or Clara could've even done it herself. She's absurdly strong for a girl. Once, in our room, she lifted my big armchair as though it was nothing."

The way she lifted the table off Milly at the Lazy Susan that night.

"Come, Trixie." I fight to keep my voice steady. "None of this proves anything."

"You didn't see how *angry* they were." Trixie shudders again.

And I come to a realization that makes me shudder, too.

Trixie believes what she's saying. She isn't making up a story to get my attention. She already *has* my attention.

She thinks this story she's telling me, about Milly and Clara teaming up to murder Mrs. Rose, is the honest truth.

"All that day, and the day after, too, they were *seething*," Trixie goes on. "They wouldn't look at anyone. I never saw them speak to each other, either, not once. Because they knew if they did, she'd see."

They *were* acting stiff that night at the faculty party. I remember that. They wouldn't look at each other, and when they did, it was fraught. As if there was something they didn't want to say.

"Milly disappeared during dinner that night," Trixie goes on. "Only a few hours after Mrs. Rose caught them. She must've gone out, to hire someone."

"She was reading," I remember. "A book on scientific discoveries. She got so caught up in it she forgot to eat."

"Did you *see* her reading?"

I pause. "No, but..."

"Gertie, I've known about all this for *weeks*. No one would listen to me. Not my mother. Not the police, either. That's why I need your help. People listen to *you*."

"Trixie." I try to sound gentle, but there's too much building up inside me. Threatening to spill over. "This is absurd."

Trixie told the *police*. And, worse, her mother.

Her mother, who could tell anyone. Who could tell *my* mother.

"They've tricked you." She shakes her head. Wipes her eyes. "Gotten you thinking they're normal. Like you."

I can't let Trixie see how much she's frightening me.

Or that I'm not normal, either.

"My mother *refused* to take them off the guest list for the ball tonight." Trixie shakes her head. "Even when I *begged*."

"This isn't possible." I've got to get through to Trixie before she tells even more people than she already has. "I've been with them every day since Mrs. Rose died."

"Have you been with them every *minute*?" Trixie peers out through her gloved fingers.

"Well, no, but..."

"Besides. I saw a man leaving Mrs. Rose's room that night. I thought he was a workman, at first, but it was too late at night for that."

I freeze. "What did he look like?"

"Tall. Wide in the chest. Dark eyebrows, like he might have been Italian. He was wearing a green jacket, and his gloves... they were so *big*. As though there was something wrong with his hands."

Blood drains from my cheeks.

"Milly must have found him when she went out the night before," Trixie goes on. "I don't know if she brought him the money that same night or if she met up with him again later, but he had to have been the man they hired to do it."

Images, memories, race through my head.

Milly, disappearing into the mouth of the alley. Speaking Italian with someone I couldn't see.

Clara, staring after her. Waiting.

Milly's handbag, stuffed with bills at the start of the night. Empty by the time we arrived at the Lazy Susan.

And that earring. Elizabeth's earring, with the two diamonds. Milly took it, to give back to her, but...but I never saw her do it.

Two diamonds, together with that wad of bills...

Would it have been enough to take a life?

Gertie, Clara said, after we kissed. *There's something I should...It's only that I don't know quite how to say it.*

All those silent, meaningful looks exchanged between them. That never included me.

"How do you know it was them who hired him?" I ask.

Trixie stares at me again, as though I'm utterly devoid of intelligence. "No one else had any reason to want her dead."

"The man you saw. What time was this?"

"I don't know. I was too upset to check. He...he frightened me."

"But it was after the faculty party ended?"

"Yes. I was going down to the kitchen for a glass of milk, and he was in the hall."

Mrs. Rose could have already been dead by then. Lying on the floor of her office, waiting for Lucy to stumble across her.

"Did you take the grand staircase?" I ask her.

"No, the south servant stairs. They're dark, but I always use them at night. They're closest to my rooms, and I never have to speak to anyone."

I nod. That was Mrs. Rose's strategy, too. Strange. "You saw him from the staircase?"

"No. I was planning to go on down to the first floor, but I heard something on the second, so I stepped out into the hall by the old library. I peered down, through the linen cupboard, and saw him coming out of her office. He didn't see me, but I nearly screamed."

"I'm surprised you didn't."

"Well, to be entirely truthful, I took him for Mrs. Rose's..." Trixie sniffs. "Companion."

"Ah, I see. You thought you'd tell your uncle about him the next day, then, and that would be that?"

Trixie's lips part, the lower one trembling. "I'm not a monster."

I don't know whether to believe her, but I nod. "You told the police all this?"

"I told Agent Perkins. I even told him about the letter. He didn't listen." Trixie climbs to her feet.

I stand up, too, the etiquette automatic. "What letter?"

"The one Clara gave Mrs. Rose the next afternoon." Trixie's face twists into a pout. "I saw her do it, before the party. Clara had this... this *glittering* look to her eyes. It was a threat, I'm certain. But Mrs. Rose must not have done whatever it was they asked for in the letter, because they killed her anyway."

"Where is this letter now?"

"I don't know! That's why I needed Agent Perkins. Mrs. Rose must have hidden it in her room somewhere. If he could find the letter, he'd have proof, but he wouldn't even look for it!"

My mind is spinning. Nothing Trixie's said sounds believable.

Yet...it fits, a little.

Milly didn't come to dinner the night before Mrs. Rose's death. She'd said she was reading. But I never saw the book she'd described.

She could have gone out that evening. She could have hired the man with the big hands, and arranged to meet him the following night to give him the payment.

And if Clara wrote Mrs. Rose a letter, and Mrs. Rose hid it in her room...

That last afternoon, before we left the seminary. After Milly and I went to see Perkins, and ran into Clara coming out of the north corridor...

She could've been coming from Mrs. Rose's room.

She could've been searching for that letter herself. Seeking that last piece of evidence so she could destroy it before the police found it.

Of course, that couldn't have been how it happened.

It's all entirely preposterous. I *know* Clara. I know Milly, too.

This is *absurd*.

"You told all this to your mother?" I ask.

"She wouldn't listen to me, either. But then, she never has." Trixie stares down at her patent leather heels. "If the police search her room and find that letter, we'll all be safe. You included. Otherwise, it's only a matter of time before you catch them yourself, and then *you'll* be on their list."

I shake my head again. "What is it you want from me?"

"I'm calling Agent Perkins as soon as I leave here." Trixie lifts her chin. Meets my eyes. "I'll have him come to the ball this evening. When he sees how important my family is, he'll know he can't ignore me, and he'll go looking for that letter right away."

"Your mother will never allow a lowly Prohibition agent to attend her ball."

"He can come through the servants' door for all I care." Trixie sniffs again.

She truly seems to believe this letter exists. If it does...and Perkins finds it...

What would happen to Clara? Milly, too?

I breathe in. Out.

I'll find a way to fix this. All of it.

I meet Trixie's gaze. Normal. I have to look normal. "You still haven't told me what you want from me."

She purses her lips. "I need you to keep me safe."

"From Agent Perkins?"

She exhales, a frustrated, impolite noise. "From *them*. We need to get Clara and Milly alone, where they can admit what they did. At the ball tonight, if you to ask them to come somewhere with you, somewhere away from the crowd, they'll do it."

"And then what? You'll go interrogate them?"

I mean it as a joke, but Trixie nods. "You can make sure they can't do anything to me."

It's then that I realize Trixie thinks we're in a gangster picture. She thinks I'm her *muscle*.

"Now, I have to be going." Trixie sniffs again. "I have an appointment with the dressmaker at my uncle's house."

"Not your own house?"

"We aren't moved in yet."

"You're...having a ball at your new house before you move into it?"

"It's no concern of yours."

314

I nod. Typical Trixie.

I walk her to the front door. "Good day, Miss Babcock. Thank you ever so for calling."

I shut the door behind her and wait until I'm sure she's gone. Then I run for my coat.

If there's a letter, I've got to find it before Perkins does.

37

It rained all morning, a mixture of water and ice. The streets grow more and more slippery the closer I get to Dupont Circle. The seminary will be empty, but if I can persuade the caretaker to let me inside, I'll slip up to Mrs. Rose's room under the guise of visiting my own.

I can find a letter as well as any fed.

But as I approach, there's no sign of life behind the seminary's bold front doors. The windows are dark, the curtains drawn, with traces of soot and dust collecting on the thick glass panes.

I trudge up the same sidewalk I did the night we came back from the Lazy Susan, watching the coppers shining their electric torches into every corner and crevice, and ring the bell. It echoes inside the entrance hall.

No one answers. The darkness behind the curtains is still and silent.

I try the handle. It's locked tight.

I step back, trying to think. The alleys on each side of the building meet at the back in a tiny courtyard that leads to the laundry door, off the kitchen. Perhaps the caretaker's in that part of the building, and would hear a knock at the back door better than the bell at the front.

I take the P Street side, passing the tree I climbed down that night with Milly and Clara, glancing up to the library balcony and our window above it. Simply knowing I'm so close to home makes me square my shoulders and lift my chin.

When I reach the wrought iron railing that runs along the

alley, though, it doesn't feel quite so familiar. The winter sunlight doesn't reach this narrow space. There's a scuttling sound behind a bush, and when I lean over to examine the source, I spot a small brown creature dining on something I'd rather not see up close.

I skirt along the fence until I reach the back door. I knock, hard, three times.

No one answers.

I knock again. If there's a caretaker here, it's a very bad one.

I try the door. It stays firmly shut, no matter how I twist the knob.

A sound rustles behind me. Another shape under the hedge.

I take a long breath. I can't be leaping at shadows. I need to know the truth. If there's no letter, that will prove Trixie's story about Milly and Clara orchestrating Mrs. Rose's murder is pure, preposterous fiction.

And if there *is* a letter, then…

Then I don't know. I'll have to destroy it, I suppose. Protect them.

Though it will destroy me, too.

But I can't think about that right now. I have a job to do.

To the left of the door, at the level of my waist, there's a window covered in a thin shade.

The glass might be thin, too. But surely I couldn't *break* a window.

Could I?

The alley has tall hedges on either side, and there's a solid brick wall at my back. No one to see me here.

I frown down at my hand, balling it into a fist experimentally. If I tried to punch glass, would I break my bones?

I glance around for a rock, but all I see are shards of broken glass and stubbed-out cigarettes.

I step close, studying the window. There's an odd angle to

the frame. The lower side isn't quite straight. In fact, there's a gap at the bottom big enough to fit two fingers through.

There's a reason the seminary's lowest floor is always cold. This window doesn't fully close.

I've gotten lucky after all.

I grab hold of the window frame and hoist upward, hard. It doesn't budge. But I keep pushing and pushing, until finally there's a long, awful wooden squeal as it begins to slide.

If anyone's inside, they'll have heard that. But there's nothing I can do about it now.

I take off my shoes and stand in my stockings on the cold cement, digging in my toes to get a better purchase on the window frame. I shove harder, and harder still, until at last there's an opening that might be wide enough.

I crouch down and gaze into the dark, cold room on the other side. The laundry. I listen closely, but all I hear are the low, quick scratches of claws under the hedges behind me.

Now all I have to do is crawl inside.

I take off my coat and push it through first, then my shoes. Finally, I slide in, feet first, praying my dress and stockings don't rip on the window frame.

Praying no one's watching me, waiting to follow me inside.

I have to wriggle to get my hips through, then my shoulders. When my feet finally touch the floor, I let out a long sigh of relief. Then I remember I haven't achieved anything yet.

I put on my shoes and my coat. My heels echo on the wooden floor as I cross the laundry room, but then, I suppose there's no reason to bother keeping quiet. The room is empty and dark, a row of sinks along one wall and not much more, and it leads into the kitchen, just as dark and cold. The smell of dust is thick. In the far corner, there's another skitter of claws.

This building is meant to be teeming with people. Girls

hurrying to class or to tea. Teachers, scrutinizing our dress and deportment. Servants moving quickly from room to room.

This quiet, this chill, isn't natural. It isn't right.

I take the grand staircase to the second floor and slip through Mrs. Rose's office. It's still littered with papers, and it still holds the faintest trace of her scent, too. Smoke and ink and warmth, in spite of the cold that grips the building.

This is where Mrs. Rose spent her last moments. It was the last place she saw as she fought to keep living.

The linen closet door looks exactly as I remember it. The jagged, uneven cuts sliced near the knob. Perhaps made with the knife the police found in Victor's office.

It couldn't have been Milly and Clara, then. They wouldn't have needed to break in.

Though Victor wouldn't have needed to, either. Mrs. Rose would have admitted him without the need for violence.

If someone brought in a paid killer, though, *he* might've needed to break in. And anyone could've done that.

If Milly and Clara spoke with that man while we were walking down Massachusetts Avenue together on our way to the Lazy Susan, they wouldn't have been there to let him in to the seminary. He would've had to use force. While Milly and Clara were out with someone who'd unwittingly provide them an alibi. Me.

Never mind about the knife. I cross the office, making my way to Mrs. Rose's bedroom.

I've never been inside this room before. When I step over the threshold it smells much like the kitchen. Dusty and vacant. The blanket over the bed is still spread tight, with only a single pillow missing. Either the servants cleaned the room after Mrs. Rose was taken away, or Mrs. Rose didn't sleep in her bed the night she died.

The writing desk in the corner, though, which Mrs. Rose

would certainly have kept in a state of perfect organization, is a mess. The drawers have been pulled open wide and emptied, with scraps of paper littering the surface and the floor around it. The untidy work of Agent Perkins and his friends.

One of the wardrobe doors is unlatched. For a brief moment an idea flits through my mind—that I could touch her clothes. See if they're still warm. If they smell of her jasmine perfume.

I open the door to see a row of two-piece suits and dresses, neatly pressed on their hangers, all of them pushed to one side. At the bottom, the missing pillow rests on top of a messy pile of high-heeled shoes. It all smells of thick, old dust. Not a single hint of jasmine.

The police have been in this room, surely, many times, and learned everything they can. Perhaps they've moved things around. Though I can't imagine why they'd put a pillow in a closet.

Still, if there were a threatening letter from Clara in the writing desk, they'd have found it. They'd have come to question her. But they haven't.

Which means the letter wasn't in the writing desk. It was somewhere else entirely. If it existed at all.

Mrs. Rose wrote letters constantly, and received even more. She sat at her desk in her office every morning, opening envelopes and sealing up new ones. Mostly seminary business, naturally. Those, she kept in her desk.

But one rainy morning, as the two of us sat sipping tea, she'd told me that when she received a truly *interesting* letter, she kept it in another place. A special place, where no one would know to look. Under a loose floorboard near her wardrobe.

Then she smiled and asked me never to repeat that.

I'd smiled back, thrilled to be trusted. Still, it was a struggle to picture my elegant headmistress stooping to peel up a floorboard.

I couldn't fathom, then, what she'd possibly have to conceal.

Now I drop to the ground and run my hands across the cracked wooden floor, catching cobwebs and dust between my fingers. The boards appear identical. Nothing's obviously misaligned.

I press along each edge, and on the fifth board, I feel it. One end is looser than the others.

I press hard, until the other side of the board rises enough for me to slide a finger underneath. Then another.

I reach inside and pry it up. Soon, the entire board has popped off, fully intact. I set it aside, my heart thumping.

Below there's a dark, narrow space, with a brown leather folder piled full of papers. Papers, it seems, no one has touched since Mrs. Rose left them here.

I carefully withdraw the folder and open its cover. The pages inside are stacked neatly. It's no surprise that Mrs. Rose kept everything neat, even under the floorboards.

The first letter is still in its envelope, written on plain white paper in sloppy handwriting. *A. Frances*, the top corner reads, with an address in Pennsylvania. I slip the letter out and unfold its creases. It's several pages, all filled in with the same careless hand. Dated two months ago.

> *My dear Jessica,*
>
> *It's the best kind of autumn day here, the sort you'd treasure, when the wind in the valley sings with the birds on its back. I'm sitting on the porch swing with my pen and paper, where you once threw a pot of fresh-made butter at me and called me daft, but you did it with such laughter in your eyes that I . . .*

I refold the letter and tuck it back into its envelope.

It's true, then, what Mr. Rose said.

I don't read any more. He was writing for *her*, not me. For some version of her I'll never know, who threw pots of butter on porch swings and smoked on the way home from the pictures on Saturday nights.

The next letter in the stack is from A. Frances, too. And the one after that, and the next, too.

He was evidently her most frequent correspondent. At least, of the letters she chose to hide under her floorboards.

If she'd needed to hide a threatening letter the very night she died, though, wouldn't it be on the *top* of the stack? Would she have taken the time to hide it among the other letters?

Perhaps. Or perhaps she'd simply burned it, and all this is for nothing. Even if I *don't* find the letter, Milly and Clara could still have done exactly what Trixie said they did.

I've got to keep searching.

I sort through the envelopes until I find another letter, on different paper. It's thick and cream-colored, the kind of stationery meant to display the writer's wealth. My mother says decent, established families don't need to bother with that sort of thing.

I sit straight up when I read the signature at the bottom of the single page of writing, though: ***Beatrice Babcock***.

Trixie wrote to Mrs. Rose?

When I lift the envelope, I discover another behind it that looks precisely the same. In fact, there's a whole sheaf of letters on that same creamy stationery.

Not only did Trixie write to Mrs. Rose, but she did so *often*.

I turn to what seems to be the first letter, from July of last year. The summer before Mrs. Rose started as our headmistress. I draw in a startled breath when I see the greeting at the top of the page.

Dear Cousin Jessica,

I hope this letter finds you well. I was delighted when my mother informed me that you had been appointed to the headmistress position at the Washington Female Seminary. I'm sure our uncle made known to you that I have been a student there for the last two years, though my mother tells me you found the position on your own, without his knowledge or assistance.

It has been many years since we have seen each other last, and I was but a child then. I consider it to be a great joy to have a member of my family as the leader of the school. I will confess that I do not, at present, count a great many friends among the students and faculty. They are, on the whole, rather disagreeable. As such, I am quite pleased to know that the situation will change in the next term.

Yours affectionately,
Beatrice Babcock

They were *cousins*?

I can't remember seeing Mrs. Rose speak to Trixie once. Or even *acknowledge* her.

Yet Mrs. Rose was the niece, it seems, of the board president. Her boss.

Was *Damian Babcock* the distant uncle Mr. Rose had told us about? The man who took in young Jessica after her parents' deaths out of charity, but sent her away to be spared the work of raising her?

No wonder she'd let her family believe her husband was dead.

He didn't want to hire her, Mr. Rose told us. *But your school needed someone fast, and when she came down from New York, she sweet-talked him into giving her a try.*

Mr. Rose didn't tell us the man she had to sweet-talk was her own uncle.

Trixie certainly never mentioned any of it, either. This very morning, when she came to tell me all about Milly and Clara's secret, she never mentioned her own.

A creak on the floor below makes me whip around backward, but it's only the wind biting through the hall. The chill has crept up from the window I left open on the first floor.

I shiver as I flip through more letters. I'm still searching for the letter Trixie seems to think Clara wrote, but curiosity about the other letters tugs at me, too.

It means something, that Trixie kept this information quiet. I need to know what.

Trixie's next few letters to her cousin are similar to the first. None of the other girls at the seminary were kind to her, Trixie wrote, again and again. She never mentioned that the reason no one liked her was that she treated us all terribly.

My own name appears in one.

> *Dear Cousin Jessica,*
>
> *I wanted to speak to you this morning, but I understand your concerns about the appearance of treating me with favoritism, so I elected to write instead.*
>
> *I see that you have chosen to change some aspects of life here at the seminary. The rule about skirt length, for example, was overdue for reform. I'm sure some students are also happy with the additional books you have added to the library and your plans to renovate the basketball court.*

*Yet you have left unchanged the situation with
regard to certain students here and their treatment of
me. I understand that you would prefer not to reveal our
familial relationship. However, there are other actions
that would be more discreet. For example, a word of
praise in front of other students, or a recognition for
my family's status, even if you prefer not to claim it for
your own.*

*In particular, there is one student, a Miss Gertrude
Pound, to whom it appears you have already taken
a liking. Miss Pound would, I'm sure, benefit from
witnessing a display of attention toward me from her
new headmistress. It is evident that she admires you.
Miss Pound is respected by the other girls here, and were
she to show esteem for me, it would encourage others to
do the same.*

*I hope you will give this, your cousin's request, due
consideration.*

> *Yours affectionately,*
> *Beatrice Babcock*

I wish I could read Mrs. Rose's replies. She must have delivered them to Trixie herself. She wouldn't have wanted the servants to know she was writing to a student.

Trixie must have truly loved her cousin to respect her request for secrecy, even after her death. It hadn't occurred to me that she was capable of such feelings.

Yet her letters are full of descriptions of her frustrations, her worries. Above all, her loneliness.

I never imagined myself feeling sorry for Trixie.

The next letter, though, is on another type of stationery.

Soft white paper, the kind my grandmother used to use. The letter is dated August 1926, a month before Mrs. Rose took over as the seminary's headmistress.

> *My dear Jessica,*
>
> *I heard from your Uncle Damian that you are coming to work for him here in Washington. I told him I thought the news a blessing.*
>
> *I regret that we have not been in contact in the years since your marriage. I was truly sorry to hear of your husband's passing. I hope that, with your return to the city, we can be a family again.*
>
> *I would like to invite you to dine with us when you are settled in at your new home, where we can begin anew.*
>
> > *Wishing you the very best,*
> > *Aunt Penelope*
>
> *P.S. Your young cousin, Trixie, will be among your new students. She gives her mother many trials, but with proper instruction, I believe she could prove a worthwhile and industrious girl. I do not advise you to show her special attention, however, lest the other families come to believe your hiring was purely a result of your family connections. Your uncle has assured me it was nothing of the sort!*

Well, that's awfully interesting.

I'm flipping farther through the stack when something white under Mrs. Rose's bed catches my eye. It's tucked underneath a bedpost, only a few feet from where I'm sitting, and covered with dust.

Another envelope. How could the police have missed it?

And why would Mrs. Rose tuck a letter there when she had a perfectly good hiding spot under this floorboard? She must have been in tremendous haste.

I reach under the bed, stretching until my fingers clasp the edge of the envelope. I'm prying it out from under the post and pulling it toward me, trying to keep from ripping it, when a crash rings out on the floor below. So loud the mice skitter back into their holes.

I leap to my feet, the leather folder and its contents scattered across the floor.

I shove it all frantically under the floorboard—I want to stack it so it looks undisturbed, but there's no time—and yank off my shoes before I duck out into the hallway, the torn envelope wrinkling between my fingers.

I don't hear any footsteps. Any voices. Any breathing except my own, thunderous in my ears.

I dash down the hall, veering away from the grand staircase and toward the north stairwell. At the top of the steps, I hear it again.

Another crash. Louder than the one before.

I run down in my stocking feet, shoes and letter clutched tight in my hand, eyes locked on the steps below me. When I reach the bottom I charge through the empty, cavernous entrance hall and around to the servants' rooms, through the kitchen.

If I can make it to the laundry. If I can get back out through the window, unseen—if I can make it without falling, without noise, without...

A shape rushes toward me. Dark, and loud, and so *fast*. Too fast to outrun. Brushing my face, with...

Feathers.

A bird. Big, and black. A crow. It must've come through the open window.

I fall to the ground and shove my shoes back onto my feet with shaking hands. A laugh bubbles up as I race across the laundry room and hoist myself up through the window.

I've been running from a *bird*.

I'm still laughing, incredulous, as I clamber out into the courtyard and peer down the dim, narrow alley to the expanse of light where it reaches the street. And the smile is still fading from my lips when I see the man, his big hands stuffed into his jacket pockets, crossing the mouth of the alley, not twenty feet away from me.

38

*H*E DIDN'T SEE ME. *H*E DIDN'T SEE ME*!*

I repeat it in my head, again and again, as I dash out onto P Street and watch the man moving swiftly away from me.

What's he doing *here*?

" 'Scuse you, girlie," says a short, white-faced man in a green ulster coat from behind his newspaper, and I realize, to my horror, that I just trod on his foot.

"Oh, I'm terribly sorry."

"Look where you're going next time. Bad enough out here with that racket over from the church."

"I will. So sorry."

I set off after the man with the big hands, keeping half a block of space between us. He isn't walking especially fast this time. By some miracle, he truly doesn't appear to have noticed me. My heart thumps inside me, and I stuff the torn letter into my coat pocket without slowing my pace. I'm desperate to take it out, to examine it, but I can't let the man with the big hands out of my sight.

He turns onto Massachusetts Avenue, and I do the same. The morning light is glaring overhead, but it's difficult to focus with the constant hammering. Laborers are nailing up an elaborate nativity display on the block behind us at St. Andrew's. I wish it were loud enough to drown out my fear.

Only when I spot the green awning do I realize where the man with the big hands is going.

Two o'clock tomorrow, he'd said. It must be about that time.

The street is full of people finishing their shopping, preparing for parties tonight and dinners tomorrow. I should be preparing, too. The Babcocks' ball is only hours away.

I lose sight of the man as the drab green awning with its faded black letters comes closer into view. Duke's is so small, so nondescript, that everyone else walks right past it without a moment's pause, as I've undoubtedly done countless times before.

A streetcar packed with people trundles past, splashing through a puddle of wet gray slush. I step aside and manage to keep my blue plaid coat from getting wet, but the icy water drenches my stockings and penetrates my boots, pooling around my toes.

I set my jaw against the chill and keep walking.

The hammering grows louder as I draw closer. St. Andrew's faces P Street, but only an alley separates it from Duke's, and there must be a dozen men outside the church, working on the display. A pair of automobile horns sound angrily as a woman laden with packages walks right out into the street, the brown paper wrappings blocking her view, and a boy on a bicycle nearly collides with her as she tries to step around a slush puddle.

The hammering is as loud as thunder when I finally reach the awning. The noon sun has plunged the steps leading down to the basement bar into darkness.

Has the man with the big hands gone inside? Could I listen at the door to hear what he's planning?

I pause at the top of the steps, composing my face, straightening my shoulders. Then I take a breath and step down in my cold, wet shoes.

Right away, I know something's wrong. The last time I glimpsed these steps, there was nothing on them but old cigarettes and broken glass. Today there's a heaviness, a darkness, that wasn't here before.

Something's on the steps. Something dark, and—and thick, and...

Wet. I've stepped in another puddle.

Then my heel skids on the slippery surface. My foot slips out from under me, and I'm falling, crashing down the steps. Pain shoots into my hip, my back, my elbow, as I fall past...

The body.

I hit the bottom, my legs thumping against the heavy, locked door, my shoulder slamming into the ground. My body throbs with pain and hammers ring in my ears as the little breakfast I ate spews out of me, vomit mixing with the blood on the steps and on my hands. The sun overhead barely casts enough light to penetrate the shadows, but I can see it all the same.

Sprawled out on the steps in front of me is the man with the big hands, face down, his head inches from my feet. Blood's pooling on the cement from the hole in the back of his head.

YOU DREW THE SHORT STRAW, TOO, HUH?" ONE OF THE OFFICERS is saying. "Working Christmas Eve?"

"Thought it'd be a light day," another replies. "Now we'll be filling out reports all afternoon."

"Shouldn't be *our* job to clean up after some hoodlum who got a twenty-five to the head outside a gin joint. We still waiting on the dry squad?"

"Nah, that's one of their guys getting here. Bonnard said he knows the girl."

"What? That one who found the stiff?"

"Yeah. None of our business, I guess, what he gets up to on his own time."

"Long as I don't have to write the report."

I'm not listening, but I hear it all anyway.

I huddle for warmth on the cold brick wall. The blood on my coat has dried, mostly, but it's grown sticky. One of the officers gave me his handkerchief to wipe my hands, but some's still lingering in the creases of my right palm. My fingers are chilled and trembling, but I can't risk getting it on my gloves.

I don't know how I got back up the stairs. I don't remember stepping around the body. I must have done it, though, because one moment I was there, at the bottom of a hole with a dead man, and the next, I was running.

Then the short man whose foot I stepped on earlier was shouting after me, asking if I needed help. If something was wrong. I didn't answer. I kept running, past well-dressed ladies who could have been Mrs. Patterson and Mrs. Paul and Mrs. Mayfield for all I know, and I did it all in a filthy coat, in boots full of icy water and a dead man's blood.

That hole, in the back of his head. It was so dark. Greasy. Inside was something gray and—bone, I think it was bone, I think it was his *skull...*

"Not dead herself, is she?" one of the coppers asks. "Hasn't said another word. Sitting there all white in the face, like she's gonna faint."

"If she was gonna faint, she'd've done it already. You working tomorrow?"

"Nah. Thought the wife'd be happy, but she only complained about the money."

The officer with the unhappy wife is the one who stopped me. I don't know how long I'd have kept running if he hadn't. He grabbed me by the biceps, shouting, "Miss! Miss! Miss!" into my face until I sagged down, my legs giving way. The officer seemed ready to leave me there on the sidewalk after that, problem solved, until I forced out the words, "Dead—I think he's dead..."

Then he dragged me to my feet. Asked me questions. Made me walk back the way I'd come.

I don't remember what I said to him. I must have told him my name, because he called me *Miss Pound* after that, steering me forward with his hands on my shoulder blades, spitting out words as he forced me back to Duke's.

Miss Pound, how did you know the dead man?

Miss Pound, what were you doing at a place like that?

Miss Pound, why can't you answer simple questions?

When we got to Duke's, he left me sitting on the low brick wall by the steps. I haven't spoken since.

Whoever killed that man must have followed him down the

stairs before I caught up to him. The hammering at the church covered the sound of the gunshot. I wonder if the nativity scene is finished.

They would've had to know about the hammering. They would've had to know the man would be going down those steps at that moment.

Who would plan something like that?

Not Milly. Where would she get a gun, or learn how to use it?

Well. Even if her parents' finances aren't what they once were, the fact remains that Milly has money. Besides, she knows everyone. She can get anything she wants. Or pay someone to get it for her. And she was with me when the two men made the plan to meet up at two o'clock today. She could've heard.

And Clara. Clara learned to do so many things in New York. Strange things. Things you wouldn't think a girl could do.

Things she didn't always tell me about.

"They find anything on the stiff yet?" one of the officers asks.

"Italian. Came over a couple of years ago. Antonio something."

"Farina," a third officer calls from the other side of the stairs. "Antonio Farina."

"Clean kill?" the first copper asks. "Single shot to the head?"

"Yeah. Somebody knew what he was doing with that gun."

"What'd the dead guy do?"

"The usual. Arrested a couple of times for robbery. Couple more for being a drunk. Worked at a butcher shop over on Sixteenth and for that undertaker, Garrett, under the table. Pickpocket, too. Had three fresh wallets on him. Probably came down to trade 'em in for booze."

I can't listen to any more of this. I lean forward, covering my ears with my hands, my elbows tucking in.

Something crumples in my coat pocket. The letter, from under Mrs. Rose's bed. I pull it out and blink down at it, the letters shifting below my blurry eyes.

There's no address. All the front of the envelope says, in a florid script, is:

To: Mrs. Jessica Rose
From: Miss Clara Blum

I tear at the envelope, ripping it into pieces, my cold fingers fumbling.

The note inside is short, the black ink smeared. Written in obvious haste.

December 10, 1927

Dear Mrs. Rose,
    You are to tell no one what you saw. If you do, you are solely to blame for what might happen next.
    Yours sincerely,
    Clara Blum

40

"JUDGE AND MRS. POUND, AND MISS POUND," RICHARDSON booms over the orchestra music, in a voice five times grander than the one he used to announce us when we visited Damian and Penelope Babcock's house last week.

Granted, Trixie's new house is itself five times grander. Her last house was a lot like my own: narrow, with a front door opening to a steep staircase and a sitting room, a pair of slim front windows to let in the light and the noise from the bustling street a few feet away. A dining room and kitchen, with a small study. A few bedrooms upstairs, and an attic with space for the servants to sleep. A much nicer home than most in the city, but nothing compared to the Babcocks' brand-new mansion in the princely Kalorama neighborhood.

Here, a uniformed chauffeur helped us out of our car and directed us to a red carpet running from the curb to the front door. The roof soared up three stories to a single round pointed turret, like something you'd expect to see on a medieval castle, though the house was constructed this year on a vacant lot. The walls are stately red and white brick, the window frames and doors a rich brown. Even with all the electric lamps lighting the path to the front door, the house resembled a vast cave waiting to swallow us whole.

I'm forbidden to dance at formal balls until my debut, but I've been to more of them than I could count at hotels, always with waiters sweeping to and fro, floors waxed to a mirror shine, and grand ballrooms draped in flowers and trailing vines. Before this year, the Babcocks' annual Christmas Eve ball was held in the Crystal Room at the Willard, with its dozens of shimmering electric-lit crystal chandeliers and thick layers of gold leaf crown molding making my eyes throb.

The ballroom Richardson shows us into tonight is smaller, but its walls are filled with mirrors, and the dance floor gleams. We might as well not be on the same planet, let alone the same city, as the wild dance floor at the East Room. Banking palms stand in each corner, and two orchestras take up nearly half the room, one playing an old-fashioned waltz while the other waits, instruments poised under chins, as the dancers rotate properly around the floor between them.

A hostess should always hire two orchestras for any ball worthy of the name, my mother told me once. That way, the dancing never has to pause. As though no worse fate could ever be imagined.

Trixie's mother is standing by the entrance to the ballroom, holding out her gloved hand to my father with a frozen smile. "Your honor. Merry Christmas. Thank you ever so for coming."

"A privilege, Mrs. Babcock. What a lovely home." My father shakes her hand and passes her off to my mother, then to me. He's already reaching for the cigar in his pocket.

"Gertrude, dear." Trixie's mother takes my hand, studying my beaded red gown and the handbag that I wouldn't let the maid store in the coatroom, however hard my mother tried to insist. She finally stopped after I nearly snapped at her. All afternoon, from the silent, painful ride home courtesy of a snub-nosed police officer through yet another dress fitting and awkward family dinner, I've managed to avoid outright speaking to my mother, a fact of which I'm sure she's keenly aware. "Lovely to see you. Do try not to run over Mrs. Patterson again."

"So sorry to hear Penelope has taken ill," my mother says, changing the subject with impressive dexterity. "Do tell her we've missed her this evening. She always brings such a kind spirit to every occasion."

"Well, she was good enough to lend us some of her household staff for the occasion. We're still getting things organized here, I'll admit. Have a lovely evening, all of you, and do try the drinks, we've devised some delightful new flavors."

As we step away, though, my mother casts me an admonishing look. I'm only days away from my exile at Lincoln Hall in Boston, that look says, and I'm to be on my very best behavior tonight.

I have no intention of doing anything of the sort, but I have no intention of my mother finding out about that, either.

She steps into the cavernous ballroom, where the volume of the orchestra makes conversation nearly impossible. A waiter swoops toward us, carrying a tray stacked with glasses of red liquid. I take one, to be polite.

I doubt Mrs. Babcock would dare to serve liquor with my father so near. Undoubtedly, though, there are trays nearby filled with glasses of imported wine and champagne. All stored in the cellar since the war years, the Babcocks would claim. *Entirely* legal. *Entirely* respectable. No need for Judge Pound to know about the man bringing those weekly deliveries to the back door.

Everything about this ball is quite respectable, in fact. Dr. Garrison and Mrs. Paul are waltzing sedately when we enter, and Mrs. Mayfield stops to compliment my mother's onyx brooch. The two of them turn silently to study another woman's overly elaborate hairstyle, trading amused glances where she probably won't see. A pair of men pat their jackets absently and pass through in search of the smoking room, where they'll ignore their wives and daughters in favor of pipes and gossip.

Nights like *this* are what I'm supposed to think matter most in the world.

"Merry Christmas, Miss Pound."

I paste a smile on my face as I turn to greet Trixie. Her gown shines deep red, so dark it's nearly black, and it's covered in beads from her neck to her ankles. It's not unlike my own dress, but hers must've been handmade in Paris for five times what my mother paid our dressmaker. "Miss Babcock. What a lovely ball. Thank you ever so for—"

"They're upstairs. Come on." Trixie darts her eyes from side to side, though it's too late to check for eavesdroppers. If anyone's paying attention, they already know something strange is going on.

Trixie's ill-suited for subterfuge. Dangerously so.

I conduct a subtler, more thorough investigation of our surroundings before I deem it safe to reply. "Both of them? Already?"

"Yes." Trixie raises the glass in her hand, pointing to the staircase. She isn't speaking quietly enough. I need to get her out of this crowd. "They came together. Milly's been drinking, and she wasn't feeling well. I told them to wait in my room on the third floor and said I'd go find help. It's quiet up there. All the servants are busy with the ball."

Why did Milly and Clara arrive together? We didn't plan that.

Milly was supposed to come with my parents and me, but I didn't see her all afternoon. My mother told me she'd called from a friend's house and would be coming with them.

She didn't say the friend in question was Clara.

Did they come... *together*?

I square my shoulders, pushing that thought aside. There's a job to be done. "Let's go, then."

"You first," Trixie says. "Don't let them leave. I'll be up in a minute."

"Where are you going?"

But Trixie's already disappeared in a whirl of silk and beads.

I check to make sure my mother isn't watching before I head toward the grand staircase at the front of the house, which is grand indeed. At the seminary, the main staircase is a little wider than the other stairs, but otherwise it's simply there to serve its purpose. In the new Babcock home, though, the grand staircase is wide enough for ten people to climb it abreast, with thick carpets, blazing electric lights, cast-iron banisters, and a landing with its own fountain where water flows from the mouth of a white marble sea nymph and swirls into a white marble bowl.

The lights dim the higher I climb. The electricity is only in use on the ground floor, it seems, and the heating, too. The temperature around me is decreasing rapidly. I wish evening gowns were permitted to have sleeves.

On the second-floor landing, I nearly collide with a maid carrying a stack of linens.

"Oh!" She regains her balance, then bobs her head. "Were you looking for the lavatory, miss? It's down off the ladies' dressing room."

I recognize her right away. She's the maid who was so kind to me at Trixie's uncle's house.

The one who told me about the bootlegger.

I smile brightly. "Thank you ever so! I'm sure you're quite busy, but I wondered if I might ask a question?"

"Certainly, miss."

"When I visited your home on Monday, you mentioned that the Babcocks had a man working for them, who brought—beverages. And that they'd once had another man before, a handsomer one. Is that right?"

Her eyes widen before she lets out a laugh. "I thought that was you, miss! Yes, I do recall saying that."

"In that case, I have an inquiry that I hope you won't find too indiscreet." I smile conspiratorially and hope she doesn't know precisely who I am, given what I plan to say next. "You see...a gentleman of my acquaintance, a family member, that is, was interested in procuring the services of such a man. Do you happen to know either of their names?"

"Well...yes. The previous man and I spoke a number of times, and we did introduce ourselves. Though I only got his first name." She flushes behind her white linens. "It didn't seem improper at the time, though perhaps..."

"I'm sure it was nothing of the kind." I smile again. "I'd be very grateful to learn his first name."

"Victor." The girl flushes again. "I believe his last name may have started with a C or a K, but I can't quite..."

"That's all right." I don't let my smile waver. This means... it means... "Thank you again."

"Enjoy your evening, miss. Merry Christmas."

"A very merry Christmas to you."

I grip the banister to keep steady as she trots neatly down the stairs.

But this isn't a safe place to linger. Anyone could see me.

I climb the steps as fast as etiquette allows, until I'm safely concealed on the stairway to the third floor. It's nearly as cold up here as it was outdoors. There must not be a single fire lit.

My eyes fall shut as I pause on the stairway, fumbling with the clasp on my handbag.

He knew the Babcocks.

But *which* Babcocks? How many?

I draw the photograph out of my handbag and open my eyes. I've had to carry it everywhere or risk its being found. I wanted to burn it, but I'm rubbish at starting fires without servants to help.

My hands are shaking, but I hold that photograph as still as I can, studying it. Every detail. Every angle.

I still can't be sure.

Only when I turn it over and see the notation in the bottom corner, a brief, neat, minute line of script I'd never noticed, do I understand.

No. *No.*

I force the air in and out of my chest. I can't let the panic take over.

I have to find Milly and Clara. We have to get out of this house. *Now.*

41

I DON'T BOTHER BEING QUIET ANYMORE.

The third floor of the house is dark and empty, but the orchestra in the ballroom below is loud enough to ring out clearly here. No one should hear my heels thundering across the thin carpet stretched over the cold oak floors as I run.

I strike each door I pass with the side of my fist, but I don't break my stride. I've just pounded on my seventh door when a soft voice calls, "Yes?" from the other side.

The room is dark when I shove the door open, its fireplace cold and unused. The space is about the size of Mrs. Rose's bedroom at the seminary, and it's devoid of furniture, rugs, or curtains. If this is Trixie's room, I don't know where she's meant to sleep.

Trixie. She could come any moment. We need to be gone by then. We need to be gone *now*. If I'd spotted the note on that photograph sooner, none of us would have ever entered this house to begin with.

The only light in the room comes through the streetlamps outside the window, but it's enough for me to see them huddled on the far side. Milly's sitting on the bare floor, her back propped against an empty wall, wearing a shimmering blue velvet gown. Her head's drooped forward, her eyes closed, her hair styled in elaborate waves that glimmer in the thin light.

Clara's bending over her, an emerald-green gown clinging to her hips. Glittering beads fall from the panels of her skirt and the neckline that brings out the soft, sloping angles of her face.

Neither of them makes a sound.

"We have to go." I shove the door open wide. "It isn't safe for us to—"

"Gertie. We need you." Clara's voice breaks. "Something's wrong with her, *really really* wrong, and I don't know what to..."

And I lunge toward Milly on the floor.

She isn't merely drunk. I should've seen it right away.

"Milly." I grab her hand. It's warm, at least, but she doesn't react to my touch. "Milly!"

"She only had two drinks." Clara sinks down beside me, reaching for Milly's other hand. "Those tall red ones. She was upset about something, I'm not sure what, and she drank them fast, but it wasn't enough to do *this*."

I cradle Milly's neck with one arm and move her gently, repositioning her on her back on the cold wood floor. Her chest rises and falls under the blue velvet gown. But she doesn't flinch when Clara and I prop her back up against the wall again.

"We have to get her out of this house." I meet Clara's eyes, trying to see if she's hiding something from me, but all I see is a fear that's close to panic. "It isn't safe."

"We can't get her down the stairs." Clara shakes her head. "Not by ourselves."

She's right. "Dr. Garrison is in the ballroom. I saw him when I was coming in."

"I'll get him." Clara's already on her feet.

"What will you tell him?"

"I'll think of something. I'll be back as soon as I can."

She disappears through the door, moving so fast in her heels I'm afraid she'll trip on the stairs.

She has to get back here before Trixie does. If she and Dr. Garrison are fast enough, we might be safe.

"Milly." I crouch down beside my best friend. "It'll be all

right. I'm here. I'm right with you. The doctor will be here soon."

"That's unlikely," says a voice from the door. "Garrison got the same dose of Veronal as your friend on the floor there, I'm afraid. Couldn't risk his getting involved. It's amazing what a few drops in a glass can accomplish. Or in a punch bowl, for that matter."

I turn to answer, and that's when I see the gun pointed at Milly and me.

42

A MEMORY FLASHES IN MY MIND.

That night at the speakeasy. The woman, Miss...I never did learn her name.

She'd come with Mr. Pengelley. She was kind to us.

When the police had him, I tried to pull her out, but she wouldn't come. She kept shouting for him. Screaming. I had to drag her, in the end.

It seemed strange to me then that she wouldn't go, even when there was no hope left of saving him. I didn't understand.

Staring at that gun, staring down at Milly, I understand it now.

"Trixie's coming!" The words come out by instinct. A garbled, uncalculated shout. "She'll be here any second! Trixie! Your *daughter*, Trixie!"

It's all I can think of that might stop him. The image of his daughter's face, watching him shoot girls her own age in cold blood.

And it might have worked. George Babcock doesn't lower the gun. But he doesn't pull the trigger, either.

"You're lying." His voice is the opposite of mine, cool and collected. His finger still holds the safety cocked. I know that much from motion pictures.

The gun in his hand is small enough to have been kept concealed in a jacket pocket, but there's something attached to it. A silencer. I know about those, too. With that, he can shoot without anyone hearing, orchestra or no orchestra.

Clean kill? the police officer had said this afternoon.

Yeah, another had answered. *Somebody knew what he was doing with that gun.*

"I've heard knives are more you girls' style." Mr. Babcock tilts his head toward the hall Clara disappeared down without taking his eyes off me. "But I don't think anyone will look askance at bullets. Women carry guns in their handbags these days. Besides, none of that will matter once they find out what kind of girls you were."

"Were?" I fight to steady my breathing. Steady my voice.

If I can keep him distracted, keep him talking, Clara might get back in time to see and get help. Though the prospect of Clara anywhere near that gun is enough to make me rock on my feet.

I lift my hands over my head and stand slowly, taking a step away from Milly. Keeping his gun trained on me. "You're planning to murder all three of us, then?"

"Nah. You're the one they're most likely to believe. A judge's daughter. The only one of your set who isn't a known degenerate." He tilts his head, as though half-heartedly apologizing for what he's about to say next. "So I was thinking I'd shoot *you* in the head, leave the gun in the Otis girl's hand, and make sure the Blum girl is the one to find you. Once she starts screaming, that should take care of the rest for me."

My heart howls in my chest. But I draw in a sharp breath. Feign indifference. "Oh?"

"But I'm reconsidering. Slightly." The gun is steady in Mr. Babcock's hand. But then, it would be. He was on the rifle team at Penn. He said so, back at the faculty party. "Once we have the public's attention focused on the ring of queers at your school, it won't be difficult to get them believing you three killed Jessica. There's plenty of evidence against the Blum girl already from her little situation in New York. Won't matter who her father is, since he won't be anybody anyway after word gets out. Once the jury hears what Trixie's got to say, they'll think it was a simple lovers' quarrel. Might even think Jessica was in on it."

"It won't work." I sniff the way I imagine Trixie might, if it were her staring down a gun. "Milly and Clara will tell the truth on the stand, and their stories will match perfectly. The jury will want to believe such innocent-looking girls."

"You may be right." His eyes never leave my face. "That's why it'd probably be easier if there's only one of you left standing, so the others can't conspire. You've proven significantly more adept at that than I expected. To be honest, I didn't want to have to hurt any of you girls, but after what you saw this afternoon, well, you took matters out of my hands. Thought you'd stop all that poking around nonsense once he left that shawl on your railing, but you didn't seem to care about keeping yourself out of trouble. Or your friends."

He tilts his head to the other side. The movement so easy.

Only one of you left standing.

"So I'll adjust the plan to a murder-suicide." He nods toward Milly without ever taking his eyes off me. "The Otis girl shoots you, then puts the gun in her mouth and pulls the trigger. Unless the Blum girl comes back first. Then it'd have to be all three. Guess I better move quick."

"Trixie will know it was you!" I lift my chin, but it's not enough to cover up how fast my breaths are coming. He's bound to know precisely how terrified I am. "You might fool the courts, but she'll never be able to look at you again!"

"Trixie only knows what I tell her." He laughs softly. "Always has been a daddy's girl."

He lifts the gun higher, his finger moving on the trigger.

"It isn't going to be as simple as you think!" I risk a glance at Milly. Her chest rises and falls, and it's enough to give me the strength to go on. I *have* to go on, for her and for Clara. "We're in a building full of people. *Someone* will know it was you."

"That's where you're wrong." George Babcock's hand doesn't waver. "They didn't know about Jessica, did they?"

He almost seems to be enjoying himself. I suppose there's been no one to admire all the effort that he's put into this scheme.

I can use that, perhaps. Turn it into more time.

Because Clara *will* come back. Even if she can't get Dr. Garrison, she'll bring someone who can help. She *has* to.

"*I* knew about Jessica." I lift my chin again. "About Mr. Farina, too."

It works. Mr. Babcock goes on talking.

"That Italian from Garrett's?" He chuckles. "Did the job for pocket change. He screwed it up, though. I knew I should've taken care of things myself."

"Garrett's," I say. "The funeral home. Is that where you found Mr. Farina? Did you have him put cosmetics on Mrs. Rose so the doctors wouldn't see the bruises? Was that part of what you paid him to kill her, or did it cost extra?"

"I hope you've found some entertainment in coming up with all these theories." Mr. Babcock smiles faintly.

"I did, actually. I saw you that night, you know. Across the street from the seminary. Watching to make sure you'd gotten the result you wanted. Was it an umbrella you were leaning on? There was quite a sizable collection of them in your brother's house."

"Indeed. Had one in the car." Mr. Babcock's smile widens. I was right. He's enjoying this. "Lucky for me, it was my left ankle that got twisted when the dry squad came storming in. If it'd been the other, the drive back to your school would've been excruciating."

"Was it you who directed Mr. Farina to fire a gun in the alley during the faculty party, too? So you could take the opportunity to go down and let him in to Mrs. Rose's office?"

"Brought him to her bedroom, actually. It's got that enormous wardrobe. Big enough for a man to hide in. I was part of the crew who got stuck moving it up there for the last headmistress. Vowed I'd hire men to do all my labor from then on."

"Including strangling your nieces?"

Mr. Babcock lets out a delighted laugh that sends a shudder down my spine. "He wasn't supposed to strangle her. The idea was to hide in the wardrobe, do her in with a pillow once she fell asleep, and toss a few bottles around. It'd look like she got drunk and died in her sleep. Easy and painless. Farina's the one who made it complicated."

I manage not to flinch, but it takes all my strength.

Easy and painless.

"You didn't count on her going out," I say. Anything to keep him talking. Though I wish with all my soul that we could talk about anything else. "By the time Mrs. Rose got back from the motion pictures, Mr. Farina must've been hiding in that wardrobe for hours. She might've noticed the pillow missing from her bed and gone out into the hall, looking for an explanation."

"Or for another drink from her queer bootlegger buddy." Mr. Babcock shrugs, still smiling. "Doesn't matter now."

I swallow. But I go on, matching his even, easy tone as well as I can. *Someone's* got to be coming soon. *Anyone.*

"By then, Mr. Farina must've been panicking," I say. "Smothering her in her sleep wasn't going to work anymore, and he wouldn't get paid if she was still alive in the morning. He went to stop her before she could call for help. But she fought back." I want to shut my eyes. Shut this out. But I can't take my gaze off Mr. Babcock and his gun. "She dug her nails in. Hard enough to draw blood. He grabbed the nearest thing he could find—the shawl she'd hung over the door."

"Strangling may not be that different from smothering, in the end." Mr. Babcock smiles again. "Not that anyone would know for sure."

He's trying to faze me, and it's working. I swallow, again. But I don't stop. "Either way, they'd made enough noise that Mr. Farina had to toss those bottles around the room and get out fast."

"He didn't do such a bad job, really. It was you girls who caused the problems. I'd told Farina to leave for New York as soon as Jessica was in the ground, but once I realized what you and your friends were up to, I had him stick around. Problem was, then he expected *more* money, that I didn't have."

"And how much debt are you in, exactly, to those fellows your brother mentioned in New York?"

That finally gets a reaction. Mr. Babcock's gun doesn't move, but his nostrils flare. "Girls like you don't know the first thing about money."

"I know who's got the *real* money in your family." I watch the anger grow in Mr. Babcock's eyes and pray I haven't miscalculated. Though it doesn't matter if I did. It's too late to stop. "Your *brother's* the head of the Babcock railroad company. You're only a vice president at a middling bank. Yet you just built a grand Kalorama mansion with a ballroom for two hundred and no furniture on the top two floors."

"You need to learn your manners, Miss Pound," he mutters.

"Your brother still wouldn't give you anything. He's such a skinflint his own servants mock him for it."

"My brother's useless." Mr. Babcock never blinks. "He despised Jessica, but he was too *upstanding* to do anything about it."

"Did you despise her, too? Or did you only care about inheriting her bank account?"

He smiles again. It's beginning to feel almost normal. A smiling face behind a pointed gun. "You should see the numbers on the Rose statements. No idea where she was getting it all from, but I don't care what schemes she got up to. Dirty money's still money. My office set up the account for her, you know. She didn't have any family left except us, and she never bothered with a will."

"And when your sickly older brother and his wife die of the poison you've been giving them since you've been staying at their home, that'll mean even more of a windfall for you, won't it?"

His smile flickers. Only for an instant, but I see it.

"Miss Pound." He recovers quickly, letting out a brief laugh. "I had no idea you were so fanciful."

"It won't have been mere Veronal for them, of course," I go on, watching as his smile fades more with every word. "Penelope's a lot like my own grandmother, you know. She wouldn't have missed a ball unless she was too ill to stand. It'll have been arsenic, is that right? A dose in their tea each morning, courtesy of that bottle of Fowler's Solution you keep in their lavatory?"

He's scowling openly now. I thought it would be gratifying to see my suspicions confirmed one by one, but it's not. It's frightening.

It's harder to think now that we're not pretending at civility anymore. Harder to breathe, too.

But I keep my chin lifted. Can't let him see me flounder.

He won't let this go on much longer.

"There's something more you ought to know." I straighten my shoulders. I have to draw this out as long as I possibly can.

"Enlighten me, please, Miss Pound."

"Not yet. First, tell me why you paid to have the Lazy Susan raided."

"Oh, that." He shrugs. "That one was cheap."

A sound echoes somewhere. Is it Milly, stirring? I don't dare take my eyes off Mr. Babcock.

"Plenty of people in this city wanted to take Pengelley down." His face is smoothing out again, a bit. Good. I want to get him back to where he was. I can't risk him panicking while his finger's still on that trigger. "I only had to arrange for it to be the same night, and make sure they got a photograph, in case anyone asked where I was. It's funny, though, nobody *has* asked. Now, nobody will."

I nod. That photograph was how I knew. The notation on the back. I was so shaky, so frightened, when it first appeared in the mail slot, that I missed it.

Leaving this with you. It was taken for a reason. —V.K.

Victor sold liquor to the Babcocks. He would've known them all by sight.

When he slipped me that photograph, he didn't mean it as a threat. He must've gotten it from his friend who worked at the paper, and when he saw the original version, not the grainy copy that appeared in print, he recognized George Babcock's blurred running face.

That afternoon, even knowing the police were after him, he'd stayed in town long enough to bring that photograph to me. To get justice for Mrs. Rose, or to clear his name of her murder. Perhaps both.

He followed me home that afternoon, but he didn't call out. Just as he always kept his hands in view when we spoke to him. He never wanted to frighten any of us.

He'd always gone to great lengths to keep us at ease, in fact. To never attract attention. He couldn't risk having the police called. But once he knew I was the one on the other side of my front door—*me*, not my parents, not our servants—he wrote that note and put it through the slot. He believed that giving me the photograph would be enough for me to figure out who'd killed Mrs. Rose, and what to do about it.

It was the last piece of the puzzle. The one I'd been searching for. Victor *was* the one who had it.

And I *did* figure it out—but too late to save Mr. Farina. Or us.

Another sound echoes, somewhere in the hall, but Mr. Babcock's eyes stay fixed on me. Waiting.

"Regarding your inheritance from Mrs. Rose." I speak slowly. Once he knows, this is over, and there's no telling what his rage might make him do. "Thanks to our poking around nonsense, we discovered something that I fear may affect your financial outcome."

Another sound comes, but Mr. Babcock's attention is entirely focused on me. "Continue, Miss Pound."

I take in a breath as the shadow comes into view behind him. It's happening.

Then, suddenly, there's a blur of motion, and the gun isn't pointing at my face anymore. It's exploding, with a muffled bang and a puff of foul-smelling smoke, and someone's crying out.

When the smoke clears, Mr. Babcock's back is to me. And Agent Perkins is lying on the ground, blood pouring from his chest.

43

Mr. Babcock's shoulders heave.

He reaches out a foot. Nudges Agent Perkins in the side.

Perkins doesn't move.

We're both panicking now.

I shut my eyes. I try to think.

Trixie must have let Perkins in through the servants' door after all.

He could have *saved* us. I despised him, but I needed him. And now he's dead.

Dead like that man, Antonio Farina, when I tripped over his body this morning.

All that blood. Sticky on my hands.

My breath comes in heavy waves.

But I can't lose control. I have to get us out of this. Alive.

Mr. Babcock is still holding the gun. Behind him, the door's half open.

"That was..." He swings the gun toward me, and I throw both hands back into the air, cursing myself for not doing something when the gun was down.

Mr. Babcock's killed two men today. I don't think he even *meant* to shoot Perkins.

He isn't acting rationally anymore. He could do *anything*.

There's no way out of this.

I'm going to die. Milly, too. And Clara—what will happen to Clara? Even if she survives, there will be a trial—she'll be devastated, her family ruined—and my family, too, and Milly's—and then they might kill Clara, too, hang her, or...

"That was *your* doing." Mr. Babcock shakes the barrel of the gun at me. "*You* shot the copper. You were in here with her, and he walked in and saw you. You knew you'd been caught in degeneracy, so you shot him, and then you shot *her*, and then you shot *yourself*, and the Blum girl—"

"Daddy?"

The voice coming from the doorway, from the other side of Perkins's body, is smaller than I've ever heard it, but there's no mistaking her.

"Trixie!" Mr. Babcock's voice blooms with fresh horror as his eyes flick to the door. Trying to calculate how much she's heard. "Don't look. It's awful. That man was crazed. Came in here swearing he was going to kill me. I had to do something. And these girls—I'm sorry, I know you thought they were your friends, but they're not right in the head. Unnatural. You can't trust a word they say."

"They killed Jessica." Trixie bobs her head fervently. Her eyes are on the gun he's holding. It's still pointed at my chest. "Don't worry, Daddy, there's proof. I know it for sure."

I stare at Trixie, my mouth dropping open.

Trixie *believed* that? Truly? *Still?*

I thought she'd been covering for her father. Acting like it was all Milly and Clara's doing, to keep him from being blamed.

I was wrong. She has no idea what he's done.

"Trixie." I need to get through to her. Before her father shoots me and claims the gun slipped in his hand. "I'm so sorry, but your father hired that man you saw in the hall that night. He paid that man to kill Mrs. Rose."

"No." Trixie shakes her head. She's staring at me, hard, but her lip is wobbling.

"That's right, Trixie. You know better than to listen to the likes of her." Mr. Babcock's still holding the gun on me. "You know how they treated you."

"Think about it, Trixie." I force myself to look at her instead of the gun. Her entire face is trembling. I feel sorry for her, now, I do, but there's no time for that. "Think about that letter you told the police to go looking for in Mrs. Rose's room. You knew they didn't have enough evidence to arrest Clara and Milly without it."

Trixie sniffs. Finally, she looks like the Trixie I know. "That's right. That letter's the proof."

I wrench my gaze back to meet her father's. "I'm going to take a piece of paper out of my handbag, sir."

When he doesn't answer, I reach down, slowly, to the bag still dangling from my arm, and draw out the letter I took from Mrs. Rose's room.

"I found it." I drag my eyes back to meet Trixie's. "I broke into the seminary this afternoon. It was in her room."

"Then you know it's true!" Her eyes light up, but only for an instant. "Why didn't you give it to the police straightaway?"

"Because it was very clear that you wrote it yourself."

A tear springs loose from Trixie's eye. "Stop it. I know what I saw. Jessica saw it, too, and look what happened to her."

"Milly and Clara aren't murderers." I lift my chin. "Being the way they . . . *we* . . . are—it doesn't make us criminals."

"Of *course* it does!" Trixie explodes.

She doesn't seem to notice that I said *we.*

It's strange that with everything else that's happening, using that word makes me quiver with fear.

"Jessica should've called the police the instant she *saw* them!" Trixie's shouting now. "I *told* her that, but she wouldn't listen! She never listened to me. No one *ever* does!"

She steps toward me, hands balled into fists at her sides.

I don't dare move closer, but I smooth out my voice. "It's all right, Trixie. You're all right."

"Don't you tell me how I *am!*" she snarls.

"Your father told me." I lift my chin. It feels as though I could fall apart at any moment, but my only choice is to keep going. "He admitted it. You must have heard. You had to have been right behind Perkins in the hall. He wouldn't have known to come up here if you hadn't shown him the way."

Trixie gazes down, for the first time, at Perkins's body on the ground. She draws in another sharp sniff.

That's when I see his chest rise, ever so softly. He's alive.

I need a distraction. If Mr. Babcock sees, he'll find an excuse to shoot him again. Perkins has to live. We'll need his testimony, badly.

That, and getting out of this room without being shot ourselves.

A shadow moves in the hallway behind him. I allow myself, finally, to hope.

"Mr. Babcock." I square my shoulders and take a cautious step forward. Then another.

I have to keep his eyes on me. I can't wait any longer.

"Killing Mrs. Rose would not have achieved your desired outcome." I draw in a breath. This information is the only weapon I have, and I have to use it right. I won't get another chance. "Her husband, Richard—he's alive."

For the first time, Mr. Babcock's hand, the one holding the gun, falls slightly. "What are you talking about?"

I take another step, forcing him to change the angle of his body to face me, and I flatten my palm against my back. "Richard Rose is still alive. I've met him."

"That's…" Mr. Babcock's chest heaves. The gun waves in the air.

I swallow hard. He shot Perkins in a panic. He could do the same thing to me.

"You're lying." His voice edges close to a shout. "You're *lying.*"

"I'm—"

"Why are you *lying* to me?" Mr. Babcock's voice rises louder still. The shadow moves again.

"I'm not lying." I can't stop now. Can't let him take his eyes off me. I crook one finger behind my back, a tiny movement that I can only hope is enough. "Richard Rose will inherit all of his wife's money, not your brother or you. You did all of this for nothing."

He starts toward me, his shadow following. The gun is so close. "*You* need to—"

"Daddy?" Trixie whimpers. "What are you—"

Then Mr. Babcock's screaming.

He crashes to the ground next to Perkins. The gun's spinning out across the wood floor, where someone's bending, snatching it up.

Clara. She's on the floor now, too. Crying out. Mr. Babcock's got her by the ankle with two hands. He's twisting it, biting it, and she's kicking out, shouting.

"*Help!*" Clara screams. "*Someone! The third floor! Help!*"

Only then, as I race toward them, does it occur to me to shout, too. *Help! Up here!*"

Clara's still struggling on the ground with Mr. Babcock. His right leg is jutting out, dark liquid puddling under his knee. Clara's switchblade is halfway across the floor, the blade red and dripping.

I grab Mr. Babcock's bloodied leg. Plunge two fingers into the bloodiest part, my nails digging in deep behind his knee, where Clara sunk the blade.

He screams, and Clara scrambles to her feet, the gun in her hand. She points it at his head.

"Get up, Gertie." Her voice is calm and even.

I climb to my feet silently. My arms, my dress, are streaked with blood.

"You don't know how to use that." Mr. Babcock's supine on the ground, panting, staring up at Clara.

"I do, as it happens," Clara tells him. "Want to take the chance?"

I take a breath. "Trixie, go find my father. He's in the ballroom. Tell him to call the police."

Trixie doesn't move. Her voice is even smaller than it was before. "What's happening?"

"It's fine, Trixie," her father says, but his voice is high, and Clara's holding a gun on him, and it's obvious nothing's fine at all. "Go on ahead. There's a good girl."

Trixie stumbles as she disappears through the door. I don't think we'll see her again.

"You heard the gunshot?" I ask Clara.

"Barely." Her eyes are locked on Mr. Babcock. "I'd been trying to get Dr. Garrison to move, but he's fast asleep in the smoking room. I finally gave up and came to check on you."

"Fortunately for us," I say.

Mr. Babcock gazes up at Clara. "Here's what we'll do, girls. I won't tell anyone about you, and you don't tell anyone about me. Everyone else who knows anything is dead."

I decide to let him keep thinking he killed Perkins. Perhaps it'll add to his torment a little. If he's capable of feeling tormented.

"I'll go get someone," I say. "I don't want to leave you alone with him, but—"

"We'll be fine." Clara levels the gun at Mr. Babcock on the ground, and I believe her, fiercely.

But before I'm halfway to the door, a hundred footsteps are ascending the stairs all at once.

My father gets there first. He stands in the doorway for an instant, taking in the scene before him, his eyes flicking to me. Then he turns and shouts down the hallway. "Ed! Call the police, now!"

Then he rushes into the room and kneels to check on Milly as a half-dozen other men in tuxedos and tails swarm in.

Clara never drops her arm. The gun stays firmly pointed at Mr. Babcock as the men in the room circle uneasily, trying to help Milly and Perkins.

Finally, the coppers arrive. My father murmurs something to them, and right away two of them draw their guns, both of them pointed at Mr. Babcock.

"It's all right, miss," one of them tells Clara. "You can stand down."

Clara looks at me. Uncertain. Shuddering.

Slowly, I nod. It's over.

We've *won*.

THE WASHINGTON EVENING STAR

Tuesday, December 27, 1927

GIRLS' SCHOOL SHUTTERED AFTER HEADMISTRESS MURDER

The board of the Washington Female Seminary announced that the school would officially close following the death of Mrs. Jessica Blackwell Rose, its former headmistress, who was allegedly murdered by a man hired by Mr. George Babcock, former vice president of Georgetown National Bank.

Mr. Babcock is in Washington Jail awaiting trial after being apprehended following efforts by a group of seminary students, led by Miss Gertrude Pound, daughter of Judge Joseph R. Pound. Another man who was previously held on suspicion of involvement in Mrs. Rose's murder, Mr. Johannes Viktor Koning, also known by the alias Victor King, has been released in light of the new evidence.

A third man, Mr. Richard Rose, admitted having been married to Mrs. Rose at the time of her death, but was released following police questioning. "The husband was considered a suspect initially, due to his having concealed his identity for so long," said Agent Samuel Perkins, who was injured in the apprehension of Mr. Babcock. "But he's turned out to be merely an eccentric. Harmless, as far as we can tell."

Mr. Edward Mayfield, White House appointments secretary, was named the new chairman of the board of trustees at Washington Female Seminary, and promptly issued a statement announcing the school's closure. The statement read, in part, "Our students are daughters of the most honorable families in the country. The behavior of one woman, who served as headmistress for only a short time, should not be interpreted as reflective of her students' character. These girls will move on to respectable futures, and we apologize to each and every family affected by Jessica Rose's actions."

The statement went on to describe procedures for the girls' families to retrieve their belongings.

One former student, Miss Elizabeth Baker, age 14, was in tears when she answered a reporter's call. "The seminary was our family," Miss Baker said. "I don't understand why they had to take it from us. It feels as though we're the ones being punished."

44

I<small>T'S THE COLDEST MORNING WE'VE SEEN ALL WINTER, BUT THE SUN</small> is rising.

I flatten my palms against the cold glass windowpane, watching the slow creep of orange over the rooftops of Dupont Circle. The sky was still black when we left this morning to catch the streetcar. It felt appropriate at the time, but now I'm glad for the thin stretch of sunlight.

"Lincoln Hall's out of the question, then?" Clara asks, her voice pitched low. It's so quiet here, so empty, that it doesn't feel right to speak aloud. The three of us made sure to get here early, so we could have the dormitory to ourselves. It's New Year's Day. The last time any of us will be allowed inside the seminary to pack up our things.

I shake my head. "I told my mother she'd have to drag me onto the train car herself. Eventually, she realized I meant it."

Milly laughs. "I don't know that I'm going to let my parents make me do much, either, after this. Or anyone else, if I can help it."

"So you're staying in Washington." Clara closes the trunk she's packing and meets my gaze. On the other side of the room, Milly's watching us.

"For the moment." I open the drawer on the writing desk to reveal a few sheets of old notepaper and a single pen. I add them to the small pile of items in my carpetbag without letting my gaze linger on the empty drawer before I shut it again, firmly, and turn away. The other girls sent their maids to do their packing days ago, but the three of us waited until the dust from the Babcocks' ball had settled. Until Clara had returned from visiting her family in New York. Until we could all be alone together, for the first time since that night in Trixie's cold, empty room at their cold, half-empty mansion. It's thoroughly cold and thoroughly empty now that Trixie and her mother and sisters have gone to stay with their cousins in Alexandria. "Mr. Farrel thinks I'm ready to pass the college entrance examinations without needing further classwork."

"And once that's done, you'll be on a train after all." Milly nods. "I've never been to California. They say the weather's beautiful."

"California." Clara's smiling, but her voice is too high, too thin. "Maybe you'll wind up marrying a film star. Or becoming one."

I force a smile to match. "Perhaps Milly will marry a lord in Cambridge."

Milly's answering laugh is markedly forced. "I've no intention of marrying anyone. My brother's flat is bound to be in a decrepit state. I'll need to spend months fixing it up before I can consider any other tasks."

"Don't delay on getting in your applications, though," Clara says. "They're certain to admit you at one of the women's colleges there."

Milly drops her gaze to the nightgown she's folding. "I won't."

"They've accepted you back at your old school for the next term?" I ask Clara. "For certain?"

"Seems there's a new principal, and no one bothered to tell him about my past." She smiles again. "Everything can go back to the way it was, since your father was good enough to make that call to the police chief. The coppers'll be leaving us alone. Though I have you to thank for that, too."

She casts a glance at Milly, who, strangely, blushes.

"How's that?" I ask. There was a time when I stopped myself from asking about odd looks that passed between Milly and Clara, but not anymore.

"Our final payment was Milly's doing." Clara smiles again. "We were ready to go begging, but she used every cent she'd saved to pay off their collector. You were there, remember? That man in the alley on our way to the Lazy Susan?"

"The one you spoke Italian with?" Now I laugh. "That man was a *debt collector*?"

"He was part of their team, I suppose. He gave me a slight discount for speaking the language." Milly laughs, too. "My father knew him, years ago, when he first moved to Washington. It wasn't difficult to track him down and make arrangements."

"Then you must have known," I say, and all our smiles fade. "About Clara, and . . . and what happened in New York."

"Yes." Milly speaks shortly. She doesn't look at Clara this time. "I heard."

I nod.

Here we are. Talking about what we don't talk about.

"The day before the faculty party." Clara sighs and looks at me. Lifts her chin. "The payment was overdue. I was crying. Thought I'd have to leave the seminary and find work. Milly found me, and when she asked what was wrong . . ."

"That was the only time." Milly's eyes dart from me to Clara and back again. "I swear it."

I nod slowly. It didn't go on as long as I'd feared, then. The lying.

Besides. I lied to them both, too.

"That was when Mrs. Rose found you out?" I ask without looking at either of them. "With Trixie lurking behind her?"

It's hard to be angry with Trixie, though. Now, when I think of her, my memory goes straight to how she'd looked that night in the doorway, when she saw Perkins lying on the floor. She'd brought him there to hear Milly and Clara's confession. Instead, she saw him nearly killed by her own father.

He's still recovering from his injuries, but he's already giving quotes to the papers. I'm sure he'll deliver quite a performance at Mr. Babcock's trial. I hope he can confirm for the jury what I've only guessed at. That it was George Babcock who wrote to the *Evening Star*, claiming to be a seminary student who'd been offered alcohol by her headmistress. That it was him, too, who planted the knife in Victor's office, knowing that it perfectly matched the markings made in Mrs. Rose's office door, but had been wiped clean of fingerprints that could've linked it to Mr. Farina or himself.

I only wish I'd thought of it all soon enough to keep us far away from that ball. I truly thought going there was the only way to get Trixie to confess. I needed to hear her explain *why* she'd tried to frame Clara with that letter. I thought she was covering for someone else, but I was wrong. She genuinely thought Milly and Clara were the guilty ones, and that it was up to her to get justice for the cousin she idolized. Even if she had to create the evidence herself.

Trixie cared about Mrs. Rose far more than I'd ever thought her capable of caring about anyone. But then, I never truly tried to understand her.

Perhaps Mrs. Rose wasn't much better. She was so determined to prove that her family connections weren't the reason for her success—*one never wants to give others cause to think their background is the sole determiner of their accomplishments*, she'd said—that she'd abandoned Trixie.

Milly nods, worry crossing her face. "I suppose Trixie will tell the whole world."

"She already tried that. No one listened. Except her father, when he thought it would benefit him." I sit down heavily on my old bed, its sheets tinged now with dust and disuse. "I doubt they'll try using that line in court. My father said his lawyers will likely advise him to say as little as possible about anything."

Milly exhales, her eyes finding Clara's. She doesn't look as relieved.

I suppose Clara's used to this. The constant worry about being caught. The intimate familiarity with the consequences.

"You *could* go and marry some man, you know," I tell Milly, trying to keep it from sounding like the question it is. "If that's what you think is best. You can move to a new country. Start a new life."

Forget your old one, I don't say. *You can decide to forget us. If that's what you want.*

"I suppose I could." Milly sits on her own bed, leaving Clara on her feet between us. The suit she'd been folding hangs, forgotten, in her arms. "Yet I don't know that I particularly want to."

None of us speaks. But I let myself hope, again.

"It's only..." I glance at Clara. "After what you said that night...the first time we went to the Seven Seas..."

"Well, I couldn't believe how foolhardy you were being! Both of you. I was only trying to keep you safe." Milly swallows. "And...I suppose I was frightened. For myself, too. If anyone found out..."

"It'd be the end of everything," Clara finishes for her.

"Look at Victor," I add.

After Mr. Babcock admitted he'd been the one to call in the anonymous tip to search the storeroom at the Capitol, the police had been forced to release Victor. No one's seen him since he walked out of the police station that day. I hope he had enough money hidden away to travel. To start over somewhere new. That's what Clara had to do, after all, and she had a powerful father to protect her. Victor has nothing of the sort.

Everyone knows about him now. He may have been deemed innocent of murder, but that doesn't mean the world will accept him for who he is.

I reach out, stretching my fingers into the empty space between my bed and Milly's. She stretches out, too, until the tips of our fingers touch.

"I truly thought it was him." Milly slides her fingers against mine, lightly. "Because we saw him that night, yes, at first. But also because I thought that it was...that *I* was...that there was something wrong with it. With *me*."

Clara nods. "I thought that, too. For years."

Years? I look at Clara. She nods again.

Years. Clara's known for *years*.

"I've made so many mistakes." Milly drops my hand. Drops her head. "There's so much I didn't understand. There were boys who I didn't...who I shouldn't have..."

"It's all right," I tell her, and I mean it. "You don't have to understand it all. I don't. It doesn't have to mean everything you've ever done was a mistake."

"I don't understand most of it, either," Clara confesses, dropping down to sit on the floor between us. I slide down to sit on the rug beside her, and Milly does, too. I reach out both hands, taking Clara's fingers in one and Milly's in the other. Clara reaches, tentatively, for Milly's other hand, until all three of us are intertwined, a quiet little loop.

"It's all right if there *are* boys," I add, to Milly. "You don't have any...obligations."

"What if I want to have some, though?"

Her words shoot through me.

"But you're leaving," I say quickly. I don't want Milly thinking she owes me anything. Owes *us* anything.

She doesn't remember the night of the ball. Still, all week, she's been making little jokes that don't truly sound like jokes. Saying Clara and I are her saviors. That she'd be dead if it weren't for us.

"You'll be in a different country by the end of the month," I remind her. "Clara's train leaves this *afternoon*, and I..."

"I know." Milly squeezes my fingers lightly, and I can see her doing the same to Clara's. The sun behind my back is slowly filling the room with a cold, watery light. "But we'll still see each other. We have to. I can't *not* see the two of you again. Together."

Warmth surges inside me.

I slide my gaze from Milly to Clara. There's warmth in her eyes, too.

"We'll find one another," Clara says. "We'll find a way."

"Is that—are we..." I don't know how to say what I'm asking.

Is this something people do? Something *we* can do? The three of us?

Is that what I want?

Yes. Yes. It's what I've wanted more than anything.

Almost.

I squeeze their hands, and I shut my eyes, and I think. Hard. What I want... what I *truly* want...

Is to make my own choices. Control my *own* future.

I want that future to include the two of them. But a journey, too. All my own. California, for a start, but more than that. More than dormitory rooms and Latin recitations and doing what other people tell me.

I squeeze Milly's and Clara's hands again. They squeeze back. We're a circle.

"I didn't know it was *possible* to want…" Milly looks from Clara to me and back. "To have any of this. I'm still not sure it is."

"We get to decide what's possible for us," Clara says.

"Certain rules are so ingrained…" Both of them turn to look at me. "Mrs. Rose told me that the day she died. *Certain rules are so ingrained, it never occurs to many to question them.*"

"It occurred to you," Milly says.

It occurred to Mrs. Rose, too.

She broke so many rules. She defied her aunt and uncle to go to college. Pursue a career. She ignored what society told her to want, how to spend her time, and with whom. The objections of others were enough to destroy her reputation, and the seminary, too, despite everything we tried to do. Yet *we'll* remember her for who she was, and perhaps that's enough.

Her marriage was unconventional, too. But that didn't mean that what she and Mr. Rose had wasn't important. Or that it wasn't love.

I want to question everything. Decide for myself what truly matters. And if other people don't like that, I want to change the way they think.

I don't know what it all means. Not yet. Not precisely. I only know I want to be the one to figure it out for myself.

Acknowledgments

Writing *Everything Glittered* meant trying my hand at a new genre, in a new historical era, and with a new publisher—a trifecta of challenges, but one that ultimately proved almost entirely delightful, thanks to the help I had along the way.[1]

To Erika Turner, thank you for bringing me in to Little, Brown Books for Young Readers and making me feel so welcome—and for making this book so, so, so much better than it was before. I'm incredibly grateful to the entire LBYR team who worked on and championed this book, including Alvina Ling, Lily Choi, Roddyna Saint-Paul, Esther Reisberg, and Mishma Nixon, as well as copy editor Starr Baer and proofreaders Lindsay Kaplan and Sarah Vostok. Thanks also to Kamin for the gorgeous and inspiring cover illustration, to Gabrielle Chang for the stunning design, and to Karina Granda for the beautiful art direction throughout, both inside and out.

Thank you to Bess Braswell, Claire Stetzer, Jessica Spotswood, and all the early readers for your extremely helpful feedback and suggestions on early drafts. Any mistakes or errors are my own.

Thank you to Jim McCarthy, who's been my agent for nearly a decade and a half (!) and who is responsible for this book—and all my books—being out in the world, and to the DC

---

[1] It feels wrong to use the word *delightful* to describe a writing process that included a body count, but as I always remind my kids when we put on a Star Wars movie, at least it's all pretend.

Commission on the Arts and Humanities for its support of my work and that of thousands of other writers, artists, and community members in Washington, DC.

I'm also grateful to the women behind some of the source material I used most frequently in my research: Ilana DeBare and her book *Where Girls Come First: The Rise, Fall, and Surprising Revival of Girls' Schools,* Debbie Sessions and her website VintageDancer.com, and Emily Post and her original, fascinating etiquette guide from 1922.[2]

Thank you to Darcy and Louisa for helping me to see the world in new ways every single day. And, as always, to Julia— my first sounding board, my best friend, and just generally my everything.

---

[2] I now know exactly how to decorate a Prohibition-era ballroom, why no one should ever bring a lady's maid to a "camping party," and why it's always wise to wear gay-colored socks with one's golf tweeds. Thank you, Emily Post!

ROBIN TALLEY

(she/her) grew up in southwest Virginia and now lives in Washington, DC, with her wife and their rambunctious kiddos. She is the *New York Times* bestselling author of eight novels for teen readers, including *Pulp*. Her books have been short-listed for the Lambda Literary Award and the CILIP Carnegie Medal. Robin invites you to visit her online at robintalley.com and on Instagram @robin_talley.